Allegiance

Allegiance

G.R. Thomas

*To my sister Emma,
who listened to my endless story ideas
and told me to write them down.
I finally did.*

*"This above all: To thine self be true, and it must follow,
as the night the day, thou canst not then be false to any man.
Farewell, my blessing season this in thee."*

WILLIAM SHAKESPEARE
Hamlet. Act 1 Scene 3

Prologue

Edessa, Ancient Turkey, 15000 BC

Lilith hitched a leather satchel over her back with rheumatic fingers, pushed her cane into the soft ground, and heaved her stiff body away from her village towards the cool shadows of the orchards — towards peace and solitude, where she could contemplate where she'd go. Running wouldn't change things, but it was all she could think of. However, running was nigh impossible. She was aged, wearied and alone, whereas Eve had retained her youthful vigour and beauty- and the love of her life.

She pursed her lips and pulled a shawl across her shoulders against the midday sun's bite. The Euphrates River trickled just beyond a thick tree line at the foot of a grassy slope. She dropped her sack of meagre belongings, and a sliver of this morning's bread slipped from the loose drawstring. She snatched it from the grass and took a bite, chewing through her anger before she moved closer to the river and plucked at the long, lush grass. The river's gentle rush mingled with distant laughter. A soft breeze calmed her hot skin, and she relaxed. With her back against a fig tree, Lilith rubbed the aches from her legs, her cane resting by her side. Sunlight fanned across her face, its warmth a contrast to the cold in her heart. She closed her eyes. In her youth, she'd played in these same fresh waters without a care in the world...

Until Ahdem arrived.

A twig snapped in the thick shadows that led towards the orchard's centre. A bird tweeted overhead, then fluttered away.

Lilith squinted and shaded her eyes, "Who's there?"

She leaned forwards and held her breath as though that would help somehow. She clasped her cane and pulled herself to her feet, needing the tree's support until her feet were sure on the ground. The breeze picked up; her wrap skirt flapped against her legs.

"Whoever you are, leave me alone. I'm in no mood for company."

She heard nothing but the soft *shhh* of the yellowed leaves fluttering to the ground.

Lilith shook her head at herself. She picked up her belongings, pulled the drawstring tight and knotted it for good measure. She inched down a small incline towards the river, where the ground was sandy and softer for her bones.

The laughter became louder as she approached the river's edge. Although she was parched, she halted, her sandals an inch away from the pale-yellow sand. Her arthritic fingers tightened around her cane; she recognised Eve's light giggles. Hidden within the trees' shadows, Lilith watched Ahdem and Eve splash about like young lovers. Her nostrils flared, and her lips thinned. She closed her eyes, remembering his lips on hers just that one time. A small groan of pleasure escaped her.

"And yet you gave him up for her to have."

Lilith dropped her cane. She made for the safety of a tree trunk, but strong hands gripped her arms. The stranger picked up her cane and handed it back to her.

"Here, my dear."

His deep voice chilled her papery skin. Her old heart raced. She righted herself and pulled away from his support.

"Thank you," her mouth had dried to leather.

He stepped away, giving her space, "My pleasure."

The man was huge, not mythical, but tall with the muscles of a great warrior. His eyes slid between her and Ahdem and Eve.

"You know them too?" Lilith snapped, a little coarser than intended.

"Doesn't everyone? The great lovers that time hasn't touched. Royalty without crowns, they say."

He smiled, but it didn't reach his unusually dark eyes. She'd seen eyes like his before, when childish innocence had her and other children nosing around an old cave on the outskirts of her grandparents' village. They'd squealed and run away when five great men like him chased them away, not on foot, but with wings. They hadn't spoken of it since, but Lilith knew from all the stories that they had been ancient ones. The thought sent excitement through her. She was so close to death. Lilith didn't fear dying, only boredom and people wasting her time.

She picked up her sack and hobbled away, hoping to find peace and quiet elsewhere.

"Leaving so soon? We're yet to introduce ourselves."

Lilith shook her head, "I know what you are. You've no use for me, and I've no desire for your tricks."

She headed back into the orchard. The trees whispered more urgently, and the birds had quieted. She dug her cane harder into the ground with each step, trying to ignore his intrigue and the soft pad of his footsteps behind her.

"I don't want anything from you, old woman. Perhaps I can give you that which you covet but never had?"

Lilith froze. Her heart hammered against her ribs. She turned around; he was mere feet away and looked at her with arrogant confidence. His brows arched with a smile that stretched across his face. This one reached his eyes, which sparkled even in the shade.

She felt vulnerable.

"Leave me alone. You know nothing about me," she waved him away and turned around.

He appeared in front of her, arms on his hips and his head tilted.

"My lady, you seem bereft."

He was taller and broader than Ahdem. His sun-kissed skin stretched across mountainous muscles that even a scared, old lady couldn't fail to desire.

He pointed at her, "You are Lilith, a strong woman of Earth who has wasted her life pining for that which nature didn't bless her with."

Lilith sniffed and licked her dry lips. "Know my name too? Clever, aren't you?" her cockiness hid the shake in her voice as she looked straight into his otherworldly eyes. "Shouldn't I know your name, too, since you're interrupting my peace?"

He bowed, "My name is Yeqon."

"Well, Yeqon, what do you want with an old crone like me? Be on your way, young man. There is much more to excite you elsewhere."

She couldn't help a glance behind her, where Eve's annoying voice trilled like a bird in spring. The voice of another joined her. Eve's daughter, Ahna. She was one of Eve's six healthy babes. Lilith rubbed her belly, forever empty.

"It must cut you to the bone to see them like that," Yeqon said.

Confusion screwed up her face, "What are you talking about?"

Leaves crunched under his feet as he stepped in her way.

A new chill touched her skin even though the air was warm. Blood rushed to her head.

"You know exactly what I'm talking about, don't you?"

His eyes hooked hers. Her chin quivered, but she tightened her lips and flicked her cane at him. Yeqon grabbed it and pulled her close. Too feeble to resist, Lilith fell into his chest. The sting and burn when he hit her back blinded her. In a flurry of fearful regrets, Lilith surrendered to death… but the pain receded and she was out of his arms, standing tall and strong without her cane. Her shallow breaths came fast. She slapped her chest, her arms, her legs; they felt straight and powerful. The ground felt firmer under her feet. The air smelled sweeter.

"I don't understand what…"

"There is much you don't understand, but you will if you allow me to show you. Let me reveal your true potential."

She searched the angles of his face, which changed before her eyes. Luminous white trails erupted beneath his right eye and curled around his cheek and brow. Yeqon glimmered with exquisite beauty. His dark waves tussled as smooth horns sprouted and curled against his head.

Her heart hammered with a mixture of abject horror and unruffled intrigue.

"I've never met one of you in the flesh," she said, "But as a child…"

"We keep to ourselves these days. I know you saw us in the caves. Your strength of character even as a child, so brave, so curious for adventure. You intrigued me. I've watched over you since then."

Lilith gulped, "What have you done to me?"

"I've reminded you of your youth and of your heart's desire." Yeqon rested his hand on her stomach. His hand felt like fire through her clothing, "You can have everything you want if you join me."

Lilith held her breath. The sounds of Ahdem, Eve, and Ahna faded.

"W-what do you want f-from me?"

His voice dropped to a deep seductive timbre, "Children. Just as you do."

"But I am aged. My body is not long for this world."

A sigh rumbled in Yeqon's throat. He plucked a fig, plump and ripe. With his thumbnail, he nicked a vein in his wrist. He squashed the fruit open in his other and drizzled blood into its pink and green flesh.

Yeqon held it out for Lilith, "Eat."

Shocked, her eyes were transfixed on the fruit, "You've tainted Eve's orchard."

"This is my love and my power that I wish to share with you."

"But… I can't steal her fruit."

He waved his arm around. "Does she not have an abundance? Has she not deprived you of enough?" he narrowed his eyes, and their light darkened. "You deserve better than to rot into dust. I offer you the chance to live on long past them both, to be at my side, to have the children you wanted. Just one bite, sweet Lilith, and youth will descend on you once more."

Dizziness glazed her eyes. Lilith shook it away and blinked only to refocus on his iridescent blood on the fig's thousand seeds. It darkened its pink flesh and whetted her appetite.

"You know you want the chance to have all that life has denied you," Yeqon's eyes darted towards the river where Ahdem and Eve continued to laugh. The breeze tussled strands of his dark hair across his forehead. The sight made her heart skip a beat or two, "Just one bite, and your pain and regret will be a mere memory."

Eve's laughter stirred Lilith's long-suppressed jealousy into a stomach ache. Lilith licked her lips. Her fingers clenched against her belly.

Yeqon took her hand and placed the fruit in her palm. The fig was heavier than she'd expected and warm from his hand. Rosy juice settled in the creases of her palm. She touched the crimson blush in the fruit's centre, and a jolt startled her. Yeqon held her steady. A hot rush washed through her and excited her mind and her body.

"What will this do to me?" Lilith's words trembled with the rising thrill.

She bit her lip and held the fig an inch from her mouth.

"It will give you what you desire, nothing more, nothing less."

Yeqon nudged her hand until the fig pressed against her lips. He unravelled dusky wings of light, and she quivered. A small drop of juice slipped into her mouth… and another jolt of electricity buzzed through her. An exhilarating breath rushed into her lungs. She felt lighter, more vibrant, than she had in decades. She parted her lips, ready to take a bite…

Something rustled. Yeqon pulled her behind him, and they sunk into the thickest part of the orchard. Footsteps crunched through the leaves, followed by laughter.

"I see you!" Ahdem called.

Eve squealed, "You'll never catch me."

They dashed through the trees, dripping wet, strong, and happy.

Yeqon held Lilith close. His smell, warm charcoal, was comforting, and she sank into him.

Eve circled a sapling. Out of breath, she bent over. Ahdem rushed up behind her and spun her until they embraced and kissed with a passion that Lilith bristled at.

Lilith crushed the fig in her palm. Its juice drizzled down her arm.

"Sickening, isn't it?" Yeqon whispered.

Eve pulled away and yanked Ahdem's hands, "Come, my love. I want to visit Lilith. I fear she is unwell."

"Do we have to?" Ahdem asked, "I am tired of her complaints. She's never satisfied and always whines about her aches."

He scooped Eve up into his arms and kissed her. They trudged away until they were lost in the shadows. Their voices drained into the breeze, which had become an angry gust.

Lilith's nostrils flared. Yeqon let her slide out of his embrace and kissed her cheek. Her eyes were downcast as tears clouded her vision. She blinked. The cooler wind dried them against her skin and left her frozen in anger. She looked at her well-used cane, which lay discarded on a thick bed of leaves.

The bulk of the fruit was still intact. She glanced at Yeqon, back at the cane, and shoved the entire blood-soaked fig into her mouth. Its sweetness exploded on her tongue. A metallic aftertaste set her mouth on fire. Her lips tingled and numbed as Lilith lost all feeling in her body and collapsed.

Yeqon picked her up and put her back on her feet.

Lilith felt lighter and stronger. She ran her hands along her body, positive that she had to be injured. A buzz lingered in the depths of her chest. Her abdomen felt different. It was taught, flat, and the tanned skin smooth. Her slender fingers were no longer rheumatic and marred with brown spots and snaking veins. Her skin was even and plump. All her teeth intact.

Yeqon took one of her soft hands and kissed it, "You are an unrivalled beauty."

His smell stirred her belly. She parted her lips and breathed deeper, faster. Her stomach grumbled.

Yeqon smiled. He opened his wrist once more and held it to her mouth. Shocked but unable to stop herself, she sucked at his blood, the rush a dizzying delight. Her eyes burned, her lips tingled, and her body trembled with strength.

Yeqon pulled away before she was sated. His thumb wiped her lips clean, tilted her chin up, and kissed her. She clung to him.

From that moment, Lilith knew her life depended on the Daimon who had tempted her.

Chapter One

I never thought I'd consider a punch in the face a great way to start the day; however, as my fist sunk into Lorcan's soft, cherubic cheek, I grunted with satisfaction. He was my allocated training partner. A dedicated choice, but an uncomfortable one. I'd never hit Lorcan's brother, but Brennan didn't grate on my nerves like Lorcan did.

"Ouch!" I laughed and shook the sting from my fingers, "Man, your face hurts my knuckles."

"Damn it, Soph," Lorcan rubbed at the rosy swelling that haloed his dimple. His chin twitched as he used some very un-angelic swears.

I spat out a mouthful of blood and rubbed my raw knuckles. As the floor absorbed it, my blood's iridescence deepened. A few micro-sparks of energy sputtered from within the droplets, reflecting the E'lan's strength in the training rooms. This rarely visible universal energy reacted to our energy, our strength, and our weakness.

The buzz and clang of others honing their fighting skills heightened the soft murmurs of this unseen power. I welcomed the burn that it drew to the surface, an invigorating flush to my skin. I watched the others, human and A'vean, drenched in sweat and determination. Angel-human hybrids; Eudaimonians and pure angels; A'vean's fallen Watchers, moved seamlessly together. At the sight of their selfless commitment, my body reignited and called the E'lan inwards. Heat prickled up my spine, and my face blossomed with A'vean's fire.

The magic broke when Lorcan continued to whine.

"You're not meant to pummel the teacher quite so perfectly," he mumbled through swollen lips.

"Oh, poor you. But *you* split my knuckles open," I waved them at him. "Not very nice."

Lorcan prodded his face. Fingertip-sparks of healing energy probed into the swellings and calmed the angry redness. He chuckled, "That's barely a scratch." He dabbed blood from his chin, "You want to play dirty?"

I was already moving. I launched a smooth roundhouse straight at his unprotected side. Lorcan wasn't as distracted as I'd thought, however. He hooked my ankle with a lightning-quick move, flipped me head over heels, and slammed me onto my back. Slightly winded, it took me a moment to get back up.

I groaned, "Well played."

He smiled and winked, looking a little more like Brennan.

A sarcastic slow clap echoed behind me. I peered back to see Jude watching every move I made. He passed a staff to Rik, his new charge. Rik avoided all eye contact with me as he twirled the weapon, ready to spar.

Since I'd rescued him from Yeqon's vile dungeons, Rik blossomed rapidly into a powerful warrior with unprecedented speed and commitment. It was a shock and a delight. I just wished he'd let me enjoy it with him; it hurt to be ignored. I'd found my brother and lost him all at once.

Gedz'iel and Koi watched from a high ledge farther back. Their expressions gave nothing away as they guided the underground army to perfection.

An impatient cough brought my attention back to Lorcan, who kneeled in front of me, offering a hand up. I smiled as I licked away coppery dribbles from the corner of my mouth.

"Give in yet?" I asked.

"You'd like that, wouldn't you?" Lorcan rubbed his hands together,

"Come on then. Let's go another round."

"You sure? You seem a little tired, buddy."

We circled each other. I cracked my neck with a few satisfying pops. He wriggled his fingers to egg me on; a sly grin dimpled his cheeks.

"C'mon then," he said. "Let's really spill some blood, Ms Earthborn."

"Ooh, I hate that name!" I flew at him.

"Sophia!" Koi shouted.

I dropped to my feet, skidded to a stop, "Sorry."

"You know the rules," Koi said, his tone amused. "No powers. The basics only, please. It hurts more now but will serve you well later. Carry on," he waved his hands at me to get on with it.

The weight of Jude and Rik's attention was too much. Embarrassment heated my skin. God, I hated attention… I really was in the worst possible job. I turned back to Lorcan, tried to pretend they weren't there. I shook out my arms, took a few breaths, re-centred.

"Come on," Lorcan said. "You're doing great. Don't worry about anyone else," he crouched, ready for me with a sparkle in his eye that was more than just excitement for the fight.

As we waited for the other to make the first move, he let slip another one of his weird glances. Each time it happened; I sensed his heart race. The sweaty sheen on his skin, the way his eyes darted away when I hooked them with mine, none of it was related to training.

Jude sniggered, in my mind, *"Good luck with that."*

I ground my jaw and gave him my best pissed-off look. Jude shrugged; needling people was his sport. He didn't need to rearrange weapons at that very moment. It was purely an excuse to amuse himself at my expense.

Brennan noticed and threw a spiked mace across the room.

"While you're laughing at her, get over here and help like you're supposed to."

Jude caught the mace, it swung in his fist, his knuckles white around its handle. He pointed it at Brennan. Brennan responded with a not-so-nice hand gesture that involved a middle finger.

Both Lorcan and I laughed quietly. The Jude-Brennan feud had taken the focus off the awkwardness between us.

"Those two are going to kill each other," he muttered.

"True. But not before I have a crack at you!" I laughed as I bounced back and forwards, fists up, ready for another round. Lorcan mirrored me. He swung a fake lunge, which forced me into an evasive back flip. Every eye was on us again, and I hated it.

Our eyes met again when I righted myself, Lorcan's face was flushed. He bit his lip in a way that made my heart race, my skin tingle. Don't get me wrong, I wasn't immune to attention, but it wasn't Lorcan's I craved. Did I have the social skills to deal with it? Of course not. Did my awkwardness make things worse… absolutely.

I didn't need his flirting, but I didn't do much to discourage it. What I did do, was encourage the training, work harder, try harder to hone my fighting skills, and Lorcan was the one to perfect this.

I wanted to fight, to get my vengeance against Yeqon. I had an axe to grind, just like everyone else. In moments of quiet, the feeling sat uncomfortably with me because vengeance drove Yeqon, and he was everything I wasn't.

I moved in for a right hook but Lorcan put his hands up.

"Let's take a break. You're too amazing for me on an empty stomach," he began to remove his armour.

"You're hungry? Now?" I threw my hands in the air.

"Yep."

"Hell no!"

Too much pent-up energy, and a dab of pissed off coiled my muscles into action. I ran, somersaulted over his head, and kicked his legs out from under him. His chest guard clattered to the floor. He boomeranged back to his feet, fire in his eyes, but I knocked him flat again with a swift uppercut.

"Never take your eyes off the enemy whilst they still stand," I rammed my hands into my hips with satisfaction.

"You'll regret that," Lorcan smiled. He rubbed his chin whilst pulling himself back up, smothered in sweaty dirt.

"Really? You're all goggle eyes and playing nice. I'm here to learn, Lorcan, not take a tea break." I sniffed and shook out my arms. Everything hurt, but in a good way.

Lorcan's eyes darkened. I'd offended him. I immediately regretted it, but covered my mistake with another jab to his face.

He grabbed his mouth, "Shit!" His eyes thinned at me.

"Give in?" I arched my brows and backed away, now he was pissed and for some reason, I liked it.

"Never will I give up with you," he grimaced, that look hooked into a half-smile. That smile sparkled in his eyes. He licked his lips and spat blood again. He ripped the last of his armour off.

"All is fair and equal in our world, Soph," his fingers wriggled, he eyed my armour.

My armour smacked to the floor too.

"Soph," Brenann screeched somewhere behind me. "Are you insane?"

Lorcan cracked his knuckles; sparks erupted with each pop. "I think she's definitely a little insane, brother," Lorcan's muscles rippled across his chest.

The energy shifted from uncomfortable to volatile, which was much more pleasant. It was then I knew I was absolutely not the old me. That Sophia would never have relished the prospect of a fight. Everyone's attention shifted for a very different reason; my safety was in question. I was going to prove them wrong.

We met with a skin-slapping, bone-crunching *thud*. Lorcan pulled my hair, twisted me around until his arm plastered my back against his chest.

"I said I was hungry, that's all," he whispered into my ear. "No need to be unkind."

My other elbow connected with his ribs, I twisted into a groin-kicking position. One crack of my knee and he fell away into a ball, trying to recover with dignity.

"Cruel… move… Soph," his faced bloomed bright red.

"You said all was fair and equal?" I cracked my knuckles, "Suck it up."

Lorcan recovered quickly, sprang to his feet and charged again. I flipped him over my head. He was heavy and it took effort, but I did it with an ungainly squeal. Someone laughed.

"Go, Princess! Man, you're doing some arse kicking today."

Lorcan sucked breath back into his chest, "Shut up, Brennan."

I rushed him again, but my cheekbone cracked when Lorcan's elbow found my face. I fell on my back, winded. A hazy, pin-pricked blackness clouded my vision.

I coughed and spluttered, "Ugh, God."

Lorcan straddled me, "Yeah, well, you hurt me too. You're getting stronger by the hour."

His voice softened; his breaths slowed. He wiped sweat from his brow and pulled me into a sitting position. His hand didn't linger like it usually did.

Sweat burned my eyes and stung the open flesh. I leant forwards, awaiting the dizziness to pass. I sniffed back the blood dribbling from my nose.

The light overhead illuminated Lorcan's elongated shadow. He offered me a hand up.

I grabbed his ankles and pulled him to the floor. I heard a crack, winced, but didn't relent. Now *I* planted myself atop *his* chest, my knees firmly pinning his arms under him. I put my forearm across his neck. Crimson droplets fell from my nose onto his face.

"This could have been a sword," I whispered into his ear. I smiled and glanced back at my mentors. My vision still swam a little, and the bang to my head muted the auditorium's sounds. Gedz'iel and Koi whispered amongst themselves as they pointed at me. Koi nodded, and they turned to address another group awaiting their attention.

"Hmph! What does a girl have to do to get some recognition?" I asked Lorcan.

I wriggled back to free his arms. Lorcan relaxed into surrender. He wiped a fresh sprout of blood from his lips, blinked to clear his eyes. I sat lighter upon him, but still pinned his torso to the floor.

"They're a tough crowd," I said.

Lorcan coughed, "Compliments aren't really an angelic trademark." He rested his head back and pulled long strands of hair from his eyes. "You need to learn to pat yourself on the back, but if it helps, you did good. I'm bloody dying here."

I slid away from him, slapping the filth from my pants which was more blood than dirt.

"Sorry about your clothes," he mumbled.

I laughed, "You see yours?" I pointed at the blood smeared all over them.

Lorcan chuckled, "Eilir won't be impressed."

I couldn't help liking him despite his awkward behaviour. He was sweet and kind to everyone. Keeping his touchy-feely tendencies in line was the only problem. I didn't want to be mean to him to keep him at bay, so I tried to be careful with how I interacted with him.

"Look at us. Must be a pretty bloody picture… literally!"

He laughed.

Lorcan rubbed something from cheek and flicked mud from my bare shoulder. His pulse bounced faster in his neck; his hand was about to linger again. I coughed. He realised what he was doing and slid it away.

"That was a clever move you pulled, Soph. You're thinking a few moves ahead now," he diverted to business rather than pleasure.

"Thanks," I smiled. "I've got a good teacher."

The sound of clanging swords and wrestling continued on around us as we pulled ourselves up and collected our armour.

"Done?" Lorcan asked.

I nodded, "Yeah, for now. I'm actually a bit hungry too."

Thomas clapped on the far side of the room. He stood alone, smiled, and gave me a thumbs up. Lorcan slapped me on the back to draw my attention back to him.

"You're doing well, Soph, really well," he said. "Wouldn't have expected that kind of grunt from you a few weeks back," Lorcan clicked his jaw. "Crap, you've really done my face in," he touched the split on his chin and winced. Fresh blood sprouted from the split in his lip. He licked that away.

I gently shoved his shoulder, near the white scars that marked how long he'd been stuck on Earth, "Aww, it's okay. You're still pretty."

Lorcan blushed beneath the mess I'd made of his face. He had scarlet cheeks more often than I did. I felt sorry for him, wished I could return the feelings he couldn't at all hide.

"Want me to heal that for you?"

"Really?" he asked. "You would do that for me?"

"Why not? Isn't that the A'vean way? We do the damage; we offer to fix it?"

His eyebrows arched in surprise. "Well, yeah," he smiled coyly.

Lorcan relaxed and sat back down, pulling his knees up to his chest. His eyes dashed between me and the others in the training room, "You sure?"

I rolled my eyes, "I can't send you away looking like that, Enl'iel would kill me!" I laughed, but it was true. She'd not be impressed if I left him injured. I patted his legs, "Get comfy."

"Thanks, Soph," his fingers laced around his knees.

"Okay then, lets fix you up," I scooted closer.

Lorcan peered around the training room again.

"Come on," I said. "Before Jude offers to do it for you," I laughed.

Lorcan scoffed and screwed up his face, "Ah, I'd prefer it if he didn't."

"So, what hurts the most?" I rubbed my hands, drew some healing light into my palms.

He pointed to his mouth, which really was a bit of a pulpy mess.

I shrugged innocently. "Sorry about that," I grimaced. "Okay, sit still."

I waited until my hands glowed soft and warm, then ran my fingers gently across each wound. Lorcan grunted and groaned where it hurt most, but was quiet and patient for the most part. His eyes swirled and sparkled every colour of the spectrum. They followed each stroke of my fingers. My stomach clenched; I hurried. I was only feeding the lust monster by touching him. Offering my help had been the right thing to do, but I should have realised that I encouraged his amorous impulses every time our skin met.

"Just going to tidy up that lip now, and then we're done," I smiled more out of relief for myself than anything. How did I get myself into these situations? I really needed Jaz and her boy skills, "Just open your mouth a little. Ooh, sorry, it's a nasty one."

"Part of the job," he mumbled. I felt guilty. Lorcan's lips were split in the middle and at the corners. I gently held his bottom lip and smoothed my forefinger across the injuries. The injury knitted together quickly. The swelling subsided and his cherubic lips returned to a healthy pout. The blood that had settled in his dimples melted away.

I peeked up through my lashes during the healing, unsurprised he was doing that thing again; the doe-eyed stare. I finished quickly; my cheeks flushed as rosy as his.

"There you go. All better," I wiped my hands together to douse the light. "I'm off for a shower."

I moved to stand, but he caught my wrists. I glanced about, noticing Thomas was gone again. Gedz'iel and Koi had disappeared too. Amongst the hustle and bustle, I spied Brennan by the doorway, watching with arched brows and an amused grin. I was looking for a distraction; clearly, he'd be no help at all. Matias, the annoying Eloi assigned to keep an eye on me, had sidled up behind Brennan and watched me also with stern, but quiet interest.

"You don't want me to heal you as well?" Lorcan asked. He tilted his head as he reached forwards and touched a tender swelling on my wrist.

I gulped, sighed, and rolled my eyes dramatically.

"You want me to rob that macabre joy from Enl'iel? I couldn't possibly do that to her. You know how much pleasure she gets from a juicy wound. She might even make me a tasty eye-of-newt brew!"

God, I was hopeless at this.

Lorcan held me a moment longer. His mouth opened and closed.

He wanted to say something more, but his hands slid from my arms. He chuckled lightly.

"Yeah, true," his gaze fell to the floor. "Couldn't take the pleasure from her," he wiped his nose on the back of his hand and slapped his thighs. "Maybe we'll catch last meal together tonight?" he asked. His eyes were less *come hither*, thank goodness.

"I'll see if I have time," I said. "I want to check in on Kristen to see how her wounds are healing. I also promised Enl'iel I'd make some poultices with her. She's teaching me how to add my energy in just the right dose to activate them."

His face fell further, so of course, I rambled some more.

"Oh, I was also going to garden with Eilir, and there's the whole study-the-Kaladai thing too!" I cringed. I'd lied about the gardening part. Was an angel supposed to lie? The rest, at least, was true.

Lorcan sighed. He pulled at a cotton thread on his pants and made good work of being interested in it.

"Okay. Maybe tomorrow then," he looked back up; his mouth set in a resigned smile. "I suppose you really should try to get that box to reveal its secrets. We'll need that portal key sooner rather than later," he glanced sideways at me as he stood. "Same time tomorrow? It's time you trained with a few more assailants. You need to handle more than one attacker at a time. You good with that?"

My brows furrowed, "How many are we talking about?"

"As many as you can handle," he smirked.

"Right, well, sounds daunting, but hey, it's better than a pack of Rogues decomposing all over me."

A shadow flitted through Lorcan's eyes at the mention of Yeqon's blood-sucking zombie army, "It will better equip you for that."

I nodded, "Tomorrow then?"

"It's a date."

Lorcan disappeared, leaving me hanging on the *date* word. With him gone, I hurried out of the training complex and handed my weapons belt to Matias.

"Okay, buddy, if you're going to follow me everywhere, the least you can do is be handy," I said. "And please, will you say something? Mention the weather? Anything?"

His ebony fingers curled around my weapons, no hint of a response across his unemotive face.

"Excellent," I said. "Don't hold back on your enthusiasm, buddy."

He narrowed his eyes, and indicated the way ahead with a well-muscled arm.

"After you, Soph'ael."

I put Lorcan to the back of my mind during my shower. Instead, I thought about everything that had occurred recently. I worried how I'd solve everyone's problems. From Kristen and Jaz to my brother, Rik. Then there were the big ones. The prophecy still hanging over my head. That great portal key to hunt down and activate without Yeqon getting his grubby hands on it. Humans were disappearing in alarming numbers, and stories of conspiracies and aliens had flooded the mainstream news broadcasts. The pressure was on.

Hot earthy water poured over my aches but couldn't reach the pains that mattered most. The general hum of my inner self had changed an octave or two. The ones I loved got hurt over and over, and something deep within me was fighting to be heard. It had been a few weeks since I'd escaped from Yeqon. Since then, I'd discovered Jaz' kidnapping and Kea's physical death. The wall of silence between myself and Rik had slapped me in the face; he remained a furious and hurt soul. For the first time, my losses hardened my resolve rather than sent me into a dribbling mess of self-doubt and pity.

Initially, I'd wanted to run to find Jaz, to avenge Kea, to finish this whole damned saga of mayhem and destiny, but I didn't. With Matias under my feet, I needed to keep my freedom and to garner all the intel and strength that I could. I needed to push myself so when I did venture out, the Daimon would be worse off for it. So, I stayed put like the good girl I'd always been, trained a bazillion hours a day and recuperated under Enl'iel's strict instructions.

But I worried about Jaz and promised myself that, somehow, I would find her.

After I'd healed my wounds myself, I picked up the iPod on my side table. It was the only part of Jaz I had left. I heard Matias shuffle outside the door. My bedroom was my only sanctuary from him, so I put one ear bud in and pressed play. The solace and comfort here allowed these private moments, where I could relax from the complicit façade I was putting on. I deserved an Oscar for how well I concealed the blazing anger in my gut. The yearning to save and destroy had developed whilst I was in Yeqon's foul grip. No alarm bells had gone off for anyone, not even for Enl'iel. Brennan, who was constantly in my face, hadn't realised it either. My change from virtuous innocence to determined advocate of the fallen was hidden beneath the daily grind.

I visited the cells most days, drawn to the prisoner they called Ben. I was convinced he knew something that could help me—after all, he had brought me home. He had betrayed Yeqon to save me. So far, though, he had remained frustratingly silent, which only spurred me on. With or without help, I'd bring down the curtain on all this.

A cool prickle ran down my spine and pulled me out of my thoughts. I turned off the iPod, wound the cords around it, and got dressed. A cool breeze wafted around my ankles. I turned in every direction, peered into the corners of my room as nerves lashed my pulse. My hands eased towards my weapons.

"Do you require my presence?" Matias called through the door.

"All good here!" Goosebumps chilled my skin, "Who's there?" I whispered.

Something moved; a shadow perhaps? I'd placed my gown over the end of my bed, but now it was on the other side of the room. I unlatched my belt and slid out the diamond dagger. It sat snug and familiar in my hand.

"Av'ael?"

The little girl who often visited me was good at appearing suddenly. I hoped it was her.

But I was alone. Of course, I was. This place was as secure as any on Earth, especially with Mr. Personality outside my door. Good luck to the uninvited who tried to get past the traps and guards waiting along a fifty-mile radius on the surface.

After a cautious poke around the room, I accepted that it was just me, a bed, a chair, a side table, and the light orb that bobbed above my head. I put the non-existent sound down to my over-active mind. I was miles underground. It was probably a creak in the earth.

I forced myself to relax on the duvet's corner with a spare dagger on the side table. Constant imminent danger called for such a macabre habit.

I plucked up the iPod and pressed play. Wrapping the white cords tighter around my fingertips, the red, white, and blue hues where the circulation cut off and then restored mesmerised me. I imagined it was my hands around Yeqon's throat.

Nessun Dorma trailed up from the small device. Jaz loved that song; only I knew that, of course. Just picturing Jaz' face embellished my dark thoughts. They sat more snuggly in my mind every day, and I pulled on those cords until my fingers turned numb. I wanted revenge. I wanted to plunge my diamond dagger into Yeqon's black heart and twist.

"Oh God, who the hell are you?" I sighed, stretched and yawned, and as I stood, my feet landed in a pile of gravel, "Where did that come from?" I mumbled.

The rest of the floor, though bare earth, was firm and smooth. I kicked the ochre mess away and picked up my boots to see if I'd trailed it in. Nope.

I reached for my carafe and splashed a handful of cool water on my face. Peering into a small mirror that hung on the quartz-rich walls, I tugged at my hair, which was even whiter than before. I traced the swirls of my A'vean markings, which now felt a part of me, across my face. Each curve glowed and tingled where my fingertips grazed them.

"Hello, you," I said to my reflection. "Do I even know you?"

I picked up my belt, heavy with my weapons. It was never far from my side. Its buckle shone in the orb's soft glow and reflected a long sliver of my face. It wasn't that I didn't look like me, just different. What was inside of me permeated to the outside. My eyes were less naïve, harsher. Maybe I wasn't so good at hiding my anger.

This was the first morning that I had a few hours to do whatever I wanted, and I would take advantage of having fewer eyes baring down on my every move. Gedz'iel and Koi were heading to Australia and Asia to reign in some Rogues, which would take a lot of attention away from here.

I wanted to dig out a little of the old me, something to balance my anger and loss of my old life. After a moment's concentration, I changed my white hair to rainbow locks and plaited them across one side of my head. I threaded lavender buds through each twist, just as Enl'iel had taught me. It felt better, familiar, but also slightly rebellious because it was different to everyone else. I felt renewed and empowered to do things my way. I stared at my reflection again. I was a new person, but I was also Sophia—a shy and homely nurse with a not-so-secret talent.

A bit of grime was stuck to the mirror, so I swatted at it.

It stayed put, seemed to sink into the mirror's surface.

I reached for it again, but the brown sliver pulled back into the reflection.

"What the…"

My reflection warped and faded until it disappeared and a black oval replaced it. I couldn't move; my arms and legs were pinned to my sides. The strange object appeared again from within the murky glass. A hand gripped what I saw now was a thin paintbrush. Every stroke brushed away the darkness inside the frame. An image appeared from a soft smudge of colours. Bright light blazed.

I was sucked into the glass and tumbled through a space-like realm of darkness and stars. I had no voice, no control over my body, as I spun about and saw glimpses of bizarre visions. A young man smiled at me, then faded away. The tap-tapping of a chisel on stone echoed as I passed a great marble effigy of a man. A woman with long black hair beckoned me towards her and faded away. A soft rain of multicoloured fluid splashed from somewhere above. My skin stained like a rainbow as the colours rained down. Within seconds, those colours faded into the feeling of being cold and wet.

I found myself at the bottom of the ocean. A warm, comforting current drew me towards an underwater cave. The sun shone through the cerulean water in subdued shards. Just as I felt like I was getting somewhere, I was yanked upwards. Erratically, I sailed through the sky over a myriad of unrecognisable landscapes— oceans, loping green hills, and rocky terrain. A vast and somewhat familiar city rushed by underneath. I thudded to the ground atop a cold slab of white marble. I stopped for a moment, like I was allowed to recuperate from the assault. I stretched my fingers. They grazed against something, and I raised my eyes to a circular bronze effigy of an elderly man's face. I was immediately drawn to it. The numbers 1519 flashed in my mind like a neon sign. The marble shifted. It fell away under me, and I fell into the cavity. Rancid hot air hit me when I entwined with a skeleton.

The unseen force dragged me away again, and pure darkness enveloped me. Screams rattled my very soul — not mine, but someone, or something else's cries of agony. Horror taunted someone as I wandered through this dark and cold place. It felt like a cave; dank, mouldy air assaulted my senses, and the ground was wet and rough. An orange glow lit the way ahead. The screams softened, as though someone had turned down the volume.

I still had no voice, so I used the only senses I controlled, my sight and hearing.

Bright wall sconces warmed my freezing skin and illuminated rocky walls that were adorned with all manner of hideous paintings. Grotesque demons with gaping maws scribbled in black ink bloomed along the walls as I moved forwards. The force pulled me more gently, like it was allowing me time to observe my surrounds. Some of the images looked like Rogues, some like Daimon. One was of a lithe and beautiful woman with wicked, dark eyes.

The force stopped me in front of the final painting. Another woman, tall and beautiful, with soft and kind eyes. The one who had called to me only moments ago in the mirror. Her smooth ebony hair fell over milky shoulders. A muslin veil draped over her hair. She smiled at me as though she knew something I didn't. Behind her, a forest was painting itself into being right before my eyes.

An aged hand appeared in the corner of my eyes and dabbed at the image with a brush, amending it here and there. It was extra careful with the highlights in her eyes, and it made tiny strokes to accent a now complete background landscape of mountains and trees.

My pendant pounded against my chest. I reached towards the painting, but a pull in my gut prevented me from touching it and brought me back through a haze of light and dark, cool and warm. I couldn't move again.

The dizzying journey ended with a thud; I was back in front of the mirror. My rainbow hair was perfectly in place, but I glistened with sweat. My hand ached from the tight grip I had on my pendant. I huffed and puffed like I'd run a mini marathon.

"Okay," I said. "Whoever you are, it would be much easier if you just said what you want."

I glanced around my room, half expecting to find the perpetrator.

"I'm not good at cryptic puzzles, you know."

No answer, naturally, and no presence either.

This had been the most vivid vision I'd had. Where had I gone? Who had tried to show me this? Was it Enoch, the human prophet I'el directed? Was it the mysterious Disciple of Learning, whose identity I didn't know?

A few deep breaths helped me to stop shaking. Initially, I'd felt that I needed to run and tell someone, but now, something told me to keep this close to my heart.

"Either you're going mad or someone is trying really hard to tell you something," I told my reflection. "Who are you?" I asked the mirror and the silver box, which remained by my bedside.

I ran my hands along the vines that grew across the walls; plants I'd helped to grow. It helped me restore a sense of calm and control. I sighed with relief and quickly jotted down what I remembered on my notepad. I was keeping track of all the visions, which, upon inspection, were occurring more frequently. With every step I came closer to unravelling this mystery, the netherworld tried to help me more. I wanted to understand them, but I was also frightened of what I might find.

"Okay. Morning off. No more scary dreams, please?" I raised my arms and spun around, daring another invisible something to play.

I created a small orb in my palm and ran it over a flower bud just as Eilir had taught me. Within seconds, a large white bloom opened. I inhaled its light scent and opened a few more until I felt lighter.

I hadn't had a chance to understand my heritage since it had crashed into my life. After we had healed the wounded, secured the perimeters, and farewelled the ascended, I had been thrown into organising the underground living spaces into an orderly and smooth operation between training sessions. It was a good distraction; an enjoyable exercise and a crash course into my own angelic heritage. I had uncovered a culture based on absolute equality. The essence of A'veans was to protect and guide, not at all about self-fulfilment. Most intriguing was their propensity to heal. Learning about the Earth's untapped resources, coupled with the use of E'lan, was my new passion and fitted into the part I'd left behind — Sophia the nurse. Under Enl'iel's tutelage and Eilir's watchful eye, I learned how to use orbs of differing energy levels to heal and ease pain.

It was also incredible, almost magical, to use its energy to grow flowers, fruits, and vegetables at an unbelievably rapid rate. It was the role of the young, teens yet to awaken, to grow the gardens guided by Watchers. Unable yet to train for battle or protection duty, they filled a vital role, ensuring the underground sanctuaries were self-sufficient. Their gardens spread through every corridor except the lowest levels, near the cells. They provided a sense of normality, like we lived in a giant underground garden of Babylon. They also produced oxygen and a sweet floral aroma that eradicated the heavy mineral air. Eilir made plenty of humorous remarks when my first few sprouts had shrivelled and died. She told us her mind when we positioned an orb incorrectly or stepped on a new seedling.

Everyone had a role, some easier than others. Jude had more than his lion's share of responsibilities, which sort of rationalised his constant moodiness. After my rescue, he had worked on resetting the Zythros stone. The large orange salt stone, Kaymakli's entry and exit point, was now closed. For now, all human warriors were stuck underground until a safe entry was established. They were frustrated, but Thomas assumed the role of peacekeeper amongst the human army. He kept them training when he wasn't by Kristen's bedside.

During the constant busyness, Jude focused on Rik, taking him under his wing, so to speak. Jude had volunteered for the task, and Rik seemed to gel with his no-nonsense manner.

Day after day, for endless sweaty hours, the training auditorium was our breakfast, lunch, and dinner. Rik learned and did what he was told, but he didn't speak to me. Despite his coldness, I coveted every moment near him. He'd come around eventually, I hoped.

I inhaled one last blossom and cinched my weapons belt into the comfy position just above my hip.

There was a light knock at the door.

"Come in."

Matias opened the door a crack and swept my room with his suspicious eyes. He nodded and fully opened the door. Lorcan entered.

"Hey,"

"Hey, Lorcan," I smiled. "You're not here to drag me to the training room again, are you? I'm stuffed," I threw my towels and dirty clothes over the bed.

Matias' gaze followed Lorcan's tentative steps without an ounce of affect.

Lorcan smiled back and shook his head. "I'm not that sadistic that I'd choose to be beaten up twice in one day," he ran his hands through his now-clean hair, which he'd plaited in a thick rope down his back like Jude's. He'd roughly poked a few Daimon-repelling cedar and sage twigs into it. He'd washed up quickly, he was normally more pedantic about his appearance.

I unnecessarily tidied my side table, "Didn't think I'd see you until later tonight."

"Just checking you're okay," Lorcan answered. "It was a pretty rough session today," he scanned my room and settled back on me. "I see Enl'iel healed you. You look great. And your hair is, um… really nice."

"Oh, this?" I flicked the colourful plait over my shoulder, "Thanks.

I thought I'd bring a little of the old me back."

"You used to look like that by choice?" his eyebrows arched.

"Actually, I *chose* this style," I scoffed, but then twirled the braid and smiled so he knew I wasn't offended. "It was tough being the only kid with white hair."

Lorcan lingered for an awkward moment. His eyes hung on me far longer than necessary. I cleared my throat, my cheeks burned.

The edges of his mouth turned up a little, "I like it."

I shuffled my belt. The weapons jingled and filled the uncomfortable silence.

"I suppose it was confusing for you as a child," he said. "Knowing you were different but not how and why," he picked up the iPod from my side table, looked bemused by it, and placed it back.

"I didn't think about it at first because Nan…um… Enl'iel, home-schooled me. It was lonely at times, but I had my horse, Grey, and then there was Shadow, my dog," my heart sank as I remembered his death. "You would have loved him. Very naughty but a great friend, kinda like you," I joked to push back the tears that prickled in the back of my eyes.

"I'm naughty?" Lorcan's expression brightened.

"You can be."

We laughed.

"Anyway," I said, "I couldn't go to school until I was old enough to wear tinted contact lenses. I thought I was nearly blind. Nan never told me it was a normal part of growing up for non-humans to have impaired vision until my teens. I was always confused as to why my eyes were different, but she very adeptly avoided the subject when I brought it up."

Lorcan glanced at himself in the mirror, "Must have been confusing."

I nodded.

"How did you cope with… you know, being different?" he asked.

"I didn't actually realise how different I was until I started regular school, when Jaz made it abundantly clear. She was constantly staring at me, but not in a nice way. She hated me until she liked me," I plucked up her iPod again. I'd find her somehow, "Until then, it had really just been me and Nan. I miss her the way I knew her, as my grandmother."

Lorcan nodded, hands clasped behind his back, and circled my room until he arrived back at me. His smile was soft, reassuring, "She protected you well, Soph."

"I know. I still miss those days though," I placed the iPod down again and flopped onto my bed. "But I have all of you now, so I suppose I'm actually pretty damn lucky."

Lorcan moved closer to the bed, hands rubbing at his sides, "I think we're lucky to have you too."

His eyes glistened; awkwardness twitched his fingers. He looked down, shuffled his bare feet. Then those warm eyes met mine again. I gulped. *Not again.* Nerves bloomed in my stomach like bubbles.

I twiddled my fingers in my lap, "Did you need anything else, or are you going to stand there until you annoy Matias?"

"I have something for you, actually," Lorcan ducked outside and retrieved something, hiding it behind his back.

"You have something for me?" I stood and pressed my hand to my chest, "What is it?"

He stepped closer again, "I hope it won't upset you."

My eyes narrowed, "What do you mean by that?"

He adjusted whatever he was holding behind him and cleared his throat, "It's just that you're taking everything on the chin, but I think you're hiding how you really feel. I need to be sure you're okay?"

"I'm perfectly fine, as you can see," I swept my hands down my body, the lie hidden in my light voice, and held up my fists. "Ready for whatever you'll throw at me tomorrow."

He nodded with a half-smile. "I don't believe you for a minute, but you look good, Soph… beautiful, in fact," his pupils dilated, and he took a deep breath. His mark glowed brighter, ever the giveaway of an A'veans rising emotions. His pale eyebrows faded under its intensity.

Oh God. Oh I'el. Oh whatever.

"Thank you," I said.

My eyes swept over his shoulder to the door. *I should invite Matias in for tea.*

Lorcan was an odd character. One moment he was a kick-ass Daimon fighter, the next a bumbling social introvert. He was me and I was him, apart from how I wasn't in love with him.

"Sorry," he whispered. "That was too forward."

"You don't need to be sorry for anything," smiling to reduce his embarrassment, I craned to see what was in his hands. "So, will you keep me in suspense or can I see what you've got there?"

His dimples deepened as he smiled, it reached his eyes, and a soft chuckle followed.

"Why don't you sit?" I spun around a chair next to the bed.

He hesitated before taking a seat. I flopped onto the edge of my bed across from him.

"So, a girl asks again, what do you have for me? It's not even my birthday," I clasped my hands in my lap.

"It's not that kind of gift," he sat awkwardly as he tried to conceal the surprise.

"What is it then? You going to make me guess?" I leaned to the left, trying to see behind him.

He chuckled, "No, of course not. I… I, ah… I found this a while ago but didn't know what to do with it. Then I thought of you."

He reverently presented me with what he'd been hiding. Across his battle-calloused palms lay a perfect and freshly polished chromious sword. An ornate handle with curved etchings held a blade so beautiful and sharp that just looking at it felt like it could slice me open. I leaned in to admire the intricate craftsmanship.

"It's very beautiful, but I have a sword, Lorcan."

"Yes, but not this one," his eyes watered and his smile waned as he swallowed his grief. "It's Kea's."

"Oh my God," my hands smacked against my mouth.

"I found it on the beach of the Blood River of Souls when I was looking for you in Oblivion."

Kea's death and being in the bowels of Hell in the Empyrean realm were horrendous memories I preferred to push away. She had lured Yeqon away to save me. My guilt was overwhelming.

"Thomas polished it up for you," Lorcan said. "I thought it would mean something to you. We all love her, but I thought it might help you with her loss. You haven't experienced losing one of our mortal shells. It's difficult even for us, but we understand where she is," he peered at the weapon and smoothed his hand across its blade, "We will see her again, but that might be hard to understand for you. Kea adores you. She's very special, and, um, so are you."

Lorcan offered me the sword. His eyes flitted between mine and the weapon.

Tears blurred my vision as he laid it into my quivering palms. A few droplets landed on the perfect silver and magnified the engravings like miniature mirrors.

"Oh, Lorcan, it's gorgeous, but I really don't deserve it."

I sniffed and tried to hand it back, but he wasn't having it. The renewed longing in his intense stare didn't escape me. His sad eyes scanned every inch of my face and settled on my lips. I squirmed, yet my heart hammered. I was stuck between my grief and the feelings Lorcan drew out of me. As much as I wished he'd look at another, I would have been lying if I'd said I didn't enjoy the attention. I was lonely, filled with an empty feeling as though I'd lost someone other than Jaz. Filling that void could only be a positive, at least that's what I told myself every time his eyes caught mine. It was selfish and indulgent, and I felt like a two-faced sow for thinking this way.

"I can't take it," I whispered as I offered it back a second time, "It's not mine."

His arms didn't move. I pushed, he gently opposed, and Kea's sword remained halfway between us.

"She was so fond of you," he said. "I'm sure she would want you to have it. Besides, you can return it to her. You're our saviour angel. You'll redeem and unite us soon. I believe that with every part of my soul, Sophia."

Lorcan's overwhelming belief in me was almost impossible to bear as I tried again to push the sword back to him. He continued to resist.

"I can't, Lorcan."

He tilted his head, "Can't or won't?" his heavy eyes softened.

"I don't know," my head fell and I cried.

"It's understandable that you still doubt yourself, but we don't. We see you as you can't see yourself. Please take it and draw strength from Kea's remaining energy."

My fingers curled around the blade, and Lorcan's fingers slid over mine. His warm palms held mine firm and still so that our skin touched the sword as one.

"Can you feel Kea's energy?" he asked. "Close your eyes. Think of her. She is still close by, ready to help you."

I closed my eyes. The metal was warm, just like his hands, and it became hotter the more I thought of Kea. I pictured her face; high, dignified cheekbones; perfect double braids; don't-mess-with-me expression. Kea had always been ready for a fight. Her determined smile always had warmth and grit. She was so clear in my mind, as though she were right in front of me. Deep-blue eyes swirled with an eternity of experience.

I looked down to see the weapon blazing white. Its energy seared into my hands, permeated my skin, slid through my veins. Incredible power shot through me. My head flung back, and I gasped. Inexplicable confidence, strength, and energy filled me.

I stared at Lorcan, "I felt her energy. It's…"

"It's incredible, isn't it?" he slid to his knees, and his stomach brushed against my legs.

"Yes. But how?" I leaned into him like it would explain things.

"Because you're you."

I searched his eyes for a better explanation, but he'd fallen back into his amorous self. His eyes softened, and a trickle of sweat beaded at his temples. He bit his lower lip. My eyes flitted between him and the door. His breathing had increased a notch. My heart skipped a beat as I fumbled for words again.

"I miss her," I whispered.

"I'm here for you, Soph. Unlike those who've betrayed and hurt you, I'll always be there."

Lorcan looked at the ground like he could see right through to the prisoners in their cells. When he looked back up, the longing in his eyes unravelled the part of me that just wanted comfort. My selfish and lonely desires erupted, challenging my common sense. With every stroke of his thumb across my hand I fell deeper into a dangerous territory that I was embarrassingly under-equipped to navigate.

"You are worth more than your destiny," he said. "You've suffered with dignity and compassion through incredible change and loss. I admire how you've risen to it all. You deserve everything."

Lorcan's lips parted, and his mark brightened. He gripped my hands tighter. The heat radiating off him felt like it might meld us into the sword.

My throat was dry and I felt giddy. The room closed in on me. I opened my mouth to breathe, but it encouraged him. His breath fanned across my skin as he leaned in. I gripped the sword until it cut my palm. I swallowed, voiceless and unsure what to do; what I *wanted* to do.

"Please," Lorcan said, "Take it as a gift not just from Kea, but also from me," his jaw was tight. His smile faded into a deep intensity.

"I… don't know what to say."

"You don't have to say anything," he whispered. "Just accept it."

He smelled like a fresh ocean. I couldn't move, and my silence encouraged him all the way.

I looked into his eyes. "Thank you then. It's so sweet. I'm truly honoured," I pulled a little on the blade.

"And I cherish you," he almost breathed the words.

I pulled the blade onto my lap, feeling another sting with its bite. Lorcan didn't let go. His hand shot up and wrapped around my arm, his fingers soft and warm on my skin.

"What are you doing?" I uttered.

He hesitated, "I'm not sure."

His hand slid up to the back of my head. My skin tingled with a yearning I didn't want to deny. His other hand tilted my chin up. With a brief, shaky breath, he peered into my eyes. I wanted to push him away. I wanted…I didn't know what I wanted.

"Lorcan, this isn't…"

His lips were a soft, warm reprieve from the battle. I had no time to stop him, and deep down, I didn't want to. The rush was instant and gratifying, and it unlocked a more human side of me; a selfish, ill-timed desire. Strands of his silken hair brushed my face. Mere seconds of pleasure ignited a flame that had been on a slow burn, but it wasn't a flame for Lorcan. My heart raced for someone else. But who?

Despite this, I kissed him back. Lorcan was comfort in a painful world, excitement in a time of dread. Kea's sword clattered to the ground when I reached for him. He groaned, and we slipped onto the floor, hands roaming to eradicate each other's loneliness.

The door creaked open, and we broke apart with the speed of teenagers caught sneaking into each other's rooms. Matias leaned into the room.

"Are you alright, Soph'ael?" his eyes swept over us. "Ah, I see you are quite well," he frowned and left, closing the door behind him.

I ran a hand down my face and glanced at Lorcan, who looked equally surprised. I couldn't think of anything to say as I touched my tingling mouth. Apparently, neither could Lorcan. We laughed awkwardly.

Lorcan rolled himself up onto his knees, "I'd better get back to my duties, and you, um… get back to being our angel."

I nodded and picked up the blood-stained sword. I bit my swollen bottom lip as Lorcan leaned in and pecked my forehead.

"I'd better, um..." I struggled for words.

"Yeah, me too," Lorcan transferred out, probably to avoid Matias.

I leaned onto my knees, "Oh, Soph. What are you doing?" I held my head in my hands.

Lorcan's kiss had ignited a need for companionship, for more than the platonic kind. I stood and glared reprovingly at my reflection.

"That can't happen again. He'll understand," I tried to convince myself.

I couldn't encourage this thing with Lorcan, and not just because of my mission. The phantom in my mind pulled too hard and too often at my heart.

I flopped back onto the bed and pondered whether I should head down to the lowest, dankest level of Kaymakli. Away from these uncomfortable thoughts and back to the more sinister ones. Back to the cells where our enemies hid in the shadows — back to Ben and Belial. I'd spent many moments sitting outside Ben's cell. It was a selfish outlet for contemplating what I wanted to do to Belial, who resided in the cell next door. He hadn't made a sound or asked for anything since we'd detained him. He'd given himself up, saved us, but I had no sympathy for him. No one else did either, particularly Enl'iel, who repeatedly told me to stay away from him and Ben and the cells all together. My thoughts were darker when I sat in the dank quiet. Were they so different from Daimon impulses? I reminded myself that love drove mine, not greed for what wasn't mine.

With my fingers grazing my just-kissed lips, I flushed, "Ugh, you're an idiot Sophia! Prison cells it is then." I glowered at Enoch's box. "I'll be back for you later," my fingers grazed it's lid. Enoch was really starting to irritate me. Too many riddles and dreams.

I double-checked that Kea's sword was well secured on my belt and headed for the door.

"Matias, I'm going for a walk. I'll be back shortly."

"You know I must accompany you, Soph'ael," he said.

My hands clamped onto my hips, "I'm not running away. Where would I go?"

Matias's eyes narrowed, "I will not argue with you, young one. You will do as Gedz'iel has commanded for your own safety."

I threw my hands up in the air, "Fine. But I'm going to the cells, and you'll just have to deal with that."

Matias cleared his throat, clasped his hands behind his back, "Enl'iel will not be pleased."

"I'll deal with Enl'iel," I said. "She's busy helping the Alchemae anyway. I'm sure we can keep this between us?" I smiled sweetly and pressed a finger to my lips.

Matias grumbled but stood aside.

On the way out, I scooped up Jaz' iPod. I hoped just having it nearby might somehow help me find her. If nothing else, it was something of hers, and that comforted me. As I pushed it into my pocket, the same scratching sound from earlier returned. It seemed somewhere near the bed.

"I'll be there in a minute, Matias. I just need to change my shirt," I didn't want to alarm him.

I flicked the duvet and pillows around. Nothing seemed to be on the bed. I bit my lip, my fingers tapped against my thighs. The sound scratched again; it sounded like it was under the bed.

"Oh God…" my skin prickled as I squatted. A wisp of air curled around my ankles, I shivered. My knees hit the floor and my heart raced as I imagined Rogues and ghouls and all things dreadful. I grimaced, lifted a corner of bed linen that draped along the floor, convinced something horrific had to be there…

"Oh … thank God!" I sighed with relief.

A little brown mouse sat on its haunches nibbling the remnants of an Eccles cake. Beside him lay another small pile of dust.

"I thought you were a Rogue, little one. Perhaps I should name you Rogue since you sneak around like one?" I shook my head and laughed with nervous relief, "I'm sure I'm going bonkers. In the space of five minutes, I've had visions, wished death on a Daimon, thought there was a monster under my bed, and…" I touched my lips. "Well, you probably saw that," I was talking to a mouse… things were really going well.

It wasn't such a surprise to see him. The mouse had begun visiting a few days ago. He was fearless and happily sat nearby, hoping for any morsel I could share. He'd just given me a fright this time, sneaking around like a… I didn't want to think about it.

"Hungry, little buddy?"

It nibbled enthusiastically on a creamy pastry flake. It was so cute I couldn't help smiling.

The door creaked. "Who are you talking to, dear?" Enl'iel was in the doorway.

"Thank you, Matias," she said. Matias wordlessly closed the door for her. She clutched her pendant as did I with mine.

"Just a little friend," I pointed to the mouse.

Enl'iel smiled, "Still finding pets, I see."

"*They* find *me*," I shrugged, stood and dusted myself off, "You're done in the stasis room?"

"Oh, no," she waved the question away. "Goodness, that place always needs something attended to. I just had a feeling I needed to check in on you," her eyes ran over me like she knew what had happened with Lorcan, or what I was planning — or both.

Heat bloomed in my cheeks. I drummed my fingers around my pendant.

"All good here," the guilty shake in my voice a dead giveaway.

Enl'iel had that pained expression she wore too often. She was worried about me; guilt clawed through me. I hated sneaking around behind her back, having secrets I never used to.

Enl'iel put her arm around my shoulder, "Are you alright?"

"That's a loaded question, but yes," it was almost the truth. "By the way, if Lorcan asks, you healed my wounds after practice."

She sighed, held me at arm's length, her eyes travelled the curves of my face, the spark of them clearly noticing the colour of my cheeks. "And why would I do this?"

I looked down.

"I don't want to hurt his feelings. He's just…" I stepped away from her, steepled my hands under my nose, sighed into my palms.

"He is enthusiastic about your, uh, friendship? It's not like the entire community can't see it. You need to be honest and kind with him, Sophia," she clasped her hands across her stomach. "He's shockingly innocent in these matters. His entire time on Earth has been in service.

You may be surprised to hear this, but I've not known him to ever follow his heart."

I ran my hands over my face, "I've done a bad thing."

"Hmm. I can imagine."

Enl'iel examined my lips as though she could see the kiss. I died a thousand deaths of humiliation.

She arched a brow, suppressed a smile. "All knots can be undone. Some just take a little more care than others," she struggled to suppress a smile.

I pouted, "This isn't funny."

"You're correct. Matters of the heart and the feelings of others are to be cultivated carefully, especially in these times. Whatever happened between you two is an unnecessary and dangerous distraction. We cannot have passions of the flesh shading the present danger. You must be true to Lorcan, as gently as you can, for your sake, for his sake, and for the sake of our survival."

I could have curled up and burst into flames.

"It's not like that," I said. "There's no passion or flesh. God, Enl'iel!" I slumped onto the bed and covered my face with my hands. The pressure of having someone crush on me putting an entire species at risk felt dramatic at best, horrifying at worst.

"Well, whatever it is, you must end it, or put it in its place for another time," Enl'iel's words were authoritative, but her eyes still smiled.

"Can we please change the topic?" I couldn't talk to her — my Nan from a former life — about love stuff. "I'd rather have some time to think on Enoch's puzzles," it was a partial truth.

She nodded, lips pursed and eyes disbelieving, "That's much more sensible."

After a pained silence, I sighed, pulled myself back up, dignity included.

I patted the bed for her to join me, "Sorry."

Enl'iel smiled and settled on the edge. My weapons jingled like deadly jewels as her weight shifted the mattress. She plucked up a strand of my hair and smiled at the familiar colours.

"How are you coping with Jaz' disappearance?" she asked, "It must be terribly hard for you."

"Awful," I said. "I shouldn't have let her be dragged into this world," tears prickled my eyes. I tried to quash intrusive thoughts, imagining where she was, what was happening to her.

"That would have been preferable, but she had already seen enough to put her in plenty of danger. And let's be honest, you could never have stopped her from following you. You're her family, and Hell hath no fury like Jasmine when she is told no."

We laughed.

I flipped the iPod in my hand, "Never a truer statement."

"Chin up, I may have good news," Enl'iel said. "We have had contact with the captors."

"What?" My knuckles whitened around the iPod. I grabbed Enl'iel's hands as though it would make the news come quicker.

"There was a note," she said. "It was intercepted in the last hour."

"From whom? What did it say?" I gripped her hands harder, yet she didn't flinch.

"Whilst you were training, someone breached the farthest boundary above ground. Elmas sensed the intrusion and warned us. The guards apprehended them just beyond the Fairy Chimneys."

"Who was it?" I held my breath, a dizzying rage coiled in my gut.

Enl'iel pulled her hands from my iron grip, cocooned mine in hers in a gentler embrace. She squeezed them, "An Afflicted."

My fists curled tighter within her grasp, "What did they want?"

"They didn't want anything, Sophia. They were merely sent to deliver a message."

"And what was it?" my heart raced until I felt nauseous.

"We think it was about Jasmine."

Enl'iel released my hands as I pulled away. I paced. My spine burned as my wings yearned for release. My mark flared across my face like a whip.

Enl'iel stood, "Stay calm, please."

"I want to see them. Did this messenger say where Jaz is? What do they want with her?"

"We are trying to establish that. The Afflicted came with a scrawled note, which had Nephr'eus's name inked on it… and a spot of human blood."

My hands shook. It took all my will to calm their fire.

Enl'iel followed me around the room, "As we speak, Gedz'iel is deploying with Koi and Lorcan to see if they can trace where she came from."

I pulled on my boots but didn't bother with the laces. "Someone's gotta know more than that!" I reached for the door, "Wake up, Matias. We're outta here, and it's not to the cells."

Enl'iel pulled me around to face her, "You were going to the cells? After I explicitly forbade it?"

"Not now, Enl'iel. I want to see this Afflicted."

She pressed her hand against my chest. Her face blossomed with anger.

"That's not the best idea, Sophia. She's not in a good state of health."

"I've seen zombies, vampires, and creatures my nightmares would be scared of," I said. "I can cope with one Afflicted. Frankly, I don't care about her condition. I just want to find my best friend."

I pushed past her. Matias tailed me up the corridor as I sped off.

"You will waste your energy on her," Enl'iel called after me. "I only mentioned it to give you hope."

"I don't need hope," I yelled back. "I need answers. If she's seen Jaz, I'll take whatever I can get!"

I transferred away, taking the well of tears with me.

Chapter Two

I fell from the quick transfer into a wobbly run. I wiped my face dry of tears as I dashed towards the stasis room. A flash behind me told me Matias was on my tail.

"We have told you more than once that you mustn't travel alone," he grumbled.

"Sorry, buddy," I said. "I need the practice."

I snatched angrily at a wide-leafed vine trailing down the wall as though it was the plant's fault it was in my way.

Transfers were becoming easier every day, as long as I knew where I was going. It was my new favourite power. I practiced it as much as I dared; the worst I'd done was end up in someone else's room whilst they were undressing. It would be good for a laugh later... *much* later.

Outside the stasis room, I turned to Matias, "Can I at least go in *here* by myself? It's full of safe people. I'm sure I can't get into trouble with you guarding the door."

He stared down his broad nose at me, but his eyes struggled to hide his amusement, the first hint of anything other than irritation.

I steepled my hands together, "Please?"

"Very well. I do, however, advise you to refrain from further transfers at present," Matias paused, he studied me for a moment. "You're going to hurt yourself... or someone else," he suppressed that near-smile further. "That is an order, Soph'ael. I encourage you to take my direction with clarity… and the safest transportation," he stood aside and stabbed his sword into the floor, poised like a sentry.

"I will work on my… transportation technique," I over-smiled, a little affronted by his criticism. His near-smile waned. "I promise I will stay in the stasis room," I said, letting my annoyance wane.

With my hand pressed to the door, I turned back to him, "Please, call me Sophia."

"Your name is Soph'ael. Be proud of your A'vean name."

I rolled my eyes and turned away, "Okay then. Soph'ael it is for you."

Hands back on the stasis room door, my heart beat furiously with hope and fear. It almost hurt to feel it all at once. I pressed forwards, the heavy door creaked, the healing aromas hit me.

The new stasis room wasn't as well appointed as the one at Katoika, yet the Alchamae had sourced all that they needed. Humans and Eudaimonians, the Watcher-Human hybrids who lived aboveground, were a priceless covert black-market. Mehmet and Elmas were particularly resourceful. They provided a continuous supply of herbs and ingredients for tinctures and poultices. They also kept me well stocked with Turkish coffee, a small plus in a miserable situation.

The dimly lit, sweet-smelling room was fairly empty. Most people had been healed after the last battle and moved back into the living quarters. The room's calm hum set my volatile emotions at ease.

A young man lay on a bed with a softly pulsating soul stone upon his chest. He was in the deep sleep of the final Right of Sevens that allowed him to transition into a full Eudaimonian. I'd heard murmurings of an upcoming twenty-first reception, this had to be the recipient. I coveted the tranquil peace he was in.

Cael was in his usual spot by Kristen. She remained in an induced coma whilst her wounds were healing from the Rogue attack. He smiled when I closed the door, but narrowed his eyes when I rushed his way.

"Slow down there, lass," he said. "Breathe. The Afflicted is secure. She won't go anywhere."

"You know why I'm here?" I asked, resting my hand on Kristen's forehead. She was warm, the shivering of infection had ceased, her colour healthier.

"The very moment the Afflicted was brought in, I knew you wouldn't be far away," Cael leaned over Kristen and threaded fresh herbs through her hair. He peered over his shoulder at the veil that secluded the intensive care room, "The Afflicted is in no condition to flee. Sit with us a while before you tend to your business."

I looked between Kristen and the back room, anxious to do everything at once.

Cael patted Kristen's mattress, "Please. Your friend needs you here more than that Afflicted needs your anger."

I fought the urge to rush to the back room and squatted by Kristen's bed. Cael repositioned her pillow and tucked her blankets in.

"Is she doing well today?" I asked.

Cael tucked her hair behind her ears, "Like a warrior."

"Of course, she is. She looks a better colour," I took a fresh bud of lavender from Cael, threading it into her mousy hair. My eyes swept over the bandages that covered the infected Rogue bite marks on her neck. A thin drainage tube poked out of the lower part of the bottom of the crepe dressing and snaked down into a glass bottle, which hung below the head of the bed. A blood-stained yellow fluid dripped out, tinged with blackness.

Cael patted my hand, "How are you doing?"

"I'm as fine as I can be, I suppose," my attention rested on Cael's legs and his wheelchair. "What about you?"

"Oh, you know, another day, another dose of nerve ending repairs," he wriggled one toe and spun his chair around. "A little here and there each day. I'm fine," he spun his chair around again and flexed his back.

"Something's happening, not sure how far I'll get, but there's more to me than a set of wings," he winked.

The blush leaflets of his spine had begun to reform. A faint glow emanated from within them, but no one was sure if Cael would ever regain his wings properly.

He spun his chair back around so that he faced me again.

"Oh, Cael," I said. "That's looking promising though?"

"One day at a time. Don't you worry about old Cael now. I've got all the time in the world to recover, or learn new ways to get around. Besides, it's a great opportunity to learn more from the Alchemae. I did that bandage myself today!" he beamed and pointed at the neatly placed bandage around Kristen's neck.

Enl'iel appeared, a bluster of annoyance, with a full basket of herbs in her hand. She handed it to Cael, who began to sort through the contents.

"Sophia, if you had waited, I would have accompanied you, you've left Matias in a foul mood."

"He's just his regular self then," I said. Enl'iel frowned at me and quickly checked over Kristen. She adjusted the drain and fiddled with the bandage. "Not bad, Cael," she mumbled.

Cael gave me a wry look and pulled some tea-tree and stinging nettle out of the basket.

Enl'iel placed a hand on Kristen's brow and pulsed a little glow of E'lan into her skin, which brought a healthier blush to her cheeks. Enl'iel nodded to herself and pulled a fresh soul stone from her pocket, replacing the dull one above Kristen's heart.

The veil's hum called louder. I ignored it as best as I could, but kept glancing in its direction.

"How long until she'll recover?" I asked.

"She's stable," Enl'iel said, "The tissues are still infected, but I am pleased the fever has subsided." She looked closer at the drainage bottle. "You just don't know where the Rogues have been; the older they are, the more likely that they'll cause purification. As Kristen is human, we're taking it slow. She can only tolerate so much of our power at once," Enl'iel sniffed a small salve jar. "We need to be careful. I haven't seen such a wound on a human who survived. We are taking things slow and steady with her, but I am quietly confident."

"She will heal well with you looking over her," I said as the energy in the room changed.

The air tingled with an impending transference. A number of Alchemae entered the room, one after the other, arms full of supplies. One re-lit an incense lamp whilst the others spread the contents of their baskets across a large preparation table that divided the room in two. They moved with ghostly fluidity.

"Here," Cael passed me a sheaf of chamomile.

I pulled apart the delicate yellow flowers into a small bowl, ready to steep into a tea. Enl'iel collected a pinch from me and added it to the salve she had been perfecting at the preparation table. She stirred it vigorously, blowing hair out of her face as she worked. The Alchemae pounded, cut, mixed, and boiled all manner of things beside her.

The veil buzzed louder. The urge to leave grew stronger by the second.

"What are you doing for the infection?" I asked.

Enl'iel pounded the pestle harder into a mortar, "Elmas has been sourcing manuka honey among other difficult-to-find remedies for our most essential poultices. You remember how Esme taught us about its wonderful qualities?" An Alchemae passed her a pinch of something that she added to her mixture.

"I can hear Esme's voice as though she was right next to me," I said, a lump squeezed in my chest. Her loss was still so raw.

"Three times a day, at the dressing change, either Cael or I pulse the wound with small bursts of E'lan to stimulate cell growth," Enl'iel's mouth pursed with disgust as she pointed at the drainage oozing from Kristen's wound. "What you see there is the remnants of the filth the Rogue bite left behind," she shook her head sharply, tapping the pestle on the edge of the mortar. "The manuka honey does the rest," she made her back towards us, mortar in hand.

"Is she in pain?" I asked.

Cael retrieved a small ceramic jar from beside Kristen's bed and uncorked it. "Not at all," he dipped a finger into it. An orange powder glistened on his skin. "Turmeric and kava keep her comfortable," his fingertip glowed. The pinch of powder sizzled as he rubbed it just inside Kristen's bottom lip. She moaned.

"It can tingle when it kicks in," Enl'iel said. She pointed at Kristen's neck, "It helps with the infection too."

I took a closer look at Kristen's drainage system. Each droplet oozed slowly down a clear length of tubing. Within the small tear-shaped purulent droplets, swirls of violent darkness snaked around, unable to escape. The fluid was tinged the same turmeric orange as it helped draw out the darkness. Each drop of infection seemed to drown as it fell into the glass receptacle below.

"She looks much better today," I said. "Her energy is definitely stronger."

I cocooned her limp hand in mine. Her pulse was steady.

"Her heart is strong and her spirit stronger still," Cael said. "Let's hope her mind is strong too when she wakes. She'll be badly scarred."

I kissed Kristen's forehead... my lips froze as a scream peeled from the back room.

I jumped up, fingers curling by my weapons. Cael spun towards the veil. Alchemae rushed through, and I remembered why I was here. Enl'iel dropped what she was doing. She rushed around to me and grasped my arm.

"Listen to me, it will do you no good to go in there," she said.

I moved away from them, towards the howling.

Cael wheeled beside me, "She's right, darlin'. Don't trust that thing, no matter what it says or how it looks."

"I need to find out if it knows something about Jaz," I said.

"It will lie," Enl'iel said. "Let the Alchemae deal with it."

I walked closer to the veil, its energy an ocean rip drawing my in. More Alchemae rushed past me towards the prisoner.

"It will tell you anything for the drug," Cael said.

I smelled vanilla and lavender behind me, Enl'iel tailed me closely.

"It may have created this as a ruse to get Thanratos from us," she said. "We need to be cautious."

I faced both of them, "You can't give me intel that could lead to Jaz and expect me to ignore it?"

"It was remiss of me, in hindsight," Enl'iel said. "I should have known you would be impulsive and rush up here," she plucked at her pendant.

Anger flushed through me, "I'm not being impulsive, Enl'iel, I'm being proactive."

"Let her go, Enl'iel," Cael said, reaching for Enl'iel's arm, patting it gently. "We'll protect her from the Afflicted's bargains and lies. Soph is going to go in there no matter what we say. I'd rather guide her through it, wouldn't you?"

Enl'iel pursed her lips and shook her head, "Sophia shouldn't go in there. No good will come of it," she crossed her arms, met my stubborn glare, "Go back to your duties or return to the training room where strength, not disappointment, will be your reward."

"I want to see the Afflicted Enl'iel. I've earned the right!" I pressed a finger into my chest to underline the point. I moved towards the veil. "I'm going in."

Enl'iel threw her arms up and huffed. "Fine. You will learn the hard way as always," she returned to tending to Kristen, her movements stiff with frustration.

Cael winked at me, "I've got your back, darlin'. But keep your head about you, okay?"

I nodded and braced myself in front of the veil's incessant hum. I was ready to breach it, hoping there were answers within.

The gentle crunch of Cael's receding wheels told me I'd won this round, "Step through the veil, Soph. Get it out of your system. Just be ready for some colourful language and no answers," he settled back by Kristen as well.

"I really wish you went back to study Enoch's box," Enl'iel said. The mortar and pestle thumped again, "Leave us to sort out other business."

"She needs to see our world in all its glory and darkness," Cael said. "Let her go. She was born for this; she was born for us. Overprotecting her will crush what has already blossomed."

Enl'iel's shoulders fell. She nodded.

"Very well," she eyed me with caution and returned to Kristen with her concoction.

Cael unwrapped the bandage as Enl'iel scooped the mixture into some muslin.

"Nephr'eus has always been notorious for sending her rabble to do her dirty work. Don't expect a rousing reception, darlin'."

"Bad language and attitude are the least of my worries," I said.

"I'm sure Jaz has softened your ears to it," he said. "You'll be right at home. Off you go," Cael smiled and tipped his head towards the veil. "Try not to be disappointed, darlin'. More often than not, Afflicted are useless, especially when they're withdrawing from Thanratos, as she is."

"I'll keep that in mind," I answered.

Nervous; I stepped through the energy curtain. It was like walking through a cloud, but the cool tingle I'd expected was a warm rush. Its song chimed like high-pitched bells, and its energy left a peppery taste in my mouth.

My pounding pendant's heat felt like a burning boulder banging against my throat. It got overexcited over everything; I didn't understand its purpose.

I touched my soul stone bracelet for comfort when the noise and bitter stench hit me. Three Alchemae huddled around the intensive care bed as others flitted in and out. There were no monitors blipping about the patient's internal workings. No intravenous drips or defibrillators on standby. Instead, this area was intense with an E'lan halo — a white wisp that bowed over the head of the bed like a pale rainbow. The air was heavy with lavender and cedar incense, but even this blend didn't mask the smell of semi-death. A sandalwood paste sat in a mortar, ready to join the defensive aromatherapy.

The healers' faces and hands glowed with healing energy. One dabbed a sheaf of sage on the struggling patient's face, who screeched in violent protest and kicked out. Her toes, caked in filth, splayed and curled back in pain. I felt agony and hate coursing through her tainted blood. I heard the growls of her desperate stomach. She spat dirty phlegm between wicked accusations. The healers didn't bat an eyelid as they continued.

"I'm burning, you bitch!" the Afflicted screamed. "Fucking whores of humanity! Help me! Don't touch me! Argh, you disgusting dog! Get away!"

I ducked a spit missile.

"Give it to me! Give… it… to… *me*!" The Afflicted made that strange chittering sound, like the clicking of summer cicadas. She heaved and spat some more.

"You will all die in the deepest pits of Tartarus!" her panicked eyes rolled back. She was even more frightening with only the whites showing. "Oblivion will eat you alive! Cell by cell, limb by limb! Your arms shall be torn from their sockets while Yeqon's scum suck the juice from your bones! Feed me or Mistress will feed you to the Blood River!"

She moaned like a dying animal. There was a French lilt to her voice. Was Jaz in France?

The Afflicted succumbed to a coughing fit. Harsh ammonia tainted the already vulgar odour.

"Ha! I piss on you!"

The Alchemae dabbed at the yellow fluid soaking the sheets. They ignored her rantings as though she were mute.

I clasped my shaking fists by my sides, ground my teeth until my jaw ached, and stepped around the healers to get a better look. The Afflicted was a horrendous, emaciated sight. It seemed impossible that she had once been a member of this community, but somewhere within that mortal shell was an A'vean soul; a dark and tainted one that I wasn't certain could be redeemed. She writhed as the healers patted her sinuous skin with moist cloths. The red energy shackles around her wrists and ankles that bound her to the bed, didn't stop her from bucking. Her skin blistered where she struggled against the restraints. Linen lay askew and drenched with too many body fluids.

Her dull, red-rimmed eyes locked onto me. She panted like a wild beast in heat. Clawing at the exposed mattress, she sucked in a surprised breath through yellowed teeth. Her eyes widened.

"I can smell who you are, Earth-born! It's *you* she wants!" her lips curled back and her eyes flared.

Deep breath in, deep breath out. Repeat.

I no longer needed this mantra to calm my nerves, but more to reign in my simmering desire to be impulsive and careless.

I stepped closer. The Afflicted shrank back as I leaned in. Despite her mania, she was scared of me. I liked it. I leaned in more and stared into her hellish eyes. Her funky, sweet smell, mixed with urine and sweat, made me gag. I breathed out and shook off the nausea.

"Who wants me?" I asked. "Nephr'eus or her sister?"

Spittle dribbled down her pasty lips. She screamed with more desperation than malice, "*Please* medicate me! I burn from within! I will descend to the worst place! Can't you help me, dear angel of A'vean?"

The blue veins in her neck pulsed like raging rivers. She began to retch. A small trickle of iridescent blood sprouted from the corner of her mouth, her nose flared, snot crusted inside.

One of the Alchemae moved in to sponge her down again, but I pushed the healer's hand away.

"Tell me who sent you," I said through still-clenched teeth. "Tell me where my friend is, or you will lie here, in pain, until you descend."

The Afflicted's mouth gaped. Behind me, the Alchemae gasped.

"Tell me where Jasmine is, and I'll let them help you," I said. "If you don't, you can rot where you are."

She screamed, easily switching from despair to anger. "You show no mercy, and you are the Earth-born!" she spat in my face. "Spawn of a whore! That's all you are!"

I grabbed her neck and cut off the insults. Her eyes bulged as my hand lit with fury.

"Drug addict or not, you will not speak to me like that," I shoved her into the pillow and leaned in further. "Tell me what you know, and make it quick," I squeezed harder as searing energy surged into my fingertips. The five glowing digits drew blisters to her cyanotic skin. It would only take a thought, and she'd be gone.

"Soph'ael!" someone yelled.

The Afflicted moaned under my fingertips. The urge to squeeze harder shocked me, but before I could stop, she began to convulse. Red bubbles foamed from her mouth. Her teeth squeaked as they ground together.

"Roll her onto her side," someone said.

I just watched, frozen. The sight triggered the part of my heart that I'd thought was one hundred percent me. The part that was kind and compassionate.

The part an evil had now compromised.

I let go. "Oh, God!" I pulled away and stared at my hand as though it was as offensive to me as she was.

The Alchemae calmed the Afflicted with pulsations of light to her temples.

"Soph'ael?" Arms wrapped around me, but I pushed them away.

The Afflicted howled. "Scourged are we who were weak, slaves to the evil sisters. No salvation," her hoarse complaints disintegrated into gibberish, and the chittering returned.

But I had my answer.

"Nephr'eus and Anjou'elle!" My loud proclamation made the Alchemae next to me jump, "Yeqon *and* those two are after me, but why? What do they want?"

I'd drawn the eternal short straw. I glared at the ceiling.
One day soon, I'el, we shall meet, and you'll have some serious feet-kissing to do.

I grabbed the Afflicted again, but this time by her shoulders, rather than her neck. Perhaps I could shake some sense into her.

"You want mercy?" I asked. "Did you show mercy to my friend? To your kindred and those who loved you? To those you killed and maimed for your addiction? And you ask me, of all people, for mercy?"

I let go before I struck her; the urge was strong.

Her eyes rolled back again, and the gibberish returned. Her limbs began to fit once more.

"Can't you do anything?" I asked the Alchemae. "Make her help me!"

They shuffled uncomfortably. One placed her hand on my arm, "Please let us ease her pain? She is a victim of the drug and knows not of what she speaks. We can no more force the truth from her than we can reverse time."

My cheeks burned at my lack of compassion. There was a ruddy smear across my arm; my hand stained with her blood. I felt sick. This was so not me.

Or was it?

The Afflicted *was* a victim, but she had also made a choice, which had entwined her journey with Jaz' disappearance.

The tallest Alchemae wiped the blood from my arm, "This is not the girl I met not so long ago. I feel your struggle. Do not let darkness entrap your heart and mind, Sophia. I feel the struggle within you."

She touched my soul stone, "Hear her soul, not the drug, just as you are learning to hear your own soul song."

My soul song; that was exactly what it was. With each touch of my pendant and each sweep of my hand across my soul stone, a rhythmic wave rocketed through me, like a song. I clung to its soothing tone.

I kept my attention on the desperate patient, who leaned into the cool relief of a fresh cloth. I tried not to listen to the sensible and moral words, yet the Alchemae was correct. That body on the bed was a person, an otherworldly person who had made a mistake. It was then that I saw how much physical and mental pain she was in. My hands wrenched as tight as my heart.

I touched her shoulder and felt for her soul song. There was a vibration, but it felt like white noise.

"That's my Princess."

My head snapped around. Brennan stepped into the room, shaking his head. It tugged at the shame in my gut. My lips quivered, and he pulled me into his comforting embrace.

"Oh, Princess. You've been through so much."

His broad hands smoothed over my back as he held me tight and kissed the top of my head. The warmth, the familiarity, was soothing as I struggled to hold back tears.

"I know what you're doing, you know?" Brennan said. "You're trying to be what you think you need to be, but don't. Be yourself. Be brave, but be you. The universe has put a big stinking bag of crap at your feet and set it alight, but you don't need to change to stamp it out. You're a good soul, Soph. Your song is pure. You can get through this without losing yourself." Brennan cupped my face, not letting my shame allow me to look away. "You, Princess, have all of us. Be that nurse, that sweet, fun, caring girl you've always been, and the answers will come to you. We're here to catch you or push you, whatever you need."

He hugged me again.

Water sloshed behind me as the Alchemae tended to the quietening Afflicted.

"So much has happened, Bren," I mumbled into him. "I feel like I'm drowning. That place I was in, it was…just… indescribable. The things I've seen," I sobbed harder. "The waking dreams are so confusing, and don't get me started on the bloody box. I don't know what to make of the damn thing or where Jaz is. And people… They're just annoying and… oh, I don't know! Everything is so confusing, and I'm a mess, and…"

Brennan held me at arm's length. "Who's annoying you? I still have these two armies to help with that," he smiled and flexed his enormous biceps. His eyes twinkled extra bright.

My frustration dissipated as he hugged me tight again. I pulled away and sat at the far end of the room, distancing myself from the Afflicted. I teased a small orb into my palm and played with it as I tried to ignore the waning moans. The orb tingled as I wound it through my fingers; it was a distraction, but not enough. I huffed.

Brennan knelt by my side.

"Come on, spit it out," he said. "Is it Matias? He really needs a personality infusion."

"He's okay, sort of," I looked through the energy veil. "Still out there?"

Brennan smirked. "Like a rottweiler," he hugged me into his side. "Come on, Princess. Get it all out."

"It's nothing and everything," I said. "I'm seeing and hearing things, worried about Jaz, annoyed with a box, and then there's that prisoner you call Ben. I can't get him out of my head."

Brennan's face fell, his mouth tightened.

"He saved me, yet you all say he's a traitor. I'm sitting outside his cell every other day like something's drawing me to him. And..." I balanced the tiny orb on my fingertip and bit my lip.

"And what, Soph?"

The orb rolled back into my palm. "It's stupid."

"What is it?" Brennan's knee prodded mine.

"I'm stupid and confused," I snapped my hand shut. The orb extinguished.

"Stupid? No," Brennan said. "Confused? Possibly. What's confusing you?"

Lorcan burst through the veil.

"What are you doing here?" I asked a little too harshly.

"Nice to see you too, Soph," he was colder in front of his brother.

"Any luck?" Brennan asked.

"Somewhat," Lorcan tilted his head towards the bed. "From that one's energy, I sensed France as a general direction."

"That's a start," Brennan said.

I wiped my eyes, hope fluttered to life in my chest.

"The Afflicted mentioned she was a slave to the sisters," I said. "Could it be Nephr'eus and Anjou'elle?"

Lorcan paused; neither of us could look at the other.

"There are no others who work like this," he said. "Even Yeqon limits his use of Afflicted. He's too lazy to feed them the drug," Lorcan snorted. "This has the sisters' stink all over it."

"You think this could be where Jaz is?" I asked.

Lorcan nodded, "I do."

Without thinking, and I was good at that lately, I hugged him.

"Thank you, Lorcan!"

We jumped away from each other.

"Just my job," Lorcan spluttered.

I sidled back to Brennan, he whispered into my mind.

"*Oh boy, what are you two up to, Princess?*"

"*Nothing,*" I whispered back. "*Shut up.*"

"*Only trying to warn you.*"

"*I don't need — Hang on. You heard me?*"

"*Yup!*"

I grabbed my face.

"*Omg! I haven't done this properly before! Can you still hear me?*"

Nothing. I swore in my head.

"*Nah, I heard ya,*" Brennan whispered. "*Just teasing. And you really shouldn't say that word, Princess.*"

"*You're horrid.*" I elbowed him.

"*You love it!*" Brennan slapped Lorcan on the shoulder, "Right, Bro, let's piss off Jude."

Lorcan quirked an eyebrow at Brennan, then grimaced at him, and Brennan did the same, they were having a private mind chat as well.

"Well, thanks for that brotherly love," Brennan said. "Duly noted. We'll prank Jude later then, hey? Let's get back to what we were doing," he directed me to the doorway.

"Soph was just about to head back to her room and have a think on Enoch's box," Brennan looked at me all serious, adding his classic wink at the end, "Isn't that right?"

"But I want to search for Jaz!" I begged.

"We'll chat about this situation later, okay?" Brennan shot a look at the Afflicted. "We'll find Jaz, don't worry. Once we've got a hotter trail, Dipstick here will find her," he laughed and shoved Lorcan out of the room ahead of me. "Don't you have a function to get ready for, Bro? You stink. Go shower."

Lorcan grunted and left.

"Now, Princess, go play with your shiny toy or I'll tell Matias that I heard you whispering about sneaking off to the cells again. You know how much he loves chasing you."

"You're a beast," I smiled despite myself.

"And it's why you love me," he said.

Chapter

Three

Lilith screamed as she clawed at Yeqon's legs, weak from hunger. The mountain rumbled above, its protests widening gaseous fissures in the throne room. Vapours and smoke gathered in a choking haze. The Unseen glowed under its lava veins, dusted in a spray of its skin.

"Help me, my King," she said. "You must!"

Yeqon, sitting on the charred remains of his throne, kicked her away. Lilith's frail body tumbled; her limbs askew.

He grimaced at her human frailty, "Get out of my sight."

Lilith shrunk away, a wrinkled shadow of herself. Age spots erupted across the backs of her hands, her skin was thinned, blue blood vessels snaking underneath. Her split nails clawed at the walls as she tried to pull herself up with some semblance of dignity. The broken heel of her stiletto flew past Kasadya as Lilith kicked it away. She snapped the other heel off so she could stand more comfortably. The red wedge in her hand made her thirst rise.

"After all this time?" Lilith's feeble voice was shrill, "You'll let me die like a wretched piece of garbage?" Her eyes narrowed; her mouth thinned.

Yeqon's knuckles whitened around his trident. He drummed the fingertips of the other on his armrest. The trident's points glimmered lava orange. His eye twitched above a satisfied half-smile. He drank from his goblet, the heady bitterness calming his nerves.

"Look at me!" Lilith waved her hands in front of him, "I rot before my own eyes. My flesh hangs from my bones. I cannot any bare more children. This isn't a worthy demise for your soulmate!"

She hissed at someone who chuckled in the shadows, "Die!"

"Don't let me wither like this? Don't make me beg you?"

"Then rot in silence, woman," Yeqon said. "I've enough brats to feed and plenty to do my bidding," Yeqon drank and belched.

Lilith's gaunt face paled; her lips as thin as her jowls were long.

"My King!" she wailed. "Do not forsake me. You cannot humiliate me so!" she heaved deep breaths.

"Finally lost your place," Asbel whispered nearby.

Lilith's eyes found him; he ran a finger down his throat, mocked her with a sweep of his tongue over his lips.

"You will regret that," she whispered.

"Where... is... she?" Yeqon growled through his teeth and crushed his cup into dust.

Lilith's attention flew back to Yeqon.

"I knew it. You desire *her*!" she crawled along the wall, lashes heavy with red tears of jealousy. "You cast me aside for the one whose blood should bathe us all in glorious victory? You want her for yourself!" Lilith ripped out tufts of greying hair, "Look what you've done to me!" She lurched forwards, arthritic fingers arched to claw at Yeqon, but her feeble legs gave way. They all laughed.

"Bastards! You filthy leftovers will regret your mockery!" Lilith glared at Asbel.

"You worry me no more, woman," Asbel said. "Why don't you just dry up and die?"

More laughter.

Lilith screamed, she slithered up the steps and fell at Yeqon's feet, a broken heap. "I gave up everything for you. I have stood by your side since that day in the orchard so long ago. I have borne you many loyal children. I have been your one true queen," she wavered between sobs and accusation.

Yeqon looked down his nose at her and tilted his head in contemplation. Lilith wiped snot along her bony arm. She sat straighter and rearranged her scraps of hair.

"One mouthful, my King, and I shall be renewed, ever young by your side in spirit and in body. You owe me that!" her hands splayed on the ground; her nails dug into the dirt for support.

Yeqon smiled, it didn't reach his hard eyes.

"You *have* been there, haven't you? Always by my side. But did I not give you more?" he swept his arm about. "I gave you immortality, Lilith."

Her dull eyes widened, a mixture of desperation and anger.

"Yes, my love. You have bestowed me with more than any mere mortal could ever hope for. I will forever be your loyal servant in gratitude," she bowed her head.

Yeqon leaned down and reached for her. Lilith scuttled forwards, leaning into his broad hand. He ran his fingers through her wiry mop. She cooed; he glared at her.

"My Ki…" Lilith screamed.

Yeqon had grabbed a fistful of her hair and yanked her forwards until she toppled over. He dragged her across the filthy cavern floor until they reached a stain, where he pushed her head into the dirt.

"Even now," Yeqon said, "Clotted and dried in the dust, Soph'ael's blood shines. It calls to me. Look at it!" he pushed Lilith's face harder into the dust. "Her power lingers long after she left. This is the power I want. This is the power I need to defeat our father!" he screamed

Lilith's nose flared at the dark stain. Her tongue flicked out for one grainy drop, but Yeqon slapped her away. His muscles twitched and his breaths deepened as he stared into nothingness. Lilith dangled from his fist. She clawed to free herself, but she was trapped in his grasp. The cold of mortal death was close and terrifying.

Colour rose to Yeqon's cheeks. His head slowly fell back as he inhaled and grasped his heart. He groaned as if in a moment of private pleasure. Lilith's cries brought him back. His pupils dilated black; evil without rival stared at her. Yeqon kneeled, lowered Lilith to the floor. He leaned into her sallow face. He plucked at the loose skin of her neck. She held his eyes as defiantly as she could.

"You, my dear human, have no hope of giving me such pleasure."

Yeqon pulled Lilith up to his face. His lips tightened as he peered into her horrified eyes. He yanked her necklace from her, and she fumbled to grab the small soul stone that had sustained her between feeds. "No!" her mouth quivered.

"It is well past time that we parted ways," Yeqon said.

Asbel smiled the broadest.

Lilith howled. Yeqon pulled his arm back, ready to throw her down. He hesitated. Something flickered through his black glare; a tiny rainbow that hadn't emerged in a thousand years. He let go, and she fell at his feet. He reached for his trident and pricked his skin. Yeqon shoved the oozing fingertip into Lilith's mouth. She sucked hungrily whilst Yeqon smiled.

Asbel groaned with disgust.

Within moments, Yeqon flung her aside. Lilith tumbled at Asbel's feet.

"The mother of my many children deserves a final meal," Yeqon said. "Consider this a parting gift, dear Lilith. From today, you will make your own way in this forsaken world. If I see you again, it will be the Pits for you until you shrivel up and die for good."

Asbel poked her with his boot. Lilith crawled away into a corner, like a bug into its shadowy sanctuary.

"Where is Soph'ael?" Yeqon gathered his trident and spun around. He fired its searing power at his brothers, who ducked and weaved out of the way. His smoke-grey wings created a flurry of debris.

"Yeqon!" Kasadya yelled, "Stop this!"

Yeqon threw orbs at random, leaving his brothers to deflect the maelstrom of his impatience.

Kasadya aimed a fiery orb at his leader, "I said *stop*!"

Yeqon's red-rimmed eyes widened.

"Stop now, or be your own army," Kasadya growled. "We are sick of your incompetent domination," Kasadya drew a sword as long as he was tall. "You assumed yourself the leader long ago, but know this, my brother: we tire of your ego."

The others followed Kasadya's lead and armed their weapons.

"Well, well," Yeqon said. "You betray me as the bell tolls on our adventure? After I have done all the hard work, have made all the sacrifices?" He punched his chest, leaving an inflamed whorl behind, "Have my ways not been enough?" Yeqon pounded down the steps towards Asbel and towered over him. "Dear Asbel, you feel the same? Do you doubt my leadership too?" Yeqon cocked his head.

Asbel's eyes darted between him and the others. Yeqon spat in his face. Asbel's mark burned white-hot with humiliation. He looked into Yeqon's murderous glare.

"You have guided us through an arduous existence," Asbel mumbled through his teeth. "As we near the precipice, though, I fear that your… enthusiasm has strained the bonds between us. We are your brothers, not your subjects."

Yeqon leaned into his trident, "And…?"

"We will do better to work with you as equals, as brothers, not out of fear of reprisal. From you," Asbel said.

Yeqon chuckled. The sound deepened and broadened into a long bout of laughter. Asbel, Kasadya, Pineme, and Ged'erel nervously looked at one another.

Yeqon took a seat on his charred throne, he continued to laugh.

Ged'erel's face darkened, "Yeqon."

Yeqon wiped tears from his eyes, "Oh, please, go on. My ever-trusted Ged'erel, do you also wish to add to this hilarity?"

"You mock us," Ged'erel's words were measured. "Stop it. Do you wish to dominate us, your loyal brothers, or to grasp I'el's soul and purge him from existence?"

Yeqon sat upright. He leaned forwards, resting his elbows on his knees, and looked about the dank and miserable cavern. He slowly nodded at each of them.

"We will dine at his table as he melts away into nothing at our feet," Yeqon growled.

They all nodded.

"Shall we continue together, or shall we part ways and seek such on our own?" Ged'erel asked.

Yeqon stood tall. The mark on his face glowed a vivid neon. A nerve quivered under his left eye; his nostrils flared.

"Very well," Yeqon said. His eyes cleared a little; the blue that had appeared receded within the blackness.

"In peace, I ask all of you — where is Soph'ael?"

"We are looking everywhere," Pineme said. "We are dispatching more Rogues than ever to sniff her out, but she is fortified well behind wards and decoy boundaries. They are expecting us."

Yeqon thrust his trident into the ground, "*That* is not an answer!"

Pineme flinched and cocked his bow again. They others re-drew their weapons.

"But…" Yeqon placed a palm up, indicating calm. "But we shall deal with this. We have many resources. I will stop feeding my children. It is time they earned their keep."

Chapter Four

I found Av'ael cross-legged in my room, drawing in the dust on the floor with vine leaf stems. When she noticed me, she jumped up and threw herself at my waist.

"I missed you, pretty Sophia!"

Av'ael's hands clung to my legs. I edged her away from my weapons and bent down for a hug. She peeked behind me at Matias, the Ever-Present, and squished up her face before giving me a tickly K'ufili kiss. The gesture warmed not only my cheek, but also my soul.

"Hello, sweet pea," I scooped her up onto my hip. "How are you? What are you doing here? I bet your mum is looking for you."

Long lashes adorned her milky eyes, which peered deeply into mine. I felt that Av'ael somehow saw me with them, rather than with her second sight. She snuggled into me, and I instantly felt better. My pendant hummed with a calm warmth.

"Ooh, pretty Sophia, Mumma is *always* looking for me," Av'ael shrugged and giggled. "I want you to come to a party. Someone is having a 'ce… 'ce…ception tonight," her face blossomed with excitement.

"A reception? That sounds wonderful," I said. "Whose party is it?"

"His name is Dam'iel, but I call him Stinky Pants," Av'ael laughed, her cheeks reddened.

"Stinky Pants, eh? Well, I can't miss the opportunity to meet someone with such a distinguished name," I laughed. She hugged my neck tighter.

Her hand cupped my ear. "The nice man said you should listen to your dreams," she whispered. "You should find the blue water and the man of pictures."

I stiffened, held her back, and stared into her innocent face.

"What man spoke to you, little one?" I asked. An intrigued chill blossomed across my skin.

Av'ael touched my cheek as though to reassure me. "You know, the man who tells me things when I sleep. He woke me up again and told me to give you his messages," her pointer finger poked her chin as her face screwed up in concentration. "The man says you must listen to your dreams and not be frightened. He's very nice; he always shows me pretty flowers and ponies and makes me laugh," her face softened into a broad smile. "He says I'm special and that I must tell you things to help you. Mumma doesn't like it. She says I should stay asleep. She says they are just silly dreams and that I should leave you alone." Av'ael pursed her lips and pressed a finger against them, looking around for anyone who might be listening. Her eyes narrowed at Matias, who stared ahead in the open doorway.

She beamed, "It's a secret."

My heart skipped a beat.

"Don't tell Mumma I'm here, okay?"

"Where is your mother?" I asked.

Av'ael's face contorted with a devious giggle. "Don't know. Mumma always wants to put me back to bed, but I'm not ready for sleep. I like it here more. I like playing hide-and-seek with her," she giggled again. "She gets so cross!" her hand slapped to her mouth to suppress another laugh.

"I can't have you getting into trouble now," I said. "I'm sure she worries when you roam these corridors."

Av'ael winked. "It's okay, I won't get in trouble. She puts me back to bed, and I sneak out again. No one ever sees me unless I want them to," she twirled a lock of silky hair through her fingers. "Anyway, I promised her I would sleep soon. I just have to do my chores first," Av'ael closed her eyes as though in thought, then gathered my pendant into her hand. "I've seen this before. It's special," her fingers stroked the opal.

Of course she'd seen it, I never took it off.

"It's very precious to me," I said.

"The man told me that it has a story to tell you."

The hairs on my neck rose. I clung to her a little tighter. Everything seemed to slow, and the air felt heavy. Back in the Katoika sanctuary, Av'ael had told us that a man had shown her Stonehenge in her dreams. It had helped us to break one of Enoch's clues. We suspected it was I'el who sent her messages, but was it? Excitement and apprehension bubbled in my gut. I had to force calm in my voice, lest I frighten her.

"What…ah…does the man look like?" I asked.

Av'ael wriggled, so I placed her down. Her white hair floated dreamily around her face as she smiled up at me.

"Have you got pencils?" she asked. "I can draw him," she nodded with great enthusiasm.

"Indeed, I do," I waved her over. "Follow me."

She bounced onto my bed and giggled more feverishly. I could have sworn that, mid-bounce, she floated a little longer than normal. Her beige dress drifted a little too slowly in the air before it settled around her knees. I paused, tilted my head in wonder as she grinned and messed up my bed.

I flipped through my sketches of waves, rocks, and scrolls before I passed her the notebook. She sat cross-legged and began to squiggle. Her tongue stuck out of the corner of her mouth as she concentrated.

Whilst I waited, I ran my hands along the walls. Sparkling gemstones erupted wherever my fingers trailed. They shone against the lush foliage that adorned the walls.

"Pretty," I whispered to myself. A new wonder evolved with every day that I lived this in strange and deadly, yet beautiful world.

I turned back to Av'ael, who swept the pencil in large strokes over the paper.

"So, when is Dam'iel's reception?"

When a Eudaimonian turns twenty-one, they attain all of their abilities, which was cause for great joy. I understood it to be the origin of the human twenty-first party. It was a coming-of age-celebration, and I had yet to experience one.

"After last meal," Av'ael said. "They have sweets to eat at the party… lots of sweets," she licked her lips and held out her picture with both hands. It was striking and familiar.

I took the paper from her chubby fingers, unable to peel my attention from her artwork. "It's last meal soon," I mumbled softly.

"Everyone will be there," Av'ael clapped her hands. "All the important people."

I dropped down next to her and scooped my knees into my hands. "Is this who speaks to you in your dreams?"

"Uh, huh," Av'ael exaggerated an enthusiastic nod.

I felt the heavy presence of Matias behind me. He smelled of a forest in Winter. Of rainwater and moss… ancient. His shadow spilled over me. I looked up to see his brows furrowed at the drawing. "Hmm…" he rubbed his chin.

"Does this mean something to you?" I asked.

Matias stared into space. "No," he returned to the doorway.

Unsettled, I returned my attention to Av'ael's artwork. It was a cartoon-like drawing of an eye. She had added lots of outward strokes, suggesting light or sparkles. The iris was a spiral.

Av'ael pursed her lips, "It's colourful in my dreams, like a rainbow."

"It's magnificent," I replied. "I can imagine its colours. You are very special for such a visitor to talk to you."

Av'ael beamed, her cheeks blossomed.

"Does this help you save us from the scary monsters, pretty Sophia?"

I scooped her onto my lap and hugged her. She was featherlight and felt like she might slip right through me and disappear. The urge to protect her was strong.

I pulled her in a little tighter and whispered into her cheek, "Something frightened you?"

Av'ael nodded. "I want them to go away," her stubby fingers pointed to the door. "Far away," her arms wrapped around my neck, her touch sent an electric buzz through me. She pulled back and looked at me with those milky eyes, seeing with something deeper than eyesight.

"I will do everything I can to make sure you never see a scary monster ever again," I said.

She snuggled closer, "Jazzy will be okay. She's special too."

I believed her. With Av'ael still around my neck, I clambered to my feet.

"Now," I said, "Who are all these important people?"

"Ooh, Ged… Ged… *Geda'ziel!*" Av'ael beamed. "He's always there for 'ceptions. He's the boss," she twirled my hair around her fingers. "Pretty. I want colours in my hair too."

Hope rushed through me, "Gedz'iel is back? Have you seen him?"

She nodded over-dramatically.

My pendant burned in tune with my mark, the news tripped my nerves. The Afflicted woman had told us precious nothing, and Lorcan had only an inkling that Jaz might be in France, but Gedz'iel might have more. I paced with Av'ael on my hip.

"He's with Koi," Av'ael said. "I like Koi. He makes nice tea. They were at the Zytos stone, talking about boring things," she rolled her eyes and sighed.

"Thank you, little one," I kissed her cheek. It was near dinner time and I'd see Gedz'iel soon, so I placed her down and took her hand in mine. I glanced at Enoch's box; the silver glimmered, inviting me towards it.

I'll figure out who and what you are soon, buddy.

"Now," I said, "Where is this party?"

The walk to the reception led us through many lush tunnels. Av'ael held my hand much of the way but skipped ahead here and there. After running circles around Matias and nearly tripping him up, she returned to me. I clasped her hand only to feel a strange coldness tug at me. She ran ahead again towards a clutch of blossoming vines. A worker raised orbs to encourage their growth. Although her hand had left mine, I still felt that something had a hold of me. My head swam, my vision stuttered, and I glanced down to see nothing at all in my palm. But something clawed at it, tried to possess it, and I yanked my hand away.

"Soph'ael?" Matias said, "Are you alright?"

"I…" The strange feeling passed, but I was chilled to the bone, "I don't know."

Matias beefed up bigger than ever and eyed every passer-by with dark scrutiny. He walked ahead around the next corner. He returned when he had thoroughly scouted the tunnel.

He gently pressed his palm on my forehead. "Beware, Soph'ael. The safer you feel, the more danger you're in, even here," he gently pushed me along when Av'ael came back into sight.

Deep breath in, deep breath out. What the hell had happened?

Av'ael had plucked some red, pear-shaped fruits from the vines. "Here, for you," she beamed and thrust one at Matias as well.

"You are strange, young one," he took a bite.

My voice still had a nervous shake to it, "Why, thank you, ma'am. I haven't tried one of these yet."

Av'ael looked at me like Matias had done. "Stay away from cold things," her face screwed up with seriousness.

"Cold things?" I squeezed the fruit until juice ran down my wrist.

"They're bad," Av'ael said. "Stay in the light."

Her words chilled me, but she took my affected hand in both of hers and warmed it with a splutter of her power. Her smile washed away the strange warning and lit every part of her face. She was such a perplexing child.

"Take a bite!" Av'ael pointed at the glossy fruit. "They're super yummy, but I can't eat them anymore. They upset my tummy," she patted her belly, and her face fell a little. "Go on," she pushed it into my hands and passed another to Matias, who nodded and gazed at her with a strange intensity.

I took a small bite of mine. Av'ael clasped her hands under her nose, her eyes eager.

"Hmmm. It's delicious, kind of like pineapple and mango mixed together. What are they called again?"

"A'vexia," Av'ael replied. "Mumma says they come from A'vean. That's a long way," she stretched her arms wide. I took a bigger bite. "Mumma said the first Watchers brought them to Earth."

I glanced at Matias as he'd been one of the first to arrive.

He shoved the last piece into his mouth, "We planted these ourselves. It is pleasing to see them grow again. They are difficult to grow above ground."

"Why?" I asked.

Matias pointed at the worker nearby who tended the vines with glimmering palms, "That would draw attention, would it not?"

"Oh," *Give me a chance, mate.*

Av'ael gave him a stern look in my defence.

"Mumma says they give us the things that keep us healthy. She says the first Watchers made a huge garden and shared it with humans. It helped them stay healthy and live for a long time," she nodded with great enthusiasm.

"Huh?" I nodded. "I've just eaten an extra-terrestrial fruit. That's… actually very cool."

"What does that mean?" Av'ael asked, furrowing her pale brows.

Her sweetness was such a balm to my bruised soul.

"It means they are wonderful," I splayed my arms and spun around, laughing. "This whole place is amazing!"

We danced the rest of the way under the orbs' soft glow. Matias didn't join in.

Av'ael and I entered the main dining hall hand in hand and giggling.

Her face blossomed into wide-eyed excitement. "Oh, look, how pretty!" she squealed and jumped up and down excitedly.

Av'ael waved to everyone. Whilst the crowd said hello to me, she went unnoticed by my side, despite her overt happiness.

Long wooden tables lined the gargantuan room. Crystals pin-pricked raw walls and caught the light of the hovering orbs in a bright and glittering spectacle. Crystalline reflections sprinkled across the crowd like stardust. Keepers zoomed around to check on everyone.

One little Keeper hovered in front of Av'ael, then floated up to me. Although it was just a featureless bioluminescent ball, it felt like it was examining me. With a pulse of excitement, it looped the loop above my head, and the others joined in.

Av'ael clapped. "They like you, pretty Sophia!"

They zoomed away and went about whatever business they attended to, but their short show had brought enough attention that many now knew I'd entered the room. Thankfully, the excitement of who I was had died down. I received several polite nods like everyone else. I relished the almost-normality.

The crowd chatted, shoulder to shoulder, in hushed tones. Clothes were crisp white in varying styles. Facial markings glowed as greetings were made. K'ufili kisses were plentiful. I received a few as I excused myself past everyone towards the room's centre. Soft-glowing pterugia flapped in place of hand gestures. Children laughed and played tag. It felt like a family gathering; for the first time, I felt part of this world.

I spotted Eilir slapping the hand of someone picking at her treats too early. Dash appeared behind her, and she leaned into him. She looked older than before. Av'ael skipped around laughing sweetly as she chased the other children. I started to walk towards Eilir, but my shoulder caught on something before I made it two steps. I turned, my breath caught, my heart fluttered with guilt.

Lorcan's warm smile felt guarded. "No one should be at a reception without a partner," the familiar twinkle in his eyes was absent as he put his arm around my waist.

My gut squirmed. The lust from this morning had dulled. Did Lorcan regret it too? Had Brennan said something?

I slipped out from under his arm, and his smile faltered. Yes, he definitely could sense I was not on *that* page anymore.

Facepalm. You're horrid, Sophia.

"Thanks," I said, "I'll be fine by myself. I won't stay too long because I need to get back to Enoch's box."

Lorcan nodded and examined his toes. His energy lulled, "Sure, of course. I should have known you'd be too busy."

"You relax and enjoy yourself," I stammered, feeling guilty all over again. "It'll be back to training and looking for Jaz soon enough, okay?"

His mouth pursed and his tongue pushed into his cheek like he was thinking about what to say. I saved him the stress.

"I wasn't even going to be here until literally ten minutes ago," I said, looking around the beautiful scene. "Jaz would have liked this," I sighed. She would have had plenty to say about the fashion.

"So, I've come for her sake. She would kill me if I turned down a party invite. She's a people person, despite what you think," I whispered the last part with a heavy heart.

"This is no place for a foul-mouthed human."

I glared at Lorcan, "I beg your pardon?"

"You heard me," he said. "We should be focusing all our energy on finding the portal and putting down Yeqon instead of looking for one human. We're ascending in enormous numbers."

Rage and hurt surged inside me. "Jaz didn't ask for this," I whispered through my teeth. "She was dragged into this madness, and I'll have you know that foul-mouthed human would put her life on the line to save your bigoted arse."

Lorcan's mouth curled up.

"Don't you dare smile at me!"

He quirked a brow.

"Stop mocking me!" I felt eyes on my back.

"Soph, I'm not mocking you," Lorcan said. He peered over my shoulder, noting the attention we'd drawn, and lowered his voice. "I love your passion. Put it elsewhere though. Let your friend go. If she is as good a soul as you say, you will see her again once you've liberated us."

My fingers curled into fists, "You mean I should leave her to die."

"I mean, you should get on with your mission and leave us to ours. This is teamwork, you know. There's no *I* in team, as humans like to say," he smirked, quite pleased with himself.

I didn't want to make a bigger scene, so I swallowed the urge to slap him.

"If Jaz is of such little value to you, why do you bother searching for her at all?"

Whispers about our argument were swirling. My heart was pounding.

Lorcan took my elbow and pulled me closer. His warm breath, despite my anger, drew tingles down my spine. I hated myself.

"Why do any of us bother?" he whispered into my ear. "Because I am loyal to my people, as are we all. I follow orders," he paused. His warmth hovered over my ear. I want this, but not with you. Who do I want this with? I hated myself harder.

"I'm sorry about your friend, but you may need to prepare for the worst. She's just a human, and it's likely she won't survive if Nephr'eus has her."

His candour shocked me. Anger boiled beneath my calm exterior.

"If you knew what a friend was," I said, "You wouldn't say that. I feel sorry for you, Lorcan. When Jaz returns and hears you speak about her like that, she'll kick more than your arse!" I pushed away from him. "Go away, Lorcan."

He grabbed for my arm again, mumbling something that may have been an apology, but I shrugged him away and hurried through the crowd. I glanced back at him; he was statue still, chewing his bottom lip, narrowed eyes fixed on me. I kept moving and shook my head.

"Ugh, why are people so difficult," I muttered to myself.

He was likely right about Jaz' fate. My heart seized at the thought.

Eilir spotted me and waved me over, saving me from a complete meltdown.

"Ah, there she is," Eilir said. "*Yn croesawu*, my sweet. Got your appetite back, my dear? I'd be glad to see it."

Her Welsh welcome was a sweet melody. Our power's multi-lingual ability was one of the more delightful abilities.

Eilir pulled me into a bosom-filled hug, which surrounded me with the scent of flour and sugar. She was easy to melt into; a mother when you needed one. She reminded me of Esme. I was so grateful for the familiarity that I hugged her harder.

"Oh, me! Your strength isn't lacking despite you eating like a sparrow," Eilir readjusted her rumpled shirt and patted my arms. "I must say, though, that I can't see at all where you keep it," she pinched my biceps.

I pulled her hands together and kissed them, "You worry too much. I just ate an A'vexia fruit. Does that make you feel better?"

"Oh, me, darling child, it does indeed," she pulled me into another enthusiastic embrace. "Be sure to keep it up. Eating isn't just a hobby for the privileged. You've got to keep your strength up, young lady."

"I'm too distracted at the moment. I'm so worried about Jaz, but I will try harder."

Eilir already had a sweet cake on a plate, which she waved under my nose. It was her own brand of superpower.

"You will distract yourself to the grave if you don't improve, and I'll have none of that! You eat your dinner and I'll let you try this, eh?" Her smile began in the corners of her pale eyes and oozed down to her mouth. It eked into every soft line of her face. "And if you don't, I'll sit you down and feed you like a babe," she nodded with satisfaction.

It was impossible not to be charmed by Eilir, even when she was chastising me. My smile, however, was weak, my fears for Jaz too fresh.

Eilir picked up my chin with rheumatic fingers.

"Oh, come now, child. You mind my word; dear Jasmine will be found. Between Koi, those two buffoons..." she nodded towards Brennan who was flapping his wings wildly, seemingly in an argument with Lorcan. "Between those two and the others, they'll bring her back. Not to mention Master Jude! Oh me, has he got his heart in a pickle for that one," Eilir laughed.

"What do you mean?" I stepped back and put my plate down. "They can't..." I tugged at my pendant.

"Oh yes, my dear. Jasmine's prickly charms have his heart in a twist," Eilir clasped her bosom and smiled to herself as she closed her eyes. "Jude never was one for the faint-of-heart types. Many a Watcher has unsuccessfully vied for his attention," she tapped her nose and winked. "Not one has so much as put a twinkle in his eye," she winked cheekily, but then her soft jowls fell and her smile waned. "Poor lad. Another love that can never blossom. 'Tis a cruelty that's difficult to bear."

Eilir scanned the room with her unseeing eyes and located Dash, who was in deep conversation with Koi. Her face bloomed with love and anguish.

"Love between us can be only in our hearts and minds. Master Jude is as grumpy as a neutered boar in a pen full of sows," she chuckled, but her eyes closed and she sighed, "Being in love with a human is as much a torture as a pleasure."

"He can't be in love... with Jaz?" Fate couldn't be that cruel, would it?

"Oh me. Are you as blind as I, lass?" Eilir chuckled again. "I've not been wrong yet. I saw it with your parents too."

"Are you certain?"

"Of course! You wouldn't know it to hear them bickering though, mind you. Oh no, no! They sound far more like two feral cats in a fight to the death in a back alley, they do, but oh, those stolen glances!" Eilir winked.

"Oh Jaz," my words were a despondent whisper. The crowd's hum grew distant. The strict rule of zero fraternisation between humans and

Watchers was heavily enforced and resolutely understood, yet it wasn't something Jaz would have been aware of. It was an awful thought, so I hoped it wasn't true. Jaz had experienced so much disappointment and hardship; I couldn't stand for her to have her heart broken again. Not now and not by one of us. Ben had already shattered her heart as her fake brother. I didn't understand it, but I knew he had immersed himself in her life and betrayed her as well as us.

Before I could dwell more on it, the celebrations started. A female Watcher called a family onto a raised dais. The crowd hushed. Gedz'iel appeared in a flash of light. The orange Zythros stone hummed and pulsed behind him like a halo. His cropped hair glistened as the silvery gems on the walls refracted across his face. He rubbed his hands together, clapped, and produced a large white orb, which he threw upwards. It hovered and warmed the room like a spotlight. His magnificent strobing wings unravelled and stretched wide.

"Good evening to you all," Gedz'iel said. "Forgive my tardiness and lack of traditional attire," he gestured to his bare torso. "These are indeed strange times. As you are aware, we have been searching for Yeqon and Nephr'eus as well as the human girl."

My heart froze.

"We have encountered increased Rogue and Afflicted activity," he said. "We have also noted scattered vampiric attacks in broad daylight. They show the lengths Yeqon will go to."

He paused. Whispered murmurs prodded at the obedient silence.

"I urge you to take extra caution, especially those who are free to leave Kaymakli," Gedz'iel pointed to one of his many scars; the silvery skin shimmered. "We all carry enough of these. I do not want to see any more on you, my kindred. I hope this will be the last reception forced upon us outside of A'vean."

His grim face lit into a gentle smile. "Tonight, let us celebrate," Gedz'iel held out his hands. "With the blessings of I'el, let this ceremony commence."

A lighter murmur travelled through the room. Some younger teens shouted a few obscenities about what they'd do to our enemies. They received cold glares from Gedz'iel and a flick of a tea-towel from Eilir.

"Considering the dire times we find ourselves in," Gedz'iel said, "It is especially wonderful to observe one of our own mature."

He peered about the audience, and the room glowed brighter as everyone's faces lit up.

Other than Eilir, no humans were present.

"Dam'iel, please step forwards," Gedz'iel held out his hand in invitation.

A gangly young man in white training pants, with bare feet and chest stepped forwards. His shoulder-length white hair was slicked behind his ears, herbs entwined through it in small twists. A soul stone hung from his neck. New wings sputtered and arced with emerging energy down the length of his spine. He wrung his hands and squinted at Gedz'iel's glowing presence. The room was silent, but for the trickle of water from the nearby underground well.

Gedz'iel opened his arms. Arcs of light sizzled out of his palms and danced above them. Dam'iel let his arms fall to his sides as he took a confident step closer, chest puffed out with pride.

"Master Dam'iel, of the line of I'el, the creator of all life, I welcome you into maturity. You have transitioned thrice through the Right of Sevens. I now welcome you as a purveyor of peace, harmony, and protection, be it here on Earth, or at the farthest reaches of the universes," Gedz'iel looked to the crowd.

"In I'el's name we give you our peace, harmony, and protection," the audience answered.

My eyes glazed over a little at this point, I let the ceremony fade into the background. I was too worried about Jaz.

Brennan startled me when he grabbed my shoulders and hugged me from behind, "This is the fun bit, Princess."

I gently slapped him as I snapped out of my thoughts, "You scared me," I whispered. "What do you mean?"

His eyes widened, "It gets a little bloody."

Enl'iel appeared on my other side. "Oh, stop it, Brennan. Watch our beautiful custom and learn, dear," she prodded my chin and turned my attention back to the dais.

Dam'iel kneeled before Gedz'iel. An Alchemae stood nearby, a sweet incense lantern in one hand and a mortar and pestle in the other. The thick cedar and sandalwood smoke encased her like a mystical fog. I held my breath as Gedz'iel leant forwards and wriggled his fingers until he had moulded a thin shard of light, which he held like a wand. He traced Dam'iel's facial markings. Dam'iel became rigid, but held his position as his face welted red. My fingers dug into Brennan's arm; he kissed my head to reassure me. Dam'iel's lips were a thin line of control. His mark began to glow from within, strong and beautiful. Gedz'iel nicked the base of Dam'iel's right shoulder blade. It didn't bleed but cauterised into a neat line. Gedz'iel stepped back and assessed him.

"You are now fully connected to the E'lan," Gedz'iel said. "You shall move in tune with the universal song which connects everything."

The Alchemae applied the ointment from the mortar to Dam'iel's inflamed skin. His parents ran onto the stage and showered him in K'ufili kisses and hugs.

Av'ael stuck her head out from behind the Zythros stone and furiously waved at me. She disappeared just as quickly.

"Okay, Princess," Brennan spun me around. "This rock star has to leave you to party alone. Got myself a gig looking for Mini Princess."

Enl'iel shook her head, but smiled with her eyes. Brennan pecked her cheek.

"Time to head off," Brennan said. "Koi is banging on in my head. He's bloody impatient, you know. You'd think I had a hearing problem the way he screams his orders."

I grabbed his arm, "Can I come with you, please?"

Brennan winked, "Princesses who are important angels must stay here and play with shiny boxes."

"But—"

Enl'iel squeezed my hand, "Let him go. They have their job; you have yours. I will help you where I can between my duties with the Alchemae. You heard Gedz'iel, an increase in Rogue activity is a bad sign. We must find and activate this portal before Yeqon has any opportunity to get his hands on you again."

I sobered at that thought.

Apparently, so did Brennan. "You really need to work out the next part of Enoch's puzzle," he said. "I'll find Mini Princess, I promise. You keep up your training and problem solving, okay?" he squeezed my hands.

"All I'm doing is staring at that damn box or improving my PB on the circuit whilst you guys are out there in danger. Why couldn't Enoch have just put a post-it note in the box?"

Brennan laughed. "See, Enl'iel? She has a sense of humour after all," he hugged me tight. "If Enoch had made it easy, we would have solved our issues long ago. You've sorted crazy stuff out before with your most powerful weapon… instinct. Listen to those visions, and if your intuition looks like me, it will be damn good looking!"

Enl'iel slapped him over the head, "Away with you."

"Well, it *could* look like my brother," Brennan said. "That would be trag…"

Two Watchers appeared in a blast of heat and light. They bore many markings on their shoulders and looked as ancient as Matias.

"Master Gedz'iel," one said, "Yeqon has breached this realm. Rogues have been spotted on three continents, and…"

The air was hot and stuffy. My mind ached with the distant sounds of crashing waves.

"Speak!" Gedz'iel said.

"By the mercy of I'el. Yeqon has released his children!"

The room gasped as the female Watcher flopped forwards and leaned on her thighs. Her pulsating wings dulled as a large wound revealed itself beneath their glow. A ragged gash oozed down her side. The male Watcher held her whilst the Alchemae ran to her and transferred, presumably to the stasis room.

Gedz'iel closed his eyes and breathed deeply. His jaw clenched, and his temples pulsed. He nodded at the other messenger.

"Leave," he said to the tense crowd. "The celebrations are over. All fit warriors report for duty immediately."

His attention landed on me for a moment whilst the room fell into well-practiced evacuation. Guards rushed to Gedz'iel with new weapons, which he quickly adjusted around his hips.

Brennan tried to pull me out of the room, but I dug my feet in. Lorcan, Koi, and Jude appeared beside me, their faces like thunder. Koi cracked his knuckles and rubbed his hands over and over. Matias shadowed me.

My pulse raced as I walked towards Gedz'iel, who was questioning the male Watcher.

"Wait, Princess," Brennan's face was taught. He patted my hand and pulled me close.

Gedz'iel inspected the messenger's injuries. He took a herb from an Alchemae and ran it across the Watcher's skin in his glowing palm. It made quick work of the puncture wounds circling the Watcher's arms, and he bowed in thanks.

Enl'iel rushed forwards and insisted he sip from a cup. He obliged her for two mouthfuls with a grateful smile, followed by the disgusted wince her tonics were famous for.

He bowed his head, "Master Gedz'iel, we've failed to contain Yeqon's spawn. Forgive us."

"Do not apologise," Gedz'iel said. "You first saw them in Mexico?"

"Yes, in the usual place at the Zone de Silencio. We remained vigilant under the eye of the Empyrean realm. Normally, the odd Rogue appears and we deal with them, but this time, we were unprepared for the flood," he shook his head.

Gedz'iel paced, "What happened after the breach?"

"We covertly diverted all human activity. The day was overcast, or so it seemed. It now appears though that we were fooled by a veil. Yeqon's mists were hidden within the clouds; they poured from the sky in the thousands. We were fifty," the Watcher's shoulders fell. He hung his head and kneeled.

I was rigid. I barely knew what it all meant beyond things coming out of Yeqon's realm.

Gedz'iel twirled a sharp sliver of light through his fingers, "Get up. This is no fault of yours. Tell me all you know of these creatures, his children, such as they are. How do they travel? I've not seen one alive in a thousand years."

"By foot," the Watcher said, "But at incredible speed."

"Do they still camouflage as human?"

"Yes, Master. Their ability to meld with the human population is disastrous. They hid amongst the mist and stench of the outpouring Rogues. It was only once the Rogues hit the ground and the fog dissolved that we saw them emerge. And… they are hungry."

"Did these hybrids show A'vean characteristics?" Koi asked.

"Some. They had partial face marks, but they appeared mainly human. Most are red-headed."

"Like their mother," Koi said. "He still breeds with her," he pumped one fist into the other.

"Brennan, what are they?" I asked.

Clearly, they weren't Rogues by everyone's reaction, they were worse.

Brennan shushed me, "They're Lilith's children, and they're bad news."

"That foul woman who Yeqon called his Queen?"

Brennan didn't answer, but I knew what they were. Lilith survived by drinking Yeqon's blood. What did that make her children? My flesh chilled.

Koi fell back and spoke with Jude. Lorcan glanced my way a few times, but only concern reflected at me.

"Where have they breached?" Gedz'iel asked.

"South America, North America, and the Alaskan border. Speculation of an Australian attack remains unconfirmed. We suspect that some can fly, but we haven't yet observed it."

"Oh hell," Brennan whispered.

"Fly?" Koi murmured. He and Gedz'iel exchanged glances.

"Human casualties?" Gedz'iel asked.

"Enough have died or disappeared that the human communication networks are broadcasting acts of terrorism across these territories. Their political leaders are creative with explanations. Panic is growing."

Gedz'iel closed his eyes and retracted his wings. He took a few silent breaths, "We must communicate with our sleeper agents in all governments. They can minimise public fear and knowledge from within."

"I will leave at once," the messenger said.

Gedz'iel nodded and waved him away. His eyes landed back on me.

"Everyone who is unable to fight is to bunker down," he said. "Enl'iel, send word to prepare for wounded humans and A'veans. We will triage and remove any witnesses or victims of the Rogues and vampires from the human world."

My mouth dried up. The word vampire spoken aloud made it true. My pendant beat faster in response to my horror.

"Koi, Jude, gather every available fighter we have regardless of age. Matias, you are relieved of your duty to Sophia. I need your skills elsewhere. Brennan, you will maintain fortification of this sanctuary and others if requested and monitor the prisoners. Lorcan, you will replace Matias as Sophia's chaperone."

"What?" I asked.

Gedz'iel transferred to within inches of me. I looked into his heavy eyes; they held an age of weariness, the weight of too much time.

"Our time indulging you is over, Soph'ael," he said. "Yeqon has unleashed an unspeakable plague and uses humanity to divide us. He is desperate. You must double your efforts to solve Enoch's puzzle. I am sorry, but we can no longer search for your companion."

With one ear-piercing crack of light, Gedz'iel was gone. And I was speechless.

Chapter Five

Lonely corridors stretched before me as I carried the box I'd quickly collected from my room. Orbs lit as I passed. I barely noticed the people coming and going after the reception had been abruptly cancelled.

Lorcan followed me, "Soph?"

"I don't want to talk."

"Slow down," he said. His tone bordered on annoyance, "I know why you're upset. Just stop a minute!"

"You don't know anything, Lorcan," I hurried around a few more turns, past the boisterous training room, and down another level where the air cooled. "I bet you're happy. How will anyone help me find Jaz with Hell ripping open? You'll be glad to hear that she's probably dead."

His footsteps stopped. Soon after, so did mine. I turned to see him begin to turn away, his wings shimmered, ready to transfer.

"I'm sorry," I said. "I know you don't like her, but I shouldn't have said that."

His wings dimmed a little and he turned back around. A cluster of guards blustered past towards the training room.

Lorcan shrugged, "It's okay."

"Nothing is okay." I leaned against the wall and banged my head against it.

"You're right," he said. "We're all on edge and scared," his face was as soft as his voice had become.

I didn't ever really consider that any of them would be scared. I continued along the tunnel and entered the prison. Lorcan padded after me.

"We don't know what'll happen," he said, "But as crap as all this is, we need to stick together. I'm sorry too. I was cruel about Jaz," his shoulder was level with mine.

"Thank you," I said. "Please let me help?"

"I do want you to help. This isn't what I was thinking though," disappointment dripped through his words as we faced the cells.

I pointed at two sets of footprints, "Someone's been here."

"*You*'re not meant to be here, Soph," Lorcan grabbed my shoulder. "C'mon, let's get outta here. I'll even look at that bloody box with you."

"You know what?" I shoved his hand away, "Kea shouldn't be dead, Jaz shouldn't be kidnapped, and vampires shouldn't exist! *That*, Lorcan, is what isn't meant to be."

I pushed through the door, feeling Lorcan's eyeroll.

"Ma'am."

I spun around, "What is it?"

A guard bowed his head, "You're not supposed to be here."

"But here I am!" I swept my arms out.

"Ma'am, my orders are—"

"My orders come from a higher power than yours," my finger trembled as I pointed at the ceiling, towards A'vean and I'el.

"That trumps Gedz'iel, Enl'iel, or whoever is telling you what to do."

The guard straightened, glanced at Lorcan, and returned to staring at the back of the room, "Yes, ma'am."

"Whose been here?" I asked.

"Your brother," the guard said.

"Rik was here?" my heart raced. "Why?"

"Enl'iel escorts him once a day to visit," Lorcan said.

My mouth screwed up. "Okay for him to be around Daimon but not for me, is it?"

Rik was an emotional wreck; I had thought he'd keep away from here.

I squatted and pulled at my pendant. The chill that had followed me for the past few days clawed at me again. Lorcan hovered close but kept his mouth shut.

I opened my pockets and laid out Enoch's box and both scrolls. The parchments curled up at the edges; I gathered some stones to hold them down.

The oppressive quiet of this place helped me focus. Apart from Lorcan's breathing, the humming red bars were the only sound. They murmured as they reflected against the chromious-lined walls. How could I sort out this box and find my best friend? Jaz would throw herself at everything at once.

The cells were dark, but I heard the shuffles, felt the changing pulses. The prisoners remained quiet, but I'd sensed Ben's pulse raise the moment I'd entered as it always did. I imagined it was hatred. I felt Belial's agitation as he moved in the darkness. Their intense unnerving interest in my presence hung heavily in the shadows.

Elizabeth's delicate scroll cracked under my lightest touch, threatening to crumble before I found answers. I turned the box upside down and sideways, but it offered no mercy. Elizabeth Woodville had clearly known something about the Disciple of Learning, but was it someone from her time? That would take me back to the 1500's, where I'd begun when I hunted down her grave in St George's Chapel in Windsor Castle. Yet Enoch, who had lived thousands of years before her, had inscribed the title in the box, too, and he had foreseen more than what was written in the prime scroll. Was this another prophecy?

"Okay, Mr. Enoch, sir, I'm cracking this code if it kills me, well, preferably not kill me but..."

Ben's or Belial's shuffle halted the creeping breeze that nagged at me more often. Once they settled, it whipped up again. A snicker whispered into my ear and brought goose bumps to my skin. I spun around, but only Lorcan stood behind me. I reached for one of the scrolls… an icy sensation scratched my knuckles.

I yanked my arm away. The scrolls fluttered up, and Elizabeth's fell upside down across Enoch's.

"Everything alright?" Lorcan asked.

"Of course," I lied.

I brushed my hands up and down my arms to quell the uncomfortable feeling that I was being stalked. Whatever it was kept a low enough profile that only I noticed it.

Then again, perhaps I was going mad from being cooped up underground.

Deep breath in, deep breath out.

I reached for Elizabeth's parchment, my attention drawn to its edge, which sat in such a way that it underlined a paragraph of Enoch's scroll. I pulled the paper closer.

The devil will be her saviour, an angel will be her downfall.

My fingers grazed over the ink.

"The devil will be my saviour, the devil…" I squinted in Ben's direction as the words repeated over and over in my mind.

I pondered the thought, staring into the darkness, catching his outline. Blood rushed to my cheeks. The scroll crinkled in my sweaty palms, and I shook my head, flicking ridiculous thoughts away. I glanced between the parchment and the cell where Ben remained ever so silent and annoyingly perplexing.

But it made sense. Ben had saved me from Yeqon and Belial's clutches, and I couldn't ignore the strange sensation that drew me to him. Did that make Pathos, the Eloi, who had betrayed us to Yeqon, the angel who would be my downfall? "But he's gone now," I mumbled.

Someone in the cells spoke, but the sound was hushed. Lorcan moved in front of me. Behind the ruby light of the cell bars, I made out Belial and Ben. I rose and walked past Lorcan.

He barred my path, "Stay back, Soph."

"They know something," I pointed at their shadows, my attention on Ben. One heart raced a little faster, and I just knew it was his.

Lorcan grunted and tightened his folded arms.

"*Enoch's words have proven true so far,*" I whispered into Lorcan's mind. "*Ben has saved me once, and he was a devil in disguise. I think he may be the one. He may be the devil who will help me. Perhaps he will be the key to saving us all?*"

"*Are you kidding me?*" Lorcan's mark glowed brighter, "*He's nothing more than the scum of Tartarus.*"

My mouth thinned. I bit back my anger and rolled up the scrolls.

"*Are you here to help me or not?*"

Lorcan's eyes bulged, "*I'm trying to stop you from getting yourself ascended!*"

"*I've done okay without you around. You didn't save me from the bad guys; Ben did,*" I regretted my thoughts immediately.

Lorcan's mouth fell open, and his arms untwined. I may as well have stuck a knife directly into his heart.

I looked down in shame, "*I'm sorry. I didn't mean for it to sound that way.*" I took his hand in mine. "*I trust you with my life, Lorcan.*" The hurt blazing under his skin abated, and he crossed his arms again, "*But please don't block my every move. This is the first thing that has made any sense in a while. If Ben is what Enoch suggests, he only has his freedom to gain.*"

Any semblance of calm disappeared from Lorcan's face, "You've no authority to set him free."

I glared at him. "For I'el's sake, Lorcan, shut up!" I pressed a finger roughly against my lips.

"*I can use any means necessary to do what you people want me to do!*"

Something, maybe a bed, scraped behind us. The E'lan rose, and footfalls followed. Ben was only feet away from the bite of his confines.

Lorcan stepped between me and the cells again. "You're making a big mistake if you trust him," he whispered.

"Out of my way. We can either work together or fight it out," I shook my arms and lit one hand.

"I'm trying to protect you," Lorcan said.

"And I'm trying to save the lot of you!" I pushed past him. Lorcan grabbed for my hand, but I smacked it away only for him to pull me back by my other hand, "Let go!" I snarled through my teeth.

"I'm not touching you!"

I shook my hand free and spun around, ready to throttle him, but his hands were nowhere near me. There was no one near me.

Something brushed past me. Husky laughter trailed unseen footsteps around me. Lorcan's eyes widened. I focused on the doorway's shadows.

"Is anyone out there?" I asked the guard.

He stepped outside briefly, Lorcan in tow. When Lorcan returned, he shrugged with an unsettled expression.

The guard resumed his position, "There is no one present other than yourself, Watcher Lorcan, and I. Do you require assistance, ma'am?"

"No, thank you," I waved him off and turned away.

A sharp chill grappled at my spine. Something was definitely following me. I was convinced of it now. No little mice friends were down here. I had quite enough attention focused on me, I didn't need anyone else, corporeal or otherwise.

"Are you okay?" Lorcan asked.

"Let me think a minute, please," I slumped and bit into an A'vexia I'd stuffed into my pocket on the way down. It was sweet and delicious, but the shine across its blood-red skin caught my eye and I flung it aside. The memory of Lilith and her red apples soured its flavour.

I reached for the scrolls again, noted every brittle square inch, every colour variation or stroke change. I held Elizabeth's scroll up and floated a small orb above my head to illuminate it. My pendant thrummed to life.

"What are you hiding, Gran?" I muttered.

"Talking to yourself is the first sign of madness," Ben's voice was honey.

I lowered the script and peered at his cell. Careful to tuck the scroll behind my back, I sat back on my heels and watched his outline sharpen.

The red glow of the bars framed Ben's strangely familiar face. It grated on me that I couldn't place it. The silvery scar along his chin evoked something in me that I couldn't put my finger on. His tattered appearance pulled at my sympathies, but only just; he *had* betrayed his kin after all.

"So, you're talking now?" I returned my gaze to the scroll; my attention, however, was one hundred percent on him.

"You turn up day after day with your shiny box and notes and talk to yourself," Ben said. "I was a little concerned, to be honest."

"You come here *every* day?" Lorcan asked.

"Every single day, pretty boy!" Ben teased. His eyes glimmered under raised brows. He nodded mockingly slow.

"You piece of…"

"Shut up!" I shook my head at Lorcan. "You too, Ben."

I couldn't look away from Ben. Within his blue eyes was something more than a Daimon. It was familiar. It was frightening. Perhaps it was for him too, because he looked away first.

Ben chuckled and pretended to unravel a scroll, "'Tell me your secrets, Mr. Enoch, sir.'"

I scowled; my heart hammered with humiliation, "You're hilarious."

Ben's mouth stretched into a half-smile. "Can you blame me? There's not much else I can do to amuse myself in here," he leaned close to the unforgiving beams.

The guard marched forwards, sword flickering with E'lan, "Stand down, prisoner!"

"That's a big weapon you have there! Okay, okay, I'm scared," Ben smirked, put his hands up in surrender, and backed away. The weapon's glow highlighted the bruises on his face.

"I said, stand down *and* be quiet prisoner, or I will silence you myself," the guard's expression left no room for compromise. He kinda scared me too.

Lorcan made a self-satisfied snort, clearly happy that the guard was on his side. I gave him a dirty look and then addressed the guard.

"It's okay. I want to hear what he has to say," I said. "He doesn't scare me one bit," that wasn't entirely true. Ben didn't flinch, rather, he responded with an annoyingly smug expression. He would toy with me if I let him. I had to be smart and careful.

"Very well, ma'am, but I advise you to be cautious. He is not to be trusted. None that consort with the Unseen are an ally," the guard dulled his sword and resumed his position, widening his wings in an extra warning to Ben.

"Listen to the guard if you won't listen to me," Lorcan said and released his own wings.

I refrained from asking why they needed to show off who had bigger wings. I scooted closer to the cell and pulled my belongings with me. My pendant pulsed, warning me to keep my distance. I stopped where I was. Everyone and everything seemed to push me back from him, yet another force was telling me to run straight to Ben. I ventured no closer, for now.

"So, Ben. What did you want to say?" I asked.

"Nothing really," he picked at his finger nails and sighed, "Just enjoying the view."

The air tingled with Lorcan's anger.

I scoffed, "Not a word? I doubt that. You look like you have a world of worry you might like to get off your chest?"

Ben's tone flattened, "There's nothing I can say that's worth anything to anyone."

"Why are you bothering me then? Go back to your shadows and sulk. I've got enough on my mind," I turned away and picked up Elizabeth's scroll.

"Then why do you come down here so often? Clearly you want to talk to me," he responded.

I huffed, "Don't big-note yourself."

"There are safer places than here, Sophia," Ben's eyes narrowed and travelled around the room. "I sense the change in the air. Something's going down, isn't that right? You guys are scared," he licked his finger and tested the air, his eyes on me. "My guess is that the King of the Daimon is up to something, so if I were you…"

"If you were me what?"

Ben shook his head, his laugh hollow. Keen eyes sparkled beneath tired lids, "I'd be looking for a safer place than this. I'm fairly certain that my head and his," he jerked a thumb towards Belial, "Our heads have a gilded plate waiting. Yeqon lets nothing go unpunished. Not. A. Single. Thing," Ben blew a lock of hair out of his eyes. "Isn't that right, my friend?" Ben called to Belial, who only grunted in response.

I gathered the scrolls and tucked them into Enoch's box.

"If you must know, I actually feel very safe down here," I said. "Usually, no-one bothers me. I'm guaranteed a few minutes to myself. And just so it's clear, I'm no damsel in distress."

"That's one thing we can agree on," his face lost its humour, fading into darkness, empathy, frustration. A myriad of emotions seemed to fleet through those eyes.

"If you've got something helpful to say, then say it; otherwise, slink back into your corner. Between trying to be *the saviour*," I made mocking air quotes as I uttered that term, "Between that and worrying about Jaz, I wouldn't mind a bit of peace and quiet."

The energy in the room shifted. A hot sting nipped at my skin.

"What do you mean, you're worried about Jaz?"

I shouldn't have said that, "That's no concern of yours." My voice hitched.

"What's happened to her?"

"Why do you care?" My pendant thrummed.

Although Ben looked cool and calm, I heard his heart fire ten times faster. He was suppressing something, and it didn't feel like anger. He stepped closer to the bars; the red glow made his eyes look blood shot.

"Is she missing?"

I clasped the pendant.

Lorcan put a hand on my shoulder. *"Soph, stop,"* he whispered into my mind.

I put my hand up to silence him. With a gentle sweep of my foot, Enoch's box slid behind me.

"Why are you so concerned?" I asked.

His chin quivered, and his eyes watered.

Ben took in a shaky breath. "She's an innocent," he whispered. "I wish no harm to innocents," his hands swept up his face and over his head. In the rusty hues of the cell bars, the unusual white streaks in his Daimon-black hair appeared bloody.

"How do you know her?" I asked.

"What does it matter?"

I stood as close to the cell as I dared. "It matters because any piece of information could help me find her," I smelled the salt in his sweat, felt the heat of his skin. He smelled familiar and it stirred something in me.

Ben kept combing his misshapen and bruised knuckles through his hair. Something inside screamed at me, but I couldn't place it.

"How do you know Jaz?" I asked impatiently.

He sniffed and straightened. "Traitor and all, you know? I've been around," he said followed by an awkward silence.

"I can help you find her if she's missing. That's it, isn't it? You've lost her? She's been taken? I'm an excellent tracker," there was an emotive urgency in his voice, as though he actually cared.

"You'll be doing nothing other than rotting away in there!" Lorcan grabbed my shoulder, urged me back, but I shook him off.

I didn't want Ben to know things he shouldn't, but it seemed that horse had bolted.

"I already have an excellent tracker," I smiled at Lorcan, caressing his ego which I knew was sorely needed.

Lorcan wasn't impressed. His hands pumped open and closed as he paced the room. Sparks jittered from his fingertips.

Ben scoffed, "Lorcan is an amateur."

Lorcan cracked his knuckles. Even the whites of his eyes seemed to glow.

I kept a close eye on the silverware at my feet, "You're looking to escape, that's all."

"Finally, she listens to me," Lorcan mumbled in my head.

"Wouldn't you?" Ben asked. "But perhaps there are other reasons. Didn't I rescue you from Yeqon?"

"Yes," I whispered. "You did. Why?" I moved closer to the cell again, suspicious of his every utterance.

I held his gaze for a second; there was so much left unsaid in his bewildering eyes.

Ben shook his head and kicked his toes into the earth. His hands dug into his pants pockets.

A chuckle came from Belial's cell.

Ben raised his fist in Belial's direction, "Keep your mouth shut!" Ben bit his bottom lip, paused, closed his eyes, and mumbled something to himself before he looked at me.

"I saved you because I've hated Yeqon from the time he took me in."

"So, why stay and do his dirty work?" I demanded.

"Because he wanted it," Lorcan said.

Ben ground his teeth and shot daggers at Lorcan, "Because I was weak. Yeqon hunts the weak, and once you're in his service, it's near impossible to get out in one piece."

"You're here, aren't you, Ben?" I asked, "In one piece?"

His eyes hooked me, something twisted inside me. My gaze dropped to my feet. Why did I feel like we were the only two people in existence? Why was my belly writhing and my mouth dry when he looked at me?

Ben sighed and paced, "Yeqon isn't as on his game as you think."

"It still makes no sense," I said. "You could have run anywhere."

"But you were what I needed to open my eyes."

My guts squirmed harder. I wanted to run to him and throw myself into his arms.

Ben hung his head, "I was a good Watcher, believe it or not."

"That's the first thing you've said that I know to be true," Lorcan said. "Why throw it away? You had all of us. We were here for you. Why would you choose him?" his question dripped with betrayal and hurt.

"Why?" The cell lit up as Ben's wings spread. Shadows consumed his eyes, and his mark blazed. He glared at Lorcan first, then at me. His hair danced in the static of his fury. Dirt whirred up and misted through the red bars, which zapped it into nothingness.

"I'el murdered my wife!" Ben bellowed at Lorcan, "My entire village, my world! And for what? Because you guys created us when you were told not to. I'el punished *my* family for *your* sin."

Ben clutched his face and roared. He squatted, rocking in his misery. His wings dulled, he heaved for breath. His hurt and rage hit my heart. Copper tainted the air when he punched and kicked the unforgiving rock that confined him.

"Stop it!" I moved closer until the bars' sting threatened me.

I felt Lorcan behind me. The guard's jangle of weapons told me he, too, was nearby.

Ben kneeled, rolling something in his bloodied fingers.

"Is that true, Lorcan?" I asked. "Did I'el really murder his family?"

"Yes," Lorcan said. "He wanted to wipe out the hybrids. He flooded the world and sent in high angels to finish what nature hadn't. He wanted to reset the planet, give humans a fresh start with a clean race."

Tears prickled my eyes. How hadn't they all turned on I'el?

"Ben, I'm sorry," I said. "I… I don't understand it."

Ben held up a bead, "This is all I have left of her. This and the memory of her flesh torn off her body."

"I understand your anger," I whispered.

He hissed, "You could never understand."

My mouth tightened. "I've lost people since this world gate crashed my life. I've lost those I love, been threatened, abused, and beaten. I could have chosen to go the wrong way, but I haven't. You chose the wrong path. That's on you," my last words barely made it out as I wiped my eyes dry and sniffed back painful memories, "If there's any part of you that can face that truth, then you can earn your redemption. I *need* help."

"Soph…"

"Just stop, Lorcan. Be helpful or go away."

Enoch's scroll had led me to the right place. I knew that Ben was the devil who would save me… I just knew it.

Ben was still, apart from his newly swelling fingers that twirled the bead. Tears slid down his cheeks as he crushed it into dust.

"I'm so far gone," he said. "All I can do is try to fix things in some small measure before I descend."

Belial laughed unexpectedly, "You have as much chance of redemption as I, Nik'ael." His deep voice was weak and dry, like he'd swallowed sand.

Ben's face glowed a little brighter, and the E'lan buzzed louder. Belial shuffled. Ben stared towards Belial's cell sand balled purple fists until they were white-knuckled where they weren't spilt open. The veins on his torso lit up and revealed a myriad of ugly scars and wounds that hadn't healed properly.

"I suppose that's true. I don't deserve redemption," Ben said. His glow softened, and he rubbed the gnarled wound on his knuckles. The static anger of the cell bars tugged at his hair; the strobing red of his confines flickered across every undulation of his exhausted looking body. Ben straightened and re-formed his fists, "But that doesn't mean I won't leave this world with a clearer conscience than I've had in a thousand years."

Belial laughed, "Good luck with that, brother."

"Ma'am," the guard interrupted. "I've allowed you more than your share of time with the prisoner."

I shuffled back. "I know, you have your orders," I bit my lip and held my breath. My fingers slid down to my belt. "I understand completely," I said.

With a subtle flick of my hand, my diamond dagger clattered to the floor. I allowed the guard to lean in first. My heart hammered. He reached for the handle…

I pulsed a bolt of energy into the base of his skull. The guard's wings sputtered and he fell heavily to the floor, unconscious.

"Sophia!" Lorcan ran to the guard, "Have you lost your mind?" he rolled the guard onto his side and checked his vitals.

I dropped to my knees to assure myself that the guard was actually okay. His breathing was calm, his pulse regular.

Deep breath in, deep breath out.

I stood, wiping my mudded hands down my sides, and sheathed the dagger.

"I'm thinking for myself," I said. "For you, for them, for Jaz, and for the here and now. He would have called Gedz'iel if I'd pushed his loyalty much further. You can see he's not hurt. He'll be fine, Lorcan."

Lorcan shook his head. "You've lost the plot, Soph," he put the guard over his shoulder and headed to the doorway.

"Perhaps I have lost my mind, but I'd say I'm in a lot of good company!" my eyes flickered over Ben's alarmed expression, one that quickly evolved into a subtle smile.

Lorcan grumped angrily as he sat the hefty guard by the door.

I checked the guard's pulse again and patted him on the head. "Sorry about that. Have a nice nap."

"I can't believe I just did that!" I thought to myself.

"I can't believe you did that either," Lorcan's eyes were wide as he adjusted the guard into a comfortable position.

"Out of my head! That's not fair Lorcan. Well, anyway…" my voice softened. "You're my accomplice now, so you'd best just go with the flow," I stroked his cheek, his pulse bloomed. It was an unfair means to an end. Lorcan gulped and grabbed my wrist.

"Soph?"

"I'm doing what I need to do to save everyone, and you damned well know it."

He dropped my hand. "You'll get me skinned alive," he sighed.

Ben moved closer to the bars. "Impressive, Soph," he said with renewed arrogance.

"So, can you help me or not?" I asked.

Ben splayed his hands, "Tell me what happened to Jaz and we'll see."

Lorcan sighed in defeat whilst I told Ben what I knew of Jaz' abduction and the Afflicted messenger. Ben's face tightened when I mentioned the dark sisters.

"You know Anjou'elle and Nephr'eus?"

Ben nodded. "I hoped they were long descended," he pumped his fists, accidently grazing the bars. They flung him backwards, leaving the nauseating smell of burnt flesh in the air.

Ben groaned and pulled himself back up. Lorcan snorted with amusement. I moved closer to his cell again.

"Are you okay?" I felt way too much concern as he pulled himself back to his feet.

"I'm fine," he groaned angrily, as he quickly healed the new wounds but strangely, he left the rest unhealed. I feared him a little just then, seeing him lash out like that with no care for his own well-being. He paced back and forth. "Are you sure it was them?" he glanced up and rubbed his temples.

"Yes," I said. "How well do you know them?"

"More than I care to," he growled. "You're a dangerous friend to have, Sophia."

The way he said my name was way too familiar. I couldn't help myself.

"Are you sure we don't know each other, apart from you spying on me and all?"

"I'm quite sure," his voice lowered.

"I don't think I believe you."

"You can believe whatever you want," he ran his uninjured hand through his hair and stared hard at me. Azure blue eyes swirled with clouds of suspicion. The ring of dark, a hallmark of the Daimon within, shadowed his irises. I crossed my arms protectively, stepping cautiously closer. My hands warmed with a hint of power, just in case.

"So, I've told you the story," I said. "Now, how can you help me, and why should I trust a single thing you say?"

Lorcan stepped between me and Ben. He tipped my face gently up. His chin trembled. "Please, Soph. You've not seen what we've seen. You don't know the lengths Daimon will go to. I can't stop you, but please don't disregard a thousand lifetimes of experience for a gut feeling," his anger had receded; worry in its place.

Ben clucked his tongue, "Pretty boy is right. You have absolutely no reason to trust me. However, I can offer an insider's perspective."

I stepped around Lorcan. He let me go.

Ben leaned forwards, "I've travelled this planet for thousands of years too. I've been to a lot of places, met many people and… things you probably wouldn't care much for. I've moved in circles your friends would never lower themselves to. There is little I don't know."

I took another step closer and tilted my head. One minute Ben was smug, the next angry. He screamed loneliness. The closer I got, the more his scent triggered a wild clamping in my gut — a comforting fragrance of spicy smoke that had the hairs on the back of my neck stand on end.

"*Who are you?*" I thought.

I gently inhaled again, raking my mind for the memory that was screaming at me. Enl'iel had told me that aromas were strong memory triggers. Why was this stranger eliciting such a response? How closely had he kept tabs on me? What private moments had he intruded on?

"Tell me who you are," I demanded.

Ben licked his lips and dropped his eyes. I heard the soft whoosh of blood in his veins as his heart beat faster.

"I am no one, Earth-born," he cracked his knuckles one by one, avoiding a blue-green swelling over the middle ones.

"You want redemption?" I asked. "You want to help me? Then you owe me the truth," I said.

He sat and rested his head in his hands. "You're boring me," he muttered into his palms.

My mark burned, "I reckon the pits of Hell won't be much more exciting."

He leaned back onto his hands; his eyes narrowed. Lorcan was silent, but his feet shuffled and his face was all manner of expressions. I could have sworn they were having a rather vehement mind chat, and it brought Ben's mark to life too. Its heat made his scent fuller, richer.

Then it hit me — ashes and spice. A dreamy fragrance that made my head swim. A rush of emotions hit me as a vague memory flashed through my mind. I was back in my old home. Ben carried me upstairs in his arms. I snuggled into him contentedly. I swallowed hard. Sweat sprung on the back of my neck.

"Who the hell are you?" my voice broke.

Lorcan nodded at Ben and stepped back behind me.

"What are you two doing?" I asked.

"I am who I said I am," Ben said. "You know me from the dreams I invaded and the shadows I hid in. That is all," he sniffed and looked away. It was *a* truth, but not *the* truth.

Lorcan tugged my elbow to coax me away from the cell, "Let's get out of here. You're getting nowhere."

I stared at Ben. Perhaps Lorcan was right. Was there any point in knowing what he had been to me? Did I really need to know the whole sordid truth? My feet toyed around Enoch's box near the faded wheelchair tacks in the dirt. Cael was probably due for his daily visit. The guard would wake soon.

I couldn't change the past, whatever it was, but I could change the future. *I* was the future.

"Keep your secrets," I said. "I want to find Jaz and help the Watchers. Whoever you were in the past won't help with that."

"First intelligent thing you've said," Ben said.

"Well, we'll see how smart I am soon enough. Either I'm a fool to even acknowledge your existence, or it's the best move to make; trusting you, that is."

Ben was sure to have intel. Progress had been glacial lately, and no one else seemed able to help me. Beneath his acidic coating, I believed he was genuine.

"Okay then. Let's start again. What do you know about these sisters?"

Lorcan sighed. The guard moaned.

"Anytime now," I urged impatiently.

Ben's eyes were heavy with a Daimon's darkness. He rose to his feet, taller and broader and broodier than even Jude. I swallowed and hoped this wasn't my worst move in this game.

"Everyone knows the sisters," Ben said. "We just haven't heard from them in a very long time. I'd hoped they'd fallen into an abyss somewhere and descended," he slammed a fist into the wall.

"Will you please stop that?" I asked. His behaviour was a grotesque, self-destructive indulgence.

"How dangerous are they compared to Yeqon?" I asked.

Ben walked to the back of his cell and kicked something, "Every bit, maybe more."

"*Everything I love is destroyed*," his words were faint in my head. "*Please, not her too.*"

I flushed, "What did you say?"

"Nothing," Ben snapped.

"No, I heard you whisper something."

His agitation was increasing again. His bloody hands ran through his hair, leaving the white streaks soaked red. The longer I was there, the more pronounced the whiteness seemed.

"If they have Jaz, will they hurt her?" I asked.

He shook his head, "Not if they need her for something, like drawing you out."

"Me?"

"Don't act so surprised," Ben raised his arms in emphasis. "The entire world wants you."

"They want to open the portal too?" I glanced at Enoch's box, angry with it and him for leaving too much unanswered.

"How the hell would I know what they want? I just know, if they're involved, they'll do whatever it takes to get it," Ben snapped.

"Would they…"

"Kill her? Yes, if it gets them what they desire. But, whilst she is of value alive, they will keep her as such," his face and voice were an equal measure of taught.

The guard took a deep breath. He would wake soon.

"Tell me how I can save her!"

"Stop this! Stop this very instant, Sophia!"

I startled. Enl'iel stood over the rousing guard, her cheeks flaming red and all levels of pissed off.

Chapter Six

Enl'iel dragged me through the corridors. I could barely keep up with her furious pace.

"Let go!"

Her grip tightened. I wrenched my arm from her, and she grabbed hold of the other.

Lorcan kept pace with us, "Enl'iel, please calm down."

She snorted at him as she dragged me unceremoniously past onlookers who seemed as embarrassed as I was.

"I can't believe you've indulged her in this, Lorcan!"

We rounded a corner.

"I…" Enl'iel cut Lorcan off.

"Don't even try to provide excuses! You're not thinking with your head, young man. I can't believe it's me — a *half-breed* — pulling her out of there instead of you. If Gedz'iel were here, he'd rip your wings out. What on Earth would you both do then?" she cursed under her breath. "If only we had the Pits here!" she grumbled furiously.

Scrambling with Enoch's box under my arm, I tripped and slid along.

Enl'iel felt a hair's-breadth from transferring us somewhere, such was the furious glow and heat rippling from her skin. I was ashamed of myself. This was the woman who'd raised me, who I looked up to the most, and she was apoplectic with me. Her strained, high-pitched voice tore shreds from me. I'd never in my life known her to be so angered.

"I can't believe you were in there again after we explained why you can't trust them," she said. "I thought you were more sensible. I thought you had more respect. And you knocked out a sentry? You may be the Earth-born angel, but you could easily find yourself on the wrong side of those red bars too," she huffed a rage-filled breath.

My gut was telling me to follow my instincts, even against the woman I called mother. Wasn't that what they'd all been telling me to do all this time? Follow your instincts! I pulled against her as we rounded another corner, but she pulled harder.

"Let go of me!" I snapped angrily.

"Enl'iel," Lorcan jumped in front of her. "Sophia was in no danger with me by her side."

Enl'iel could have slayed Yeqon with the look she gave Lorcan. "You will romance her to her grave, you fool," she pushed him out of her way.

Lorcan fell back behind us, but I felt his humiliation.

"She didn't mean that," I whispered into his mind.

He didn't respond but kept up behind us. A few gardeners scattered at the commotion, leaving baskets of produce behind.

"Honestly, do you care at all about anyone but yourselves?"

I'd had enough. Yes, Lorcan was a pain in my backside at times, but he was at no fault here. I dug my feet in and pulled free, toppling into the wall. A gnarled cluster of charcoal crystals sprouted from the damp rock, as though the earth mimicked my anger.

I pulled myself up, "Calm the hell down! Enl'iel!"

She tapped her foot and rammed her arms across her chest. Her eyes reddened; moisture filled her lashes.

She spread her arms, "Well then, what do you have to say for yourself?"

My cheeks flamed. I clutched my belongings to my chest as a dozen choice words flooded my mind. I was tempted to use a few of the juicier ones, but I fought back the urge to say something I'd regret later. I peered over my shoulder at Lorcan. He was in a difficult position. I know he agreed with Enl'iel, but he wasn't impressed right now either.

Deep breath in, deep breath out.

"Well?" Enl'iel demanded.

The quiet corridor, the cold air, and the nip of E'lan cleared my head.

I passed the box to Lorcan. A group of Alchamae wandered around the corner to harvest the fruits and blooms. They took what they needed, collected the previously abandoned pickings, and made a hasty retreat along with the two little Keeper souls that trailed them busily.

That distraction gave us both a moment of pause to calm our tempers.

Enl'iel sighed and let her arms fall to her sides. "I know you're trying to be more independent," she said. "Impatience is an easy master to surrender to. You want to fix things like you've always done and I love you for that, but you must listen to me. You cannot trust Ben. He could use the information you gave him against you," her mouth pursed.

She'd listened too long for me to deny anything. Self-control was usually our forte, but today, I felt less inclined to chill out.

"I've been pent up underground and kept out of the loop," I said. "You want me to do a huge thing without all the information and resources that are available to you, hoping I'll just work things out, but maybe, just maybe, my journey isn't what you think it should be."

I clenched my pendant, a habit I'd picked up from her. The opal teardrop hummed in rhythm with my emotions. I puffed out a frustrated breath.

Enl'iel tapped her foot again, "You don't know what you're facing, Sophia."

"I am well aware of the dangers," I said. "I've felt Yeqon's wrath up close and personal, if you don't recall?"

She winced; a tear evaporated against her mark's fire.

"I'm not on a suicide mission, I actually quite like being alive!" I held my chest, emphasising the fact. "Now, as horrid as it may sound to you, I feel somehow connected to Ben. I can't explain it. Perhaps it's because he rescued me… I don't know," I threw my hands in the air. I thought it best to keep the whole devil-who-will-save-me thing to myself lest she combust on the spot.

Another tear bloomed on her lashes, but she wiped it away and twiddled her pendant.

"Ben handed himself in, knowing what he would face," I said. There was no guarantee he wouldn't be descended on sight. He stood up to Yeqon. He made sure both Rik and I got home. He has betrayed Yeqon, protected Rik and I, and delivered himself to us, all in one move," I said.

Enl'iel opened her mouth, but I spoke over her. Her eyes flared; her anger was refuelling.

"He knows these kidnappers. Jaz is in real danger if they have her. I can't ignore this!"

Enl'iel's hands clenched by her sides. The E'lan tugged at her hair. It fanned around her head, she looked foreboding.

"You stand here and regurgitate your justifications, but you, young angel, know *nothing* about our world, nothing about our enemies, nothing about our history, just a mere skimming of the surface. Subterfuge is a specialty of the Daimon. Enduring a beating for their cause is nothing to them," she said.

As she wrung her hands, impatiently awaiting my reply, a cool breeze wafted down from the upper levels and blew Enl'iel's hair around her face. She fussed with it and tied it back impatiently into a rough plait. A static tingle shifted in the air, and a white flash followed.

Brennan marched towards us, "Will you two keep it down, please? How is a Watcher supposed to sulk in peace?" He shook his head.

Enl'iel lurched towards him. "Is everything alright? I thought you left with Koi," she took his hand.

Brennan hugged her but quickly held her back to examine both of us, only a cursory glance at his brother.

Brennan rolled his eyes. "I'm perfectly fine apart from the fact that I must remain here as the guard dog…again," he huffed. "Not allowed to go behead any Rogues. However, by the looks of it, you feisty maidens need my calming charm."

Enl'iel sighed. "Oh, for I'el's' sake. You really are tiring at times, Brennan," she pinched the bridge of her nose.

He smiled and smacked Lorcan over the head.

"What the hell!" Lorcan pulled back a fist but lowered it just as quickly.

"Did you cause all this, bro?"

Lorcan sneered. "I swear on both our lives that this isn't my doing," he glared at me.

"Owning your mistakes should be a strength, should it not?" Enl'iel snapped, her stare hard on me.

Brennan's face lit with intrigue.

"And you can stop your nonsense, Brennan. I've just tried to explain to Sophia that we have rules for a reason. I'd think it an honour to oversee our safety?"

"Of course it is, Li, Li," Brennan said. "It's just bloody Jude interfering, you know? Still gets under my skin. It's a whole lot of big, dirty bollocks. He convinced Ged that no one is as amazing as me at protecting the sanctuary's boundaries. There is truth to that, but," he winked at me, "I've trained some damn fine guards. Thanks to me, this place is tighter than a cat's—"

Enl'iel placed her palm on his chest. "I get your point. I'm sorry you couldn't go, too. I know how much you've missed field work. Perhaps they'll call on you when our safety is more assured? You know how important it is that we maintain order for the good of us all," she glanced at me.

Brennan winked at me again. "The good of us all would be yours truly in the field. Anyway, what's this weirdness oozing from you two like Daimon ichor? I thought Jazz had magically materialised with all the colourful language floating up through the ether."

I crossed my arms.

"Oh, they were your unladylike thoughts, were they? Well, Princess, I have to say I'm shocked." he gave me a thumbs up. "Good to get your feelings out though," his brows arched. "Tell me, what's going on with you two… or three?"

Enl'iel scrunched her mouth in thought. Lorcan picked at his nails with his dagger.

"You and I are in the same boat," I said. "I want to help Jaz, but I'm not allowed to go anywhere or do anything besides sitting in a designated corner doing puzzles," I glowered at Enoch's box.

"That's not entirely correct," Enl'iel said. "You are over-dramatizing things and missing the important details of where you've just been."

"Where *have* you been?" Brennan asked. One finger rubbed his chin, his eyes alight. "No, don't answer that. I can guess," when the smile faded from his eyes, it hurt more than Enl'iel's anger.

I was about to explain, but Brennan silenced me with a finger pressed to my lips. His eyes lit again.

"So, we'll sulk together?" he clapped his hand to my shoulder. "Excellent. Nothing like a pity party for two. I'll take her for a run in the training room, Li, Li. We can sweat out our frustration while you grab a cup of tea."

Enl'iel cracked her knuckles in a very un-Enl'iel like manner. Her biceps flexed taut. She looked suddenly stronger than ever. I'd never considered her as physically strong, she had brought me up as my Nan, after all, but now, she looked tough and mighty pissed off.

"I don't feel like tea. Convince me that you can look after yourself, Sophia, and I will give you space within reason," her hard eyes didn't give an inch. "Pick up your things, *we* shall train together."

Kaymakli's training room wasn't as big as Katoika's, but it was still enormous and decked out with enough shiny weapons to make any dark-ages torture house proud.

Enl'iel waved me forwards. I trailed her across a small make-shift running track. Enl'iel, Brennan, and I stepped over the scorch lines that marked the track, which hugged the perimeter with a variety of workout set-ups. A metallic echo drew my attention upwards. Workers were welding chromious sheets to the ceiling.

"What are they doing?" I asked.

"Extra protection," Brennan answered. "Koi saw to it. That will stop anything from burrowing down to us."

The workers heated and flexed the metal sheets with their bare hands before pinning them to the rocky ceiling with white-hot energy blasts. Two energetic Keepers pulsed in tune with each other as they decorated the panels. They swirled across the installations and inscribed the unique designs we all had as our facial markings. Each one was slightly different, like a fingerprint. The result was a shining protective dome, an artwork in fine etching. It was a portrait of all of us.

"Clever little things," I mumbled.

Enl'iel clicked her fingers and pointed a few feet away. "We aren't here for fine art appreciation. Put your things down. I don't even want you to warm up, Sophia."

"You really want to train with me?" I asked.

"Train? No. Fight?" she glared at me. "Yes."

"Oh crap," Lorcan muttered behind me.

"Is this really necessary, Li, Li?" Brennan pleaded.

"Entirely," she flexed her arms again and shook out her shoulders.

"This is ridiculous," Lorcan said. "She's your daughter!"

"I'll fight you if you don't mind yourself. And you!" Enl'iel snapped her fingers at the workers, who'd stopped what they'd been doing to stare at us, "Out, *now*!"

There was no way she'd actually fight me, so I let her play out her anger.

"Clearly you haven't had your morning tea yet!" Brennan chuckled.

"Will you just stop fooling around for one moment, Brennan?" Enl'iel glared wildly his way.

"What the hell have you done, Princess?" Brennan whispered into my mind.

I snorted and stopped myself from transferring away.

"Prepare yourself," Enl'iel said.

I turned and walked away, "This is ridiculous."

"Don't you dare turn your back on an enemy, Sophia!" she called.

"You aren't my enemy," I called back. "C'mon, Lorcan. Let's go."

He hesitated. I was about to turn around to question this exercise of her ego when a hefty *thump* pummelled my back. I lurched face first into the floor. Spitting out a mouthful of dirt and coughing, I pulled myself back up.

"What the hell was that?" I yelled.

Lorcan tried to help me, but I slapped him away.

Enl'iel chuckled, her sharp eyes bored into mine, "A Daimon won't invite you first. You've had it too easy until now. We've babied you to the point that you've got no sensibility. It's my mistake, and I'll fix it."

Enl'iel crouched like a predator. The swirls around her eye pulsed rhythmically as she prepared a new orb in her hands.

I was still trying to figure her out when I fell on my butt again. The hot sting of that extra painful orb burned my chest. I scrambled up quickly. Lorcan and Brennan looked gob smacked but didn't intervene.

"Stop this!" I yelled. "*I've* had an easy time? Are you kidding me?"

I stormed towards her; fists clenched. Enl'iel lit her hands again, threatening more pain. She couldn't have looked further from the woman who'd raised me.

"You've made quite the point of telling me you can do more than I know, so show me," Enl'iel said. "You want to work things out yourself? Let's go then. Do you think a Daimon will wait until you're ready? Will you be prepared when Ben attacks you from behind?" Another sputtering orb hovered over her hand. Energy arced in blue and white wisps around her.

"Enl'iel, please calm down," Brennan's voice echoed around the deserted room.

With lightning speed, she threw a half-formed orb at his feet.

"You stay out of this!" she commanded. I'd never seen her behave this way before. Her grandmotherly softness was far away, as her face hardened to stone.

"Are you waiting for my permission, Sophia? A Daimon would have seared your head from your shoulders and ripped your heart out by now."

"Li, Li! What are you doing?"

"What I should have a long time ago!"

She answered Brennan, her eyes as steely as Jude's.

"Come on Sophia, you have an advantage over me, you know I can't fly. So, show me what you've got!"

I shook my head. "I can't fight you," my pulse pounded in my temples.

"Can't or won't?" Enl'iel's veins glimmered in her arms as they filled with white-hot power. Her E'lan forged two intimidating red orbs, which slowly spun in her open palms. The display drew spectators. "Well?" she demanded again.

"I can't," I said, "Because you're my… you know."

A blast to my abdomen flung me into the air. I crashed back down and slid to an embarrassing and abrasive stop. A hole was singed into my shirt; I rubbed the pain away and dabbed out embers.

I looked to the boys for support.

"I'm not getting between you, Princess," Brennan whispered into my head.

Enl'iel badgered me with a rope of light, which twirled expertly. She whipped it by her feet, "Get up, Sophia."

"I'm warning you," I said. An instinctive pull and yearning outside my control churned in my gut.

"Will Ben stop when you warn him? Will you hesitate when he drags you back to Yeqon?" Enl'iel's honeyed tone became a slow drip of acid.

She swung the rope of E'lan at me. It nicked my forearm and left a scalding burn.

I screamed. Rage bubbled up. I needed to hit something other than her, so I slapped the ground.

"For I'el's sake, Li Li!" Brennan snapped, "It's not funny anymore!"

"Don't worry, boys." I pulled myself up and healed the burn. "I've got this," I sniffed and flicked my hair out of my face.

Within seconds, my wings were free. My face burned and it felt good. I rose into the air with a gentle sweep, eyes fixed on Enl'iel's furious but proud face. Shaking, I hovered over her. My lip split between my teeth as I tried to quell its quiver.

Lightning flew from Enl'iel's fingers. I dodged, but two stung my hands and feet. If she were a Daimon, those hits would have been a whole other world of pain and danger. She had dialled her energy down to training mode, but it was no picnic.

Shaking with anger, I rose higher. Enl'iel peered up at me with a scary intensity.

Two red orbs zoomed towards me. Training and hunting orbs. Weapons that seemed to be conscious. I swooped down and shoved at Enl'iel's chest, knocking her to the floor. She somersaulted backwards and shot more arcs at me.

Enl'iel's speed and agility were incredible. She parkoured off the walls and equipment like a nimble athlete. It was all I could do to keep up with her assaults. Finally, I lost it and threw an orb at her. It missed... the first time.

She threw her head back and laughed, her hands on her hips.

"Fine!" My body exploded with light, and I welcomed it. I drew every atom I could touch from the air until the E'lan magnetised to me. Energy swirled around my fiery skin, encircled me like a protective cage. The air buzzed. I took a deep breath. My eyes felt like fire.

Enl'iel smiled wider, "Come on, baby angel."

"Run," I growled from my core.

I drew my palms across themselves to form a blazing white shard. Sharp and deadly, I aimed it straight at her.

"I shall not run!" Enl'iel didn't seem concerned about my new weapon. She started to form a new orb...

My shard flew from my hand like a javelin and landed at her feet. It blew her off balance, and I descended on her.

Enl'iel ran after that. I chased her with my own wave of energised arcs and orbs. They hurled her forwards, and she tumbled until she came to a stop against a pile of hessian sacks. Blood sprouted from her mouth, but she jumped to her feet, heaving for breath. For a nanosecond, I felt guilty, but then I was back on my own backside, sliding towards the door.

Bloodied and bruised, my wings extended to their fullest. My pain was more than skin deep.

Kea's sword was in my hands, though I didn't remember drawing it. I rose higher, one angry stroke of my wings at a time. The boys were yelling at me to stop, but I was done. I'd had enough.

"You will never live up to your true potential," Enl'iel shouted.

Enl'iel watched me swoop down, fear didn't stain her eyes. Brennan and Lorcan were a mere blur in my periphery. Right before we connected, she surrounded herself in a ball of light. It spluttered a constant barrage of munitions my way. None hit their mark.

She produced a massive red orb and launched it at me. I swung Kea's gleaming sword across my body. The red beast blipped out of existence. I throttled into her through her wall of protection. We tumbled, a fusion of pain, anger, and confusion.

Sitting astride Enl'iel's heaving chest, my knees pinned her arms flush to the floor. She was caked in dirt and red with welts. Her left eyebrow had split, blood pooled in her lashes. I clenched a handful of her hair and held Kea's sword millimetres above her throat. She fought for breath. Blood crusted around her lips. Sincere surprise and resignation dawned in her eyes.

Panting, I leaned in, "I'm not your little girl anymore."

Chapter Seven

Concealed in the clouds, Gedz'iel was fuming. He circled the Watchers faster and faster until he had fenced them into a tight band. His dazzling aura melded into the sunlight, glistening within the vast white of the upper atmosphere.

"You've explicitly disobeyed me," Gedz'iel said.

Jude eased forwards, "We owe the human one last chance before we abandon her. Yeqon and his detritus are contained for now. She did save Sophia's life once, after all, and with nothing other than a gardening tool. I've deployed a number of units to the infringement zones in Australia and America. We have time for Sophia's human."

Gedz'iel's mark flared, his dimple deepened as his jaw ground, "My decision was final. Your opinion on one human does not negate the needs of the many."

Jude averted his eyes, "It's on our route to the Americas anyway, Master Gedz'iel. It will take us but an hour to follow the trail Dash has picked up, and Lorcan had a good lead from that Afflicted."

"You over-step your station." Gedz'iel rushed closer to him, "Do you not understand what Yeqon can achieve in one minute?"

Jude bowed his head, yet his lips were a tight line. "I do, Gedz'iel. I have witnessed it more times than I care to remember," Jude's fists clenched; he drew a centring breath. "However, we are here to serve all humans. We fulfil I'el's intent when we protect all innocents where we are able."

Koi's eyes narrowed on Jude. He ushered the others back with a wave of his hand.

Gedz'iel eyed Jude with suspicion. Jude usually followed orders without question. "You have spoken ill of humans for as long as I remember," Gedz'iel said. The glow of his wings caught a defiant gleam in Jude's eyes.

"Your unspoken assumption is erroneous, Master," Jude grumbled.

"It had better be," Gedz'iel glided closer, and Jude raised his head. Their eyes met, Jude's swirling with an intense fervour.

"Master," Koi said. "I, too, believe we owe the girl a debt for saving Soph'ael. We will pass over one of the suspected hostage sites anyway. It will not deviate from our route. In fact, we may have the chance to descend a few Afflicted."

"If we do not find her," Jude added, "Then I defer to you to end the search. Jasmine's fate shall be her own."

Gedz'iel spun around, "Do you all wish to defy me?"

The Watchers bowed their heads.

Gedz'iel stretched his wings and flew up into the sun's glare. He stared into the stratosphere, the cold air calming his anger. He had renounced his freedom to help his kindred, had always expected unwavering compliance. He looked down at the Watchers; they, too, were battle-scarred in as many ways as he, and possibly more. Was I'el still listening? A'mageddon was coming, and I'el hadn't shown mercy for the longest time except for Soph'ael's birth.

Gedz'iel reached out to the elements. The E'lan felt different these days, its energy pulling at him stronger and more deeply. He gazed at the wilting stars of the fading night, looked to his creator for strength and guidance. The sun rose higher, its rose gold beams blazed across his body, fanning out through his wings.

Koi floated up to him, looking towards the heavens, "Sophia will find a way to search for Jasmine if we do not find her first, and that will put her at significant risk. It is who she is, Gedz'iel."

"I do not doubt that," Gedz'iel sighed and ran his hands across his wearied face. "She does not realize her power."

"No. It is a blessing and a curse whilst she learns her way," Koi added quietly. "The tighter we bind her, the more she may push back at us."

"Very well, brother. A pure soul well guided is far greater than one constrained."

They sunk back to the others, hovering in front of Jude.

"We will make a single sweep for the human on our way to the Americas," Gedz'iel said. "I do not want Sophia to know of this, it would renew her hopes, and she has more important matters to focus on. It would have been helpful to have Lorcan here, Jude. He knows the girl's energy better than we do."

Jude flushed but held his words back.

"Call Lorcan back, Koi," Gedz'iel said. "Tell Brennan to glue himself to Sophia until Lorcan returns. Gather more infantry to meet us ahead."

"*You are a fool,*" Gedz'iel whispered into Jude's mind. "*Learn from Dash's torment.*"

Jude blanched before pride thinned his mouth and hardened his already fiery eyes.

"*I am many things, but a fool is not one of them,*" Jude bowed. "Finding the girl, who is so close to Sophia's heart, may well keep her more focused on her mission."

"You keep telling yourself that, Jude, and perhaps you will keep yourself out of trouble," Gedz'iel turned his back on Jude. "Move out." He swept around the group and continued through oncoming thunder clouds towards the French border.

Camouflaged in a fork of lightning, Lorcan joined them. The merging of two powers, Watcher and Mother Nature, taunted thunder and released rain. Lorcan was soaked as he bowed to Gedz'iel.

"Track the Afflicted that brought news of Jasmine," Gedz'iel commanded. "I wish to return the girl to Sophia, if at all possible, as soon as possible."

"What?" Lorcan flicked water from his surprised face.

"Just do it!" Gedz'iel growled.

Lorcan tucked his wings in tight and dove ahead, darting in a zig-zag pattern as he tracked the fragmented energy the Afflicted woman had left. The others kept pace behind him.

Lorcan circled and returned, "I'm getting bits and pieces. She must have been intoxicated on the drug; her signature is a bloody mess."

"Try again," Gedz'iel said.

Lorcan circled back and forth.

"Brennan would have been helpful too," Koi said. "He knew Jasmine for many years."

Gedz'iel furrowed his brows.

Jude snorted, "Brennan can stay with the ladies and wear his apron."

Lorcan waved them down below the clouds. "It seems we are headed for Anjou," excitement quickened his voice.

Gedz'iel's face softened, "There is a known Afflicted den in Anjou."

"Perhaps this may be of benefit after all," he added.

"Neph'reus and Anjou'elle likely source their Afflicted from there," Koi said. "We have a good chance of getting helpful information unless the Afflicted have not been fed well. Then we may just find corpses."

"I'll descend them all either way," Jude growled.

Gedz'iel glowered at Jude.

"Sort him out, Koi, and quickly," Gedz'iel snapped. "Errant emotions equal an ascended soul; we have precious few resources as it is."

Only a white plume remained as Gedz'iel disappeared after Lorcan.

Heavy silence hung between the remaining Watchers and the Eloi as they kept a steady pace towards Anjou. Koi dropped back to coast alongside Jude.

"Don't," Jude grunted.

Koi understood the conflict of love and betrayal, and the romantic enticement of revenge. His fingers rubbed across the faded words; *love* and *hate*; his knuckles adorned forever.

"I know what it is like to love the wrong person," Koi said. Jude's eye twitched. "We have all done it. That is why we find ourselves here. Now is not the time to allow personal grievances to get in the way. Clear your head so we can find Jaz. This is our only chance. Yeqon will afford us no further luxuries," Koi said and banked to the left into a thicker cloud cluster. Jude sped up behind him, his face as grim as a Daimon's.

"Fine," Jude sighed. "I'll sort it out."

"Good, because we are nearly there," Koi grimaced and rubbed his eyes. "Their stench makes them water every time. Would you believe a damned smell brings old Koi down?" he slapped Jude's shoulder.

Jude moaned and peered through the streaking breaks in the clouds. "Those wenches have been here with their drugged-up army since Anjou'elle seduced that foolhardy Count five hundred years ago." Koi said. Jude grunted in response.

"It's when they developed a taste for toying with European royalty," Koi added. "I suppose we could thank them in a way. Their meddling led to Sophia's parents fleeing. If they hadn't run, Sophia could have been born inside the devil's nest."

They emerged below a high-altitude mantle of rumbling clouds. Lightning pierced the darkness, thunder followed.

Lorcan, Dash, and the Eloi floated up to them.

"Ready when you are, brothers," Lorcan nodded at Koi. "The Afflicted came from directly below us; her signature is strongest here, where that structure is," Lorcan pointed to a dark blob against the ground. "Gedz'iel has gone in first to check it out."

"Let's get on with it," Koi said. "Damage control has never been more important," he nodded at Jude. "Do you want to take the lead?"

Jude nodded sharply in response. He pulled into a smooth hovering stop, turned, and faced the others.

"We're a few miles above Anjou. Check your weapons while we wait for Gedz'iel. There will be no mercy where compliance is not afforded to us," Jude ordered.

Clouds collided overhead, igniting a dazzling lightning show. Wind whipped up below them and tossed them about as they honed their sights on Anjou.

When the lightning next bathed the sky in white, they transferred to the ground.

Gedz'iel landed outside the bluestone ruins of Castle Pouancé. His feet sunk into fresh snow under the bare branches of a Hawthorn tree. The cold air captured his breath in rhythmic white puffs. It wasn't a well-visited site, which gave him an advantage. Still, he altered his appearance to appear as a tourist. His robust frame hid under a loose hoody, denims clung to his legs, and his signature crew cut shimmered into darker dreadlocks. Even the cleft of his square jaw faded.

Hands in his pockets, Gedz'iel pretended to read the opening times of the tourist site on the information board, but he took in everything of the surrounds. A flock of birds landed on the craggy branches of wintery trees. Woodsmoke wafted over from the town. He listened to the swift footfalls of folk going about their early morning business. A group of children cycled by; their light giggles a strange contrast to his dark mission. Every breath of wind carried a fluctuation of the E'lan; his kindred were waiting overhead.

Gedz'iel was familiar with the mighty stone structure of Pouancé. Six hundred years ago it had been a handy placement for his spies, and it had enabled the Watchers to keep tabs on any Daimon interference. This place had been one of Neph'reus' favourites, and Anjou'elle's namesake. Previously a Watcher called An'jael, Anjou'elle had melded Anjou into her name so long ago that few remembered her real name. Gedz'iel envisioned her and Nephr'eus gliding across perfectly appointed gardens, wooing unsuspecting humans. Why they were causing trouble now perplexed him.

Gedz'iel screwed up his face, pulled his hoody down, and rubbed the smattering of stubble on his chin, "Why are you two sticking your noses in Yeqon's business?"

Nephr'eus and Anjou'elle had never been part of Yeqon's plans. Had they destroyed the Kaladai? The lack of intel left his knuckles white. Gedz'iel cracked them one at a time and made his way towards the ruins, following the fetid smell of Afflicted.

Naked trees fringed the old moat. Gedz'iel stopped and sniffed under each leafless giant. His facial mark glowed brighter as he followed the tainted honey aroma.

"Make your way down," he instructed the faint lights amongst the flashes of lightning. *"The path is clear."*

Gedz'iel moved towards the rear of the ruins. He felt the negativity infused into the surroundings and rubbed his hands to draw energy. He ducked under scaffolding and found what he was looking for. He wasn't sure he would get anything out of this lot, but he'd try. He needed to get his subordinates back on track.

Koi's strong energy signature materialised behind him.

"They're still here," Gedz'iel said. He leaned into the battered doorway and took a deep breath. A growl rumbled in his throat. "T'el, give me strength to show mercy where it is due," he glanced skywards for reassurance that his creator was watching over them.

A scorching punch to the heavy padlocks opened the wrought iron gate with a high-pitched squeal. Elemental energy peaked as the others followed Gedz'iel in simple human clothing.

Koi glowered at the doorway and pinched his nose, "The stench is unmistakable. I'd have thought the fools would have moved on like the others frequently do."

"Being an addict doesn't an Einstein make," Lorcan muttered.

"Indeed," Koi said. "The drug rules them, which is advantageous to us. There must be a reliable source. Who do you suppose that might be, given recent events?"

Koi ducked under a frameless doorway into a new corridor. Their feet padded silently across slippery stones.

Jude pounded a fist along the walls as he squeezed through the narrowing corridor, "Those stupid women have practically sign-posted they're nearby. They've been the greatest supplier of Thanratos for the better part of the past thousand years."

"But why now?" Lorcan asked. "Weren't they happy enough with their corpses in servitude?"

"Why indeed?" Gedz'iel asked. He led them into a fetid, crumbling room. Water dripped into stagnant puddles. Rodents scurried around their feet. They continued through the murky stink in determined silence, down towards the underground remnants of the old ice rooms.

Gedz'iel stopped and raised his hand. He cocked his head to the side, listening through the walls. His eyes widened, and he nodded to the others.

"*I hear them,*" he whispered. "*They are moving,*" his face brightened like a dimmer switch had cranked up his markings, and his disguise melted away, "*Be on your guard. They know we are here and will feel cornered.*"

Jude cracked his knuckles. "*Good. Let's let them sweat a while. They'll panic and make mistakes,*" he pushed forwards. "*I'll be damned to the Pits if they don't know where Jaz is,*" Jude drew his sword and peered into the blackness ahead, his hunger for a fight burning bright.

Chapter Eight

"What the hell was that and where is the Princess I know?" My shoulders jiggled under Brennan's fervent questioning. Ignoring him was no easy feat. He was the overly enthusiastic puppy bouncing at my heels when I felt like rubbish, but he was more guard dog than puppy right then.

"Let me go, Brennan!" I wriggled until he released me.

"I'll let you go, but I won't leave your side. How does that suit you?"

"Just leave me alone!" I stormed away, confused and overwhelmed. The power that had emerged from within my body had frightened me.

Enl'iel had yelled at Brennan to keep an eye on me and left swiftly, so he dutifully trailed me back to my room despite my efforts to evade him. He even cheated by transferring ahead and waiting around every single corner.

"Personal space, Brennan! Do you not understand the concept?" I wanted to throw Enoch's box at him.

"Um, no, I don't, especially when young ladies walk around in bad moods with giant pointy swords."

I hadn't realised that I was still clutching Kea's sword. I tucked it back into my belt. My pulse rushed wildly in my head. I'd made my violent point to Enl'iel, and I was still pinching myself about whether it had been real. I wasn't proud of my behaviour, but enough was enough.

The box was heavy in my arms and on my mind as I neared my room. Ben's face flashed through visions of caves and blue oceans, whilst the scrolls words whispered in the recesses on my thoughts. My wings took over and I zipped around a few corners, Brennan in tow.

"Soph, will you calm down, please? You'll break something or someone!"

"I'm going to my room to work on this bloody box, okay? Just like I'm supposed to!"

"Good, but I might tag along until you calm yourself down a few degrees."

A surprisingly rude insult rumbled through my mind and made me feel slightly better.

"I heard that, you know. I'd prefer not to do that to myself."

I groaned, "Get out of my head!" I spun around and shoved at his chest, box and all.

"Woah, okay!" Brennan held onto the edges of the box. "Sorry, Soph. I shouldn't pry. It's bad manners, but hey, I'm here for you just like you were there for me back home," his eyes softened. "You know I've always been in your corner, don't you?"

The question was rhetorical, his sincerity hard to ignore. My fingers dug into the ridges of the box, as tight as my mouth was pursed.

"If I let go of this, will you hit me again?" Brennan narrowed his eyes with suspicion.

I shook my head. The box slid from his grip.

"I understand why you're upset," he said. "If it were up to me, we'd go kick butt and find Jaz. Poor Mini Princess," he shook his head.

My anger softened a little, but I pushed around him and stomped through the bustling corridors, deftly avoiding eye contact with everyone.

Outside my room, I took a deep breath. I leaned back against the wall and closed my eyes. A sense of control was starting to overwhelm my inner egocentric toddler who wanted everything her way.

Deep breath in, deep breath out.

My face continued to burn, but my emotional outburst petered out. Enli'el had been out of line, but she was still, in my heart, my Nan. What kind of person holds a sword to their Nan's throat?

I groaned. "What have I done?" I'd apologise once we had both calmed down. "Shouldn't you check on her?" I asked Brennan, who flopped next to me against the door.

His eyes widened with exaggerated apprehension, "*Now?* Are you kidding? Do you even know her?"

"I thought I did," I felt like I'd lost someone; someone comforting and constant.

Brennan plucked at some vines along the wall, "You know part of her, just not all of her."

"I'm not sure I like the other part."

He touched his shoulder to mine and pushed away a vine that kept swatting my face. "Enl'iel is a strong and powerful woman. She doesn't suffer fools," he pointed at himself. "Have you ever known her to enjoy not having the last word?"

I glanced at him; his face dimpled with a smile, "No."

"Have you ever known her to admit she was wrong?"

"Never," I said.

"If I went up there now to calm her, I'd end up with an orb up my butt," Brennan chuckled. "Learned that the hard way."

I laughed, too, despite trying not to. It felt wrong after what had happened, but Brennan had a way of making everything lighter.

I pulled on some leaves, "She is pretty scary when she's angry."

"Best we all cool off a while. May I?" he pointed at my door. "I'm much more entertaining than my brother," he winked, knowing he was embarrassing me.

My face burned. I was about to tell him to go somewhere particularly rude, but with one look at his puppy eyes, I opened the door.

"C'mon then."

Brennan threw himself onto my bed. I put the box on the floor and hung up my weapons.

"Why do you get the big bed?" Brennan asked. "This is lush," he rolled onto his side and leaned on his elbow, fiddling with the pillow tassels whilst I eyed Enoch's box. He pointed at it, "You going to have another crack?"

"Well, I've got to do something," I leaned in and examined my warped reflection across the silver.

"I hope that doesn't involve Ben."

"Not now, Brennan," I flung a sock from the floor at him.

He caught it and flung it back, "Now that would kill a Daimon with one sniff."

I threw the other one at him.

"Enl'iel does have a point," humour waned from his voice. "You've only been in our culture six weeks. There's so much you don't understand yet."

I sighed and leaned against the side table. It was a little out of place, so I pushed it back a couple of inches, "I just can't stand by if there's another possibility to help Jaz and…"

I slumped to the floor and pulled Enoch's box into my lap, "And this dammed thing."

My fingers smoothed across the frustrating silver lump.

I'm going to work you out. Just watch me.

Brennan slapped one of my pillows, "Oh crap."

"What is it?"

He'd broken one of the tassels; the threads tangled in his fingers.

I laughed as he tried to knot the frills back together, "Can't take you anywhere, man-child."

He belly-laughed, "Sorry, Soph. My bad."

I shook my head, "It's just a pillow."

He whistled and looked away as he tucked the threads under the pillow.

"You are the biggest dag I've ever met," I said.

"I assume that's a good thing?"

I winked at him, "It's an endearment, trust me. Surely, you've heard it before?"

He squinted, "Nope. I prefer Demi God, Casanova, blah blah. You get the picture?"

I snorted, "Yeah, that definitely sounds like you."

His smile spread as he fell back and rolled over the duvet.

Whilst he messed up my bed, I noticed Jaz' iPod on the floor.

"Someone's been here!" I picked it up. It was covered with red dust.

"Lemme see," Brennan moved to the edge of the bed and reached out. I gave it to him. He turned it over a few times. The longer he inspected it, the more unease rose in my gut.

"Do you see something?" my pendant hummed a little.

"That's odd," his mark flickered. He smudged some of the dirt between his fingers and sniffed. "This soil isn't from this region."

My heart hammered a little faster.

"Seen or heard anything odd?" Brennan asked, eyes arrowed at the dust.

"Yes, actually," I fiddled with my pendant. "What is it, Brennan?"

He shone light from his fingertips and sniffed again, "Not sure."

"I've been feeling like something is around me," I said. "I thought it might be Av'ael, she comes and goes like a ghost, but I'm really not sure."

Brennan continued to roll the grains; his fingertips now stained ochre. "She is an odd little thing, isn't she? Here and then not," he straightened, legs dangling over the bed. "It could have been brought in on the boots of someone bringing in supplies."

"But how did it get on my stuff?" I took the iPod from him and wiped it clean on my pants. The iPod buttons were stained where the dirt had settled into the grooves.

"Well," Brennan's voice was all cheek again. "This place is like your teenage room back home. You clearly don't let anyone in here to tidy for you, and that…" he pointed at the iPod, "Is probably your own grotty habits." Brennan hooked his arms behind his head and rested on a pillow.

I swept the room with a glance, "I like things as they are, thank you. This iPod was spotless when I last touched it, and it definitely wasn't on the floor."

"I'll call in a few Keepers to scout the corridors for rodents then. Sometimes they get into our stuff," he shrugged and I felt somewhat better with that suggestion.

"I've been feeding a mouse. It pops in most days," I peeked under the bed, but it wasn't there.

Brennan clapped his hands. "Ah, I'm sure that's it then. I'll have some Keepers on the prowl. Can't have the crops chewed away. No more feeding the mice, 'kay?" he waved a finger at me and rested back on his elbow.

I placed the iPod on the table but noticed Brennan's attention dashed around the room. We were both pretending it was a mouse but worried it was more sinister. I rubbed my hand, remembering the cold pull on my fingers. I looked over the room until I was satisfied that nothing was there but Brennan and I.

I returned my attention to the box, "It doesn't want to tell me anything." A dozen different reflections of myself danced over its surface.

Brennan slid from the bed and sidled in beside me. "It wants to tell you everything. It was made for you, Soph," he tapped it with his fingers and it hummed a little with his touch. "If you ever want to visit A'vean, you need to get your butt into gear. Go on, don't be scared."

My attention hung on the many swirls and undulations expertly carved into the silver, "I'm not scared, I'm frustrated."

"Take a deep breath and let your instincts take over."

I rolled my eyes, "Gee, haven't heard that before. That's what I was trying to do when Enl'iel went all crazy mother bear on me."

"She does that to everyone," Brennan nodded at the box. "C'mon now, you can do this."

I adjusted the shiny conundrum in my lap. My fingertips glided over the lid, willing it to reveal a secret drawer or something. Why hadn't my blood worked on this like on everything else? I sighed.

"Oh Soph," Brennan said. "I get it, I really do, Princess. All this cloak-and-dagger-secret-message mumbo jumbo. Can't tell you the dark times I've had whilst trying to heal myself for five hundred miserable years. I'm getting tired of the old man up there and his games. It's lucky I have a winning personality or I might've gone all Darth Vader ages ago."

I bit my lip, "I've seen the dark side, Brennan. Trust me, you've chosen the better deal."

The light orb overhead mirrored metallic prisms off the ornate edges of Enoch's box. I ran my palm along the box's inner edge, recalled its emptiness in Yeqon's lair, my dreams of the ocean, and the Disciple of Learning who seemed to be the key to the box's heart. My eyes became heavy and closed.

Heat pulsed though my hands, or through the chromious they clung to? I wasn't sure. It scored up my arms and forced my eyes open. My veins flashed white, rivers of power flowing towards the box. I tried to let go, but my fingertips blazed and grasped it tighter of their own volition My pendant thrummed, and my face burned. The box, my hands, and my energy were connecting… and I let it happen.

My fractured reflection stared solemnly back at me, as did Brennan's as he hung very eagerly next to me.

His breath warmed my shoulder. "When we defeat Yeqon, he mustn't have the opportunity to try again on other worlds. There are many underdeveloped places that are vulnerable just like Earth, and he's got the taste for power now," he touched a finger to the lid but pulled it away when the box vibrated harder.

A deep burn spread from my gut into my chest. It wasn't uncomfortable, just a warm rush. I closed my eyes and pictured Yeqon having free reign. My nails pressed into the lid's edges.

"You haven't spoken much about what happened in Yeqon's realm," Brennan said. "I went there in the past, but not to his dungeons. I can't believe that's where Kea's body died."

His voice hitched. My heart lurched, and I held the box even harder. His words were working, drawing my fears, emotions and power together.

"We'll see her again, right?" I asked, my voice tight and raspy. "Lorcan promised."

"Eventually, Princess. When you open the portal, the Cavern of Souls will release our kindred and they will return home. I'm sure she'll be the first at the door, just bursting to see us."

"Where exactly is the Cavern of Souls?" I couldn't feel my fingers anymore, the burn had numbed them. I clamped my eyes shut, begging the box to connect with me, to reveal its secrets.

"I used to know, now it's just a vague recollection of Peru," Brennan answered. "After I'el closed the portals, he wiped the knowledge from our memories. We only see it if we, you know, die a mortal death. There are a lot of good friends who I miss. They must be aching to be released."

My fingers inched along each metal nook as Brennan prodded a little more at things best left tucked away.

"Did you want to talk about it?" he asked.

"Not really," I said. "I'd prefer to forget it all, particularly Lilith."

His energy spiked. I opened my eyes, surprised to see his mark sear through the darkest expression I'd ever seen on his face. The shine was gone from his eyes; his mouth was tight.

"She's really still there?" he asked. "Alive?"

I stretched my neck. "Alive enough to do this," my hair fell away from the silver scar across my throat.

Brennan shook his head. "Of all the unnatural pieces of filth. I can't believe he still keeps her around," Brennan's fingers curled into fists, and he slammed one into the floor. He took a deep breath and calmed his anger.

I refocussed on the box, "He treated her pretty badly, actually. Not that I felt at all sorry for her."

"Despite her wild claims and dramatizations, Lilith is nothing more than a prize of pride for Yeqon. Her lover used to be one of us. She was a decent woman then, believe it or not," he snorted. "Until greed and lust clouded her humanity."

My hands fell away from the box. Enoch could wait another minute. I nodded, encouraging Brennan to continue.

"It's not my story to tell."

"You can't drop snippets like that and then leave me hanging. It's past time to play coy or keep any more secrets."

Brennan eased back and slapped his hands on his thighs.

"Well?" I shuffled forwards with my lap full of treasure-hunting paraphernalia. The box remained fiery; my pendant thrummed harder like they were in tune with each other.

Brennan cleared his throat and rubbed his palms together, "Well, Lilith was Eve's best friend. They were the real deal a very long time ago. The humans got that bit right."

My mouth hung open, and I might have forgotten to breathe. Myth and fact came together. It delighted and frightened me.

"She grew up alongside Eve, in the primary human settlement," Brennan said. "This was the first place where the Eloi openly helped humans. It was an innocent time for them to learn and evolve from cave dwellers. Prior to this, we had hung in the shadows like we were supposed to."

I leaned forwards as though it would accelerate the story. For that moment, I was just Sophia, enraptured by a story no one on Earth really knew.

"Lilith and Eve unfortunately fell in love with the same man, Ahdem. It was awkward, as you can imagine, but Lilith was ever the best friend and allowed Eve to pursue him. They got together, and the rest should have been history, right?"

I nodded and bit my lower lip, "But that's not what happened?"

"Hell no. Lilith was down and out and hooked up with the Watcher who managed the settlement. He taught her how to become a healer. To cut a long story short, the poor lad fell off the A'vean wagon and in love with her. Even as she aged, his love didn't dwindle, but Lilith grew dark, angry. She began to resent the ageless Watchers as she grew frail, and she had never lost her flame for Ahdem either. She grew to hate Eve, whose beauty had prevailed over time. According to her lover, Lilith came across a strange Watcher passing through the outskirts of town one afternoon. He sensed something dark within her and promised her immortality, to restore her youth, and the revenge she coveted against Eve if she became his lover. Most of all, he promised her children, something her other lover hadn't allowed."

I was on the edge of my seat, "What happened?"

Brennan's eyes sparkled. "It's said she drank his blood, which restored her youth. She was immediately addicted but didn't realise it. Over time, the constant infiltration of his energy changed her into an inhuman hybrid," he shook his head. "She had the children he had promised, and they all retained her altered genes," Brennan's mouth pursed, and he ran a hand though his hair. "Apparently, they rank in the tens of thousands. What do you suppose those babies turned out to be? Cherubs? Puppies or kittens?"

"I don't know," I did know, but I waited for him to say it because I didn't want to. I'd seen enough in Yeqon's lair.

"Vampires, Soph. Filthy things with an insatiable blood-lust. Somehow, Lilith's metamorphosis caused their offspring to mutate into something like the Vam'pria we've seen on other worlds. And, Soph, that's exactly what he wanted. I'm damned sure Yeqon planned it this way. He has created an immortal army of monstrous creatures with no allegiance to I'el, only to him and Lilith."

"Yeqon created vampires?"

Brennan sneered. "On Earth, at least. It was a repeat of another mistake we've made, an accident on another world. Some higher Watchers had saved a colony of humanoids from pandemic disease by infusing them with their blood to cleanse them, but it changed the structure of their blood and digestive system. They couldn't consume anything but fresh blood and flesh. We named them the Vam'pria — creatures of blood. We quickly sealed that world, crashed the portals, and punished those Watchers. All of them are now part of Yeqon's pack, because he was one of them."

"I've seen Lilith drink from him," I said. "She looked fresher and younger afterwards." My back ached with angry tension. My wings needed freedom, but not yet. "That must be why she does his bidding. She'd rather see his vile future than die," the fire in my stomach churned. My excitement for the story waned into disgust. "What happened to the other Watcher? The one she was with before Yeqon?"

"He was devastated," Brennan said. "Never took another mate. He was so full of hate that he disappeared for hundreds of years. I was worried he'd turn up on the wrong side, but he returned to us, damaged, but okay."

"Oh, the poor thing," I touched Brennan's arm. "Who was it?"

"That's not for me to say."

My arm fell away.

Brennan tapped my knee, "It is his story to tell, Soph. You understand that?"

I nodded.

"Anyway," Brennan said, "That's not the worst of it. What do you suppose happened after that little hook up?"

I shrugged, fearful and unable to take my eyes off his.

"Filled with ungodly power and lust, Lilith took her long-repressed vengeance against Eve. One night, she cut her own wrist and bled onto Eve's favourite fig tree, spoiling the fruit with the poison in her veins. She wanted to change Eve to be like her so Ahdem would reject her. The next night, she had Yeqon whisper to Eve in her dreams. Eve rose, half asleep, and ate a fruit from the tree. But instead of becoming like Lilith, she lost her memory. She became a shell of herself. Her love for Ahdem, their children — all forgotten. She and their little world crumbled away. Eve eventually lost her mind and was locked away for her own protection. Chaos in their oasis mirrored their marriage falling apart as others had eaten the poisoned fruit too, hence the story of Ahdem and Eve."

We stared at each other. This explained more than why Lilith was a sadistic lunatic.

"I can't believe it," I said. "Everything I thought I knew…" I hugged the box in tighter, my fingers ran along the smooth silver edges.

Brennan sighed and slapped his hands on his thighs again, "Tell me about it. Some crazy crap has gone down on this little rock we call home."

So much myth was derived from facts, just jumbled over time. There was an element of truth to all the stories I'd ever heard and they were all linked to my own secret heritage. That fire stoked inside me.

My skin tingled with a new excitement, an urgency to undo what had already begun… to put a stop to the evil orbiting us. I opened the lid of the box and peered into its emptiness. So many images pushed to the forefront of my mind. Watchers, gardens of Eden… Yeqon's leering grin, Belial's mockery of Esme's corpse and decomposing Rogues.

That stranger who lay shadowed in my memories and made my heart flutter, a back drop to it all.

I thought of Jaz and her strength. She wouldn't have given up; she'd have kicked this box's butt and then some.

I pushed it back onto the ground, closed my eyes, and gripped its edges. Infusing objects with my energy had made things happen before, like when I melted open the prime scroll. I emptied my mind and imagined the box opening an unseen latch or a secret compartment. A cold breeze swirled around me; its fingers fussed around my ankles. I opened an eye; ochre dust powdered my toes. I gulped and encouraged myself to believe that it was the mouse at play again; there was no logical reason for a breeze to exist in my room.

"I don't know what will happen," I said as my hands lit.

"No one does, Princess, but I'm here. I've got your back."

Deep breath in, deep breath out.

The draught faded from my awareness. I relaxed into a pre-sleep paraesthesia. A hot coil unravelled in my gut, curled its way through my body, as though it knew where it was going. I breathed deeper to draw it up towards my hands. It flowed until my hands were luminous with the feverish heat of E'lan. My nails dug into the box's edges as I willed it to give me its secrets.

My subconscious pulled me in. I fell backwards until I hit solid ground. Everything was darkness and heat. A sliver of light sliced through that dark. I stepped towards it, one step at a time. For every step, that sliver inched open like a door. My heart thrashed, but there was no fear in this place, so I kept going.

"Hello?" I called.

The door opened fully, soundless on its hinges. A crisp silhouette filled the frame, the light behind haloing around a figure. In utter silence, Enoch held out his hand to me. He nodded. A smile pulled up soft jowls, adding softness to brown eyes. I let my hand sink into his.

We stood atop a rocky outcrop, a wild sea raging below. The sun warmed my shoulders, the sky a clear blue. A man with cropped hair stood on the cliff's edge and stared out to sea. He wore the earthy tones of a distant era. Paint splattered the length of his pants; paintbrushes stuck out of a back pocket. A satchel hung over one shoulder. A silvery box in his hands glinted in the sunlight.

"Under the water?" he asked me in Italian. "Are you sure, your Highness?"

I answered, not in my voice, but in the smooth tones of English aristocracy. I held something small and knobbly in my fist. I wanted to look at it, but I felt compelled to speak instead.

"Yes, dearest friend," I said. "Deep beneath the waves, amongst the ruins of Tiberius, where the evil ones no longer tread. I am at your service should you require further assistance. Call me on dawn's breath and I shall be by your side."

I pointed at the box, Enoch's box. He released it. The box rose at the behest of my power, hovering in the air. His eyes widened in wonder as they followed its path.

"Come," I said.

He bowed his head, "I am not worthy of such an undertaking."

"You are most worthy indeed. Born a bastard, pure of heart and scorned by your father, yet a soul so true that it drew the great angel Uriel to your side. By his grace, you will save your kind and our people."

I finally recognised the voice. It was Elizabeth Woodville, my regal grandmother and Regent Queen of England.

I tried desperately to see who the man was but he didn't turn around.

"Follow my guidance," Elizabeth said through me. "In time, she will come and retrieve your work."

"Very well," the man said. "I commend my life's works to you."

He reached for the box, it settled back into his arms and he dove into the ocean, pulled quickly under by its weight. I slowly moved forwards and watched him disappear beneath the crystalline blue. White water broke wildly against the rocks below.

The sky darkened, walls closed in around me, and Enoch reappeared. He bowed and stepped back into the slivered doorway. I retraced my steps, and the connection closed.

"Princess?"

I blinked, "What?"

I shook my head to clear the fog. My hands were still alight.

"Another vision?" Brennan asked.

I nodded.

He leaned in, took my hand, his fingers lost in its light, "Was it helpful?"

"Yes, I think so."

His face lit up, "What did you see?"

I shook my limbs out, drew reality back.

Deep breath in, deep breath out.

"Well, I started in a dark room, it was really hot. It was kind of a full house in there. Enoch, my grandmother, and a man I didn't recognise but, she certainly knew him."

Brennan narrowed his eyes, his fingers curled tighter around mine, "And?"

"Enoch guided me to a cliff by an ocean. Elizabeth was there. I didn't see her, but I saw through her, I spoke as though I *was* her. I think she directed this man to hide clues. He had one of these boxes," I closed my eyes and pinched the bridge of my nose, willing thoughts forward. If Elizabeth was speaking to this stranger, perhaps…

"What if he was the Disciple of Learning?"

Brennan leaned into his knees, "Think harder, Soph."

"If he was, he lived when she did," I leaned back towards Enoch's box. The heat from my hands drew a luminous red to its surface. Left in their wake were fingertip-sized spots of melted chromious, "I've bled on the damn box, but…"

I concentrated on fire in my hands, the delicious anger that grew in my heart, stoked it with the ugly images of Lilith and Yeqon. I was transfixed by those little melted spots of metal.

"C'mon!" I urgently whispered to myself, hoping I was right.

The box began to vibrate harder than ever, so I pushed harder.

"Um, Soph?"

"Shh."

The pulse of the orb above was a loud thrum. The trickling water from my thermal shower crashed like Niagara Falls. And then there was the deep drumming of my heart, its beat in my temples, a train hurtling towards a precipice. An image of Jaz tied to a bed flashed through my mind. For a second, I heard her moans…

E'lan burst from my heart. It seared through my fingers and into the box. Sweat stung my eyes as I urged the power out. I doubled over, my teeth ground as a scream rumbled inside my chest.

The fire was too much. I fell forwards into white-hot flames.

The maelstrom in my head quieted. My body heaved and I was panting with exhaustion. The burn ebbed away into the background.

Brennan's excited pulse thumped against my shoulder as he slipped his arm around me, "Princess, you might want to look down."

My hands felt empty and wet. I opened my eyes; they felt sticky, like I was waking up from deep sleep. I rubbed away the blurriness — my heart seized.

"Oh no!" Panic shivered through me. I couldn't breathe, "No, no, no!" A silver puddle pooled on the ground where the box had sat mere seconds ago.

I clawed at my face with shaking, silver-tinged fingers. I pulled Brennan's hand into mine.

"Oh my God, Brennan. What have I done?"

He gently pulled his hand away.

"Shh, Princess, it's okay."

I shook my head. The box was gone, I couldn't even look at the mess left in its wake. A puddle, like liquid mercury, shimmered atop the woven grass mat underneath us. A smattering of orange cinders was all that remained of the internal woodwork. I was in a numb haze, dizziness overcame me. A mortified pulse thrummed in my temples.

Brennan tugged at my arm, "Look!"

I sobbed, "No. I can't believe what I've done!"

"Neither can I. It's bloody amazing," Brennan pulled a little harder, urging my hands from my face.

I blinked away tears and focussed on his, searching for disappointment. His eyes, however, sparkled with excitement.

I sniffed back another sob, "Why aren't you angry?"

"How in I'el's name could I be angry with you?" Brennan glanced at the floor, "Old Enoch and this Disciple dude had more up their sleeves than we thought. Bloody clever stuff! Open your eyes properly and look down."

The metallic puddle was more than just that. The melted chromious had hardened into a solid plate. Parts of it drained away and revealed a silver cog. Flat teeth hugged the edges, each a dazzling and precise receptacle awaiting a mate. Swirls, like those on the training cavern's roof, were etched around the curves. A neat script hugged its circumference. In its centre, was the engraving of a man, his arms and legs splayed towards the four spokes. Something familiar about the image poked at my memory.

"For the love of I'el," Brennan whispered. "I think that's a piece of the Kaladai."

He picked it up, carefully turned it in his hands. It sparkled like diamonds. It was so perfectly beautiful, not a smudge, not the tiniest imperfection and it seemed to glow from within. There was something almost sentient about it.

"Oh, thank God!" I sighed and reached for the mysterious object. It was warm, impossibly smooth, and heavy. Its energy hummed against my skin; it shimmered like a gossamer aurora.

I passed it back to Brennan.

"It's been a long time since I've seen a portal," he said, eyes wide with curiosity. "The last one was destroyed so long ago, but I'll be damned if this isn't part of its mechanism," he held it up and traced a finger across the tiny words. "What does it say, Soph?"

He passed it back.

"Um…" I bit my lip. With a shaky finger, I traced the image and the fine words, which were the same ancient language as the script from the Prime Scroll chamber.

"Drowned Vitruvian where Tiberius dost play." I hugged the silvery disk to my chest as wild oceans and underwater caves swept through my mind. "It's my dream — my vision," I drew a sharp breath. "I think it might lead us to the portal."

Chapter Nine

Goosebumps swarmed across my body. The E'lan was so strong that wisps of energy snaked and popped around me — a sign of an intense connection to this elemental power. I hugged the piece of the Kaladai closer to my chest. It felt right somehow, and my body relaxed.

"Brennan?"

"Soph?" he leaned closer.

I rested the cog in my lap. "What does it mean Brennan?" I heard the ocean's soft splash as the image clung to my mind.

"I have no idea, but you're bloody awesome," Brennan tilted the cog to get a better view, "How did you know to do that?"

"The Prime Scroll cylinder melted when I concentrated on wishing it open," I said. "I just tried what worked before."

We huddled closer on the floor.

"Chromious does have a memory," Brennan whispered. "Extreme heat will restore it to its original shape, that's how we repair our weapons. But to completely change form?" he whistled. "This is some awesome concealment by old Enoch. Maybe he was more angel than human?" Brennan shook his head.

I unravelled a scroll, running my finger down the swirling script.

"'Three chests of knowledge must be sought'," I read it in a thoughtful hush. "I've found two of the chests and now a piece of the

Kaladai. I've only one more to find, Brennan!" I smiled as I rolled up the document and placed it back in my pocket along with Elizabeth's scroll, "I feel like I'm actually getting somewhere."

I chewed my thumbnail, searched the engraved script on the cog for anything that could unlock its mystery. At the barest touch, its elemental pitch washed up my arm, entwined with each beat of my heart. It spread like a wave; it was connected to me in some inexplicable way. I stared at it, into my own reflection.

My pupils expanded, the mark on my cheek burned in pleasant victory. Its swirls bloomed brighter where they wrapped around my eye, as though urging me to see something more. I peered deeper; the blue of my irises intensified. Something reflected within them.

A dreamy warmth urged me to fall into it again, so I did.

A blue ocean, craggy rocks, and Av'ael's knowing face flashed through my mind. I sank to the bottom of a warm sea and landed on soft sand. The current pulled at me to follow it.

Brennan was far away, his voice dulled by the water.

"Soph? Are you okay?"

"I'm fine. Wait for me."

I moved with the flow along the ocean floor. Corpses lay scattered here and there, limbs askew or missing. The water's crystal-clear blue rippled over the bodies, softening the macabre scene. A few feet ahead, a shadow slowly changed into a human form. Its outline became crisper as the current moved me forward.

"Soph?"

I ignored Brennan as a familiar voice drowned his out.

"Follow me and you will find what you seek."

I sped towards the figure. Behind it, a rocky expanse came into view. I reached out, desperate to get to this spectre.

My grandmother materialised, bobbing and ebbing upon the current at the mouth of a cave. White robes wafted around her. A small golden crown sat atop her milky hair. Her hands, stretched out in front, held a small skull. There was a shiny object beneath it, but I couldn't see what it was.

My pendant magnetised towards her like she was a beacon, but with each stroke I gained, she retreated.

"Beneath mine atlas, souls twin doth dwell," she said with the soft tones of an elderly man.

"Help me understand!" I called.

An invisible pull dragged me away. The ocean bed erupted. Gnarled claws reached up through the sand, scrambling to grab me. Blood and bone, muscle and sinew. Foul Rogues reanimated from their watery graves. They slithered up amidst effervescent bubbles which exploded from their gaping jaws.

The water was too thick. There was no mist, no foul wet and grisly growls… the ocean silenced their screams. My wings refused to open whilst I scrambled to break the surface. I glanced down, fleshless fingers tugged at my ankles. Fear rose its paralysing head. Panicked, I breathed, water filled my lungs, burning and constricting my chest. I flailed and spun, unsure which way was up. The water was white and fizzy. I spun over and over losing my sense of direction. Light, dark, light, dark, until sunlight finally streamed down.

A hand reached for mine, but the foul creatures still tugged at me and yanked me back into the depths.

A long-dead face burst through the bubbles, its bony maw wide for a bite. Barely any flesh clung to its salt-bleached bones. I punched it away in a strange, slow motion. It launched forwards again, and I caught it between my charged fingers.

Bones shattered under my knuckles. Festering grey flesh fluttered away as the Rogue sank towards another rising shadow.

I swam with all that I had towards the surface, clawing faster, rising above the frothy surrounds until my hands reached the first rays of fragmented light. The surface was so close, yet I couldn't break it. Sharp bones plunged into my feet, ripped at my calves, and pulled me back to the darkness. A toothless smile rushed closer; its grip tight as it clawed up my legs.

My consciousness faded; my eyes rolled backwards. I tumbled over and over, curled in a ball to protect myself as much as possible.

More corpses floated upwards and obscured the beautiful light.

Through the chaos, amidst the pain and horror of my body being ripped and bitten, E'lan's gentle vibration tapped into mine. It strengthened me, beckoned my instincts into action. I tightened my body against the attacks, grit my teeth, and pushed fear away. I let the Rogues think they had me, let them pull me a little deeper… until the burn reached my heart and exploded with the next beat.

"Princess, come back! You're safe. I got you."

I fell into the safety of Brennan's arms, swatting at myself. His breath warmed my skin, the reassuring thud of his heart comforting. He held me until I calmed. I looked up into his wide eyes, framed by a tight knit in his brows.

"You scare me when you go all catatonic," Brennan said. "I don't know where you are."

I squeezed his hand and sighed through my nose. My attention fell on the silver cog shining by my knees. I hugged it possessively.

This vision had been an extension of the one that had plagued me for weeks, but it had given me a snippet more. I had to find this place. It was connected to this new artefact. Along with it came danger too, but I had a piece of the Kaladai, and that was empowering.

I straightened and held up the cog, "You know, I worked it all out when I was Yeqon's prisoner. I trusted my instincts and found a way. I can do this too."

A smile returned to the corners of Brennan's mouth.

I felt strangely calm, even content. The cog's song drew me in, buzzing as it had done when it was disguised as the ornate box.

"I hear you," I whispered.

Brennan shook his head.

"What?" I asked.

"You amaze me."

"I'm just doing what I was born to do," I said with more conviction than before.

His eyes glistened. He leaned back on his hands, looked me up and down, and nodded with that broad, dimpled smile.

"And to the world I say, welcome the saviour of man and beast, the light of all angels, for the daughter of I'el has risen."

Chapter
Ten

Gedz'iel knew that no amount of stealth could conceal the Watchers. The energy emanating from Castle Pouancé's depths rose quickly. A dozen rats scattered past them towards the surface.

"Something has upset the locals," he muttered. His hand rested against the wall and ignited a soft white as his E'lan joined with that coming from somewhere deep below the old structure.

"They're here," Gedz'iel pointed down. "Watch yourselves, there are probably sleeper Rogues around as well," he nodded to the ever-quiet Eloi to go ahead. "Try not to bleed."

Theus, Amais, and Serail blended into the darkness.

Gedz'iel held Matias back, "Is she safe?"

"Brennan is with her."

Gedz'iel nodded, relieved, and released him arm so Matias could follow his brothers.

They sneaked through the ruin's first dingy corridors.

Dash glanced around the dank interior. "Yeqon's had a long time to leave zombie cluster bombs around," he whispered as his eyes swept swiftly around the dank interior.

"Don't worry about those now, but he's right, the less bleeding we do, the better," Koi reassured.

"Don't worry, young Dash," Jude said. "I'll make the bloodletting quick. I don't take shit from these cretins," Jude hissed. "I'll be in and out with Jasmine or with intel about her whereabouts and the bones of the descended behind me."

Koi's mark glowed in warning, "Jude, less talk and more action or I'll transfer you out myself."

Jude grunted but kept quiet and followed Koi.

Pinpricks of daylight beamed though the crumbling walls, creating a starry-night effect. A frigid draught whistled through the cracks. The corridor narrowed where it spiralled down thinner stairs, which were slippery with moss. More rats rushed through their feet.

Gedz'iel stopped, "Do you hear that?"

They pressed their ears against the icy, bluestone wall.

"Groaning," Koi said.

"That doesn't sound healthy," Lorcan added.

Gedz'iel drew his sword. "Withdrawing Afflicted won't be an easy fight," sparks sizzled from his knuckles.

The others followed suit; weapons readied.

E'lan flashed through the air over their heads, sizzling like fizzing soda. A bird rushed out of a crevasse and knocked its nest to the ground. Three small eggs smashed on the stone. The bird flew past them towards the exit. A thin line of bugs rushed out from the same spot.

"I'm pretty sure this isn't because of us," Dash said.

"Of course it isn't," Lorcan shoved past Dash. "It's them. Can't you smell that sweet stink of Thanratos? Let's move. I've got other places to be," Lorcan twirled his sword in his hands, the chromious gleaming with his power.

Jude pushed Lorcan's hands down, "Settle down, you fool. Don't poke that where it doesn't belong."

"Both of you settle down," Gedz'iel said without looking back at them, "Or you both can head back to Kaymakli to babysit the children."

Lorcan chuckled, "Don't want to go join Brennan, do you?"

Jude, his knuckles white, pushed past Lorcan and settled near Koi.

Koi sighed, "You two have taken on too many human traits."

Lorcan rolled his eyes, Jude just grunted some more.

The soft squelch of Gedz'iel's footsteps halted, and he faced them. The glow of the Eloi's faces behind him lit him up like spotlights.

"When we reach their chamber, look for Afflicted who appear sated," Gedz'iel said. "The best-fed ones are most likely to be on the drug payroll. That's where we'll find intel. Anything that looks like a corpse, leave it be. Don't provoke them unless it's necessary."

"We should descend them all," Lorcan snapped.

"Sometimes," Jude said, "I want to descend *you* and that love-sick clunk-head you've got!"

Lorcan lunged at him.

Gedz'iel grabbed them by their throats, "Enough! Do you wish to help or to spend time in the munitions room so you can sharpen blades for real warriors?"

Lorcan's shoulders slumped, Jude bowed his head and quietly cursed to himself.

Koi shook his head at them.

Dash patted Lorcan's shoulder and urged him forwards, "C'mon, let's find the girl and get out of here."

Lorcan nodded, his face beet red.

"Apologies, Gedz'iel," Jude muttered through gritted teeth.

Gedz'iel leapt over a wide fissure at the base of the staircase. "Ignore the weak, they will be useless. Don't waste your energy on unnecessary battles. Those of us who have taken the wrong path suffer every minute for their choice. If they cause us no harm, leave them," he glared at Jude and Lorcan. "We are not murderers."

The tunnel widened, and Gedz'iel hurried with feline stealth. Koi and Dash followed him whilst Lorcan and Jude pushed ahead from the rear.

Gedz'iel stopped outside an ancient wooden door. Curls of wrought ironwork were all that held it together. His fingers traced the thick hinges and long-rusted lock.

Gedz'iel rushed forwards, splintering the thick door into a thousand pieces. Dozens pierced his torso, he didn't flinch.

The others rushed into a stinking, ramshackle room. They took up defensive positions by the doorway and by every corner. Theus coughed on the stench.

"For the love of I'el," Dash muttered.

Skin-and-bone bodies lay around the room in various states of consciousness. The more aware scattered into the shadows, their eyes wide with shock. The rest lay askew, some high and mumbling to themselves, others unconscious. One lay in vomit.

One tried to flee for the door.

"Oh no you don't," Lorcan flung an orb at him. "Fool," he picked up the frail, stunned male, bound him, and dropped him against a wall. Lorcan's nose wrinkled, "Hell, you stink worse than arse!"

The rest didn't bother trying to run, they simply watched on through vacant eyes.

Gedz'iel inspected each of the occupants from a safe distance. An Afflicted could turn from a dribbling mess into a viper fast, no matter how degraded they appeared.

"You know why we are here?" Gedz'iel asked.

One Afflicted coughed and spat on the floor.

"Who sustains you?" Gedz'iel asked. "Do you cavort with the Unseen? With the witches of Anjou?"

Two rolled over so as not to see him.

Jude shoved at them with his foot. "Sit up. Show some respect!" he pointed his sword at them. It glimmered with E'lan, yearning to release its pent-up force.

They sneered but complied. They took their time whilst grumbling and groaning, as if the simple task of sitting was too much effort. Their filthy rags barely covered the emaciated remnants of what they had once been. Dull grey eyes with pupils in various states of dilation darted back and forth, looking for a way out.

Koi pointed to a scruffy male against a wall, "This one seems most alert."

A weak light orb hummed above the Afflicted. Its dull glow exaggerated his sunken eyes and protruding cheekbones.

"We are looking for a human girl," Gedz'iel said. "We believe she is with Nephr'eus and Anjou'elle. We know someone feeds you. Is it them? Do you hide a human for them?"

The Afflicted rolled his eyes and stared at the ceiling.

Gedz'iel kneeled on one knee by him, "Do you hide a human girl? If you don't help me, things won't bode well for any of you. We will drag you back to our cells, where Thanratos won't wet your lips."

The male smiled. One front tooth was missing. Poorly healed scars hatched his skin. His wild eyes goggled with the touch of insanity. He pulled himself up onto an elbow, yanked a clump of hair from his nearly bald head, and teased Gedz'iel with the tuft.

"Shall I call for tea?" he lisped through the gap in his teeth. "Scones, perhaps?"

Someone coughed a laugh.

An unconscious female lolled onto the Afflicted's shoulder. He elbowed her away, and she groaned as her body hit the floor with a dull crack. Next to her, another eased herself into the shadows, sliding along her backside. Lorcan watched her as she fumbled through her pockets while watching the intruders.

The male Afflicted chewed at his fingernail stubs without looking up. "What... do we care... about a lowly human?" he mimicked Gedz'iel's deliberate tone.

Jude grabbed him by the scruff of clothing around his scrawny neck. "Did we ask you to care, you traitorous letch?" Jude glanced at Gedz'iel, his eyes flickering.

Gedz'iel nodded, giving Jude the freedom to interrogate in his way.

"We just need a simple yes or no, *brother*," Jude said. "It shouldn't be too much of a challenge for you."

Jude hoisted the Afflicted aloft with one fist. Wisps of raging energy flickered around Jude's head; it caught his hair in the static. A halo of strands pulled free from his thick plait. The white tendrils whipped at the Afflicted, who seemed uninterested. He grimaced, yawned, and rolled his eyes, then spat on the floor near Matias.

"Do that again and it will be the last movement you make," Matias hissed.

The male cleared his dry throat with a cough. "Perfect. Descend me now. I will prefer oblivion, I think, because I don't much care about some random human. None of us do," he laughed, and a chorus of laughter echoed around the room.

Jude lifted him higher, shook him like a rattle, and dropped him to the floor.

The more aware pulled themselves into crouching positions. Their weak facial marks flowed around watery eyes.

Matias, Theus, Serail, and Amais moved towards the shadows. Koi covered the doorway, and Dash backed up Gedz'iel. Lorcan sheathed his sword and side-stepped towards the female who continued to sidle backwards. She crawled; the matted hair across her face didn't hide her gaunt pallor and darting eyes.

"You have one opportunity," Gedz'iel said. "I offer anyone who assists us the chance of recovery. We will welcome you back and seek the Great Healer. If we can't find him, I guarantee you painless ascension with your own kind," he made eye contact with everyone who had the courage to meet his stare.

"Do not make us fight you," Koi said. "There is a better way."

Someone chuckled. The Afflicted Jude had dropped reached into a depression in the floor. An old masonry channel ran the length of the room, a drain to draw melting ice into the moat outside. He poked around inside it. When he withdrew his fingers, they sparkled with specks of Thanratos. He slowly licked at it; amused disdain aimed at them.

"You judge us?" the Afflicted asked. "Is that not for our most beloved I'el to do? You place yourselves too high and mighty," his face lit weakly, his nostrils flared with the drug's hit. "Anyway," he flicked his hand towards the ceiling, "He isn't interested in us. I don't fear him or you. You suffer in your way; we survive in ours. You don't approve of this? Then leave," the Afflicted laughed.

The female retreated to the rear of the room, where she melted into the shadows.

"You," the Afflicted said to her. "Get me something to drink. This burn is killing me," he clawed at his throat, his tongue swept over his dry lips.

She nodded; eyes downcast.

"Halt!" Lorcan moved quick and blocked her.

"No one moves until we get answers," Gedz'iel said. "Know that our patience has ended." An orb materialised in his hand. He dipped the tip of his sword into it, igniting the weapon.

The Afflicted all pulled themselves up, suddenly alert.

The E'lan peaked, snapped and snaked through the cold air. A sizzling blue-white glow resulted and caused the Afflicted to appear even more corpse-like. Every face glowed in a haze of static swirls.

The female ran. She ducked around Lorcan, rushed past Theus. Every Afflicted popped their wings. Some glowed from face to foot, others with mere sparks sputtering from their fingertips. They all rose into the air.

The Afflicted who had ignored their questions was surrounded by a twine of electrical ropes, which snapped and lashed at the Watchers.

The Watchers released their wings too.

The male flicked his scrawny wrist towards Gedz'iel, "All is not what you see, brother!"

A bloody wound peeled open across Gedz'iel's brow. The Afflicted chortled, his dilated eyes held the darkness of a Daimon.

"Nothing comes without effort, brother, especially survival!"

The Afflicted lunged again, but Gedz'iel dodged the strike. Jude slashed the sliver of light into nothingness, his eyes ablaze.

Gedz'iel blinked away the blood that had pooled in his lashes. It curdled above his lip and in the small cleft of his chin.

"You simple fools!" Gedz'iel bellowed. "Watchers, engage!"

Gedz'iel soared towards the leader and grabbed his throat. The Afflicted moaned, struggled to breathe. He yanked at Gedz'iel's arm, shaking and quivering with effort. Spittle bubbled from his mouth.

"You had a choice," Gedz'iel twisted the Afflicted's neck. A sharp crack followed, and the body slumped to the floor.

Gedz'iel leaned against the wall, shaking, his head bowed. He drew a long breath and joined the growing melee.

Jude and Koi were back-to-back, spinning their swords like propellers to deflect burning arcs coming their way. One cut through Koi's defence. He grabbed his side to cauterize the ooze. They spun when one of the more robust Afflicted set eyes on them. The attacker's pale wings flickered. Jude cast an orb before they got too close. It struck his shoulder and the Afflicted spun backwards and hit the wall, his skin paler under a fine dusting of debris. His ripped shirt fell in shreds from his torso as his arms and legs flailed.

"I've got this," Koi said. "Drop back and help the others."

Jude slipped away and screamed a war cry as he dove down.

Koi dipped his sword into his wing and aimed its glimmering point ahead. An Afflicted jutted back and forth, barely aloft. His hands rolled over themselves, a small orb formed in his bony palm.

"Wrong choice, brother!" Koi's sword found its mark first. The Afflicted dropped. His wings sputtered out, and his eyes bulged as he hit Serail's sword below as well. It protruded through his stomach, and he grunted, sucking in a last laboured breath before bursting into flame.

Koi nodded grimly at Serail, but he'd already turned away to back up Theus, who was knocking the weakest ones unconscious with the handle of his sword.

A woman rose within the growing body heap. Her hands grasped for anything; a curdled scream chorused her rapid breaths. She elbowed her way through the decrepit, pulled herself to her feet, and lunged for Serail.

Koi's sword speared through her heart, "Watch the ones on the ground!" he yelled.

She fell in a tuft of blue flames. Serail swooped in, scooped up the sword, and flung it back into Koi's hands.

Orbs thudded into flesh and stone. Blood stained the ice channel and washed away specks of the drug. A red trickle journeyed to the outside as blow after blow refilled the coffers with more scarlet offerings. A river iridescent with angelic power flowed beneath them.

The souls of the Afflicted howled like wolves on the full moon, mournful cries when they emerged from their fleshy shells. Their opaque spectres disappeared through small cracks in the surrounding masonry.

Inches below the roof, Gedz'iel deflected a handful of weak orbs towards a woman who had replaced the leader.

She screeched. "Get out of here! You're not wanted!" she frantically worked on his attack. Her skin paled with each effort.

"Give me the information I seek and I will spare you," Gedz'iel said.

She sobbed. "You *killed* him," she spat at Gedz'iel and threw a small, weak orb. It exploded into nothingness before it reached Gedz'iel.

He hovered closer. She backed away until she hit a corner.

"You make a grave mistake, sister," Gedz'iel said. "This bloodshed brings me no satisfaction. Does anyone here work for Nephr'eus?"

The woman held her head high and smiled, "You've given us nothing, brother. You can suffer as we do."

She reached into her wings, pulled a filament of light into a club-sized weapon. It hummed as she brandished it.

Gedz'iel drew his hands across each other, drawing out a long shard of his own light. It pulsed when he aimed its needlepoint tip at her.

She laughed and jutted her weapon at him. Her wings failed with each effort she made to stay aloft. She bounced awkwardly in the air, trying to mirror Gedz'iel's movements.

"Who feeds you the drug?" Gedz'iel demanded.

Something exploded. Gedz'iel dodged falling rock. It bit into his flesh. He groaned and spat out the air's sour taste.

"I owe you nothing, so I will tell you nothing," the woman screamed. "I regret the day I tripped over myself to get to this disappointment of a planet."

She threw her club. Gedz'iel's shard pierced it into nothingness. Its remnants rained like firework embers.

Gedz'iel growled. The blood-stained cleft in his chin deepened, his lips thinned in anger. Sweat glistened through his thick buzz cut. Azure fires burned where his brothers had cut down her kin, but he tuned out their screams.

"I am done tolerating your ill choices," Gedz'iel said. "If you are this weak-spirited on Earth, you were never a true warrior of A'vean. Earth has always been an anaemic world, and to fail on it shows your soul's true merit," he glided a little closer.

She backed up, "We were tricked!"

"There were rules, as there have always been. You were just weak," Gedz'iel answered.

She screamed and lunged towards him. A small whirlwind of E'lan whipped up around her and teased her hair into Medusa-like strands. Her clothing scraps clung to her with the sweat of withdrawal.

Gedz'iel rushed at her, grabbed her the same way he had her mate. The energy maelstrom engulfed them both. She tore at his flesh, her dying energy blistered his skin. He squeezed her neck tighter. She sunk her white-hot thumbs into his eyes. He roared and flung her across the room. Ancient mortar puffed into alabaster dust from their encounter. The air clogged with it as it coalesced with blood and sweat and electrical static. Through the haze, she tumbled back into him. He caught her twiggy arms and tossed her over his head, but she kicked off the far wall and aimed for him once more.

Gedz'iel shoved her away with a swift kick to the gut. He spat blood. His mark burned so brightly that it hid the right side of his face. Just a hint of his blue eyes visible. The gaping gash to his brow bled anew and he spat blood again.

The Afflicted shook her head and leaned into the wall. She didn't take her wild eyes off Gedz'iel, who hovered only feet away. Blood oozed down her neck across the sallow skin pulled too tight over her ribs. Her heels dug into divots in the wall as her wings sputtered and flickered like a light bulb trying to survive. Her lips quivered; her eyes watered. She looked for support but found none. Gedz'iel let her flail.

She screamed in frustration. Her body was dying and her power fading, yet she refused to yield. She pushed off the wall, wobbling on wings that didn't obey. She conjured a small, pale orb, but when she threw it, the force unbalanced her and it spun away, hitting an unconscious Afflicted in the head, descending him. Her body jerked as it tried to counter her almost-gone wings.

She plucked a small vial from her neck, opened it, and held it out towards Gedz'iel.

"Bottoms up, Watcher," she tipped the sparkling grains of Thanratos onto her tongue. Her eyes rolled back, and her body flared bright white, just enough to boost her wings one last time.

With one huge sweep of them, she crashed into Gedz'iel and smashed them both into the opposite wall. Mortar sliced the delicate leaflets along his spine.

Morning light shone through the new cracks in the walls, which sucked fresh air into the chamber. The smell of fresh snow cleared the fog in Gedz'iel's head, and the winter sun's warmth eased the pain of his wounds.

Gedz'iel dragged the Afflicted into the melee. Her legs scraped along the slippery stones, and she screamed through the cold, blue fire of descendance.

He landed near the diamond bones of her leader and held her head down, "Look at what he chose!"

She kept her eyes closed and struggled for freedom. Her nails scored his thigh.

Gedz'iel spun her to face him, "Who has the human girl?"

She spat bloody phlegm into his face. The Thanratos burned his skin, whipped his heart and terrified him. He leaned into his shoulder to smear it off his skin.

Another explosion overhead. Gedz'iel ducked and dragged her along with him. She choked on the thickening air, her cough hoarse, her body slack.

"Where is the human girl?" Gedz'iel yelled over the cacophony.

She half coughed; half laughed. Her head lolled back, too weak to hold up.

Gedz'iel's fist shot into the face of a male Afflicted who rushed him from the side. The female Afflicted shrieked.

Sorrow filled Gedz'iel's heart and anger cocooned it, but empathy made it beat.

"Sister, forgive me as I forgive you," Gedz'iel said.

A point of searing light pierced the middle of her back. It melded with the morning sunlight that cut through the haze. The skin around the wound bubbled as Gedz'iel hugged her closer and twisted his weapon until her coughing eased and her limbs went lax.

"Go now, sister," he whispered into her ear. "See if you find something more to your liking on the other side of mortality."

He yanked the shard out. She fell to the ground, a convulsing mess of flesh that erupted into flame. Her soul unravelled from her mortal flesh and melded with many others.

Screaming souls surged through the underground war. White spectres circled above those still in battle. Disoriented and fearful of where they were headed, they dashed around with increasing speed until they relinquished themselves to fate and slipped through the cracks to the other side

Gedz'iel expelled blood from his broken nose, cracked it back into place, then lurched forwards to pull an Afflicted off Matias' back.

Amongst the fighting, Lorcan darted after the girl who'd earlier tried to disappear in the mayhem. He dodged a shower of fiery munitions, ducked embers that dripped from old oak beams… and slipped in congealed blood. He fell into the ice channel and bruised his hip, but the fall had been advantageous, he caught a glimpse of her dulling her light.

"Hiding your energy won't help!" Lorcan yelled, "I'd find you if I were bound and gagged!"

He got back to his feet and sidestepped an orb that exploded to his right. It singed the tips of his hair. Ash darkened his face.

Lorcan sensed she was making her way towards the corridor they'd entered from, but Theus was blocking it. His mountainous torso shimmered, slick with his own blood. His right eye was swollen, a deep wound glistened beneath his collarbone. Theus descended one Afflicted, spun and summersaulted in front of another assailant who hovered just off the ground, screaming as she tried to draw an orb into her palms. Theus crouched and shook his head as though he were dizzy.

Lorcan drew his dagger and whistled, "Hey, Baldy!" He flung a red orb.

The skeletal woman buckled at the knees and hissed, her wild, grey eyes rivered with red. Her pale wings raised her into the air. Despite her charred legs, her hands were quick and her orbs small but true. She flung one after the other at Lorcan.

He launched his dagger straight into her eye socket. She collapsed, clawing at the weapon, howling in pain. Lorcan held an orb over her. E'lan's crackle teased light onto her face. She looked up at Lorcan with her good eye, blood streamed from the other.

A tear shimmered down her cheek, "Please?"

Lorcan hesitated. He smelled the sweet drug, the sourness of death.

The heartbeat of the girl who slunk away in the shadows was fading. He needed to follow her, there was no time for mercy.

Without looking down, he released the orb. Blue flames licked at his legs, cold and hungry. The pleading Afflicted's soul was set free.

The distraction enabled Theus to recover enough to get back to his feet, only to be struck with a lash of light wielded by another. Theus roared, holding his belly with one hand, staggering towards the perpetrator, a woman blackened with burns, her mouth a garish, toothless hollow. She screamed an insane pitch. Her arm wound back, the fluid rope of white energy regaining momentum for another strike.

It sailed through a snowstorm of ash, its tip skimming an ancient oak pillar, setting it fully alight. It cut towards Theus only to be met with his sword. He caught the energy, flicked his hand, quickly coiling it around the razor edge of his weapon, then yanked her in. With a quick thrust, both weapons burned through her belly. She slid down into a convulsing heap.

The air was thick with the beefy smell of cauterized flesh. Someone retched, it was Theus.

He dropped his weapons and fell to the ground. A half cast orb fell from his hand, fizzing away into a char by his knees. He clenched the mortal wound across is abdomen. His wings flickered out as he began to heal himself, palms alight, pressing firmly, holding the wound together. He grimaced.

Lorcan, attention still on the one fleeing, couldn't leave Theus to ascend. He took the opportunity to reel in another woman's attention to Theus, to cleanse another from the world.

"C'mon! Over here. Nice and fresh!" Lorcan yelled, pointing at Theus.

"Some nice bones to grind here, shortly! This big old Watcher looks about to burn!" Lorcan teased, his face flushed, his eyes wide with battle frenzy. The temptation was too great. The drug commanded her. She launched towards Theus; her tongue swept eagerly across pasty lips. Her feet slid along the slick floor where she fell, skidding to a stop just in front of Theus, who remained bent over, healing himself. She scrambled up, just in time for Lorcan to javelin her sternum with Theus' sword. She gaped in shock. Hollow eyes wide, her mouth fell slack as she sucked hard for a breath. Patting desperately at the searing weapon, she attempted to extract it. Her hands slipped in her own blood.

Lorcan leaned in and pulled it free, leaving her blood to pulse into her shred of clothing. Her eyes rolled back. She collapsed to her knees. She didn't see his arms sweep towards her. She didn't see the wildness of his eyes.

Lorcan's sword swept in a low smooth arc, severing her head. Blood spurted across his grim face. The heat of it hit his eyes, he winced. His nostrils flared at the metallic stench that clung across every curve and hollow of his body. He wiped the blood from his eyes with his forearm, then offered Theus a hand up. Theus finished knitting his wound, and shook his back to recall his wings.

"Are you alright, brother?" Lorcan asked.

Theus nodded. "Let this be done," he turned from Lorcan to run at the remaining affray.

Lorcan watched the last of the Afflicted cut down. The screams subsided; the air now soft with the crackle of blue flames. The sweet smell of the Afflicted was replaced with a gut churning barbeque. Koi spat ash from his mouth. Matias wrinkled his nose as he kicked through remains. A great crack pierced the now relative quiet as the smouldering oak beam fell. Shafts of sunlight played with the debris in the air. Lorcan squeezed his hands, felt the stickiness of his skin. In this moment of calm, he looked at the blood on them. His heart thrashed and bile filled his throat. This planet had promised great adventure, but instead, it had spiralled into killing his own people.

He punched a wall, closed his eyes. He breathed in deeply and tracked the girl. She was still near; he tasted the salt of her panic. He forged through the cool licks of flame towards the room's deepest shadows. Why wasn't she high or fighting like her comrades? Her nervous energy lent an odd chime to her signature. It was that particular strangeness that drew him to her in the first place. It had piqued his curiosity from the moment they'd entered the dungeon. Still, if she hadn't run, if she'd behaved as he expected of an Afflicted, he wouldn't have paid her any attention. Afflicted fought when they were cornered without fail. That she hadn't, was a glaring red flag.

Lorcan followed her energy, melted into the blackest corner in the rear wall — a fissure. Bearded with a prickly thatch of winter-browned vine, the opening was large enough for him to squeeze through. Most of the floor had sunk under the weight of the old structure, making footing tricky. Slipping though the ancient walls, he heard her grunting somewhere ahead. The coarse masonry and foliage tore at his flesh with every step. She must have been weak and confused to take this difficult exit. It was not the easiest escape route.

"Stop running," Lorcan's voice echoed back. "You know I'll catch you."

Her energy and speed rose, and her panic intensified her chime. Her exhausted grunts bounced down the walls. Her energy changed into a buzz and became a higher, more urgent frequency.

Lorcan hurried, "Don't you dare!"

He burst through branches into a thunderous morning. A gale-force wind blew wet leaves into his face. His feet reddened as they sunk into a fine dusting of snow. Pregnant clouds began to ease their burden. The rain's force dampened his ability to feel nuances in the E'lan.

Lorcan stood at the base of what had once been the moat. A burgeoning flow of water rushed through its middle. He scanned the area, but the rain belted at him sideways and diluted her signature to almost nothing.

He neither saw nor felt her. She was gone, probably transferred in time with a lightning strike to hide her movement.

Lorcan rammed his fist against the moat's wall, "Damn you!"

A small waterfall cascaded down the walls and over his head. It soothed his bloodied hands and cooled his anger.

Lorcan wished for Kea. She had always been so level-headed.

He pulled himself together. If she were here, Kea would have kicked his butt for being too emotional.

"I know exactly what you'd say, Kea. *This is bigger than you, pretty boy. Get on with it.*' And you'd be right, as always."

He smiled and shook his head, wiped his face with his forearm and smoothed his wet hair out of his eyes. He rinsed the blood from his hands in the trickling water but screwed up his face at the sight. He hated the sight of blood. It was why he preferred tracking to all-out warfare. He gulped and rubbed his hands together to spark a healing pulse, leaned towards a gash on his leg.

There was something in the bloody puddle by his toes.

It looked like nothing, really, but the wisp of black fibres drew him in. He plucked it up out of the water.

Recognition raced through his veins. The others fighting inside were a diversion, they'd needed this Afflicted girl, not their leader. He knew this because the black remnants in his palm was hair.

And it belonged to Jaz.

Chapter Eleven

My room was pin-drop quiet. The orb overhead warmed us with its soft light.

"Brennan?" I asked.

"Yes?" he replied.

I giggled, "You're full of crap. Saviour of man and beast?" I slapped my palm to my forehead.

"Ah well… I gotta sound somewhat mature every now and then. This moment deserves an Academy Award performance, don't you think?" he jumped to his feet and held up the silver artefact like a prize. "And I'd like to thank Sophia, Angel of all Angels and thief of Eccles cakes, for making me who I am today!" he bowed and slipped back next to me.

I punched his shoulder. "Idiot," I laughed again before focusing on my prize.

I turned the cog over in wonder. The precision of its lines, the smooth-mirrored surface, the beautifully detailed figure, the perfect inscription…

"Who could have made this?" I asked.

Brennan shrugged, "Mysteries of the universe?"

"We need to keep it safe."

"I've got the perfect place," he clapped and rubbed his hands together. "The Zythros stone has a cavity underneath, safe as houses under there. Just don't go advertising that it's there."

I frowned, "I'm not an idiot."

"No, you're not. Sorry."

I smiled and gave my full attention to the weighty mechanism.

"So, I have a new delightful puzzle," I bit the inside of my cheek as I pondered this new layer in my path. My brows tightened as my fingers trailed along the teeth of the cog's perimeter, "It looks like it comes from a machine. We also have the mysterious Vitruvian whatever, and the Tiberius person?"

Brennan tapped a finger against his chin. "Hmm, something's familiar. May I?" he took the cog and ran his hands over every inch, even sniffed it. "Hmph?"

"You're smelling it?"

"I've met some very stinky people over the years," Brennan said. "Smell sticks in your memory, trust me. Take Cleopatra, for instance. Yeah, she was glamourous, totally erotic and all that, but she smelled as sour as a month-old cream cake with all those milk baths she took," he crinkled his nose. "I'll never forget her."

"You knew Cleopatra?" my brows arched.

Brennan admired his reflection in the metal, "Well, let's define *knew*. I hung around her for a while, kept an eye on her constant bickering with the Romans. Fun times, Princess."

I rolled my eyes, ever surprised by all the things I didn't know.

"Okay then, I suppose I have nothing to add to that other than why?"

Brennan relaxed back and leaned onto one of his hands. "Things were quiet for us back then. Yeqon was in hiding and the humans were trying to conquer everyone and everything. Nothing's really changed there, so we all kinda just hung around in the shadows and watched them be total idiots."

"Right, well, that's amazing and bizarre," I leaned into my clasped hands. "I can't get my head around how long you guys have been here. It's so hard to comprehend."

"In the grand scheme, it's not so long for us," Brennan said. "It's the whole trapped-on-one-planet issue that's been hard. Watchers are wanderers who travel the universe, keeping order here and there. This has been like a really long detention," he sat up. "Anyway, Princess, I have an idea before we tuck this beauty away," he saluted and passed the cog back to me.

"What is it?" I asked.

"Hang ten, I'll be back shortly," Brennan transferred out. The sudden flash made the orb above sway.

There was a faint knock at the door.

"Brennan?" I spun around, expecting to see him burst through. "What are you up to?"

Another faint knock, "Who is it?"

"It's me, pretty Sophia!" Av'ael said.

I popped the cog under my pillow before I let her in. She was a kid, after all, and she was a sucker for gossip.

"Hello, my sweet."

She bounced into the room and up into my arms. Her cherubic lips pecked my cheek, soft as a butterfly.

"I can't stay long," Av'ael said. "Mumma is cross that I keep talking to you, but I need to show you something."

Av'ael wriggled out of my arms and beckoned me with her hand. She drew a circle on the ground. Place a stick figure inside. Her eyes were narrow, and her tongue pointed from the corner of her mouth as she concentrated.

"You have to find this," she said.

There was another knock at the door, and Av'ael's mother entered with one arm pointing into the corridor.

"I've told you to stop disturbing Soph'ael. Return to bed at once Av'ael!" she glared furiously at Av'ael.

"She isn't disturbing me," I said. "Actually, she has been a great little helper! Why don't you come in? We haven't properly met," I didn't even know her name.

Av'ael's mother turned to me and dropped her arm from the door. Her eyes swirled with a Watcher's rich blues, but not their warmth.

She pulled the girl into her arms, "Your destiny is your own to unravel, Soph'ael."

Av'ael wriggled against her, but her mother whispered into her ear and Av'ael settled so snuggly into her side it was like they'd melded together. Her mother walked out with Av'ael looking deflated over her shoulder. The door slammed hard enough to rattle the weapons on the nearby hook.

I sighed. How had I offended this woman?

I glanced between the closed door and Av'ael's picture on the ground, then took my notepad and copied the image. Why was it familiar? I also jotted down what I remembered of the last vision.

Brennan popped back in with a sharp white flash.

"That was fast," I said.

"Of course!" Brennan said. "Who do you think I am? Lorcan?" he rolled his eyes.

I shook my head, "Why are you so mean to him?"

"Oh, I just mess with him. He's had personality constipation for at least a millennium," Brennan screwed up his face as if… well, as if he were constipated.

I nearly choked on a laugh, then felt guilty. Lorcan tried so hard to be nothing less than sweet to me.

"Brennan, be nice," I waved my finger at him.

"He's way too serious," Brennan said. "Full of himself. Lives with his heart on his sleeve, and don't *you* know that?" he winked.

I blushed.

"Don't you worry," Brennan said "You know, brotherly love and all that," he crossed his hands over his heart, fluttered his eyes, and made a lovesick face. He fumbled in his pocket. "So, anything happen while I was gone?"

"Funnily enough, yes."

I explained the unexpected encounter with Av'ael and her ill-tempered mother.

My shoulders slumped. "I bet she thinks Av'ael is in danger if she's near me," I pointed at the picture.

"Sorry to say it, Princess, but that just might be the case," Brennan's eyes softened, and he glanced at the image. "You know, I can't say I know who they are. I tend to know family lines, but I can't place those two. They just appeared from nowhere," he stared past me. "Perhaps they're from Finland or Russia? Don't see that lot much. Not a large community that way. Too cold for me to visit as well," he mocked a shiver. "Might have made their way here for safety in numbers with all that's been going on. Oh, and you are *the* drawcard, don't forget."

He pulled a palm-sized rectangular object from his pocket.

"I'm sure it's for safety," I said. "There's something special about Av'ael though. This kid has some kind of clairvoyance. She knows things no one else does."

Brennan fiddled with the object, "That can be a trait of Av'ean heritage. You have your visions, quite powerful ones. She may well grow up to have that as her speciality."

I pointed at the sketch, "That could explain this. What do you think of this picture?"

His head nodded ever so slightly, as if he might recognise what he saw, but he said nothing. Instead, he opened a black case to reveal a shiny new smartphone.

My mouth fell open, "Where did you get that?"

"I'm like a scout, always prepared," he said. "I figured we might need a little Dr Google again to help us. It was very handy back at Windsor Castle."

"I'd hate to inflate your delicate ego further, but that's exactly what we need." I snatched the phone and held it to my chest.

"Shall I?" Brennan's fingers arced with static.

"Nope, I got this."

I pressed the *on* button. The phone blinked open to the front screen, and I dialled up energy until my finger glowed like a magic wand. A light voltage snapped and sizzled from under my fingernail into the device. The screen stuttered…and reset with full reception.

Brennan beamed at me, "Impressive!"

"I've had a good teacher."

I began typing before he could compliment himself further.

Brennan tipped the phone with his finger to get a better look, "What are you looking up?"

"That Tiberius playground thing. Seems like a place I need to find." I scrolled until I found something besides pop-up ads.

"Look!" I held the phone up for him to see. "Roman emperor, 14-37 AD, blah blah. Reluctant leader, hated gladiator games…"

"Ahh, yes, now I remember him," Brennan said. "Bit of a weak leader, apparently. Suffered terribly from skin infections, poor sod. Never met him, just heard about him," Brennan rolled his eyes in thought. "Sounds like Italy may be your place."

I scanned the page. "But what is the connection between him and this clue?"

Brennan shrugged, "Ask Google. I don't know everything."

I returned to the main search and clicked on another link. Nothing specific popped up, just lots of images of Italian coastlines and references to the Isle of Capri.

"Do you know much about Capri?" I asked.

Brennan hung over my shoulder, "I've been there a few times. Brilliant coastline, spotted with loads of ruins. There were some amazing cities along there in its heyday."

"Yes, but does anything stand out to you?" I held the phone closer to him hoping it might jog his memory.

He scratched his temple, "Not really, kiddo."

A tear, perhaps two, sprung into my eyes. Brennan gently wiped them off my cheek.

"What is it?" he asked.

"Nothing," I said. "Sorry, it's nothing."

"Wrong answer. Tell me what's making your eyes leak."

I sighed and flopped onto the bed. "It's silly, really."

My shoulders slumped. "Kea used to call me kiddo. It reminded me that she's gone," I stared at the blurry screen in my lap.

Brennan pulled me into a firm hug.

"Hey, she's not gone, remember? She's just hanging out elsewhere for a bit. She's rocking her natural form. We'll see her again, just in a different place and in a different way."

I sniffed back the tears and leaned into his shoulder, "Thanks."

I returned to scrolling through the phone. More references to Capri, but nothing specific.

"Type in *Vitruvian*," Brennan said.

I did, and up popped a picture of *Vitruvian Man*, Leonardo da Vinci's famous image of the male body.

"Will you look at this?" I held the cog high. "It's the same picture!" I jumped up, mouth agape. "That's what Av'ael drew!" I kneeled and held the phone next to her stick figure. "Why would something Leonardo da Vinci created have anything to do with what we're looking for? Why would Av'ael know about something so human?"

I glanced up at Brennan, whose face furrowed in concentration. Whilst he was thinking, I googled Leonardo da Vinci, but there was way too much to search through quickly. His birth date, his famous works of art, but nothing that linked him to my new world.

"Maybe it's a mistake?" I sucked in my lower lip, tipped my head this way and that, and concentrated on the cog and the drawing.

"Hang on, Princess. I think not," Brennan paced between the bed and door, head down and fingers steepled just under his nose.

"You won't have heard about this, but the Kaladai has been made twice before, once by I'el and once by a human. The original was destroyed long ago. Uriel entrusted an intelligent and creative human called Archimedes with creating the second Kaladai. We can't rebuild the Kaladai ourselves, and we'd never be able to activate it even if we did. It had to be created by a human we 'sullied', as it's so grossly put, and then activated by you."

I paced alongside him. "What happened to the one Archimedes made?"

"Archimedes had received plans only known to Uriel to recreate it. He was ready to hand it over while we awaited you," Brennan stopped. His face was flushed, but then it darkened and he paced some more, "Unfortunately, Anjou'elle murdered him and destroyed it for reasons unknown.

"The first one was stolen from the last functioning portal and lost in a shipwreck off the island of Antikythera, even further back in human time. Some archaeologists dug it up early last century. They've got no idea what it is," Brennan rolled his eyes. "They think it's some ancient Greek computer," he chuckled. "They call it the *Antikythera mechanism*. Gedz'iel poked around the Athens Museum years back hoping it could be in working order, but the ocean had completely destroyed it. We thought, just for a moment, that we had recovered a portal key."

Brennan tapped his temples, deep in thought. My skin tingled with the thrill of their history.

I grabbed his arm, "What if it was Leonardo who was entrusted to recreate it?"

"He certainly was a brilliant human," Brennan's pale brows knitted until they almost met int the middle. His eyes darted between the drawing and the cog.

I let his arm go and typed with quivering fingers.

"Oh my God, look!" I said, "It fits perfectly!"

I flipped the phone around. Brennan pried it from my white-knuckled grip.

I clasped my hands over my mouth and held my breath, "Read it out loud? I can't do it."

"Leonardo da Vinci," Brennan read. "Born April 15th, 1452. Died May 2nd, 1519. Renowned artist known for his curiosity about science. He devoted his life's work to following many disciplines of study, leading him to be referred to as the 'Disciple of Learning'."

I jumped up and down and took Brennan's hands, "That's it! It's him!"

"Leonardo is the Disciple of Learning!" I squeezed both his hands and continued to jump.

"*Thrice created, twice destroyed,* Leonardo must have made the third Kaladai!" I squealed.

Brennan grinned. He held my hands tight, let me jump some more and have my moment.

I let go and picked up the gleaming circle from my bed.

"I've got to find the rest of this," I moved to the door, and a tingle of E'lan tickled my skin. "I need to get out of here."

Brennan's grin waned. His wings blazed to life, the smile in his eyes gone.

"Don't, Brennan. You've got to let me go. It's time for me to be the Earth-born angel."

Chapter Twelve

With the storm beating down on him, Lorcan timed his energy with the weather. He concealed his signature within a crack of lightning, held the lock of hair to his chest and transferred back into Chateau Pouancé.

Koi, Gedz'iel, Jude, Dash, and the Eloi were wiping bloodied ash off themselves. The darkness was alight with the glow of their energies sealing their wounds and sterilising themselves of the filth. Cauterized flesh and the dissipating sweetness of the drug-addled fallen made the room thick and pungent.

Gedz'iel looked up, his face inflamed and bloodied. He tended a more serious abdominal gash. He gritted his teeth as he knit his flesh together. Blood had dried and settled in the crescents under his eyes.

"Where have you been, brother?" Gedz'iel asked.

"We needed you here!" Jude snapped. He kneeled by Amais and helped him heal a blistering burn that ran the length of his back.

"I was doing my job, Jude," Lorcan snapped back.

Jude snorted. "More like…"

"One of them got away, Master Gedz'iel," Lorcan said. "I saw her sneaking out and followed her to the moat. She transferred away," Lorcan turned towards the others and opened his hand. "She dropped this in her haste."

Gedz'iel touched the lock of hair. His eyes lit with understanding. "They remain a step ahead of us," Gedz'iel growled.

Koi leaned in to inspect the hair. He touched it, his mark ignited with recognition. "Damn it," he grumbled. "Poor young thing. We were wrong to bring her into our world," he shook his head.

Gedz'iel pushed Lorcan's hand away. "Too late for regrets, Koi," he gathered his weapons. "We have wasted enough time. Let us return to Kaymakli to assure everyone that all is well and double the global deployments to pull Yeqon into line." Gedz'iel glanced about the smouldering room, but his eyes were drawn to Lorcan's fingers, still clutching Jaz' hair. His nostrils flared, his mark glimmered, and he looked to the ceiling, "We cannot save every human. I will inform Sophia myself."

Jude wrestled some of the lock from Lorcan's fist. Lorcan shoved him in the chest. Jude staggered back, his attention on the delicate hairs.

"This isn't right!" Jude closed his eyes and tilted his head as though he was drawing something from the hair. He focused on Gedz'iel, "This is proof of life, a message to entice us to bargain."

Gedz'iel took Jude's wrist. Plucked some of the fibres between his fingers. "It was undoubtedly meant for us," he rubbed the black fibres together. "However, I said we could afford only a small diversion for her, and we have done so, Jude. Jasmine is gone, and we have more important things to attend. I know she is important to Sophia, but it is unreasonable to risk everyone else for one human," Gedz'iel rested his hand on Jude's shoulder, "I am sorry."

Jude's face glowed with anger, his eyes red-rimmed and moist. "Then we must intercept the Afflicted girl. We can take her in for interrogation. She'll yield quickly for a taste of her drug, and we can bring Jasmine back to m…" Jude coughed and shook his head. His eyes darted between Gedz'iel and the others, "Back to Sophia."

Gedz'iel strode past Jude, picked up an errant dagger, and placed it into Serail's hand.

"Answer me!" Jude yelled.

Lorcan slid back towards the Eloi. Dash's mouth fell open.

Gedz'iel drew a long breath and cracked his knuckles. He spun around, his mark alight and eyes swirling with colour.

"And then what, Jude? Ignore the bloodshed? Leave the human leaders to quell the mass hysteria alone? Let the whole planet go to literal Hell for the sake of one girl?"

Gedz'iel's wings blazed to life, ready for transfer.

Jude licked his dry lips, squared his shoulders as he stared at his leader. "We've enough soldiers. All major governments with our agents on staff have been debriefed. This is just as important. If we find Jaz, we might circumvent whatever the hell Nephr'eus is up to. She wants Sophia. Everyone does," Jude's knuckles were white around Jaz' hair. "Whoever has Jaz is a potential threat to Sophia's immature heart!"

"No, Jude," Gedz'iel answered. "If the Afflicted girl makes it to Kaymakli, then perhaps we will interrogate her. I will not deviate any longer."

"But…"

Gedz'iel's wings flickered. He rose off the ground and hovered above Jude, nostrils flared and fists clenched. "I've given my orders. Do you wish to live amongst a planet of zombies and vampires; a meat factory? The dead outnumber us," Gedz'iel pointed to the remains that littered the floor. "Given the chance, Yeqon can rise an insurmountable army of the living and the dead. Lilith, if she is in cycle, can birth hundreds of children at a time that will unfailingly do Yeqon's bidding. There is a line that once crossed, we cannot recover from Jude! This is not even taking into account Neph'reus and Anjou'elle! They are potentially more dangerous because I do not know what their motivations are. If Jasmine is to be saved, it will be by sheer luck."

Gedz'iel glowered at Jude, everyone remained silent.

"Now, clean up this mess, lest we leave too great a calling card for Nephr'eus. I do not wish to provoke her any further. And Jude?"

"Yes?" Jude muttered through his teeth.

"Do as I command or you will be scrubbing Eilir's pots and pans."

Jude's face tightened. He slammed his dagger into his belt and nodded.

Lorcan inclined his head, offering Jude a sympathetic look, and startled when Gedz'iel addressed him too.

"Return to your duties looking over Sophia, Lorcan," Gedz'iel said. "See to it that she is working on her mission without interruption. If you must confine her to her quarters, so be it."

Thunder penetrated the castle walls and Gedz'iel transferred amidst its rumble.

Chapter Thirteen

My room felt like it was closing in. The orb darkened, yet the gleam of the Kaladai cog shone like a beacon under Brennan's hardened expression.

I passed him the cog, "Put this safely under the Zythros stone."

He nodded and moved towards the door, but I stepped in front of him.

"Ben will know something about this," I said. "He's been around a long time."

Brennan shook his head at me, "We've all been around a long time. He doesn't top my list of people to discuss any of this with, Princess."

I waved the phone at him. "This has its limits too. I need to know where the Tiberius Playground is," I took another step back. "Ben is exactly who I should ask. He's got everything to gain by helping me."

Returning to Yeqon after Ben had brought me home wasn't an option for him. It made no sense. Working with me was his only option, apart from being descended, and for some reason that thought drew a nauseous twist into my gut.

Brennan was just a bit taller than me. When he was serious, he seemed larger. He never really looked anything more than an adoring big brother to me, but right then, he was as foreboding as Gedz'iel. The orb above flickered with the change in his mood. He crossed his arms, and his voice dropped an octave.

"You are powerful and clever, but you are also young and naive. You don't know when you're playing with fire," he passed the Kaladai cog back to me. "This needs you. Ben doesn't."

I flushed. The nausea in my gut clamped a little tighter, and I snatched the cog back to my chest. Its hum soothed me.

"You're right," I said, "I am inexperienced. But my instincts tell me Ben knows something. The way he looks at me… there's something there. You're starting to sound like Enl'iel, Brennan," I snapped.

He scowled, "Yeah, there sure is something when he looks at you. It's called bloodlust. He's desperate to be free so he can continue his misguided vengeance," Brennan's mouth tightened and he shook his head wearily at me. "I offer you some leeway and you straight away try to take more."

I shelved my rising anger, "That's not true. I do understand what you all say about him. I'm not that naïve that I don't realise he's done some terrible things, but he brought me home, so that's something." I looked to the floor, back into Brennan's stern face, then back to the floor, "I know it sounds stupid, but I feel something when I'm around him. A strange connection. It's like I know him." There was an uncomfortable pause.

Brennan's face had darkened further, a twitch flickered under his right eye, and he looked away.

I began to pace.

"Yeah, well, I feel something strange every time I'm around someone who wants to ascend me too," Brennan said. He didn't smile.

"Can't you feel it, though?" I asked. "There's truth in his aura. The E'lan surrounding him feels… I don't know, different to the other Daimon. I was around them plenty to recognise their vibes," I said.

Brennan cracked his knuckles; I just knew he wanted to say more about it.

I rolled my pendant through my fingertips, "There's something incredibly sad about him."

"That would be regret for one very bad life choice," he mumbled.

I leaned into my door, fatigued by the constant fighting.

"But there's a difference between that and wanting to make things right, isn't there?"

Brennan rested his hands on his hips, "You think he wants forgiveness? How could he possibly prove himself? How could he be of any help to you at all?"

"Ben's been moving in different circles to you," I said. "In the darker places you guys avoid. It's possible he knows something we don't. We can only google so much, you know. I'm pretty sure there isn't a search engine specialising in all things angelic and demonic."

Brennan's nostrils flared with frustration, "Of all the people to seek answers from, he is not my number one pick."

"Well, you know my thoughts on this now," I pointed at him. "It's time to think outside the square. I know that because of these visions I'm having. Something is calling to me, and I need to follow it."

"Yes, but…"

"You can come along and puff out your muscles at him if you like. I'm sure he'll behave with you breathing down his neck. I'm going to the cells with or without you."

"This is not…"

I stepped up to Brennan and called a little power to my mark. The heat intoxicated me with bravery, "Are we gonna fight too?" I clenched my fists. "I don't want to mess up that pretty face, but I'll do what I need to do."

My fists heated; my wings sputtered to life.

Brennan glared at me. "You sound too much like someone determined to win," he said, the tension in his body seemed to lessen.

"I will win," I passed him the cog. "Here, go hide this for me."

He dangled the cog between his hands, "You'll do whatever you want, won't you?"

"Yes," I put my hands on my hips too. "And I'd prefer to have you by my side, no matter where I go and what I do. I trust you more than anyone."

Surprise flickered across Brennan's eyes. A more comfortable silence hovered between us.

"I'll always be by your side, Princess," he said. "I don't agree with this, and Ged will ascend my arse for it…"

The E'lan flared hot and sharp.

"Why would my brother get his arse kicked for you?"

I startled as Lorcan emerged from the E'lan's light.

"Damn it!" I said, "You scared the hell outta me!"

"You should've sensed my transfer," Lorcan said. "You're clearly distracted. That needs to change."

His tone grated on me, and I didn't know how much he'd heard. Lorcan looked Brennan up and down. Brennan just nodded a greeting.

"Well, hi, and thanks for bursting in with criticisms," I said. "Where have you been, anyway?" I noticed he was covered in blood. Freshly healed scars covered his arms.

"Have you been fighting?" I asked, concern tempered my annoyance.

"You okay, bro?" Brennan scanned his brother, before nodding to himself, satisfied Lorcan was okay.

"All good," Lorcan said. "Just a scrape helping out Gedz'iel."

That I smelled the sweet stench of Afflicted eking from him told me it was more than that. I didn't push any further though, he appeared fit and well, and I had more important things on my mind.

Lorcan searched through his trouser pocket, but stopped and strode towards Brennan, his mouth agape when he saw the cog in Brennan's possession.

"Is that...?"

"Yep," Brennan responded.

"By the blessings of I'el, how did you do it?" Lorcan turned to me. "Where did you find it?"

I recounted the story and the power of my instincts, including my plan to see Ben.

Lorcan pinched the bridge of his nose, "I've taught you to know your enemy, not to consort with them."

I crossed my arms, tired of this dance, "You've taught me to follow my gut, so that's what I'm doing. Brennan can fill you in."

Lorcan's eyes narrowed. "Gedz'iel wants me here to make sure you're safe and on task," his eyes narrowed.

I pointed to the cog, "Am I not? You hold in your very own hands part of the Kaladai! You want to control me, but you can't. I'll do what I feel is right, and Brennan is with me on this. Right, Brennan?"

Brennan's face contorted.

"Have you been encouraging this stupid idea of hers?" Lorcan asked.

I huffed with offense.

"No, *Bro*! I absolutely have not encouraged her wildly human urges of stupidity."

"You know what? Try to stop me!"

My arms burned, and my wings sprouted, "I'm following my own rules from now on." My wings released wider. Their power made me feel stronger than ever.

"You're a friend," I said to Lorcan. "I'd rather work with you than against you. So, what will it be?"

I swayed my wings gently. The breeze toyed with their hair; my light paled their skin. Lorcan looked to Brennan, who shrugged.

Lorcan slipped between Brennan and I.

"I could just summon Gedz'iel," he threatened.

"Do it!" I drew my diamond dagger.

Lorcan half-smiled, "You going to poke me with that?"

"If I have to," I opened the door. "Are you coming?" I recalled my wings and peeked outside.

A lazy orb bobbed in the distance.

Lorcan held the edge of the door and glared down at me.

He sighed heavily.

"You're dangerously brave and stupid these days. If Gedz'iel knew what you're up to, he'd ascend you."

"No, he wouldn't," I said. "Who would find the portal and open it then?"

"Hmm. Well, he'd ascend me," Lorcan lamented.

"He'd ascend us both," Brennan added.

My hands were back on my hips. "I'll rescue you from the Cavern of Souls when I'm done then. Come on. I know you both want to hear what Ben has to say. You're curious, aren't you?"

Brennan took the cog back from Lorcan. The veins in his neck reacted to its hidden power, glowing like faint streams.

"Let me offload this first," he flashed out with the Kaladai.

Lorcan was still leaning over me, his breath warm as it washed over my shoulder.

"I don't want anything to hurt you," he said softly.

I took his hand in mine. "I've got your back and you've got mine. Everything will be fine," I said.

His fingers laced through mine and he planted a soft kiss on my hand. "I know your heart beats for another, but mine beats for you. I'll follow you into Hell if I have to."

"Lorcan…" I couldn't breathe.

"It's okay, Soph. Just let me protect you?"

My mouth was dry. He squeezed my hand but let go when Brennan returned sans the artefact.

Brennan whistled, "Glad I missed whatever that was!"

My cheeks flushed hard. Brennan rolled his eyes and spread his wings, "Righto! Let's shake down Ben before I have to put on mood lighting in here!"

Chapter
Fourteen

The air tasted the musty flavour of gloom the closer we came to the cells. It got colder the deeper we went. Four guards rushed by in a dizzying flash of wings, as well as two Alchemae clutching herb baskets to their chests. A few Keepers zipped past. Brennan and Lorcan hung so close to me that we were practically conjoined.

The Watcher guarding the entrance didn't bat an eye as we entered. He was a different one, thank goodness. I wasn't sure I'd have got past the one I'd knocked out.

Cael's wheelchair marks were fresh. He was a quiet achiever, sitting for hours as he waited for Ben or Belial to give up important information. I suspected he also came to here keep an eye on me, though he never told me that I shouldn't be here.

There were other footprints in the soil.

"Huh, practically downtown," I muttered.

Belial's cell remained dark. A collection of upturned plates with uneaten food lay discarded under the glowing bars. A fat rat was enjoying what Belial hadn't.

Belial was lying on the floor with his back to us, a shadow of himself since he'd surrendered to Koi. Ben, however, sat under a small light orb, eyes closed like he was meditating. He rubbed the swollen knuckles on one hand, flexed it open and closed and winced as they moved.

He opened his eyes a few moments after I'd entered.

"You're really testing your limits, aren't you?" he said.

Lorcan tensed behind me, his hand on my elbow.

"You don't have to do this, Soph. We can work this out ourselves," he whispered.

"He's right. Look what you've already achieved," Brennan added.

"No," I pulled my arm gently away.

"He knows something, he knows a lot of somethings. I just somehow know he can help."

"Help with what?" Ben's smooth deep voice floated over, making me lose my train of thought.

Deep breath in, deep breath out.

I made my way over to the humming bars. Their glow illuminated his face, giving it a slightly reddish hue. His piercing blue eyes held mine with unnerving ease. He tilted his head and raised his eyebrows.

"I need your help," I said.

Ben yawned, "How flattering. Couldn't do things alone, so you come back to the dregs. What do you want, Earth-born?"

Ben leaned over. His hair fell forwards, he swept it away with his hand. He licked his dry and bruised lips.

My heart raced. *Just my nerves.*

"You look thirsty," I reached for a jug on a nearby table and poured a cup of water, "Here."

Ben took the cup, careful not to touch the bars. One of his fingers grazed mine. I jerked back against one of the bars, which sent burning pain up my arm.

I jumped back. "Ow! Fu…" I caught myself before I swore like Jaz.

For a second, Ben's eyes flickered with what looked like concern.

Brennan leaped in front of me. "What did he do?" a deadly orb glimmered in Brennan's hands.

Lorcan shook with anger as he pulled me into his chest. The guard's sword sung a metallic chorus to my right.

Ben grimaced. "I didn't do anything," he flung the cup to the floor. It cracked; the earth dampened underneath.

"Stop! Calm down," I gently pushed Lorcan aside. "I got too close to the bars. It's my fault," I held up my blistered arm.

Ben sat down on his unkempt bunk. Brennan watched him whilst Lorcan fussed over the scorch mark, which was stretching up my forearm.

"May I?" he asked.

I rested my arm in his hand. It stung like fire, and I pulled away.

"Don't be a baby. Let me heal it," Lorcan said. "It's easier and quicker than doing it yourself."

"Just hurry, please?" I put my arm back in his palm.

The veins in his hand blazed to life as he drew forth his energy. White rivers flowed along his forearm, into his hand, and burned bright at his fingertips. Without touching the injured skin, his hand swept up and down my arm.

I winced. It felt like a hot knife at first, but a soothing warm replaced it. My skin was inflamed, but smooth pink tissue covered where the blisters had been.

"You haven't even begun, and you're already injured," Lorcan grumbled.

I swatted him away.

A small smile emerged at the corner of his lips, "Try not to maim yourself again."

I gathered my thoughts and cleared my throat, trying to look as confident as possible.

I stepped closer to the cell.

"I want to ask you a strange question."

"What? Is it why Rik's still sulking?" Ben asked, "There's a short and a long answer to that one."

Now there *was* a problem. Whatever relationship we had built as Yeqon's prisoners was now on life support. I'd chosen to let Rik fall to Earth from the Oblivion portal so I could save Enoch's box. This instantly damaged our relationship as brother and sister. I'd saved

Enoch's box out of utter necessity, but seemingly lost my newly found brother.

"It's not about Rik," I said.

I watched my tone and kept my feelings sealed. Daimon took advantage of anything they could to manipulate you into getting their way. Yeqon had shown me when he'd used my brother as bait for me.

Ben looked up, a strange expression in his otherwise blank eyes. "You've found Jaz then?"

"I won't discuss her with you either," I said.

He opened his mouth as though to argue, but caught himself and leaned his head into his palms.

"What is it then?" he sighed and rubbed his eyes. "My schedule is rather busy. Make it quick."

"Have you heard of Emperor Tiberius?"

He arched his brows and straightened, "That's rather random. Yes, I've heard of him. Why do you ask? He's been dead a hell of a long time."

Ben leaned closer to the threatening bars. His dark eyes showed no shame as they stared straight into mine. It was unsettling, but I matched his stare.

"I just want to know if you know anything. Did you ever have anything to do with him?" I asked.

The corners of his mouth turned down, making him look non-committal. My hands clenched. How hard would this be?

Ben leaned back onto his hands and stretched his legs. "I never met him," he squinted. "But I know of him and where he used to hang about," he brushed his legs as though dusting them off. "Will it help me get out of here if I tell you?"

"Tell me what you know or I'm out of here. I've no time for BS, Ben."

He snorted and threw his head back, "Yeah, okay, but what do I get for my trouble?"

"You'll stay in your skin," I said through my teeth.

Ben rubbed his injured hand again. His head fell forwards, and a thick clutch of hair hid his face.

"You've changed," he said.

"What's that supposed to mean?"

"You're different from the old Sophia," his eyes flashed at me from behind his black fringe that was now streaked thick with white.

"You don't know me."

My pulse quickened. What *did* he know about me? I glanced at the boys again, who offered nothing but hearty scowls in Ben's direction.

Ben smiled. I blushed and shivered all at once.

He swept his hair out of his face, "The prophecy is true. You're getting stronger by the hour."

"Shut up and answer her questions," Lorcan said. He leaned into my ear, "He's trying to get to you, Soph."

I eased away from Lorcan, "Well, he's not. I've got this."

Ben cocked his head and stared at me. The corner of his mouth tugged up, he almost smiled.

"You do, don't you?" Ben nodded to himself. "You're finally standing up for yourself. About time," he kicked away a shard of the cup.

I sighed with frustration, "Just answer my questions or be quiet. I don't have the time or the interest in your opinion and silly mind games."

"Who's playing games?" Ben asked, "Just stating what I see."

"Fine," I turned to leave. "Let's go, guys."

"Wait! I might be able to help," urgency stained Ben's voice.

I slowly turned back and crossed my arms. Ben stood just behind the bars; fists clenched by his sides.

"Alright then," I stepped closer. The boys shadowed me, their bodies close enough either side of me that I felt their energies flicker up and down their arms, "How can you help me?"

The red bars hummed louder as though they, too, were wary. My pendant pulsed. I rubbed my soul stone and felt an instant boost of reassurance.

"I might be able to guide you in the right direction with Tiberius," Ben picked at his thumbnail, his cockiness waning.

"Okay, tell me," I crossed my arms, stared hard… impatient.

He shook out his arms and took a deep breath.

"I didn't know him in person, but I know two Daimon tormented him for fun. It turned mutual once Tiberius realised the enjoyment he could get from them. He spent as much time as he could sequestered in his castle in Corsica. I was sent to drag the AWOL Daimon back to Yeqon."

Ben's heavy eyes held mine a moment too long before he looked away. Relief flooded me, and I couldn't say why.

"Tiberius' dirty little playground became well known as a den of debauchery," Ben said. "It had become attractive to bored Daimon. Even Afflicted made their way there. It risked exposing us to humans and the Watchers, so they all ended up in the Pits."

"What did you just say?" I stepped closer, leaning towards him.

"He was tormented, mad, and I…"

I twirled my hand at him, "No, no, the part about his playground." The inscription flashed through my mind.

Ben smoothed his hand across his mouth, and his forehead wrinkled.

"Well, there was some cesspit where he hung out known as Tiberius' Playground."

I clasped my hands to quell their excited tremble, "Tell me more."

"It was where he enjoyed his pleasures away from prying eyes," Ben answered.

"In Italy?" I glanced at Brennan, who shrugged with wide eyes and an unconvinced face.

"Yes, in Corsica," Ben replied. "I can't be sure where exactly. I picked up the scum as they headed back inland, so I assume it was somewhere along the coast. Could have been his castle, could have been elsewhere," Ben's head tilted to the left. His eyes sparkled a little brighter before a black flash rimmed his irises, "Have you uncovered more of the prophecy?"

"That's none of your business," I said.

I turned to Brennan, "Can I have the phone again, please?"

He passed it over. I powered it up and hurried through a few pages. Nothing new about Tiberius' Playground popped up, just references to his bizarre behaviour and secluded lifestyle. I'd hoped to find a link between this playground and my visions, but there was nothing.

Ben pointed at the phone, "There's one place you could try, but it won't be in your little search engine."

"Where?" I let my hand drop.

"Not that I've seen it personally, but they say the Keepers stocked the library at the southern sanctuary well. They documented all important events. Perhaps there's something there that might help?"

Enl'iel had told me about them. I'd seen the incredible array of scrolls, hundreds of thousands tended into the niches of the cavern walls. A hive of history, documented by A'vean Keepers of knowledge. Perhaps, just perhaps, what I was looking for was a dusty old parchment underneath my own backyard?

Brennan pulled me aside. "I don't think we should discuss this with him any further, especially with Belial in the same room," he jutted his head towards the ever-quiet cell to the right.

"He's right Soph," Lorcan whispered. "You've given over too much already, and Belial has heard every word."

I remembered the horrors Belial had done to me and my beautiful Esme all too well, but I was buzzing with the possible connection between the information I had and what might lie under a layer of time in the old Australian sanctuary.

"But Ben might know more," I whispered.

I studied Ben from a distance who, in turn, scrutinised me as well. I just felt that he could help — that he *would* help. He had three choices. Rot in that cell, be descended on Gedz'iel's order, or help me. How much did he want to survive? I'd heard of the death of his family and tried to pull some small semblance of empathy from my heart. Perhaps he'd do the right thing to honour the memory of his lost love?

I pointed at the doorway, "Let's take him out of the cell, away from Belial."

Brennan choked, "Are you mad?" He felt my forehead and gripped my shoulders. "No temperature, so I can't blame your insanity on a feverish delirium," Brennan glanced at Lorcan. "I think she's lost the plot," his eyes bored into mine. "Have you lost your marbles. Soph?"

"Perhaps, but the world is mad and on the brink of going to Hell, so we need to be a little braver instead of hiding from everything scary," I peeled Brennan's hands from my shoulders.

Lorcan crossed his arms and stood in front of Ben's cell.

Brennan's brows knotted until two lines formed above his nose. He tugged at my chin so I'd look into his eyes, "Listen to us, please?"

"C'mon, guys," I said. "We have to try something other than cowering in the shadows trying to solve ancient puzzles. Perhaps this journey is about more than just cracking a code. Perhaps it's about trust and forgiveness?"

"You sound like a Hallmark card," Brennan puffed.

"I believe in redemption and I also believe in allegiance. We've got to work together," I said. "If my challenge is to forgive the unforgivable, to ally with the lost for the greater good, then that's what I'll do, no matter how hard it seems."

"It's not hard, Sophia, it's ludicrous," Lorcan spat the words like they were poison. "You're toying with a traitor."

"You not feeling enough pressure already, Princess?" Brennan asked.

"Of course, I am! The thing is, we're sneaking about, hunched in corners, trying to find the solution. What if leaving our comfort zone gets us to the finish line sooner? Aren't you tired of hiding, Brennan? Aren't you sick of taking the safe option?" I pushed back from Brennan and caught Ben staring at me. Belial's giant shadow also rose; his hulking silhouette different since he'd lost his horns.

"I quite like the safe and quiet life," Brennan answered. "I've had thousands of years of battle upon battle. You, my princess, have had but a few weeks," his jaw feathered. "You shouldn't complain about being tired of waiting."

I felt like a complete cow.

"Sorry," I said. "That was thoughtless, the way I said that."

"Forgiven," the smile returned to Brennan's voice. "You know I love you. The worry about Jaz is pushing you. It's pushing all of us. There's merit in using whatever resources we have, but making alliances with an enemy is dangerous. I'm not sure I can stop him if he turns on us."

"But he's outnumbered," I whispered. "It's worth the risk. I'm sure of it," I pleaded to both of them.

Lorcan raised a brow at his brother, "He wouldn't get past both of us."

"*Three* of us," I said. "I've learned a thing or two," I made my mark burn bright. These past days, it was brighter than anyone else's, like a barometer of my growing power, "I'm getting stronger every day. Help me utilise that strength."

I brushed past Lorcan and Brennan and weighed up how dangerous Ben could really be. The bars lit the battle scars across his battered body. Our eyes met again. The blue of his deepened, keeping those black demonic rings at bay. His expression was a hybrid of pain, an eternity of struggle, and it gave me an idea.

"Ben?" I strode up to the cell bars.

Brennan tugged at my arm, "I won't allow this. I'm sorry."

I shook his hand away.

Lorcan edged in front of me, "You can't just do whatever you like, no matter who you are."

I put my hand up to hush them, "Calm down, I'm giving him more water. Can't you see how dehydrated he is?" I picked up another cup and filled it, "Move. Please, Lorcan?"

Lorcan took one small step to the side.

Ben moved closer to the bars.

I held out the water and caught Ben's attention.

"You look thirsty. Here," I nodded and extended my hand carefully through the bars.

Ben was probing to get into my mind, but I shut it tight. He reached for the cup… I grabbed his wrist as tight as I could. With one slow breath out, my wings expanded and my body blazed.

"Sophia! No!"

Brennan and Lorcan screamed in unison.

Ben's eyes flew wide open as the pull in my gut wrenched us both backwards.

Lorcan's hand ghosted through my ribs a nanosecond too late; I transferred Ben and myself out of Kaymakli.

Chapter Fifteen

The insulting chill of Winter was replaced by the warm embrace of a summer night. I stumbled out of Ben's reach, unsure how we'd become embraced during the transfer. His heaviness still wrapped around me like a phantom. Ashes and spice lingered and teased memories that refused to reveal themselves. I checked myself quickly. Everything seemed fine. Ben too, was turning his hands over, checking on himself, looking a little surprised by the sudden change of circumstance.

Hands on his hips, Ben checked out the house behind us. His eyes settled on mine.

A smile curled the corner of his mouth, "Well, aren't you in a shitload of trouble?"

"There's nothing amusing about any of this," I turned on my heels and walked up the back steps of my old house.

"Get inside before anyone sees us," I ushered him along with an impatient wave of my hands.

"Hmph!" he bit his lip but didn't erase the amused smile. He took a deep breath of the fresh air and stretched his arms over his head.

"Ahh. Good to be outta there."

I pointed at the house, "In. *Now.*"

He jumped onto what was left of the back porch. The screen door hung from one hinge. Black-and-yellow crime scene tape fluttered in soft pre-dawn breeze and clung to what had once been mine.

Ben entered first. I was glad to have him as a shield if the need arose; I certainly wouldn't have allowed him to be in my blind spot behind me.

My old kitchen had been reduced to cinders. The wooden floors groaned underfoot. The fridge lay on its side, door flat open against the floor. The smell of rotting food mixed with the new rodent population was beyond foul. I covered my mouth. This had once been be a place of comfort and happiness.

"Through there," I said.

I followed Ben to the lounge, keeping an eye on his every move. My hand hung ready above my diamond dagger. Its energy soared and hummed, on guard and ready for anything.

I ducked through the door frame, and a piece of a Blue Willow saucer nicked my skin. I plucked the porcelain splinter out; my heart heavy with the memory of simpler times.

Ben kicked at an upturned couch that was shrouded under one of the drapes, "It's a bit of a fixer-upper, wouldn't you say?"

I pointed to the stairs, "Just shut up and keep moving."

I noticed the circular hole scorched into the lounge floor, but I didn't dare look into it. A shredded curtain concealed part of it. The taped shape of an axe hugged the left curvature of the burn. Little yellow crime scene flags were still impaled into the surrounding floor.

That was the last time I'd seen Esme.

The dark shadow that had accompanied Belial, the one that had cut Esme in half, it lingered at the forefront of my mind. If I ever found out who that had been, I'd unleash all I had on them.

"You coming?" Ben asked, "Look like you've seen a ghost."

"Just keep going, will you?" the memories flickering through my thoughts left me vastly less tolerant.

I maintained a safe distance behind him as he padded up the splintered stairs. We could have transferred or flown up, but history had taught me it was a risk to send out that elemental cry to things best left buried. Ben trod as carefully as I did.

On the landing, we stepped between strewn clothing and shards of windowpane. Mould had taken hold of the floorboards, and my foot slipped. I righted myself only to see a charred photo of me holding up the first coffee I'd made at Miss Marples. Alfie smiled in the background. Nan had snapped the pic.

I kneeled and picked it up. My thumb smoothed across the image. Rainbow hair, brown contact lenses, and a smile so unaware of the truth of who I was. I sniffed and let it flutter from my grasp. It slipped over the balustrade and disappeared into the blackened hole.

"Your room then?"

I startled. I'd let my guard down.

"Um, yes," I said.

Ben pointed to the right.

My heart thundered. My skin prickled.

"How the hell do you know that's my room?"

"I didn't bide all my time with Yeqon by knitting," Ben said, peering through the doorframe.

I glared at him, "You've been in my room? Whilst I was there?"

"I've been a lot of places, and there's a whole lot you don't know. Probably best to keep it that way."

I felt nauseous.

Deep breath in, deep breath out. Swallow that fear, Soph. Push it way down.

Ben leapt over the remnants of my door and sat on the askew bed, leaning back on his hands and dangling his legs over the edge.

He smirked, "Not as comfy as I remember."

My gut lurched again, but this time with excitement and disgust entwined.

"Get up," I said. "You're here to help me, not to gloat about the crap you've done."

Had I ever seen him here? A thudding ache grappled the back of my head as I tried to remember. So many blanks dotted my memory. Were those gaps where he fitted in?

He bounced up from the bed and returned to my side.

"What do you want then? Why are we here?" his arms were wide, his smile waned.

It took my breath away a little as he loomed above me. He had no sense of personal space. He glared so unapologetically straight into my eyes. I took a protective step back but stumbled over something. His arm shot out and saved me from falling. I tried to push myself away, but he held me against him for long enough that I felt the firm ridges of his chest against my hands. His familiar scent carried on every pulse of his heart. I wanted to look away, to run from his touch, but in that moment, I simply couldn't. My eyes rose to his. There was no darkness in them, just a deep, blue sadness.

"I've got you," he whispered.

The warm goose bumps I'd had when Lorcan kissed me rippled across my skin, only a million times stronger. I wanted to say something, but my brain was in a flurry. Ben reached out with his injured hand and plucked something from my hair with his swollen fingers. He twirled a dried lavender blossom between them. His eyes swept over my face. My pulse beat so hard it hurt.

"Sophia…" his voice seemed to catch, he released me and it felt so cold as he stepped away. He turned around. I couldn't see his face. "So, before we're hunted down and ascended or worse, will you tell me what's going on?" his tone was back to bored and flat.

"Um…"

My throat was tight, my mouth too dry, and my face burned for reasons other than a flare of my power. I thanked the universe no one had witnessed that.

I moved to the window and peered down across the overgrown lavender hedges. Phantoms of my past were down there. I almost saw Grey and Shadow running up to greet me.

"I need you to help me look for anything that might lead me to Tiberius," I said. "Something that will point me to wherever he hung out with those Daimon."

The quiet outside unsettled me. The breeze no longer rustled through the eucalypt leaves, no early morning cockatoos screeched, no parrots chirped. No crows or magpies warbled as they scouted for their breakfast.

Ben looked over my shoulder, scouted the surrounds as well. I held my breath, my fingers bit into the window ledge. Ben quickly stepped away as that feeling between us became almost tangible. He plucked up a small bottle from the floor.

"You should always trust nature. It knows when to keep its head down," he turned the bottle upside down. A purple label was under his thumb and finger, "Here. It might help a little."

It was a vial of lavender water. Weaker than the oil, but the essence made Daimon and Rogues violently ill.

Ben unscrewed the golden lid and tipped a little onto his fingertips. It dribbled along his skin… there was no adverse reaction.

"What are you doing?" I asked.

He reached for me, but I jerked out of the way.

"You can keep your hands to yourself!"

How was he touching lavender without a reaction? I snatched the bottle from his hands and sniffed. It was pungent, certainly strong enough.

"You only had to ask. I did try to share," he said.

I grabbed his hand, but his skin was intact. No redness, no blisters, and definitely no retching. I sucked in a breath… Ben looked as healthy as a Watcher.

My hand curled over the handle of the dagger; my fingers relaxed as I scrutinised his guarded eyes. His jaw clenched; his eyes flitted away from mine; he seemed uncomfortable as I stared at him.

White tendrils of hair fell across his forehead, pale highlights thickened across the ebony that had once been fully black.

He pulled his hand away, "You can keep your hands to yourself too."

My cheeks tingled. Why did he have no reaction to something that should have repelled any Daimon?

He leaned into the window frame and surveyed the area below. "Any day now, Earth-born. What the hell do you want so I can get outta here and back to my cell?"

I dabbed lavender water along my pulse points, just in case Rogues were close by. I tossed the bottle away, it clinked and rolled into a cavity between broken floorboards.

I followed Ben's gaze to the bottom of our garden, where the battered old shed lay half submerged in the pond. I stayed a safe distance behind him; confused, unsure… intrigued.

"I want us to look through the library," I said. "You told me the Keepers document everything, but I don't know where to begin. Help me find where I need to go. I know you know more than you'll tell me and I know you'll probably lie, but I'm giving you a chance anyway. If you help me, I'll try to help you."

Ben snorted, "You have no right to promise that. You don't know what I've done."

"I've heard all I need to know."

"The edited version, I'm sure," he sniffed the outside air. "It's too dangerous. You don't know what's down there… well, you do, and that's the problem," he glanced back at me, his eyes narrow, his mark glimmered softly. "You're either very brave or utterly stupid."

"And the Kaladai falling into the wrong hands isn't dangerous or stupid?" I asked.

Ben leaned further out of the window. He looked left and right, his fingers clung so tight to the ledge, the wood splintered.

"Well, tell me what's more dangerous here than what I've already encountered in Yeqon's realm. Tell me it's impossible, and I'll still do it."

He sighed, he shoulders relaxed and he leaned back in, attention still on the unnatural quiet outside.

"Belial was instructed to stash sleepers around the southern sanctuary to intercept someone," he pointed past the lavender hedges. "He followed your grandmother here in the early 1500's when she showed an unexpected interest in this library. She was who his sleepers were supposed to intercept, but she never returned here. I assume she found what she was looking for. Those sleepers, those Rogues, they will still be down there. You'll have to be careful not to rouse them." He snorted, "With her blood in your veins, you're like a neon sign in Las Vegas. They'll rise just from you being nearby, probably even the smell of your breath, and that will be like texting Yeqon to join you for dinner."

"My grandmother was here?" the vision of us in the ocean came rushing back.

"Yes," the first blush of dawn warmed the moon's icy hue on his skin.

"What was she doing here?" I asked.

Ben shrugged and pushed himself back into my room. He picked at the splintered windowsill as he spoke.

"I don't know. There were suspicions that you had been born and she was travelling to you. It was a strange change of her movements, especially as she'd been seen travelling Europe with an unidentified man which was rather unusual for a Queen Regent of England. To see her travel to a remote place so far from home raised red flags. She was under surveillance for a time, but she was elusive. Yeqon left a number of soldiers to wait for her return, but as I said, she never did return."

My mind was racing. Elizabeth was so much more involved in my life than I ever imagined, but what had she been doing here? My pendant — *Elizabeth's* pendant — thrummed to life. My vision, her connection to every step, the revelation that Leonardo da Vinci was involved… Elizabeth was integral to the prophecy.

I leaned against the wall.

"You look pale," Ben said.

"I'm fine, just thinking."

"About?"

"The meaning of life," I rolled my eyes. I wouldn't tell him just anything, I wasn't stupid.

A shiver rippled down my spine. An unwelcome cold tugged at my hands, and I jerked them away. My eyes darted down, there was nothing there. A nervous pang hit my belly as I rubbed the feeling from m skin. Perhaps that sensation was the remaining doubt about Ben's intentions and allegiances? Perhaps it was the mysterious presence that had been following me all around Kaymakli.

Perhaps it was a bug.

Ben's eyes narrowed, "You're not okay."

"I'm fine!"

But I wasn't. The cold fingers clawed at my legs, scratching, grabbing, reaching up for me.

Ben quite suddenly pounced forwards, "Outta the way!" His arm shot out and pushed me behind him.

I grabbed at his shirt when I stumbled. It ripped away from his spine, his wings blazed to life.

"Stay behind me," he said. "We aren't alone."

"You feel it too?"

"No, but I can hear it," Ben threw an orb at the en-suite, and it exploded in a bright flash. "Come out!" Ben yelled in that direction.

"It's here!" I leaped out from behind him, swinging my dagger at the invisible intruder. Ben spun and searched around me, his face flushed, eyes wide and wild. We circled back-to-back. I jumped every time the invisible thing touched my legs.

"It's been around me for a while," I said. "What is it?"

Ben's hands lit with a new orb, "Show yourself, you thieving coward!"

The door to the en-suite rattled shut. A cold cackle echoed inside the small room.

"What is it?" I hissed.

"Something you brought back from Yeqon's world."

Ben's hands moulded a red orb.

I nodded at it, "Won't that get us found quicker?"

The en-suite door rattled louder. The taps turned on and off.

"Yes," Ben peered over his shoulder at me as though to make sure I was okay. I held my dagger higher to show him I could handle myself.

"But it wasn't me who let an entity follow me back. It's here for you, Earth-born, not me."

The taps screeched. Water gushed under the door into the bedroom.

"We are here now," a scratchy voice drawled behind the ensuite door. "We are ready to play again."

I gulped, "Oh my God!"

The door flung open. Hairs rose on my arms, bile lapped at the back of my throat. The bed scraped across the floor and flipped onto its side. We lurched out of its way.

"Well, isn't this fun?" Ben grumbled. He rolled his eyes at me and waved for me to head towards the doorway.

I stepped towards it, sending blazing energy into my dagger.

"She didn't finish her game with us," the entity bellowed, "She owes us."

Chills surged though me. Heavy footsteps scraped along the floor like sandpaper. They came from my left, then my right, closer, then farther away. A terrified rat scuttled past my feet. My bed flipped again and landed upside down. My old school bag swung from its upturned leg.

"What the hell is it?" I asked.

"Of course, you don't remember," Ben mumbled. "It's an Asmodai. A Daimon that lives on emotions and memories. This one wanted you back then, and it still wants you enough now that it's following you."

My eyes bulged with horror, "Back when?"

Ben jumped over the bed, which was spinning towards us. I leaped across as well and landed next to him.

"It doesn't matter," he yelled over the chaos.

"What did it want then?" I asked breathlessly, "What does it want now?"

The walls groaned; the ceiling sprinkled plaster. The whole room rumbled.

Ben jumped in front of me, "It wants your memories. Your mind is a gold mine of emotion. I'd stay near me if I were you."

"How do we kill it?"

Ben pulled me towards the hallway.

"It needs to lose its head. Hard to do because they crumble to dust when they feel cornered!" he said.

The en-suite's wood panelling twanged. Splinters whipped across the room and thudded around the window frame. Air rushed around us, a stale and sulphurous gale. It flung Ben and I over the bed into the far wall. Pain seared across my back. Ben groaned as he slid down next to me. Clothes and towels sailed over my head. We pulled ourselves up. I snatched up my dagger from the floor whilst Ben shook his head clear.

The Asmodai screamed in triumph.

"We don't die! We live!"

A swirling vortex of dirt emerged from the howling wind. Ochre peppered with black danced along the sagging floor. The entity coalesced into a humanoid shape. Half my height, its features morphed into a nasty ogre-like face. A hunch at the top of its spine lessened as it stood taller as wide feet formed.

Ben helped me up and pushed me behind him. He pitched an orb at the vile creature. It dropped to dust and reformed in another place.

I formed an orb, "Get out of here! There's nothing here for you!"

"She owes us more," it said. "We grow so well because of her."

Its beady eyes widened with delight, and it lunged at me with clawed hands. I dodged and threw my orb way off target. It scampered up the wall like a bug and skittered along the ceiling. I grabbed my sword and poked towards it, keeping my eyes on the scuttling target.

I was running out of time to find what I needed in the subterranean library. I needed to get away from this thing, I lunged but missed.

Ben formed an orb into a spear and pierced the creature's leg. It screeched and laughed to itself as it crawled away.

Ben cursed, "It's stronger than before."

The Asmodai darted around the walls, leaping from wall to ceiling and back again. Its foul draught followed it. It cackled to itself and circled back to me.

I drew in a deep breath, infusing my sword until it glowed like a light sabre.

"I'm here," I said. "C'mon, you evil bastard!"

Ben elbowed me back and threw another electrified javelin, which missed. I ignored Ben, I didn't need a man to save me. I lunged at the Asmodai's head. It dissipated and reappeared on the wall opposite my bed.

"It's starving and its desperate," Ben yelled. "Give me your sword!"

"No!"

I swung out, but it lunged towards me, hopping like a cricket, dodging my swipes. Forming, collapsing, and reforming. It made me dizzy trying to keep up with it.

It grabbed my ankle from behind. I kicked at its scratchy grasp, but its hands collapsed into dust and reformed. The particles sought out its limbs to reform, like a magnet sought metal.

"Give me a weapon, Soph," Ben yelled. "We'll only attract worse things using orbs!"

"No! This is Kea's sword; you're not having it!"

The Asmodai raged my way. Ben's orb hit it square in the chest, it exploded in a great puff of dust.

The air settled. I fell to my backside and Ben kicked through the remains.

I gasped, exhausted, "Is it gone? Why did that thing want me so much?"

Ben wiped red grit from his eyes. The room quieted as the gusts from the Asmodai's presence dissipated.

"It knows your power, and it wants your memories," he glowered, still looking around the room for it. "It's strengthened a lot. Wonder who it's been feeding on?"

My skin chilled.

"Let's get out of here," I said.

Ben nodded.

"*Nooooo!*" the Asmodai's voice surrounded us. "We are hungry for more."

Ben spun around, and I jumped to my feet. We circled together. I waved my sword at the invisible laughter.

"Bastard!" Ben said. "Where are you?"

"We are everywhere." It screeched. A frightening, high-pitched drawl.

The whirlwind resumed with unforgivable fury. A tornado of my old belongings disrupted my line of sight. The bed jostled across the floor again, scraping deep into the wood. Heavy footsteps vibrated along boards. A maelstrom of clothing wrapped around my face. I panicked, fumbling to peel it away.

Some of the swirling fabric blanketed the hulking shape of the Asmodai, making it visible in the chaos. It loomed above Ben and slapped him to the ground. Its gnarled hand opened wide and, quick as a flash, it had Ben by the neck.

The Asmodai laughed and sniffed Ben's hair, "You will be our entrée!" Its form solidified. It could've been a gargoyle ripped from Notre dame, but this statue was alive, and it salivated sandy dribble as it hungered for us.

Ben struggled to free himself from its grip. His eyes bulged under the pressure. He tried to produce an orb, but his arms flailed and his skin paled.

The Asmodai's hand fully enclosed his neck. It squeezed.

"Keep still," it said. "We don't want you dead, we'd have no memories to find then." Its other hand splayed across the top of Ben's head. The Asmodai turned its head and smiled at me with rubble teeth. "And next we'll have you."

Ben couldn't seem to fight the sandy limbs that held him still. He groaned, twisted his body, but the Asmodai's vice only tightened.

I was too stunned to move. I gripped my sword tighter; my hands shook.

Ben's eyes rolled back; his body slackened.

"Nice," the Asmodai said. "Lovely. Ooh, love and sadness. We like these things the most."

My wings spread and my mark blazed.

"Let. Him. Go." I raised Kea's sword.

"We never let go," it said. "No, no. Too many too disappoint, too many to feed."

I edged towards it, and it dropped Ben like a piece of trash. He rolled to the side and coughed as the Asmodai glared at me.

A thick tongue swept across its lips. It salivated more dirt. As it moved one thumping step at a time, it grew even larger. Its head nearly scraped the ceiling. A gargantuan ogre that wanted to strip my mind.

"She is all powerful now," it said. "She will restore us."

I reinfused the sword with all I could muster until it shone over every vulgar bulge of the Asmodai.

"No, she won't!" I yelled.

Giant, rocky hands grasped for me.

I screamed and lunged at it. The sword pierced the centre of its chest where a heart would have been. The stench from the puncture was nothing short of putrid; I fell back, the sword wedged in its chest.

It laughed as it pulled the sword out.

"She cannot defeat…"

I didn't know what made me do it. My right wing swooped around and sliced the Asmodai's neck. Its head teetered, its mouth gaped wider and wider until its head cracked open and it split in two. The head lurched to the side; the two halves fell into dusty heaps. The body dropped to its knees, fracturing the floorboards.

I fell to the floor with a heavy thud. Ben and I glanced at each other.

"Is it dead?" I asked.

Ben crawled closer to the rocky corpse.

The body rolled to the side. Ben jumped back, and I lunged for my sword.

A cacophony of screams emerged from the Asmodai's open neck. Where blood should have flowed, black and white entities flew from the wound as the corpse collapsed into a pile of dust. The entities twirled above us like a thousand ghostly comets.

One snapped around and plunged straight into me. It knocked the air out of me. I fell onto the floor. Ben screamed. I grabbed my chest, where a deep aching pain was spreading. I tried to draw healing power to my hands, but nothing worked. My hands were numb. I gasped for air, faint and terrified.

Ben ran his hands all over me, searching for wounds.

"You're okay, you're okay," he said over and over.

The pain spread further up my chest, climbed up my neck and into my head.

"Something… is in me…"

My mind fluttered. An ache pounded behind my eyes. I grasped at my head whilst my heart — my whole body — shook.

Ben shushed me, "It's okay, trust me."

"What… did it… do?" I patted at my torso. Something had to be bleeding.

Ben hesitated and let go, but I grabbed his arm.

"What did it…" One glance into his sombre eyes, and I shoved him away. I backed up against the wall and pointed my sword at him.

"It was you!" my arm shook violently. I felt like I was falling backwards.

His shoulders slumped; his skin paled.

"I remember you, Ben. You killed Esme!"

Chapter

Sixteen

Nephr'eus placed a small vial on her cabinet's top shelf and shut the fine glass door with a gentle chink. She cupped one hand across her belly and reached for a wine glass with the other, then turned to her sister.

"She escaped?" Nephr'eus asked.

"Yes, and they descended the rest. Ugh, the mess they left!" Anjou'elle dabbed at Jaz' feverish forehead and wiped her hands on a lace kerchief. Her brow furrowed, "They were some of the better help, too, you know? Such a shame." Anjou'elle shrugged, tucked her long skirts under her, and sat in the chair by Jaz' bedside.

"There are always more where they came from," Nephr'eus said. "I have never been left wanting for desperate kindred," she smiled. "I might call on cousin Yeqon, stroke his ego a little. He's always been forthcoming with extra helping hands," Nephr'eus sipped from a thick-stemmed goblet.

Anjou'elle shook her head. "We can't trust him, sister. You know his ambitions," her eyes rested on Jaz, and she twisted the kerchief in her hands. "If he knew our plans… well, I would rather try my luck knocking on I'el's door."

"This is where your naivete holds you back, my love," Nephr'eus said. "To own a man, to own a great leader, you must know their weakness. Understand their desires and feed those urges. Play the fool, the desirous lover or worshiper, and you will see how you can manipulate even your worst enemies to fulfil your desires," Nephr'eus' smile flushed her cheeks and sparkled her eyes. A black ring intensified around her irises.

"I've never been good at that," Anjou'elle stared into her now soaked kerchief. It was thoroughly knotted through her fingers. She sighed as she unwound the cotton.

"Perhaps you would improve if you focussed a little more on your womanly attributes and played less with tiresome human pets you keep, Anjou'elle?" Nephr'eus pointed at Jaz. Her wine sloshed as she sipped again.

Anjou'elle pulled a fresh cloth from her pocket and dabbed at Jaz. "There, there," she cooed.

"You fuss about her too much," Nephr'eus said. "I told you not to get attached. Look what happened with that troublesome Count!"

Anjou'elle rolled her eyes. "I did so love the idea of being paired with a Count. Humans are so fun and full of themselves. I mean, it was so dramatically romantic, don't you think? He did rather adore me," she giggled, but her expression quickly sobered.

"Pity it couldn't last. I did detest being called the Demon Countess of Anjou. How abhorrent! I gave him so much, but this one…" she gently wiped Jaz' forehead as she twitched feverishly. Anjou'elle sponged fresh water into Jaz' mouth, "She is rather adorable. I want to keep her."

Jaz' eyes darted beneath their lids. Cyanotic blue tinged her peeling lips.

"You had no such trouble with that Roman centurion," Nephr'eus said. "You shadowed and dispatched him and Archimedes with a minimum of fuss," her skirts whispered as she sauntered towards Anjou'elle. "You did some of your finest work with those ones, my dear," her smile widened, but her eyes narrowed and rested on Jaz. "Her purpose is the same," Nephr'eus passed Anjou'elle a cup of wine.

"That was very different," Anjou'elle said. She sipped the wine and placed the cup aside. "The humans were so close to handing part of the Kaladai over to Uriel. I had no chance to really get to know that Roman. That said," she pursed her lips, "I couldn't respect a man who cheated on his true love. He was too easily tempted by me," Anjou'elle caressed Jaz' cheek with her fingers, then patted her hand.

Nephr'eus tutted. "Will you stop that? She isn't a kitten. You couldn't even look after one of those, remember?" Nephr'eus drained her wine.

"I like the fire that burns in her soul," Anjou'elle responded. "There is something most interesting about her. She entertains me, well, she did until you did this to her," Anjou'elle pointed at Jaz' pallor. She pushed away hair glued to Jaz' sweaty forehead, "If you'd had a little more patience, sister, I'm quite sure we could have been fast friends."

"Oh, for the love of Hell itself, Anjou'elle! Listen to yourself! The only interest I have in that girl is her value as a bargaining chip. She is a means to an end, sister, nothing more, just like that centurion," Neph'reus looked into her empty goblet with disappointment.

Anjou'elle straightened; she blinked as a memory resurfaced. Her hand fell away from Jaz.

"Lucius!" she said.

"What?"

"That was his name. He was a handsome fellow; I'll give him that," Anjou'elle's brows arched, and she squeezed the damp cloth in her lap.

Nephr'eus laughed, "You really are tiresome at times."

They made eye contact, wryly smiled at each other and laughed together. The black of their irises grew until even the white of their eyes melted away. Energy sparked around them, snapping and snarling its luminous white tendrils.

Anjou'elle glanced between the Jaz and Nephr'eus. She batted her lashes, pleading for her sister's approval.

"For the love of…. oh, I don't know!" Nephr'eus face-palmed and sighed. She sauntered back to her medicinal cabinets where she poured another two glasses.

"I will indulge you, as I always do, Anjou'elle," she swished between her cabinets. "However, she must settle, lest she begins to holler again.

I will not tolerate that at all." Neph'reus opened another cabinet, "Now, what do I have in here?" She moved a few vials around, pushed aside a small brass crucible and reached right to the back. "Ah!" Neph'reus plucked carefully amongst her collection with a glassy clink.

"I knew I had a little something left to calm her until we can be rid of her," Nephr'eus swished back to the bedside.

"You shouldn't have given her the drug, sister. We could have just put her into a slumber," Anjou'elle readjusted Jaz' head on the pillow. Jaz' mouth slacked open. Anjou'elle gently nudged it closed.

"I could have dressed her up and brushed her hair. I hate to see her so. You've seen the effects of Thanratos on humans. I fear she will die horribly," Anjou'elle pouted.

Nephr'eus huffed, cupping a fine vial in her hands. She pushed an errant curl from her eyes.

"They are weak, that's not my problem or yours. Once we have this planet to ourselves, we will be queens together and you will have a world of choice. Stop fussing, sister," she waved Anjou'elle off. "I'll find you another pet, I promise. You may have a whole zoo if you like."

Anjou'elle dropped the cloth and clapped, "Really?"

Nephr'eus quirked a brow. They cackled in unison.

"So long as she survives until we get that box, what does it matter if this one expires? There are billions more, a plague of them, really!" Nephr'eus wrinkled her nose and bent over Jaz, inspecting her more closely, "Hmm. She is rather pretty though."

Nephr'eus pushed back her lace-tipped sleeves and dispensed a blue liquid from a dropper under Jaz' tongue. Jaz' torso twitched a few times; her limbs became flaccid. Her breathing slowed to deep, rattling sighs. Anjou'elle grabbed Jaz' hand to feel for a pulse.

Nephr'eus tutted, shaking her head.

"Dear, dear, perhaps I did give her a little too much Thanratos too soon. It wouldn't do at all if she died before that wretched Earth-born hands over her treasures," Neph'reus lifted Jaz' lids; her eyes had rolled back. "It's beyond my expertise unfortunately. Human dynamics never interested me enough," she smacked Jaz' cheeks and frowned. Neph'reus sniffed the vial. "Hopefully, this tincture of Vitriola, Fennel and Cloves will ease her discomfort," Nephr'eus straightened, her face pinched in thought. Her fingers clenched, and she frowned.

"Sister? Where did you say you'd heard of the Great Healer? I might have him hunted down if she worsens before we can use her."

Anjou'elle took Jaz' hand in hers and stroked her limp wrist.

"Those who believe he exists say he resides underground somewhere across the channel. As far as I know, no one has ever seen him. I have yet to meet a cured Afflicted, let alone a human. He has always been a rumour, perhaps even just a figment of hope for the hopeless," Anjou'elle lamented,

Jaz coughed hoarsely. Blood-stained phlegm pooled in the corners of her mouth.

"Go," Nephr'eus said. "See if you can find out information about him, but don't be too long. Our position is compromised. The perpetrators of that mess at Pouancé will most assuredly return, and I'll need you at my side."

Anjou'elle shook her head, "I mustn't leave you then. Not if we'll be attacked with a depleted army on our side. We'll make do with the remedies we have."

"Do as you're told, Anjou'elle."

Anjou'elle closed her eyes and took a calming breath.

"But…"

"Hurry, sister."

Anjou'elle's fingers clenched. "Fine. But I must change out of my dress first and rest. Psynostris is upon me. It may take me some searching, and I'm not sure where to start. It has been many years since he has been spoken of amongst the Afflicted. You'll need to be patient, sister."

Nephr'eus struck her, shattering the vial against Anjou'elle's cheek. Anjou'elle quelled a scream and pressed the back of her hand against the sting. Blood oozed between her fingers.

Nephr'eus's face softened, and she promptly healed the wound. "There, there, my love."

Anjou'elle flinched as her sister kissed her forehead.

"All better now?" Nephr'eus cooed.

Anjou'elle nodded, but stared at her feet.

"Good girl," Nephr'eus said. "Now, when did you say you were going to look for this mysterious healer?"

Anjou'elle stood and sniffed back tears. "Now, sister. I will depart immediately," she looked up at Nephr'eus and forced a smile. "May I change out of this heavy dress? It is cumbersome," her hands rolled over each other in front of her belly.

"Of course, my darling. It will be prudent to dress more comfortably and more human. Leave your dress with me. I shall wash it for you and care for the human whilst you are gone."

"Thank you," Anjou'elle bowed her head and disappeared in a pulsing flash.

Chapter Seventeen

My stolen memories of Ben flooded back; an entire childhood of fakery. Everything from holidays to him abducting me at Stonehenge, to the confusion of him guiding me out of Yeqon's realm.

And of course, worst of all, the feelings that smashed into my heart.

"It was you all along! Why didn't you tell me who you are?" my voice wavered. "You lying murderer!"

Ben was as ashen as I was angry, his hands raised in surrender.

"Please, let me explain?" he cautiously stepped forwards.

"Get away!"

Kea's sword shook with my fury.

"Sophia…"

"Don't speak!"

"Please, listen to me?"

"Listen to you? You murdered my Esme! You fooled me. You betrayed me. You, you…"

I grabbed my head and screamed, dropping my weapon, I sank into the Asmodai's remains.

It was Ben who I'd been pining for when Lorcan kissed me. It was Ben who I wanted to kill.

Ben kneeled next to me, reached for me, but I shoved his hand away.

"Soph... I..." he sat back a moment, then leaned in again to take my hand. I punched him as hard as I could, and he let me. I slapped his face, pounded his chest, and cried so very hard for the betrayal.

"I'm sorry," he whispered.

I fell against him, and his arms wrapped around me. Ashes and spice infused my senses. My heart raced. The clues had been everywhere, but that Asmodai had stolen enough of my memories that I hadn't been able to put it all together. Everyone else had kept the secret. How many times had I wondered why they changed the subject when Ben came up? Their deceit fuelled the burn in my gut.

Ben let me go, but not quick enough.

A scream that came from some deep and dark place filled the room. I realised it was me when I found myself atop him, my dagger at his neck, blood dribbling down his skin onto the floor.

"Do it," he said through clenched teeth.

His eyes were wide and wild, yet strangely they held none of the blackness that betrayed the Daimon within. I knew he was chameleon. Was he still pretending? I searched his eyes for evidence of his evil nature. More blood sprouted under my quivering hand. I wanted to do it, to slice until he went slack, to feel the blade hit his bones.

He didn't so much as wince. There were no black rings in his clear eyes, yet my anger was as dark and muddy as ever. I grabbed his face with my other hand, pushed against his mark and dug my nails into his stubble, trying to find a reason not to become a murderer like him.

"Do it, Earth-born. You know you want to."

His cheeks flushed hot under my hands. More blood trickled to the floor. His mark's bright glow pierced through my fingers, but it felt good... clean and clear like a crisp winter morning. My tears fizzed into steam where they hit his skin, which was still marred from the beatings he'd suffered. The ones I now remembered he'd taken for Rik and I. My head was pounding with all I remembered.

I screamed. Raised the dagger. With all my strength, I plunged it down into the floor an inch from his head. I backhanded him, added to his bruises and swellings. He didn't fight back.

"Fight me, you coward!" I yelled through fresh tears.

But he wouldn't.

I shook his shoulders and slapped him again, "Fight me, damn it!" I slapped him hard again.

He lay there and took it with silence.

I landed blow after blow against his body. Ben ignored every painful punch. My anger didn't make a single bit of difference, it only drew shame to the surface. It didn't bring Esme back; it didn't restore my trust; it pained my heart more to hurt him.

I stopped and sobbed. My arms exhausted, my knuckles bloodied, but I kept him pinned to the ground, angry and confused.

"Why would you do all this?" I cried. "Why poor Esme? She never did anyone any harm!"

My tears fell onto his chest and mixed with his blood. They sizzled over a bruise, healing it. Ben sucked in a breath and wiped a thick clot of blood from his lips.

"There is no why. There is no reason," he said. "Not that it matters now, but I actually saved Esme."

My fingers dug into his chest, the dagger back at his throat.

"Liar! I saw you kill her with the axe. It was you in the shadows that day!"

"She was already dead. Belial had gone against my orders and possessed her. He was impatient. I'd been trying to stave him off without it seeming obvious, but he was too eager to impress Yeqon. The day I went to the market to shop for Enl'iel, I thought he was up to something. Unfortunately, Esme was there at the wrong time," Ben sniffed and spat to the side as more blood ran from his mouth.

My lips quivered, "I don't believe you."

"Believe what you want, but her soul had already departed. I saved her body from further mutilation by forcing him out of her," Ben looked me straight in the eyes. No shame, no fear.

"No! You killed her!" I slammed his shoulders into the floor.

"No, I didn't. You saw what she looked like. She was already a corpse... a Rogue in the making. Would you want that for her?"

His voice hitched when I pressed the dagger hard against his throat. I didn't want to believe him, I wanted to blame him. The problem was that I did remember Esme's appearance. Her voice hadn't been hers. Her face had been purple and bloated, and everything other than the beautiful soul she had been.

She hadn't been my Esme at all.

But I couldn't rationalise what I'd seen that day as an act of kindness.

Tears obscured my vision. Salty snot dribbled over my lips.

"How could you do any of this?" I asked. "I grew up with you. I trusted you. I… loved you."

We both held our breaths.

The words had slipped out before I could stop them. Light and darkness filled my heart. My jaw clenched until it ached. I couldn't believe I'd said it, yet Ben seemed to drink it in. He gulped as he gently unhitched my nails gouging into his chest. Five half-moon welts were left behind. His thumbs circled over my skin before he abruptly let go.

"Well, more fool you then," he muttered.

I screamed, rolled off him, and stomped back and forth between him and the glass shards that had been my window.

"You disgust me!"

He snorted, sat up inspecting his chest, "That's fair, given the circumstances."

The air was thick, not just with the impending stench of evil, but with the proximity to him. He was too close, I couldn't stand the sound of his voice, the rapid beat of his heart and the bloody ashes and spice.

I threw an orb at his feet, he rolled out of its path, only just.

"Just go," I said. "I'll do this on my own," he rubbed his unhealed hand. It had to have been that way for weeks now.

"Go! I never want to see you again!" I yelled.

"Firstly, it won't look good for you to just let me disappear, and secondly, I won't leave you alone. Not here."

"Why the hell do you care if I die? I'm a means to an end for you."

I stared out the window; a murky fog was thickening below. Time was running out. I turned away, not wanting to acknowledge what was coming.

"That was true in the beginning," Ben sighed and rubbed at his temples.

"Soph, I've done more bad shit than I could ever be forgiven for. I've lied about almost everything. The one thing that *is* true, the one and only thing I want you to believe, is that everything we had was real," he held his hands out as though pleading.

"Before all this happened, when it was just us kicking about here, I let myself live again. I was secretly protecting you, almost from the moment you were born. I kept Yeqon from you for as long as I could. I'm a rotten soul, and I'm not worth a second thought to anyone, but that much was real."

I folded my arms tight, "Rotten soul? That's generous."

"Perhaps, but here we are," he said. "You want this over with? Let's look at the scrolls, and then you can do what you want with me. I really don't care."

What I wanted was to kill him and to kiss him all at once. My nails clawed into my arms. I glanced out the window again. The fog was thicker and fouler. I collected Kea's sword and my dagger and secured them into my belt.

"What does it all matter now?" I asked. "I may as well keep running down the wrong road with a goddamn Daimon while the whole frigging world is after me," I wiped more snot from my nose.

"I know the feeling well," he said.

My skin prickled with anger, yet the cadaverous smell outside overpowered its need to rise against him.

"Let's go then," I snapped, "Before something worse than you is all up in my face."

I could barely look at him. E'lan's buzz was short and sharp, like glass bells being struck, then it changed into a deeper droning. I didn't understand it. A ray of morning sunlight dried the last of my tears. I sniffed and wiped my bloodied hands down my pants.

I shook my head at myself, feeling like an utter fool, "I'm surprised Lorcan and Brennan haven't already found us."

I pointed at Ben, "Know this, if you are deceiving me again, my dagger will do its job properly next time."

He headed to the window, his good hand probing the mess I'd made of his face. "We'll have to transfer, and quickly. We've disrupted the E'lan enough already. Can't you smell it?"

"Of course I can," I screwed up my mouth and breathed for what felt like the first time in a while, "I'd prefer to be back in Kaymakli before Lorcan drags me back."

I pictured the library and released my wings. They were brighter than ever, which undoubtedly made this crumbling old house a beacon.

"Wait!' Ben raised his hand to stop me. He leaned out the window and beckoned me over.

The foul fog's tendrils reached into the house's lower level.

"We're out of time," he said. "We'll need to transfer together; it will be quicker and less noticeable. Your wings are too strong, put them away. My energy can camouflage you for a little while," he offered me his hand. "Let's at least slow them down a little?"

I stepped away, "You're kidding, aren't you?"

"Not for a second," he pointed down. The first pale mists eked up through the floorboards.

My nostrils flared. My childhood home didn't smell the same anymore. The salt and pepper of the bush was gone. Instead, the air carried death and fear, and I saw it coming in.

I crossed my arms, and my wings slunk away, "Fine!"

"You know we have to touch to transfer together," Ben reached out again. "If I try anything, you could descend me in a second and you know it, Soph. You're not fooling anyone. My destiny isn't a good one, but I'd prefer not to be mauled by a bunch of Rogues," his fingers wriggled impatiently.

Tendrils of sunlight caught wisps of white hair across Ben's forehead. He looked more like one of us than ever. His eyes were a bright blue; no black rings, no Daimon hatred peering through.

I shivered as I let my hand slip into his.

His wings stretched with a soft hum, "Scroll room?"

I nodded, "I don't trust you."

"Experience says you shouldn't, but I won't ever betray you again." Ben pulled me into his chest, his head fell forwards, and he whispered, "One… two… three."

He took away my breath and my body.

Chapter
Eighteen

Under an ambient jade glow, the gem-laden dome overhead twinkled like the night sky. I stepped out from behind the Zythros stone's green hue and threw an orb high into the air to illuminate the many shadows.

The full beauty of the cavern blazed into view.

Crystalline frescos glistened in their colourful glory. Story panels spanned the walls, new ones brilliant next to time-wearied ones. Images of me holding Enoch's box loomed above, large and skin-tingling. Yeqon cowered beneath me, an image that was most satisfying and, I hoped, prophetic. A shadowed figure, the mysterious Unknown Satan, hovered behind me. His arms were wide as though ready to catch me. I knew now, without doubt that it was Ben.

"No time for art appreciation," Ben tugged my hand, his touch an unsettling assault to my skin. I slapped it away, both wanting to touch him and not.

He widened his wings and grabbed me around the waist. We flew up to the next level and landed by one of the ornate staircases.

For the briefest moment, time froze. Daimon didn't exist. Nobody hunted me. All that mattered was his skin against mine, feeling his heart pulse under my fingertips. I wanted to sink into his chest and forget all pain, care, and destiny. My eyes travelled up his scarred torso to the dip at the base of his throat. His strong, square jaw and those lush lips he pressed together. His nostrils flared ever so subtly. There was a light sheen across his cheeks.

And those eyes; deep blue that glistened with shame and desire, secrets and fear. They were sky and ocean with hints of green meadow and plum.

Ben opened his mouth, but no words came.

Then I noticed the strip of dark hair, a hint of the blackness that still hid in the recesses of who he was. It slapped me in the face, bringing me to my senses. Shame stung my cheeks, and I pushed him back.

"My wings work perfectly fine, thanks. Touch me again and you'll lose a hand," I flicked my wing at him in warning, not wanting to touch him again. His skin on my skin seemed a dangerous thing. It made me want to strangle the soul from his mortal body. It made me want to put my lips on his.

"Just help me so we can get out of here. There's still a cell waiting for you back home," I said.

He scoffed and shrugged, "Can't wait. Miss those home comforts."

He turned away and paced along the boardwalk. His wings sunk into the neat leaflets that lined his spine. His good hand grazed along the wall, poking into each dip and undulation of rock.

It occurred to me then that I couldn't see the scrolls. Not anywhere.

I leant over the balustrade and scanned the cavern. There should've been a thousand cavities, neat diamond rows of carefully tended history. I ran my hands along the rocky surface to feel for any sign of them, a vibration or energy secreted away within the ancient layers of earth.

"Where are they?"

"Oh, they're here," Ben replied. "You just need to find them."

I remembered the Keepers hiding the scrolls behind a misty veil when the cavern had been evacuated.

"They're hidden," I bit my lip, and looked up, down; everywhere.

He chuckled, "Isn't everything hidden?"

I placed my ear against the cool wall and listened, hoping the earth would speak to me. "Where are you?" I whispered.

I slowly moved along, keeping an eye on Ben and probing just as he was. I found a small fissure and reached in. My fingers touched something furry, and I pulled my arm back out quickly. I grazed my hand, and a small sprinkling of diamonds erupted where my skin had caught. My mark zinged, and my pendant hummed against my chest.

Ben wandered back to me, "Found something?"

"Maybe?" I pointed at my hand and the gem cluster.

He arched his brows.

"Do I just...?" I grabbed the dagger and nicked my thumb.

Ben scratched the back of his head, "You'll have none left the way you're going."

"Won't Yeqon and Lilith be disappointed," I grumbled as I smeared blood across the rock.

A brackish fog-like substance leached from the walls within seconds. Dark, silent swirls puffed and rolled across the surface, claiming it greedily. Small wisps of white static sizzled within it, tickling at it until the vapor heeded its demand and slowly began to rise. Like a theatre curtain, the nebulous haze retreated into nothingness.

Laid bare was the entire collection of scrolls. Thousands of lifetimes of human and A'vean history, right there in front of us. I was right where I needed to be, but I was so out of time.

"Sophia!" Brennan bellowed. I shuddered.

Brennan and Lorcan swooped up from the Zythros stone, a duo of determined fury.

"Of all people, *you* skip on us?" Brennan fumed.

I'd never seen him so mad. He was like Enl'iel 2.0.

They both took hold of me, one arm each.

I struggled between them, "Let go of me!"

My eyes flashed to Ben, who had become very still and quiet.

A vein pulsed in Brennan's temple; his eyes blazed.

"For the love of I'el, what the hell do you think you're doing breaking a prisoner out of the cells and returning to a place that's likely ridden with Rogues?" Brennan was one decibel short of deafening me.

I yanked myself free of both of them.

"This is so ridiculous! I knew you wouldn't let me come here, so I took a risk because, goddammit, it feels like A'mageddon is on the way and someone has to do something other than hide underground!"

"No one is hiding, Sophia," Lorcan's voice a shaky, a barely veiled anger. "We're working around the clock to protect your butt and keep the bloody human population safe, not to mention our own kin!" his cheek feathered as his jaw ground.

I crossed my arms. "It seems like that's all we're doing," I said. Brennan's chin twitched. They stared at me with such anger; two dangerous, powerful Watchers pulled coils of unease from my insides.

However, instead of bearing down on me further, they turned on Ben.

Lorcan lunged at him, hands ignited and ready to strike.

"This was your idea!" he growled at Ben.

I hurled myself into Lorcan's path and elbowed him hard.

"Stop!" my mark burned in warning. "Step. Back. Now!" I pushed back on Ben's chest and held one hand out in warning towards Lorcan. "Either help me or get out!" I snapped.

Cool tendrils of E'lan materialised around us. Thin fingers of static reached out, tasted our energy, tested what was causing the elemental disruption. I breathed it in, savouring the buzz in my veins.

My eyes flicked between the three men. Who did I need to be warier of? The Daimon I wasn't sure I could trust, or the Watchers who treated me like a child?

"Do you even know what you're doing?" Lorcan asked. "Do you have an actual plan?"

I shrugged, "Sort of."

Brennan's eyes bulged. Lorcan shook his head.

Anger bristled more urgently under my skin, "And just so you know," I said, "I remember everything. I know who and what Ben is. You all lied to me. Yet again, I had to work things out for myself."

They glared at Ben.

"I didn't tell her," he said, hands raised in defence.

"How did she find out then?" Brennan's eyes darted between Ben and I until they came to rest on me, a little calmer. Concern pushed his angry blush away.

Lorcan punched his fists together and bounced on his toes. He looked fit to explode.

"She killed the Asmodai," Ben said. "That's how she remembered."

"What?" Both glared at Ben.

"It's been stalking her and attacked us. Was about to descend me, actually, when she decapitated it and voila, memories returned."

"Is that what you sensed in your room?" Brennan asked, brows furrowed even tighter.

"I imagine so," I said. "But it's gone now, and I don't have time to talk about it. Ben can help me work through the scrolls. Unless you both know how to sort through them, let's get on with it," I edged backwards, encouraging Ben to move away with a flick of my hand.

Lorcan jutted a finger towards Ben, "No! He needs to return to Kaymakli."

"Sophia, you need to take him back," Brennan agreed. "Right now."

"No!" I held my ground.

"You know I'm onto something," I whispered into Brennan's mind. *"I haven't told him anything critical. For I'el's sake, will you just go along with me, Brennan?"*

Brennan's nostrils flared, and a deep line creased his forehead.

"You can't just disappear like that, and with him! An enemy of the state! I need to be able to trust you," Even his thoughts sounded angry.

"Trust? You betrayed mine by not telling me about my lost memories," I shot back. *"I had to find it out by myself and I nearly murdered him for it! Your deception put me in an awful situation."*

"I'm sorry. We were trying to protect you."

"Stop trying to protect me and help me!" I snapped out loud.

Brennan's shoulders slumped, but Lorcan remained a seething ball of rage.

"Okay. Calm down. Let's discuss the situation?" Brennan opened his arms, inviting a truce.

Lorcan scowled at his brother, "Are you mental?"

Brennan pinched the bridge of his nose.

"Settle down," Brennan waved him down. Lorcan spun and punched the wall.

"Save that for Yeqon," Brennan said, shaking his head.

"So," Brennan looked back to me. "Can we discuss this calmly?"

I nodded. A cautious relief loosened the knot in my chest.

Lorcan turned back around, his mark had settled, his bloodied fists less clenched, but his eyes swirled; his mouth a tight strip.

The boys exchanged glances. An urgency shimmered in Lorcan's eyes. I worried they'd snatch me back to Kaymakli. My wings unfurled just enough to be handy in a snap.

"Don't provoke them," Ben whispered behind me.

I moved carefully. My bare feet sunk into the light dust as I made sure Brennan and Lorcan stayed where they were.

"You can be quiet," I whispered back. "This is half your fault."

"You dragged me here if I remember correctly," Ben said.

I glanced over my shoulder, "Will you just shut up?"

"Instead of arguing, can we talk this situation through, please?" Brennan asked again. "I'll indulge at least listening to your plan, okay?"

Lorcan swore in frustration.

I relaxed my wings a little and quietened the fiery threads between my fingers, "Promise me you'll leave him alone?"

Brennan screwed up his mouth and nodded, "For now."

Lorcan's fists were white, "Bloody hell, Brennan."

"My last breakthrough was an accident," I began. "But I can't rely on accidental discoveries anymore to solve Enoch's riddles, not with everything that's going on. The longer I take, the more people die and the more the world falls into a chaos we can't reverse. Ben has used this library before. He knows how it works, and he's familiar with Tiberius's story. Unless you two are more adept librarians?" I crossed my arms, waiting for a response.

Brennan scanned the millions of scrolls embedded in the walls.

"Well?" I asked, shrugging my shoulders.

"I've never been much of a reader," Brennan mumbled.

Lorcan paced between Brennan and I and pointed at Ben.

"I won't be ascended for the likes of him, and that's exactly what Gedz'iel will do to us!"

"Put a lid on it, Lorcs," Brennan snapped.

Lorcan clawed through his hair, and Brennan stared hard at me. He wasn't happy, but he had an open mind if ever I knew one.

"Please, will you just help us?" I asked.

"So now it's us, is it?" Lorcan's tone dripped with sarcasm. "Holy shit, Brennan. This is bad news."

I spun around, grabbed Ben by the throat and flung him to the ground. I sat astride his chest, his eyes dark from shock and the black rings around their outer edges re-emerged. There it was, the Daimon was still in there.

"I'll kill him myself if he makes one wrong move," I said.

Ben growled, "Get off me."

An orb erupted in my palm. I rolled and shook it until its shape had changed. I pointed the shard over his heart.

"You will betray us no more. Got that?"

His nose flared. Uncertainty coloured his eyes, which locked onto mine.

I leaned into his face, our skin a mere kiss apart, "Say it."

His chin quivered ever so slightly from humiliation. It was raw and pained, and some distant part of me pitied it.

"One shot, Ben," I whispered into his mind. *"I don't understand why you chose this path, but I understand it was from pain. If you help, I promise I won't let you suffer again."*

His eyes became glassy, the edges rimmed red. He sniffed and swallowed whatever this emotion was. Exhaustion touched every hollow of his face, from the dusky bags under his eyes to his sunken cheeks. Every swelling and bruise drained him into an anaemic pallor. His pupils contracted under the light of my wings, and their darkness retreated.

I pushed the weapon against the skin just below his collarbone. It was part truth, part show for the others. A small blister erupted, yet Ben didn't react.

"You have my word," he whispered. "Now, would you kindly stop burning me?"

"Promise me on Neren'iel's memory."

His eyes dilated once more, not with darkness, but with pain. Tears welled on his lashes.

"I do listen and I do remember. Honour her memory the right way," I demanded.

He swallowed hard.

"Promise," he blinked the tears away.

I hauled him up and pressed the shard out against the wall. I placed my hand on his chest, healing the wound I'd created. His breath caught, and he looked away. Our pulses raced. Self-consciousness kicked into overdrive, and I urged the wound to repair faster.

"Nice show," Lorcan said. "Are you two quite finished?"

I turned back around, leaving the wound a little underdone. "Give me a little credit. I'm the one who's suffered because of him. If I can see past my own ego for the sake of us all, so can you!" I said.

Lorcan's jaw looked about to snap. Brennan tried to calm him with a brotherly shoulder squeeze, but Lorcan shoved him away.

"Your way it is, Sophia," Brennan said. "But it will also be my way." He formed red-energy shackles and cuffed Ben in an instant. Their burn bit into Ben's skin, and he grimaced.

"Don't think of questioning it Soph!" Brennan's face was dead serious.

I nodded.

Brennan moved towards Ben. They were equal in size, but I wasn't sure about strength. "So, is it Ben or Nik'ael? Who are you today then?"

With his signature smug smile, he said, "Ben will do."

"Doesn't really matter, I suppose," Brennan said. "So, is it true you know how to navigate these records?"

I kept close to them, unsure whom I was protecting.

"I can't promise anything," Ben said. "I only know what I know and nothing more."

"Just tell us what you know," Lorcan hissed, "Or those shackles will be around your neck, and you'll be back in your stinking cell."

"Stop being an idiot," I said to Ben.

Ben leaned back against the wall. He held his wrists gingerly and shook his head, then stared right though me as though he could see my soul. It was just a second, yet it felt like an intrusion, like he saw a part of me that even I didn't know.

"The Keepers don't log the scrolls the way humans do," he peered around the cavern. "It's been a long time since I was here, but I'm pretty sure they're sorted by region. I know of Tiberius and his general lifestyle. If we can locate any reference to him, we'll likely find this place you're looking for," he sniffed as though he was bored.

The ground rumbled, a deep, earthy groan. Rock ground on rock, cracking through the decorative façade. Dirt drizzled down from fractures in the ancient ceiling.

Ben lurched forwards to shield me. I didn't need his protection, yet I didn't move out of his way quick enough; Lorcan pushed in between us.

"Hands off!" Lorcan elbowed Ben away and elevated a little, shielding me from the debris with his wings.

I was no maiden in distress. I rose in the air, too, and joined the boys who were scanning the cavern for danger.

Two Keepers appeared from within the Zythros stone. They buzzed and blinked on and off as though waking up. With quick precision, they pulled down another misty veil to hide the scrolls.

I flew up to them. They stopped and hovered above me.

"We need to find some information," I said. "Just a few minutes, please?"

The Keepers swirled around me, dancing through my hair and tickling my scalp. Light tendrils flickered over my face and probed my mark. They regrouped, pulsed brighter a few times, and drew the veil back. They retreated near the ceiling, their light quivering and flashing like a pulsar star, ready to bring the curtain down as soon as we were done.

"Thank you," I called.

The ground moved again. Cracks opened beneath us, defacing the perfect floor tiles. A filthy stench filtered through the air. Wider fissures yawned open with subsequent quakes and drew in a thicker, more pungent odour. It wasn't unlike the stench of Yeqon's underground hellhole.

They'd found us already.

"I told you they'd be here," Ben yelled through the noise.

Gems rained down like million-dollar hail, leaving the murals pockmarked. Some of the paintings were now eyeless and garish; the faces implored me for reprieve through sightless sockets.

"Hurry up and find what you need!" Brennan shouted.

"Okay, okay!" I yelled as air vents of steam screamed opened to my left. They sounded like the thuds and pops of exploding soda cans.

"Today Soph, or we'll be breakfast lunch and dinner for Rogues!" Brennan added impatiently.

"And you," Brennan bellowed at Ben. "If you're gonna help, bloody well get on with it," he pointed his sword at the lower level. "You see what's coming? I'll push you front of the line when they arrive!"

A dense fog, putrid and grey, oozed upwards. Far away, but not far enough, the guttural slurps and snarls of waking Rogues echoed.

Ben floated across, poking through pockets of scrolls, "They've sniffed you out quick this time!"

Lorcan prodded him, "Less talk, more action, Daimon!"

Ben clenched his shackled fists. His mouth curled, and the veins in his neck tensed as he glared at Lorcan, "Won't be long before they're here, pretty boy. There'll be more than a handful, I'm guessing. Why don't you grow a pair and…"

Lorcan wound his arm back.

I flew between them and pushed Lorcan away from Ben. "Instead of behaving like meatheads, will you help us?" I said.

Brennan pulled Lorcan by the shoulder, "C'mon Lorcs. I want to get outta here in one piece, bro. What are we looking for, Soph?" Brennan hovered close to Ben.

Between me and them, Ben had nowhere to go.

"Tiberius, an ancient Roman ruler," I said. "He had some place called a playground of which I can't find any geographical reference to. That's all I have, and visions which are pointing me towards Italy. Oh, and then there's the Leonardo da Vinci connection."

"Leo, huh?" Ben mumbled more to himself. He looked away as though in deep thought. "You worked that out being stuck underground?" Ben asked.

"Just help with the Tiberius thing, buddy," I said.

Without a clear sign of where to search, Brennan and Lorcan floated along the walls. I followed Ben, who seemed more systematic, floating up and down in a sequential fashion. The scrolls were tightly packed; pulling them out proved difficult. Nothing so far was at all relevant.

"How much do you know about the other Kaladai?" I asked him.

"I know only a human of worth was allowed to re-create it. Ridiculous, but I didn't make the rules. Archimedes was the only one I knew of, but those stupid sisters saw fit to destroy it," Ben snorted to himself. "Fool of an old man hid it under his floorboards apparently."

The cavern shuddered again.

Brennan ducked out of the way of a huge mud clump. "Old Uriel would be bloody helpful right about now!" he yelled over the cacophony.

"How would he help?" I flicked through the next section, less care by the second for the delicate, immeasurably valuable parchments. Nothing about Italy or Tiberius popped out.

The fog brewed harder. Its fingers reached across the ground and sought something to snatch onto.

Brennan heaved an armful of scrolls out and showed them to me one by one. I unravelled an aged document. Small flakes flittered from its edges despite my careful touch.

"Nope," I said. "Put them back. Uh… what do you mean about Uriel?"

The cavern shook again.

Brennan grunted in annoyance. "He comes and goes, helps us here and there with snippets of info, but not so much that we could actually help our bloody selves."

My heart began to pound, "If Uriel has been communicating with you since the portals closed, is he also stuck on Earth? Can't I find him and ask for his help?"

"He's a whole cut above our station, Princess. Archangels can cross any barrier through time and space, he's only here when he needs or wants to be."

Brennan held out a battered scroll. I shook my head, and he tossed it.

"God, this is so messed up," I said. They could have stopped this right here and now if they'd wanted. "When I sort this, I swear I'll bust someone's angelic arse for this. You couldn't write a more stupid story."

"I wonder if the old man even remembers us," Brennan pointed upwards.

Lorcan threw a few scrolls in my direction. "This probably got old for him so long ago he's moved on to some other world to torment."

"T'el knows exactly what's going on," Ben called down to us. "We did everything he told us not to do. He'll watch us suffer until we either descend or repent. It's not over when the portal opens, you know. We still need to return home and face His judgement."

I halted, "How do you know this?"

"We all know it," Lorcan said.

"Being trapped here is merely our prison term," Brennan added. "Next is parole."

I was about to swear the worst word I could think of when an almighty crack tore through the air. A jagged line snaked across the ceiling, and the chromious that lined it buckled. It screeched under the weight of shifting earth.

Brennan shielded me with his wings. Rubble sizzled into nothing as it sailed through the heat of his wings.

"No more yacking," he yelled. "Ben, show her the way, and bloody well do it now!"

"I'm working on it!" Ben hissed back as he struggled with his shackles. The smell of his flesh burning did not escape my attention. He flew left and right, then backtracked. I started to wonder if he really knew anything at all.

Dread creeped over me. Had I made a big mistake?

I glided along the honeycombed walls, my attention more than ever on what Ben was doing.

"Can't you read any of this?" I asked.

"Nope," Ben said.

"You two?" I asked the boys.

"Not a letter!" Brennan pointed at me and Ben. "We need you to guide us, and he needs to guide you." Clumps of rock and dirt sizzled into ash where they sailed through his wings. The unsettling thud of it pounding into his back set me into the next gear. Brennan didn't moan, but I knew from the sheen across his reddened face that it hurt.

I grabbed my head, willing my brain to think harder and trying to understand what I was looking for. I grabbed random scrolls. They were light yet thick with grime and heavy with words I wanted to know. Some were a pale cream, others a darker shade of antiquity. Each one was delicate and priceless, and all contained the special current that connected them to the E'lan. A buzz travelled through my fingers with every touch. My hands shook as the cavern crumbled and the smell of Brennan's blood carried down to me.

"I'll just start reading them out loud," I shouted. "Tell me if anything sticks out!"

A'vean script swirled and dotted both the scrolls and their storage spaces. It trailed the length of each scroll, perfect and precise. The more I focused, the more I noticed a pattern.

"They all have a name and a date. Ben, how does this work? You said there was a system."

His eyes lit up. "Dates! That's what we're looking for! Let me see," his wings glowed brighter as he rose higher, dodging debris left and right.

Lorcan grabbed his leg, yanking him back down.

"Right here, mate!" he growled.

"You want to get outta here before we have to fight off a thousand hungry Rogues? Let...me...go!" Ben grunted.

"Lorcan, let him go, he's outnumbered. He can't transfer with those on anyway," Brennan pointed at the restraints. Lorcan huffed and let him go.

There was a reprieve to the rumbling but the earth was still shifting.

More walls cracked. The fog thickened, and the snarls and screeches got closer. A few scrolls fell away into the opening abyss.

Ben's brows furrowed in thought. He moved left and right, then back again as he scanned the wall.

"Are you sure you know what you're doing?" I asked with an increased sense of urgency.

He scowled at me, "It's been a while."

"Think faster!" I snapped. "Think or we're dead!"

Ben hovered higher, blankly staring at the walls. "Got it! It's like old Greek and Roman calendars. The Keepers use time periods coupled with location and rulers of those times. They allocate a date, in A'vean values, to every hundred-year block."

"What, that sounds confusing," I motioned for Ben to come closer. He did so with Lorcan at his heels. The cavern rumbled again. Ben stretched his wings wider, shielding me from a new hail of debris. Lorcan followed suit, seemingly trying to take more hits, like it was a contest.

"You guys don't need to do that!" I rolled my eyes and stretched out my own wings quite effectively, showing them both up. They looked with disgust at each other.

"What date do I need?"

Ben winced when a rock hit his right cheek. "What do you know? I need a starting point," he blinked blood away.

"I need the place Tiberius used for residence or leisure, I'm not sure."

"That could be anywhere," Ben said.

"I have visions of being underwater with bodies on the seabed."

Ben narrowed his eyes in thought, "That's familiar for some reason. It should be easy to find if the Keepers documented all significant events of his life. Tiberius was controversial during an important time in human history, you know, the whole crucifixion thing? I can tell you, that was one that the humans invented, not us," Ben burrowed his arm deeper into a crevice. "Tiberius was all over that. The brutality of it attracted the attention of Daimon, and he liked a party with their women."

Ear-splitting screeching roared from below.

"I'll see how long we've got until were screwed," Lorcan snapped. He flew down into the stench and disappeared in the foul gas, which was resurrecting things that should have stayed dead.

"Keep an eye on him, Brennan," I said. "Don't let him go alone."

Brennan snorted. "I'm always picking him up from scraps," he turned on Ben, his face tight, eyes narrowed. "Touch one hair on her head and you're Rogue chum."

Brennan whipped his wings close by Ben's face and followed his brother.

I was once more alone with Ben, and I felt surprisingly in control.

The quakes began again, more intense this time. The updraft tossed us about. We had to work our wings hard to stay in position, but it still banged us into the walls. The subsequent bumps and grazes pounded.

Ben took over where the others had left off and cocooned his wings around me. I was about to argue.

"Don't be self-righteous," Ben said. "You concentrate on the scrolls, and I'll concentrate on this place trying to smash us to pieces. You're free to get pummelled later if you so desire."

I flicked a wing at him to push him back, "You don't need to be that close."

His smile reached his eyes.

"Tiberius was the emperor of his time," Ben's voice strained as he took every hit without complaint. "That should make it easy. He lived in Italy and ruled around the first century."

Numbers were engraved above each refuge.

"This one says 225," I said.

"What's the region?" Ben yelled over the noise.

I floated a little higher, past thousands of dusty cylinders crammed together. Southern Oceania had been etched above the section, the large script ornate with the remnants of ruby and sapphire embellishments. I plucked out a few scrolls and discovered references to the indigenous cultures of New Zealand and Australia.

"Nope, this is wrong," I said.

Ben pointed to the next section, "Over there then."

I flew over, he shadowed my movements.

"No, this seems to be…" I coughed. The rising fog stung my eyes. I yanked out random scrolls faster. "This mentions Incan tribes and the Spanish invasion, but I don't understand the name of the region."

"The Americas aren't what we want. We need an earlier time, too, closer to the first century," Ben added as we glided further along.

Lorcan and Brennan returned, their eyes red from the fog's bite. Their hard stares bored into Ben.

Brennan flicked ash from his face, "Any luck? We've got minutes at best."

I coughed and tried to ignore the filthy odour engulfing the cavern. "We're getting closer," I said.

"Hang on, I remember now," Ben glided back and took in the crumbling cavern. "The Keepers divided human affairs into northern and southern records. This wall is the southern end of the globe!" Ben sped across to the other side.

The four of us dodged tumbling clumps of earth. Shadows moved in the fog below, and I flew faster.

The Zythros stone cracked in half as we passed over it; I felt the break like a sting in my heart. Its energy blazed out. A white sheet, bright like a thousand suns, spilled across the floor. Intense heat seared my skin and burned the fog away. The screams below dissipated as it incinerated the encroaching zombies, giving us a momentary reprieve.

Brennan massaged his blistered arms, "Painful yet helpful."

"It won't last long," Lorcan said as he rubbed at his own burns.

The Zythros stone's energy faded. The crack widened and one half fell to the ground, an ethereal sentry, dead. The ancient edifice lay a mere unimpressive grey lump of rock, upended from its pedestal, no dignity afforded to it. Its inner light oscillated. It faded and shrunk slowly back into the hollow of the two halves of expired jade. Like a mini supernova, it quietly imploded, vaporising the stone. In its wake, a small oblong, as black as ink, undulated and wobbled where the stone had been.

The cavern rumbled deeply. More fissures opened and spewed volcanic gas and lava.

"That's not good," Brennan shouted over the piercing noise.

I pulled up next to Ben in front of the wall. "Why?" I asked, hairs on end again.

"Because that, my dear princess, is a goddamned mini black hole!" Brennan said.

"What? Is it dangerous?" I asked, my heart thudded faster.

"Is it dangerous she asks?" Brennan laughed. "That's a bloody affirmative. Self-annihilation is its next move and it will take everything in its path with it. All that down there, well…" Brennan's regular sarcasm quickly waned into blunt fear. "We'll be joining it in less than oblivion if Ben doesn't pull his God damned finger out and help you just a little bit faster!" Brennan pitched a scorching red orb at something below that only he had seen.

Ben clenched his teeth and moved quicker as he passed me scroll after scroll, his hands black with debris.

"He's not kidding. Read Sophia, read!" Ben urged, pushing the scrolls at me more urgently.

My hands shook as I scanned every tube, but my eyes kept wandering below my feet, which dangled just meters above A'mageddon's nightmare.

The ground was rapidly splintering. Heat radiated up from the fissures and singed my hair. Every breath burned my throat. Everything smelled wet and hot like a just-put-out campfire. The glowing magma tinted the grey smog. The scrolls I disturbed began to crumble in the heat, specks of historical ash drowning in the earth's fury. Had the cavern already claimed what I needed? I doubled my efforts. High-pitched squeals of subterranean gasses melded with the grind of rock on rock.

All the while, the little black hole pulsed quietly to itself.

A torrent of water rushed into the cavern near the stairway that exited below the old shed entrance.

"Look!" I yelled, accidentally dropping an unread document. I pointed down.

"Damn it! Hang on a sec!" I beelined quickly with two furious flaps, catching the scroll before it rolled into the burning abyss.

The stench increased tenfold as the fog reformed its thick, putrid blanket. It was hard not to gag. A skeletal hand squeezed through an ever-widening fissure. I smashed the bony digits with a single punch. The forearm fell away but it hooked the radial bone into the ground to pull itself up. I retreated upwards and left that thing to burn under a flurry of orbs I launched with my free hand.

Brennan met me halfway. "We'll deal with them!" he gestured to his brother.

"Damn it, I hate these bloody things!" Lorcan raced down past me and rained a small firestorm along the ground. An explosion of bones and flesh blew up through the smog. Roasted meat now added to the stench.

"A hundred more are coming up!" Lorcan yelled.

"Help him," I said to Brennan. "And take off Ben's shackles. He can help me better without them."

"Nope. He can talk but not touch," Brennan flew down and picked off the stragglers that had started to emerge.

Ben and I dodged the constant pelting of rubble. The shrapnel had nicked my skin all over, and it stung.

"Sorry," I called across to Ben.

"I'd do the same," he punched a rock away from his head, but dozens of smaller strikes had bloodied his face.

I threw another useless scroll away, all guilt for history literally going up in flames gone. It was the parchment or us.

"Fifth century, eighth century, second century, God, it doesn't make sense!" I pounded at the wall. "Nothing's in order! I don't recognise any of these strange names!"

The noise below sounded like jet engines firing up as the boys fought to keep us safe. Beyond it were the Rogues' incessant screams.

The black orb was smaller and denser than before, the air heavier.

Ben observed from afar.

"What are you doing?" I asked.

"Wait, just a second," Ben held up his pointer finger. "Tiberius should have had a large section. There was a lot of Daimon activity around him, which means the Keepers will have written many entries during this time. They never miss a detail. Look for the word Italy and a reference to his reign, anything important should be under his primary place of rule."

I flew out next to him and took a few seconds to take in the entire wall.

It was definitely sectioned off. Some areas yielded many scrolls while others were almost empty. More strange names emerged from the sweeping inscriptions. Albion, Hellas, Rus.

"I don't understand. What are these places?"

Ben dropped ten feet and kicked a straggler Rogue that had been scurrying up the wall like a spider. It sailed to a bony crunch below.

Ben's eyes blazed, "Time's up, Earth-born."

The putrid air stung like acid. My eyes watered constantly; my head thumped. I grasped the edges of an empty crevice trying to draw a clear breath, but it was too much.

"I can't do it," I cried.

Ben's wings encapsulated me from the terror.

"You can do anything," he whispered. "I'm right here."

His breath sent shivers along my neck.

Deep breath in, deep breath out.

He drew back, and the noise and foulness returned like a punch in the face.

"Now stop being a baby and do what you were born to do!" Ben's eyes were cold again. His hands clenched over and over, blistered from their burning confines. "The countries will be listed by their old names. Whenever the Keepers started documenting a region's history, they used the names of that era. I'll know them if you read them out loud."

"Err… Albion, Hellas, Rus," I yelled again.

"Those are Great Britain, Greece, and Russia. Keep looking."

Below us, Brennan and Lorcan fired a barrage of orbs into the crevice. The thunderous roar of the cavern's demise nearly muted their furious screams. I no longer saw them, only the flash of their wings.

My fingers quivered as they glided across the rough depressions of the names as I called them out. "Judea… Kasmir… Vitalia…"

"That's it! Stop where you are," Ben coasted over. His face was flushed and he almost smiled, but he blinked it away. "Vitalia is Italy. Now, look for Tiberius. It will be in alphabetical order."

The waterfall gushed faster behind us. Bugs and other slithering things fled through every nook and cranny, which my gut was telling me to do as well. The wall in front of us cracked and one of the scroll crevices fell away, leaving a gaping hole.

"Hope that wasn't the one you needed," Ben said.

"That's so not funny!" I scoured faster, swiping dirt and sweat from my eyes. "F, G… umm… R…"

"Hurry up, Sophia!" Lorcan bellowed. I barely heard him over the noise.

Another deep rumble caused the stale air to shift. My hair billowed in the current.

I glanced at the little black blob. It was moving faster, and its energy was pulling me away from the wall. I flapped my wings hard to compensate, but it dragged me along to a section packed with older looking scrolls, which rolled around as their snug home shifted. Thick dust clung to them.

"Where are you?" my fingers rushed over the surface until they found a crevice with just the right accent and dots above a swirling 'u' shaped impression. "I've got it! I've found T!"

An explosion threw me against the wall. Ben hurried over, but another shudder smashed him into the wall next to me. I pulled him towards me. Our wings intertwined; we shielded each other.

The ceiling over the original stairwell entrance caved in. The golden gates blew inside and twisted around what had been the Zythros stone's base; a gnarled metal web. Glittering rock, dirt, and tree roots washed in with another gush of water. The far wall bulged and disintegrated as the remnants of the old shed crashed in from the world above.

And within that mess, things were moving, Not bugs and worms, but big, unwelcome things. Withered arms and legs reached out of the sludge. Bone and skin, muscle and sinew, stretched like liquid horror. Amongst the twisting roots of upended trees, long-dead Rogues slunk out one by one. Their jaws clattered and their joints clicked.

Ben and I unravelled and lit up neon-white, ready to defend ourselves. I rose higher, summoned two orbs. I launched them. Long-suffering souls released, howling like dying fireworks as they zoomed around the cave, looking for escape.

"Keep searching!" Ben shouted. "I'll keep them away from you!"

"There's too many!" I yelled back.

Our eyes met.

"Trust me, I'll protect you," he pleaded.

I believed him with every fibre of my being. I didn't understand it, but I felt it. His hands moved towards me like he thought about holding mine, but the shackles hissed and burned into his wrists. He pulled back, roaring through his teeth, and his eyes lost the softness they'd had for that fleeting moment.

Ben shot down towards the Rogues. His light brightened as he stopped above the encroaching zombies. Bony arms pulled their torsos up and out of the earth, but a fresh quake shattered the more ossified ones. Ben flung himself into this writhing pit. The fog almost swallowed him. Rogues snapped and clawed for him. His bound fists pounded their bones into splinters; his feet powdered them into nothingness. Slick wing swipes seared heads from cervical bones.

But still they kept coming.

There was so much chaos. Shadows could have been heaving earth or lurking Rogues. With shackled hands, Ben wasn't at full power, and they had started to pull him down.

"*Brennan!*" I desperately skimmed the wall.

"*Bit busy right now,*" he screeched in my head. "*Are you done?*"

"*I'm close, but you need to unshackle Ben, he's fighting Rogues tied up like a damned Christmas turkey! They'll kill him!*"

Brennan swore and appeared at my side, his face sooty and burned. He gave me a quick once-over.

I caught another glimpse of Ben whilst I tossed scrolls here and there. Ben was barely keeping above the fog as the Rogues clawed at his feet. They were swarming along every wall and through every crevice. Ben kicked them down as best as he could, but fresh blood ran down his feet. He couldn't stop them.

"Help him!"

"Oh shit!" Brennan ground his teeth and transferred to Ben. He yanked Ben up by his hair. Ben drew a wing back to strike, but Brennan pulsed away the shackles and pushed him away. Ben drew back, looking shocked when Brennan threw him a spare sword. He turned it once, twice, passed it from hand to hand. His mark seared to life and lit the darkness. He glanced up at me, a wicked smile replacing the surprise. He nodded at Brennan. As though all was suddenly rainbows and unicorns between them, they turned in unison and dove into the devilish onslaught like a well-trained duo.

I rushed back to the scrolls. Three Rogues crawled my way, but I dispatched them with a handful of orbs.

Whilst Ben and Brennan were incinerating the other creatures in strangely perfect harmony, my desperation kicked up a notch.

"Tiberius, where… the hell… are you?"

Discarded cylinders littered the floor of the balcony. I threw a dozen more scrolls to the ground, some right over the edge and straight into the flames. There were hundreds of documents under Tiberius's reign. I skimmed the parchments, looking for the word playground or something close to it. I only found encounters with various people and places within the A'vean world. Key words jumped out at me and they were the A'vean names of Watchers I knew. Kea was listed on one, as well as Dash and Koi. More than a few inscriptions hinted at damage caused by Rogues and Daimon that had run amok outside of Yeqon's watch or for his amusement.

Interesting titles fleetingly caught my eye.

On Tiberius' renunciation of Sejunus (Daimon consort) and the relief of the Human Jewish population.

A very telling title read,

On the crucifixion of the Nazarene…a study of Pontius Pilot and Tiberius. Human greed as a pathway for Daimonic infiltration.

"Wow!" I muttered.

Another read,

On Caligula, (Daimon consort) and the perilous death of Tiberius.

That seemed to be the wrong end of the pile. I filtered back a bit further, but found nothing of interest until I came upon a tightly wound scroll wedged right in the corner. It read, *On Tiberius (Daimon Consort) and the Eradication of said Daimon. Destruction of the Oikos of Perversions.*

Oikos was Greek for house. My skin tingled with anticipation. Tiberius… Daimon…. house, and perversion all in one title had to refer to his playground. I melted the seal with a short energy pulse and unravelled the scroll.

Steam shot up from below. I wobbled and hit the wall face first, groaning as my face numbed.

The scroll slipped and teetered on my fingertips. A flick of my wing brought it back into my shaking palm.

"Holy shit Sophia!" I scolded myself breathily.

I tasted blood. Feeling returned as a painful throb at the top of my nose.

Still trying to ignore the horrendous affray that raged on below, I hastily scanned the fragile parchment that referred to Tiberius fleeing to the Isle of Capri at the end of his life. It stated it was there that he became involved with Daimon who concealed themselves as courtiers. They caused upheaval in his political life, but were only taken note of when they drew too much public attention to themselves. The Watchers were sent to Capri, but the Daimon had been dealt with by one of their own. The document's author referred to it as, *the one and only act of compensation afforded by the followers of the darkness.* The last line ended in a flurry of sweeping script:

… and upon their departure, I'el's humblest servants sunk the Blue Grotto into the ocean, Capris' dark moments eternally hidden from the weak and naïve human populace. No further could Tiberius play with the fire of Yeqon's horde.

"I've got it!" I shrieked.

I spun around, shaking with excitement; however, what I saw wasn't what I'd expected. Behind me, in a haze of dull E'lan, a panting Afflicted bore down on me, dagger in one hand, orb in the other.

Chapter Nineteen

The Afflicted and I stared at each other for mere seconds. He was out of place, out of energy, and out of luck, for in that moment I pulled myself together. He slashed towards me, drooling through spaces where teeth should have been. Desperation garnished his vacant eyes. I launched forwards.

"Oh no you don't!" I screamed.

With one hand clutching the scroll and the other fumbling for my dagger, I used my chromious chest guard as a battering ram. Its power singed the Afflicted and blistered his skin. He screeched and withdrew. His wings were dull, the E'lan in his hands faint as he frantically patted at his body, trying to heal the blisters without success.

"Get out of here before things get worse for you," I growled.

The Afflicted shook his head, licked his lips, and widened his wings. He flew at me, crazy fast. I held my position until he was almost upon me, then shot up… he crashed into the wall behind me. Bones cracked. He clung to small holes where the wall had fallen away.

"Help… me…"

The Afflicted scrambled for a foothold. His muscles were thin and sinewy. Slipping inch by inch, he called for help again, his voice a withered mew. His wings sputtered out and revealed a back so disfigured he was unrecognisable as ever having been one of us. Where the gentle wing leaflets should have been, there were black scabs.

He slipped again, holding on by one hand.

I glided up behind him, "Who sent you?"

He grimaced; his fingers white.

"No one," he whispered, struggling for breath. "I've languished here… since you left, feeding on… Andr'eal's scraps. I was on watch for Master until… you left. Then everyone left and… forgot me," he slipped again and yelped. "Please, feed me."

Anger boiled inside me, "Who is your master? Was it Nik'ael?"

"Belial. He did not trust his own master."

I recoiled. Ben had spoken the truth. Belial had been working his own agenda.

"Tell me more about Belial and I'll help you."

More debris smacked into us.

"Please, I'm falling!"

I sheathed my dagger and shoved him into the wall, making sure he wouldn't fall.

"Well?" I whispered into his ear. I twisted his arm behind his back until he yelped again, "Tell me all you know about Belial."

"He fed me, so I did as he wished," he suffered a coughing fit. "Until he left me forever," he spluttered again.

"And what did Belial wish?"

I pushed my armour harder against him. The burn made him speak quicker.

"He wished to deliver you to the Unseen himself. He wished for the reward. He knew that Nik'ael was…"

The Afflicted slumped, dead against the wall.

"No! You can't do that! Tell me about Nik'ael!"

I tried shaking the life back into him, but he was dead for sure. His body heated up. I pulled back and let him go. He plummeted, engulfed in flames before he hit the floor somewhere below.

The cavern rumbled like peels of thunder. The energy in the room had changed, the pull of air intensified as though gravity was concentrated solely on that little black hole. It spun faster every second. A whirlwind developed around it. The velocity collected high speed pebbles and dust.

Time to go.

"Guys, I've got the scroll," I yelled. "Let's get out of here!"

"Be… there… in… just a minute," Lorcan shouted from somewhere within the fog below. His wings flashed in its haze.

Brennan appeared beside me, followed by Ben. Both were panting and covered in blood and filth and radiant burns.

Brennan puffed hard.

"Look!" I held the scroll up.

"About time. This party is getting too excitable for me. I'm too old for this crap," Brennan whistled between thumb and finger. "Get up here, Bro!"

Lorcan appeared. Blood and burns covered his face too. His eyes were wild with battle frenzy. He saw the scroll in my hand.

He drew me and Brennan in. "Let's get outta here," Lorcan pointed at Ben. "We should leave him here."

Ben ignored him, as did I.

A gust pulled us towards the black hole. I reached for Ben against its force.

"Is group transfer the safest?" I asked.

"Yep," Brennan yelled over the howling air. "Quickest way with the least signature trail."

Brennan pointed at Ben, "Hands, mate. Sorry."

Ben obliged and held out his hands so Brennan could re-shackle him.

"Behave yourself," Brennan muttered, "I might let an Alchemae heal that mess for you."

A scream erupted behind us. A skeletal Rogue clawed up the wall and launched towards me. My dagger sunk into his skull before I realised it had left my hand. I followed up with an orb that incinerated the remains mid-air. The wind scooped up the ash…along with my weapon.

"My dagger!"

I flew after it, dodging the falling rocks and burning steam. The boys screamed at me to stop, but I couldn't leave it behind. It had opened the world to me. It had saved me. Its glimmer guided me. My pendant swung left and right as it followed the dagger's energy.

It landed near the broken remains of dozens of Rogues. One twitched underneath the mural of the creation of the universe. Only the large star representing I'el remained intact.

The ground shifted. A hand shot up from a small fissure and reached for my dagger, which teetered on the edge.

"No, you don't!" I pulled it away from the skinless hand and sliced off the appendage. It screeched and sunk away into the depths, leaving the dismembered hand wriggling behind.

That's when I saw the Afflicted's diamond skeleton. Another Rogue was clawing towards it.

I kicked it away just as Lorcan grabbed my arm.

"Enough, Soph. This place will implode any minute."

I yanked myself free, "I can't leave this."

"What?"

I stepped through stinking muck, leaning against the growing gale and squatted near the skeleton. I held onto a nearby boulder for balance.

"Are you kidding me?" Lorcan yelled. "Let's go *now*!" he rose from the ground, his hand waiting for me. He bobbed about, flapping hard to keep from being swept away.

"It'll only be used for evil," I screamed through the blaring noise. "I've got to destroy it.

"Soph…" Lorcan landed back down about to grab me again.

"Stand back!" I lit my hand.

The cavern's destructive winds buffeted me hard as my fingers tingled with white heat. I held tight with my other hand, to the boulder. The Afflicted's bones incinerated under my power. I caught as much Thanratos as I could and rammed it into my pockets. Some of it flew away and the sparkle of it caught my attention where it glued itself into the grooves of my hands. Its energy sent a rush through my mind and body that excited and terrified me. Something deep inside urged me to touch it to my lips, just a little — it'd be a good thing. As the air pushed and pulled me, so too did my conscience as I felt an irresistible urge to taste the iridescent temptation. I bit my lip. My hair lashed about in the gale which licked at my hand, just as I wanted to do. Was it sweet, like sugar?

Lorcan grabbed my hands, his face dark. We wrestled to stay upright. "Even you can be its slave," his voice floated away on the wind as he burned the remnants from my hands, leaving my palms inflamed but intact.

This instantly cleared my mind. The horrendous pounding and surrounding stink came back into focus.

"Was I about to…?"

Lorcan's voice and eyes were sympathetic. He nodded.

He wedged a foot under the boulder for balance and drew the leftover Thanratos from my pocket with a quick sweep of his hands. Millions of glistening molecules swirled upwards in a dazzling display and disappeared into the maelstrom.

Never ever touch the raw drug with your bare skin, okay? Lorcan said gently in my mind.

I nodded, but shame engulfed me. Was I that weak?

It's not so easy to ignore, is it? The challenge is to not let it call to you. If it does, walk away and call for help, he grabbed hold of me and looked up for the others.

A gaseous seam exploded. We ducked its boiling stream, which hissed from its widening fissure. Its hot moisture melted the fog and revealed the destruction around us. Another thunderous rumble. The ground surged beneath us. I fell heavily against Lorcan, and he held on tight.

"The gravity is too strong!" he yelled.

The cavern lurched. Everything blurred. Large boulders sailed overhead, crashing their way towards the spinning anomaly. Dirt clumps bit hard. Water defied physics as it stretched horizontally over our heads and pulled towards the spinning black orb. We held on tight to each other. The magnetism was unbearable. Our wings were useless.

Ben and Brennan were screaming in my head. I called to them in my mind, willing them to me, but I couldn't tell if they heard. I just kept calling.

Sound warped into a strange rhythmic thrumming. Lorcan's face distorted. Our bodies pressed harder into each other, yet mine felt floppy. My limbs were rubber. Rocks pounded into us from all sides. I tasted blood, felt muscles snap. My weapons pushed against my legs and sliced into me as the force jostled them like propellers.

Lorcan's fingers dug hard into me. I felt him trying to transfer us, but he couldn't match the might of the black hole.

I let the scroll go, I'd seen what I needed. I held tighter onto Lorcan. The scroll followed the million others as it was ripped to shreds.

The noise hurt my ears. The pulsing increased to a fever pitch. Every part of me ached. Every cell pulled in the wrong direction.

Ben and Brennan pressed into our huddle, and their warmth gave me strength.

"*Don't let go!*" I shouted.

I couldn't let them die, couldn't let my mission destroy them. I thought of Nan, Esme, Grey, and my dog Shadow, who'd been brutally mauled by Rogues. I recalled Jaz picking Nan's flowers in the garden. The sounds and smells of my old life beckoned me to a comforting place. I drew energy from somewhere deep inside me and urged it to erase the terror. It rushed through every artery, every cell and follicle, until my power eclipsed all pains. I willed us away from certain death.

"*What's she doing?*" someone said in a faraway voice.

My eyes fluttered open and closed. A flickering light show of reality and memories flashed through my mind. Ashes and spice. I was shaking, breath forced in my lungs by the pressure. My head fell back into someone's chest. The gravity vanished, and I felt light. My eyes opened just as the green door of the old shed hurtled towards us. Its peeling, slimy wood smacked into my face, and everything went blank.

Chapter Twenty

"Is she waking up?"

"She'd better be, scum bag!"

"She's beat up pretty bad."

"No thanks to you, dipshit!"

"Soph, please, wake up. You're okay."

"Okay? You think she's okay? If you think a shit storm in a tea cup is okay, you go on and believe that, pretty boy!"

All the voices jumbled together. They irritated my ears, but one was more acidic than the others.

"Jude?" my tongue was thick and tasted like dirt. My head felt like it had spilt open. My temples throbbed. Where was I? Fresh air calmed the fire under my skin. A magpie warbled in the distance.

A rough hand held mine, "Yes, Sophia. I'm here."

I opened one gluey eye, but the glare was too bright. I closed it again and clamped my hands over them before peeking through my fingers. Every part of me hurt.

Lorcan and Brennan hustled by my sides. Lorcan breathed too heavily, I wanted to shove him away, but didn't have the strength. Brennan's smile was pained and overshadowed by Jude's glare. Ashes and spice cleared the fog in my head, and I breathed in deeply. He was here, somewhere.

I scrambled to sit up and push away from the claustrophobic fussing. "Move. I'm fine," I coughed and spat out the taste of dirt, wiping my mouth on the back of my arm.

"There she is," Brennan said. "C'mon, Princess. Time to go home before the constabulary arrives."

I grabbed my head and pressed hard against my temples to quell the thudding pain. I fell back to the ground. They shuffled around me. A kookaburra laughed in the distance, and I shifted on what felt like dry leaves and twigs. Where the hell was I?

I opened my eyes and shielded them from the warm sunrays. Blue patches and numbers moved below cloud tufts. The numbers hovered in a circular pattern. I studied them and realised they were police helicopters. The blades thudded rhythmically. Sirens screamed desperately in the distance. Voices rustled closer through the bush. Walkie-talkie static blared on and off.

"What happened?" my voice was dry, and it hurt to swallow.

I didn't have to see myself to know I was bruised and battered. My back was especially excruciating. Leaves and sharp twigs crunched beneath my backside. I sat up to inspect myself. My nails were caked in mud and blood. My right thumb was swollen and numb, whilst my forearms were cross-hatched with deep scratches. I'd lost two toe nails; those toes were pounding dreadfully. My clothes, more red than white, looked like they had murdered someone.

Jude kneeled close; his face as dark as sin.

"What happened she asks? What bloody well didn't happen?" Jude's narrowed eyes were a world of anger. "You are in a crap-load of trouble. Thank I'el you're alive so Gedz'iel can ascend you! Get up!" he pulled on my hand.

The boys tried to help, but I slapped them away.

"I'm fine!" I was wonky but more aware with every moment.

A strange quality was in the air. Out-of-place odours, fungus-tinged earth, pungent mineral water. The charcoal of fresh burns. The ground was more uneven than I remembered, and there was too much space.

Where were the shadows, the nooks and crannies? Where were all the trees?

The kookaburra quieted. The bush was silent apart from the nearby emergency sirens. The E'lan felt unnerving; unnatural.

My old house was gone, everything was gone.

"Happy with your handiwork?" Jude asked. He spun me around until I saw it all. Anger perfused from his palms into my arms and jolted me fully awake.

"She saved us," Brennan said behind me.

"Shut your mouth!" Jude pointed down, "I like what you've done with the place, Sophia," he added sarcastically.

We balanced on the edge of an enormous hole. A hole that had swallowed my entire property. It was deep and so dark I couldn't imagine its depth. A few scattered gems glittered near the rim.

"Oh my…"

"You bet, oh my! You won't believe the backtracking and trickery Gedz'iel is having to go through to hide this lovely little black hole incident from the locals. And this?" Jude pulled Ben in front of me and shook him. "What the hell is this?" Jude's jaw was so tight I thought he might crack a tooth.

Everything flooded back.

"Well…"

"Waiting for an answer," Jude grumbled impatiently.

I rubbed my hands across my weary face and felt for my weapons. Everything was where it should be except the unwelcome swellings and pains. My pendant was warm, and my soul stone sent a sense of well-needed calm through me.

"Hope you've got something impressive to say to Gedz'iel," Jude added.

I massaged the lump on my forehead where the door had hit me just as I'd transferred us from the cavern. Anger rushed in, dulling my aches, firing up a warmth in my belly.

"Well, Jude, I didn't get a manual for the job, so you'll just have to go with the flow. And you know what? I do have something to say to his royal highness… a lot actually. The first thing will be, *you're bloody welcome!*"

Ben smirked, Brennan coughed, and Lorcan paled, but Jude repressed a smile.

"Well, we'll see about that, won't we, Miss?"

With another group transfer, we arrived in Kaymakli's underground safety. The stasis room was to my left; the heady smells of healing wafted under the door.

I pointed at Ben, "You'd better take him back to the cells."

Ben's face was emotionless.

"So, there *is* a brain between those pretty ears!" Jude said. "Thank the angels!"

Jude clicked his fingers. A bulky guard appeared, re-shackled Ben, and marched him away.

"*I'm sorry,*" I whispered into his mind.

"*It's what I would do,*" Ben whispered back.

"Do you want to rest before you see Enl'iel?" Brennan asked. "Before Ged shows up?"

"I've got this, Brennan," I said, not wanting to put off an inevitable confrontation.

This was the moment that would define the rest of this journey — *my* journey.

I shoved my hair out of the way and took one deep breath. I was aiming for cool, calm, and collected, despite my body feeling like a train wreck. Jude pushed on the door; it creaked way too loud. I tried to look as benign as possible, not like I was about to do something stupid like break more rules. He stayed near the door while I went farther inside.

Through the smoky haze, a few more teens slumbered through their last Right of Sevens. They slept with a soul stone on their chests and a myriad of herbs placed at various energy points around their bodies.

Alchemae moved between the beds to check on them, including the person I'd hoped to see, and hoped not to see all at once; Enl'iel.

I clasped my hands in front of me and cleared my sore throat. An Alchemae stopped to see what I needed. I shook my head and pointed to Enl'iel. She knew I was there; her body had stiffened; she didn't turn around. I took two steps towards her until I was at the end of a bed. She continued cleaning the arms of a cherub-faced girl with a wash cloth whilst rearranging fresh herbs around her. Enl'iel moved methodically from head to foot as she thoroughly ignored me.

"Enl'iel?"

She stopped dabbing the cloth for a moment, then continued.

"Enl'iel, I'm back."

"I'm well aware of that," she plaited sage leaves through the teen's white locks without turning around.

"I'm sorry for fighting with you," I said. "I took it way too far."

"I think you've gone well beyond our disagreement, Sophia."

I bit my lips. They were split and hurt, so I licked them instead.

"Things are moving quickly. Our world is falling apart," Enl'iel reached for a new twig of sage but put it down again. Her shoulders slumped; her voice softened.

"The expectations of others can empower or cripple. I've crippled you, Sophia."

I immediately felt guilty, "You haven't. You've empowered me to be a strong woman, Enl'iel, and a brave A'vean."

"So I hear from Jude's report," she sneaked a look at me over her shoulder and smiled. Tears welled in her lashes as she took in my battered body.

My head dropped at the memory of holding a weapon to her neck.

"I took it too far yesterday," I said. "I'm so sorry."

Enl'iel reached for the sage again and crumbled the leaves into a small bowl. The flush of annoyance had waned from her cheeks.

"No, it's my fault," she said. "I should have expected as much. Despite everything, I forget sometimes that you're no longer a child. You're no longer human, either, yet I treat you like both. I spent such a long time hiding your destiny from you that it's been hard to relinquish you to it."

"No, I…"

She held up her hand, "We had a beautiful life together for a time, but now it seems but a fleeting breath to me. I mourn that. I will always protect you wherever I can, but I realised yesterday that you have outgrown me," Enl'iel placed the herbs at the end of the bed. "You've done me proud, even though my nerves are frayed to breaking point. I hope Gedz'iel can see past your infractions of his rules," she sighed and faced me.

"I want you to have the best chance. And, to be perfectly honest, I want you to have more than this. I want you to be more than your destiny, more than this prophecy. I want you to have a happy life, whatever that may mean."

My neck and jaw were tight; I gulped.

"Enl'iel, I…"

She pulled me into a tight embrace. "I love you," she whispered into my ear.

"I love you too."

The vanilla, lavender, and tea aroma that clung to her loose hair brought visions of my childhood rushing back; better memories than I'd just left behind.

Enl'iel turned back to the girl and plucked new herbs from a wicker basket.

She held out a lantern, "Light this, please?"

I set it aglow with my pointer finger. It began to release its fresh aroma, and Enl'iel hung it on a hook above the bed.

"Now, what are we going do about your little excursion today?" she asked. "I understand you've progressed with Enoch's mysteries. Unorthodox methods, I must say."

"I had to. My instincts lead me along that path, and it worked."

"With a Daimon, no less!" her voice had no anger, just tired resignation.

"It was a risk, and it worked."

"See how far that argument gets you with Gedz'iel."

She passed me a muslin poultice that I held to my head. It immediately relieved the pain.

"You *are* a mess," she tutted as she ran her palms over my arms to heal the scratches. The sting was sharp but short, "Please, stay away from Ben until Gedz'iel can assess the situation?"

"I'll do whatever I need to," I said. "You have to accept that."

She ran her hands over my legs. They stung a little harder as their wounds knitted closed.

"Hm. You are so very strong now," she stood, put her hands on my shoulders, and looked into my eyes. "It's prophesised that you'll be the strongest of us, but I suppose I'm like any parent, overprotective and scared to let you grow into yourself. We're all scared to let you go. I only ask that you consider our safety when you follow your heart, Sophia?"

I nodded.

"Now, tell me what you've…"

The bright flash of a transfer cut her off. Jude hurried over and pushed us down.

The door smashed open. Needle-sharp splinters flew everywhere and caused the healers to throw themselves over the slumbering patients. Nasty pins stung my freshly healed arms. I crawled cross the floor to shield Enl'iel.

Cael sped out of intensive care and skidded to a stop near us.

"What the hell is going on?" he yelled.

Guards kicked away the two halves that had been the door. They scuffled with someone who screamed like a wild animal until one guard knocked them out with a bright pulse to the head. The body flopped limp in his grasp.

I pulled Enli'el and myself up and out of the way. Lorcan and Brennan appeared, healed and in fresh clothing.

The guards carried a limp female to a spare bed, well away from the children.

"Help us," one guard said.

Lorcan dragged the bed closer to the ICU. Brennan picked up her legs so they didn't drag along the floor. Together, they lowered her.

"Sorry about that," a guard said. "She got away from us. Feisty devil."

Enl'iel clasped her jaw, shaking her head, "Oh my. Another one."

Jude and Lorcan helped the guards secure the woman's arms and legs with red shackles, whilst Brennan checked over Enl'iel and gave her a peck on the cheek.

I knew from the sickly-sweet aroma and pasty skinny frame that this was an Afflicted. But why was she here, in Kaymakli's safety?

"Where did you find her?" Cael asked.

"Elmas and Mehmet discovered her on the outskirts of Nevşehir," one of the guards reported. "We were on duty nearby. Put up a damned good fight, too!" he dabbed at a scratch on his cheek.

"Well done," Cael said. "Change your posting to the main entrances of Kaymakli. I want double postings along all the tunnels."

"Call up my reserves," Jude said. "Place them in civilian attire around Nevşehir. Patrol a further twenty-five clicks past the current boundary."

"Yes, sir," they thumped their armour with closed fists, bowed, and left.

Enl'iel ran her hands over the woman's head and heart. The Afflicted was barely conscious after her frenetic entrance. Her chest rose and fell rapidly, her skin sheened with sweat. Enl'iel felt the woman's skin, opened her mouth, and lifted her fluttering eyelids.

"Hmm, she is not at all well," Enl'iel mumbled to herself.

"Who is she?" I asked.

Her hair was threadbare and matted, her cheeks too prominent. There were fresh scrapes all along her arms. That little voice inside me, the one that tells you bad news is coming, teased the back of my mind. I wanted to ignore it, but I stepped closer knowing I couldn't ignore fate.

Her clenched fists caught my eye. Whilst the rest of her seemed flaccid, they were white-knuckled and rigid. Perhaps it was the shackles causing her pain…or perhaps it was whatever was poking out between her fingers.

I reached for it, but Lorcan shoved me aside and rushed towards the unconscious woman.

He snatched her fist and tried to pry open her iron grip, but she resisted even in her delirium. Her bleak face twitched, and a guttural moan escaped through grinding, yellowed teeth.

"Open your hand or I'll break your damn fingers," Lorcan growled.

Jude leaned in, sniffed, and screwed up his face in disgust.

"Is that the one who escaped in France?" he asked.

"Yes," Lorcan said.

Jude held her wrist for Lorcan.

"What's going on?" Enl'iel asked. "Who exactly is she?"

Cael wheeled between the bed and Enli'el.

"Careful. This one is big trouble," Cael nursed an orb, ready to help.

Lorcan nearly had her fingers pried open, Jude's grip had the Afflicted's hand nearly purple.

"Just sear her bloody hand off!" Jude demanded.

Enli'el flinched.

The Afflicted woman began to pant. Her eyes flung open. She turned to Cael and glared, screaming incoherently.

"She's withdrawing," Cael said. "Do you need her alive?"

Lorcan smiled as her fingers released, "Not anymore."

He held his prize close as the woman began to tremble. Her scream waned to a wispy cry. Sweat and pallor overtook her body. Her head lolled backwards, and her eyes twitched behind the lids. I touched her forehead and felt the shadow of goodness beneath the drug.

Cael leaned the back of his hand against the Afflicted's skin as well.

"Can you treat her at all? I'd like to know where she's been and why she's here."

"I can do a little, but not much," Enl'iel said. "Just enough to ease her suffering."

"No!" Jude snapped. "Let her face the fate she imposed on herself!"

I was ready to support him, but then I recalled how I'd behaved to Nephr'eus' messenger and the lure of the Thanratos, and shame resurfaced.

Jude watched her writhe in pain, "She chose her fate, and that includes harm to Sophia and Jasmine."

My head shot up, "What do you mean?"

"She's another messenger for Nephr'eus," Lorcan said. "I flushed her out in France when we were on a brief mission yesterday. She was here for this."

Lorcan held out his hand. A lock of black hair rested in his palm.

With the Afflicted's rasping breaths to my left, and my thudding pulse in my temple, I stared open-mouthed at Jaz' lock of hair.

Cael swore. Enl'iel, too, uttered words of horror.

"She's not here to be fed or for redemption, be very clear on that," Lorcan said. "Gedz'iel gave us one chance to help Jaz, Soph," his fingers curled back around the fibres.

I plucked some from between his fingers. It tingled in my palm and sent a surge of nausea through my gut. My face flared, and my back ached. The fire in my gut stirred.

I was overcome with a vision of Jaz lying strapped to a bed in glowing, red shackles. She was pale and panted like the woman on the bed.

Chapter
Twenty-One

I didn't realise I was shaking the unconscious Afflicted until Enl'iel wrenched me off her.

"Where is she?" I yelled over and over.

Enl'iel's fingers dug into my shoulders, "She is of no use in this state, Sophia. Leave her be."

"Jaz needs me!" I held her hair close to my chest, "She's alive somewhere! This is a message to me!"

"Calm down, darlin'," Cael said. "This is good news. We have a great deal more hope now."

"Calm down? Jaz is a hostage and bait for me. I've got to find her, and now!" I paced, tried to reign in my fear with some deep breaths. "Here!" I thrust the black hair at Cael. "Do you feel that?"

He held it between his palms and closed his eyes.

"Hmm. She's in pain," he opened his eyes and handed the hair back to me. "But this is also proof of life, Sophia, and whilst there is life, there is hope. Nephr'eus wants to tempt you and us. Everyone this side of Saturn's rings understands that your weakness is your family and friends. It's no surprise she has taken the easiest course of action to get what she wants. It's what Daimon do."

I pinched my nose whilst Enl'iel hovered nearby, her nervous tension adding to mine.

"Their laziness is our strength," Cael said. "Daimon have this ridiculous need to send word of their ill deeds, leaving us clues that more often than not, lead us to them," he shook his head and chuckled. "They're egotistical fools. We will bring Nephr'eus down as we always have."

I looked into his warm eyes, "So, we can just go find her?"

He took my hand in his, "Not quite. Jasmine is a human, her plight more delicate, and you… well, you're neck-deep in other business. Let's think on how to handle this and wait for Gedz'iel."

I screamed in my mind.

"I can't know this and wait. Jaz is my family!" I snapped.

Tears blurred my vision and pooled atop my lips. Jaz had saved me from that Rogue so long ago. She saw me in trouble and didn't flinch, didn't question the horror of what she saw, just knew a friend was in trouble. She'd picked up a shovel and lopped the head off a Rogue without a second thought.

I squeezed her hair harder, probed her energy to imprint the vision to memory.

"I'm sorry, I can't do as you ask," I turned away from Cael to leave. "I'm going to find her. I need to save her."

A terse voice carried in from the broken doorway.

"It's nice to hear you'll save *some* of your family."

The comment stunned me, and I stopped.

Rik leaned against the remnants of the doorframe, hands in his pockets. His hair was newly short, a copy of Koi and Gedz'iel. A tight black shirt hid the array of old and new scars Yeqon had left. The fine white ones on his face blended into his mark, making them almost imperceptible. He looked older and stronger, but also bitter as hell.

His insinuation flamed my cheeks with a deep ache. He'd barely left his room since arriving here, and then only to see Ben or to learn combat with everyone but me. I'd heard he was a natural. Jude raved about him.

"Settle down, Rik," Brennan said.

"No worries, I understand," Rik replied. "*She* is important to you, *sister*."

Words died in my throat. How could I ever come back from letting him fall to Earth? Regret ran cold through my gut. His anger was so raw; it hurt like a knife to my heart.

Enli'el leaned into my side and hugged me.

"Are you okay?" she whispered. I nodded. "Don't go just yet," she said.

I nodded again, paralysed by the situation.

Enl'iel let go.

"Can I help you, Rik?" Enl'iel asked.

He glanced at her before retuning his icy stare to me.

"I was just wondering when training will be on. Koi has been gone a while," annoyance stained his tone.

"I see," Enl'iel cleared her throat. "We're a little undermanned at the moment," her hands clasped in front of her stomach. "There are a few issues to deal with first. Koi is very busy helping Gedz'iel keep abreast of several issues. There are plenty still here to help you if you wish," her manner was no-nonsense headmistress.

Rik made good work of not making eye contact with her either. He seemed to prefer kicking his feet about in the dust and glaring sideways at me.

"I'll meet you when I'm finished here," Jude said. "Go run a few laps."

"You look too busy with your monster there, I'll wait," Rik peeled a piece of wood from the doorframe and pointed it at the Afflicted.

Jude walked over to Rik, bunched his fist on his hips, "Watch your manners, Rik."

A veil of pissed-off fell over Rik's face. "I'm perfectly polite," he slipped his hands back into his pockets and sniffed. "I'll just go find a corner somewhere and pretend I belong here," his eyes swept the room but fell like a slap back onto me. He smirked, nodded to himself, and disappeared.

"That's cold," Brennan said.

Jude squeezed my shoulder as he walked back past me, "It's bloody ungrateful."

"It's fine," I said. "He's hurting."

"It's bloody well not okay, Soph," Jude grumbled.

"I'll go to him later when I have a moment," I said, but didn't at all feel it would make any difference. Rik hated me, I felt it in my bones.

My attention returned to the woman, who was fitting and frothing at the mouth. The Alchemae tended her without success. I kneeled beside her and watched on.

"Is this how you torture my friend?" I mumbled.

Numbness tingled beneath my skin. Despite now understanding the strong pull of Thanratos, I found it hard to pity her. Not when her private battle caused the suffering of others.

The irony was that my battle had caused Rik to suffer. Perhaps I deserved his hate?

"Soph? You okay?" Brennan edged nearer.

I bit my lip, nodded when it really was a lie, I wasn't okay at all.

"I don't understand this," I swept my hand across the Afflicted. "But I understand him. I understand that he's hurting and lashing out, but…"

Enl'iel dropped in beside me, "It hurts because you love him. Unfortunately, he's been so devoid of love, he cannot see the truth of your heart as we do. He cannot understand the sacrifices you've made."

I hung my head, "I did choose to save Enoch's box whilst he fell from the portal. Maybe I should have let the box fall instead."

Cael wheeled closer, "You did what your destiny dictated."

"Well, this destiny sucks," I blinked a tear away.

"No, sweetheart," Cael rested his hand on mine. "You do the greater good. You do what's right and necessary to protect millions of lives. You have no guilt to bear. Be kinder to yourself."

I closed my eyes and sifted through the thoughts baring down on me. I switched off the ambient noise; the Afflicted's unintelligible grunts, Jude's angry barks to someone, the constant murmuring of the Alchemae, until I found something calming. Kristen's soft breathing two beds away changed the tone. There, at least, was something to lift my spirits. She was out of immediate danger and recovering slowly.

I moved across to her bed with Enli'el padding behind me. I placed my hand above her fresh dressings, "It's still bad, isn't it?"

Enl'iel smoothed out Kristen's blanket, "Yes, but I'm certain now that's she'll recover. I don't think she'll speak again, I'm afraid. The damage to her neck was too extensive."

"Poor Kristen," I slipped my hand around hers. She was warm, the soft olive tones of her skin glowed healthier.

Poor Kristen. Poor Esme. Poor Kea. Poor Rik. And, somewhere, poor Jaz.

"Everyone around me suffers so much," I ran my hands over my face. "I've got so much more to do more."

"Yes, you do!" Gedz'iel's voice boomed through the ether a nanosecond before he materialised.

A dozen warriors including Koi and Dash followed him. They were all doused in the sickening odour of warm blood; their appearance horrified me.

"What happened?" I asked.

"I have had to split the Eloi across the Americas and Oceania," Gedz'iel spoke to everyone, just not to me. It stung. "They're recruiting for us from all regions. The world is at war."

My blood drained; I think I went numb.

The Alchemae gasped, seemed to increase their pace as they worked.

Gedz'iel made his way to the Afflicted, his face a thundercloud.

"I see she made it here after all, Lorcan," Gedz'iel's nostrils flared.

Dash glared at her with unashamed disgust.

"Are you okay?" I asked Dash.

"We're all fine. I cannot say the same for her den mates," Dash glanced at me, his eyes hollow with fatigue and his skin taught. "I'm sorry we didn't find your friend," he sighed and ran his hand over his coarse stubble.

"You really were searching for Jaz?"

Dash nodded and looked to Gedz'iel, whose hands hovered above the Afflicted. E'lan sparked from his fingertips, its crackle like fire. He paused over her heart and forehead, nodded to himself.

"I would not have authorised it if not for Jude," Gedz'iel said. "Neither did I authorise your little outing, Sophia."

My heart raced. Gedz'iel was yet to look at me. I concentrated on the Afflicted again, uncomfortable and unsure who to look at now Gedz'iel was mere inches away. Funny how intentions seem easy until you have to follow through. Whilst I thought I had a perfectly good argument, Gedz'iel seemed so… almighty up close. I bit my lip, drummed my fingers on my legs. Was now the right moment to stand up to him?

Jude cleared his throat, "This Afflicted might still be able to help find the girl."

Lorcan swore under his breath, "She's a corpse Jude, you'll never…"

"You can't give up!" I butted in, my voice trembled. "Are you saying you've got no intel about Jaz at all?"

No one answered.

I pulled the lock of her hair from my pocket and waved it around.

"Surely this can help? Please?" I glanced between them all. Lorcan took some of it from me and passed it to Gedz'iel.

Gedz'iel held the fine hairs, unemotive and still refraining from actually laying eyes on me.

"We've got nothing," Jude finally said. His nostrils flared, the darkness of exhaustion underpinning his eyes added to his foreboding appearance. Jude's palpable rage made me more anxious.

"We were so close, Sophia. I'm sorry," Dash said.

I searched his eyes for a different answer, but the weight of loss tugged at my shoulders. A tear slipped from my lashes and steamed away across my mark.

"You'll keep looking, won't you?" I asked.

"No!" Gedz'iel snapped.

I startled; my body went cold.

"One life is not justifiable for the death of many. That is where we find ourselves, Sophia!" he said, with no room for argument.

"But…" my words faded.

Gedz'iel's hard eyes fell on me, swirling with impatience. Their glimmer pulsed in tune with his mark. I felt the weight of his indignation.

"Rules exist for the greater good, not that you appear to respect that. Yeqon rains death upon this world. He uses all his evil against us like never before," Gedz'iel's face seemed more angular, more deadly. "You will leave Jasmine to her fate and follow your own," he pointed solidly at me. I could feel his finger's power as though it actually poked my chest.

The walls pushed in on me. *Death* — that word reverberated through me. Would I expect them to save me instead of thousands of others? I'd never allow it. The cold of Gedz'iel's anger at me was replaced by the heat of my own.

I didn't realise my fingers were digging into my head until I felt the warmth of blood trickle past my temples. The room had become too bright. I couldn't control my right hand as I reached out for Gedz'iel. I certainly couldn't stop the lash of energy that whipped around his waist.

"Sophia!" Enli'el screamed.

"Stop!" Lorcan yelled.

Brennan waved for me to stop, but I was in a dream, my attention fixed on Gedz'iel. His defiant eyes hooked mine as I lifted him off the floor. Gedz'iel didn't resist.

"I will *not* abandon Jaz. I will not abandon anyone. I will fight to my death for you all. I will do whatever I need to, but I will no longer be dictated to," I don't know where my voice came from. It didn't sound like me… but it was me.

I rose to Gedz'iel's level. The mist of the lanterns coated us as though we sat amongst clouds. My arm shook with the intense energy. It took hold of my body, and it felt amazing.

"My destiny is set, yes. But my morals are my own and so is my will. You need me, Gedz'iel, but I don't need your rules. Darkness is everywhere; I will bring light wherever I go. Let me do so."

For a moment we hovered, a lash of E'lan connecting us.

A smile softened Gedz'iel's unreadable face.

"You mock me?" I twisted my wrist. The lasso of light squeezed tighter around his waist and jerked him higher. Gedz'iel winced. Gasps echoed up from below.

"No, Soph'ael, Earth-born angel. I do not mock you. I welcome you," Gedz'iel replied.

I narrowed my eyes, loosened the snarling light a little.

"You have been a naïve, scared little girl," Gedz'iel said. "You needed your eyes opened. Now, they see as they were meant to. I have been here, a mere servant, awaiting an agent of I'el. That High Angel now stands before me."

My hand dropped to my side. Gedz'iel fell to the floor with a heavy thud. He smacked away an overenthusiastic Alchemae. I lowered myself until my feet sank into the soft floor.

What had I just done? My skin was hot and tingly.

My eyes found Enli'el who wrung a cloth which was well dry. Her brows knit tight, her eyes flitted between Gedz'iel and I.

I nodded at her, *I'm fine*.

She released the cloth and let out a breath. A soft smile held her quivering chin at bay and caught a tear before it fell to the floor.

Gedz'iel dusted himself off, standing proud once more.

"Continue," he said, as though nothing of importance just occurred.

Deep breath in, deep breath out.

"Where were you looking for Jaz?" I asked.

"In France, as you've heard. Nephr'eus and Anjou'elle hold her captive for unknown reasons," Gedz'iel pushed away a cup from an Alchemae and glowered at the fuss.

"They'll want the Kaladai, of course," I said. "Doesn't everyone?"

"Jaz will be close to where this one resided. Afflicted stay where they can easily source their drug," Jude pointed at the writhing Afflicted, who looked a breath from death.

I brushed past Gedz'iel to the bed, "How do we interrogate her?"

All eyes were on me, and for the first time ever, I wasn't scared. I studied this barely-there woman as I spoke.

"I would like your help, Gedz'iel. I want to find Jaz. We need to find her. She is as much a weapon for them as she is an anchor for me. As much as I possess the strength of an angel, I have a human quality they don't but know they can exploit — love."

I faced everyone.

"We brought Jaz into our world. This love I have for her, I have for all of you. I would fight just as hard for each and every one of you," I paced while the others were silent. Not even the Alchamae shuffled about. "Let's take out the sisters. Yeqon is more than enough to deal with. I only need two people to help me, the rest of the warriors are yours. The war is ours; the fight is theirs, and the solution is mine."

Gedz'iel embraced me. I was shocked, but melted into him. There were no words, just a coming together of energies that felt like I had graduated.

He put his hands on my shoulders, "Pick your soldiers, Soph'ael. I only ask that you take their guidance where your experience lacks?"

"And what about Ben?" I asked.

Gedz'iel bristled. "You just told me you are the solution. Make it so," he squeezed my shoulders and nodded sharply.

"Ah, Ged?" Brennan called. "This one is toast," Brennan pointed to the Afflicted.

Her convulsions had worsened.

"Perhaps," Gedz'iel smacked Brennan over the head as he walked to her bedside. "Do not call me *Ged*."

Brennan shrugged and smiled at me, rubbing his head and smoothing his hair back into place.

Gedz'iel kneeled by the Afflicted. A handful of Keepers whizzed around him as though interested in what he was doing. He closed his eyes and placed his hands over her head and heart again.

Enl'iel clasped her hands under her chin, her eyes flitting between the woman, Gedz'iel, and me.

I watched Gedz'iel's actions intently. My heart hammered, not because of the Afflicted, but because I felt like I had just achieved my independence.

"If only one would survive," Enli'el whispered to herself.

I took Enl'iel's hand, and she held it tight.

Gedz'iel rested his hands.

"She is indeed close to the end. There is nothing we can do," Gedz'iel leaned back on his heels, running weary hands over his face. "This taxes my very soul. But for the choices made, paradise is right in front of us. It is within every breath and upon every sunrise, yet they choose to suffer," he shook his head with a despair and fatigue that I felt as though it were my own.

Gedz'iel and Enl'iel stepped back from the bed. We retreated behind some unoccupied beds a few feet away. I wasn't quite sure why. Enli'el took my hand.

"Let what is coming be yet another lesson," Gedz'iel said.

My body buzzed, overwhelmed with a rush of adrenaline. Something unseen plucked at my skin. I wanted to unfurl my wings. My pendant hummed, and my face seared and pulsed. My body coiled and tensed. It was that fight or flight feeling you get when your instincts know something bad is about to happen. It seemed it was not just myself either, who felt this way. Every face shone, marks ablaze.

"May you find peace and redemption in your next existence," Gedz'iel said, his attention upon the Afflicted. "May the Throne of A'vean forgive you," he placed his hand over his heart. "My forgiveness is yours, dear kindred."

The others repeated the gesture. I copied them but didn't quite understand this custom, or why we were doing it.

We held hands, our marks illuminated in some form of mourning ritual; a silent reverence, deserved or not, for a lost soul. The E'lan burst to life, sparkling like fireworks. Intense power drew goose bumps to my skin. Soft wisps of white energy flickered through the room. The Keepers danced along with the Earth's tune.

Being a part of this made me feel connected to them more than ever. Every time I learned another tradition from my heritage, I felt grounded to something so very intimate, something that words really couldn't define.

An Alchemae dabbed cool cloths along the Afflicted's skin despite her poor prognosis. Care continued, no matter the outcome. Another replaced withering herbs with fresh ones around her body. They massaged her hands and feet with tenderness. One of them noticed me watching intently.

"It is to ease her soul from this mortal vessel," the Alchemae said with a smile.

The Afflicted looked almost serene in her death throws, like a languishing woodland fairy. Greens, purples, and earthy tones decorated her death bed. Her wispy hair, entwined with lavender, rosemary, cedarwood, and sandalwood, glistened with scented oils. Sage burned thick from the ceiling lanterns. A soul stone lay over the Afflicted's heart. It pulsed soft and white.

My heart felt heavy as I watched the scene play out. I was safe and warm whilst Jaz was lost somewhere, scared and perhaps hurt. In that moment, I didn't give a damn about puzzles, keys, portals, and freedom. I just wanted Jaz back and the pain around me to stop.

The Afflicted ground her teeth, the squeak of them pierced the reverent silence. Blood dribbled from the corner of her pale lips.

"Is she in pain?" I asked.

"She is close to ascension and feels nothing. These are mere reflexes of the dying shell," Gedz'iel turned away from her and urged us to do so too. "We have shown our respect. It is time to move forwards. Dash, scramble extra soldiers. No humans, just us," he commanded.

"Are you leaving?" I asked.

"There is no time to waste, young one. I trust you to discharge your duty and choose your warriors wisely whilst Koi and I attack the scourge," Gedz'iel responded.

"Who can I take with me?" I asked.

"Other than Koi, whom would you like?" Gedz'iel sounded more like himself again; impatient.

"I would like Lorcan, Brennan, Jude and… Ben."

Jude cursed to himself.

I was going to bite my tongue, but I couldn't.

"Jude, didn't Ben help me just today? I've a new set of information because of him. And, did I not send him straight back to the cells the moment we returned? I'm not a fool anymore," I pressed my lips tight, frustrated with the uphill battle that seemed to follow my every move.

Jude inclined his head and bowed, "As you wish, Earth-born. Just don't expect me to save his arse."

"I'll take care of him, don't you worry about that," I said, completely pissed off.

I bet you will, Lorcan whispered into my mind.

"So, you truly choose a Daimon, Sophia?" Jude scoffed. He sounded confused and accusing in a single hit. My fists clenched, I felt inclined to punch his mouth.

But…I took a breath, closed my eyes before I snapped. I forced tension from my body. I inhaled in the heady aromas of healing, opened my eyes and watched the ever-forgiving nature of the busy Alchemae. They never judged; they just went about whatever their duties required.

I hooked Jude's guarded eyes.

"I believe Ben has changed, or is changing. I used to feel literally sick around him, Jude, but not anymore. My chromious doesn't burn him. His eyes aren't ringed with Yeqon's darkness, and his hair is returning to white. I believe he's reverting to what he used to be."

"That's impossible!" Enl'iel said. Her hands fell to her pendant, she twirled it rapidly, her brow furrowed, "It can't be possible. He is a Daimon, Sophia, and Daimon remain as such."

"Actually, it has happened before," Gedz'iel waved Koi over. "A long time ago, my most trusted soldier was on the cusp of darkness. Is this not true, Koi?"

Koi nodded.

I quietly gasped, as did Enl'iel.

"Why is your hair so short, Koi, and why do you keep the markings on your knuckles?" Gedz'iel asked.

Koi glanced at us all, his eyes lingered on me a little longer.

"Because I was turning. Darkness overwhelmed me," Koi looked at his hands, rubbed the letters tattooed across his knuckles. He took a breath and looked back up, eyes clear and bright.

"My eyes once ached with the pull of revenge. My hair blackened to soot. I hovered on the edges of the Empyrean realm for decades. It was only with great willpower that I remembered why I was here," Koi looked at Jude and nodded at his shocked expression. "I called for Gedz'iel, and he took me in. I asked him to cut the blackness from my head, and he kept cutting, perhaps for a hundred years, until the dark had relented to the light. Once my soul accepted the purity of E'lan once more, and my eyes no longer ached, I determined to keep my hair short to remind myself of how close I had come to the precipice. Gedz'iel does the same as a sign of solidarity with me."

A humble smile replaced the sombreness of Koi's confession. He held out his hands for all to see. The word *love* across one set of knuckles, *hate* upon the other.

"I marked myself to remind myself each and every day. Love and hate have the same power. They can do great good or great evil. Love once turned me to hate, and hate turned me back to love."

There was a muttering of surprise around the room.

Lorcan screwed up his face, "You're serious? You trust a Daimon can rehabilitate?"

"Yes," Koi replied. "That's not to say we should be lax around Ben, but he was once, as Nik'ael, a good citizen of the Earth, just like I was. His sins are greater than mine, his redemption more uncertain, but I've seen the other side, felt it, yearned for it, and yet returned to you. If what Sophia says is true, then Ben would be a valuable tool against Yeqon. He will have seen and heard much that we have not. Sophia has proven, if not a little uncouth, to have so far served her destiny well, and I trust her instincts. Support and protect her, and we will succeed. Of that I am certain," Koi smiled at me. It warmed my heart to know he supported me.

"Succeed? We have precious little to go on so far," Lorcan muttered through his teeth. "Sorry, Koi, but I don't want to consort with Daimon."

"Neither do I," Jude grumbled, his face pinched tight.

"Precious little to go on?" I bristled. "Let me fill you in on what I've achieved. Back in a sec."

I transferred to the Zythros stone, retrieved the Kaladai cog, and returned to the Stasis room, stumbling to an undignified stop in front of Gedz'iel.

Interest brightened his eyes; he leaned closer to me. "What is this?"

"Nice transfer Soph, very nearly ladylike," Brennan gave me thumbs-up to which Ged'ziel frowned.

"I have something to show you, all," I held my backpack out for Gedz'iel and winked at Brennan, who smiled encouragingly. I pulled out the brilliantly silver cog and held it out for all to see.

Gedz'iel took the prize gently from my grasp, eyes wide, and held it aloft. His face lit.

"By the blessings of I'el, Sophia. This is a dial of the Kaladai," his fingers smoothed along the surface as he turned it over, his eyes a swirling cosmos of delight.

Enli'el gasped. The keepers were drawn straight to the cog. They buzzed to it like bees to a flower. Cael's wheels ground across the floor and underpinned their hum.

"It is the purest virgin chromious from the mines of A'vean," Gedz'iel said. "Only the great Uriel has ever possessed its building blocks. He would only pass such knowledge to the worthiest and most intelligent human."

"And I think I know who created it," I said.

"Who?" everyone asked, almost in unison.

"I'll keep that close to home until I'm a hundred percent sure, but my little adventure to Australia with Ben has pointed me towards the next stop."

Gedz'iel passed the dial to Koi, whose reflection glimmered in the perfect surface.

"My dear, Sophia. Where did you find this?" Koi asked.

Gedz'iel retrieved it from Koi and held it with reverent care, "Indeed, where did you uncover it, young one?"

Jude *hmphed* and gave me a sharp nod, his version of a pat on the back, I assumed.

"Well, actually, it's what's left of Enoch's box. It was somehow concealed as the box, which is probably why it was empty. It kind of melted into this," the memory still gave me chills.

Brennan pulled me in for a quick hug.

"Incredible," Koi said.

"It was bloody amazing," Brennan added.

"You were with her?" Lorcan asked. "You saw it?"

"Of course!" Brennan squeezed me tighter and winked. "She chooses her company wisely," he slid his arm away.

Lorcan scoffed and returned to idolising the Kaladai dial.

"You never cease to amaze us, Sophia," Cael said.

"Well done, dear," Enl'iel said. "I am so proud of you," she hugged her waist and rocked contentedly.

"You have done well, young one, but there is much more to discover," Gedz'iel said. "This is an excellent beginning, but even more so now, you must concentrate on the task at hand," he held the dial under one arm and pressed it into his battle-bruised chest like he was trying to absorb its energy. He took my chin gently in his other hand. "You have our fallen so close to redemption. My faith in you grows every day. I'el believes in you, and…"

A cry cut Gedz'iel off. There was scuffling in the background. Something shattered.

"Enl'iel, she is lost!" an Alchemae cried.

Enl'iel rushed back to fitting Afflicted and placed a hand to her forehead.

The rest of us watched, helpless.

"Such a dreadful shame," Enl'iel whispered. "If only we found the Great Healer. If only we knew if he were real."

The Afflicted twitched and jerked; her mouth gaped wide in a silent scream. Veins pulsed to the surface, twisted rivers of blue strained under her skin. Welts hatched across her body, gnawed without pity down her limbs. The Alchemae continued to fuss despite there being nothing they could do.

The Afflicted's A'vean mark sputtered on and off. Her veins paled into white.

"What's happening?" I asked.

It was like watching a car wreck. I didn't want to look at the terror of her demise, yet I couldn't look away either.

Cael squeezed my hand as he wheeled further away from the Afflicted, urging me to do so as well. Enli'el followed suit. The Alchemae dropped what they'd been holding and backed away behind the preparation bench. Gedz'iel fanned his wings out in front of us, and we watched through the haze of his protection.

"Keep your distance," he instructed.

Enli'el dashed in next to me, saw the look of confusion on my face. "Once we pass a certain corporeal temperature, the mortal vessel cannot survive. I'm afraid this is what happens to those with severe Thanratos withdrawal," she squeezed my hand gently.

The Afflicted's gaunt frame fluctuated between rigor and flaccidity. Her eyes flung open, her mouth loose, a high-pitched scream echoed around the room.

The Alchemae lit fresh lanterns of smoking herbs, using large herbal sheaves to waft the smoke towards her.

Tension caught the E'lan, and its tendrils flickered around us. Brennan, Jude, Lorcan, and Koi huddled closer to Enli'el and me. The Alchemae backed further away.

There was a loud *pop*, like cracking bone.

Brilliant incandescence beamed from the Afflicted's eyes. The torch-like sabres scored the ceiling and left charred circles when they dulled. Her chin slackened into a grotesque yawn as the same light shone from within her throat and bounced off a metal lantern, zigzagging above us and glancing off anything shiny. A melancholy moan followed, a heart-wrenching, frightening drawl.

The light shot towards me.

Brennan pulled me out of its way and yanked me down. We weaved and ducked dozens of blistering shots. Every hair on my body stood on end.

The Afflicted set into rigor and elevated off the bed. Her lithe form hovered a few feet up. Long wispy hair billowed across the sheets.

"May you find peace now," Enl'iel said.

Power burst from the centre of the Afflicted's chest. It fanned out and sucked back into her with another *pop*. For a fraction of time, there was an eerie quiet, as though time had stopped. There seemed to be no air, only a soundless void. No one moved. I was frozen, horrified. My pendant beat wildly.

A spinning light coalesced around her… and she exploded into a million diamond shards. Her luminescent remains collapsed onto the bed. Blue flames licked at a macabre, but beautiful, diamond skeleton. My fingers dug into Enl'iel's hand.

The screech of her inconsolable soul zoomed around the room. Its pained drawl chilled my blood anew. Her soul circled faster until she found the door — where she pierced through an accidental witness to the event. A tray with teacups and scones cluttered to the floor.

The soul disappeared.

I screamed. My head fuzzy, my throat tight.

Eilir collapsed, her chest charred where the Afflicted's soul had seared clean through.

Chapter
Twenty-Two

Eilir still clasped a red, blue and white tea towel in her hand. Dash had returned just in time to see her die.

"No!" he cried. Dash collapsed next to her, dragging her body into his lap. He shook her gently, called her name over and over. He pulled her head into his chest, stroked her hair, not giving an inch of her away.

I was frozen, gripped by shock, I couldn't breathe.

Enl'iel was the first to move. She rushed over and covered Eilir's gaping chest wound with a sheet.

"Please don't go?" Dash said. "Please, dear Eilir, my love?"

Enl'iel kneeled and draped her arms around his shoulders. She said nothing but shared his tears.

My eyes burned. My chest was too tight. Lorcan hugged me close, and I leaned into him. When he let go, I sank to the floor, my knees unwilling to hold me up.

Alchemae kneeled around Eilir and wailed for her. Their smooth ululations of mourning pierced my heart, shuddered through every cell of me. Gedz'iel and Koi gathered behind Dash, their heads lowered. Cael's hand on my shoulder reminded me that I was awake, that this wasn't a nightmare.

Jude's hard eyes rimmed red as he edged close behind Dash. Brennan and Lorcan followed. They all swiped their hands across their foreheads and raised them to the ceiling. It was a great honour that showed how loved Eilir was. A human amongst angels.

Gedz'iel leaned down and placed his hand on Dash's shoulder.

"It is time, brother, I am truly sorry for your pain."

Dash blinked up at Gedz'iel. His lips quivered as he let go of his strength. Tears pooled around his mouth.

"Why?" Dash asked. "Why are we to love only those that He chooses?" his mouth trembled, his body crumpled around Eilir.

Gedz'iel shook his head, "It is not for us to question the Throne."

"Does she not have a soul? Did he not make humanity in his own image? We look the same, feel the same. We fit together and love the same. We are all souls of A'vean!" Dash sucked in his whimpers, trying to regain control. "Our origin is the same. Please?" he drew Eilir closer. "Gedz'iel, please. Bring her back to me?"

My heart broke. I felt his agony like glass slicing though my chest, and I was angry. Who was I'el to decide where love should blossom?

"Beyond your grief, you understand the answer," Gedz'iel said to Dash. "We poisoned the apples by giving humans knowledge they couldn't comprehend or control. It was never our place to allow emotion into our mission to protect them. Our weakness led to theirs. I am sorry for your pain, Dash'iel. She was special to us all."

Dash sobbed. "I don't accept that," he pressed his cheek to Eilir's. "Forgive me, sweet Eilir, for dragging you into our world," Dash smoothed her grey hair and kissed the top of her head. "I will never regret loving you, no matter the consequences."

Eilir had paled into the pasty yellow of death. The Alchemae seemed to know what needed to be done. They began to chant a low melancholy tune, reminiscent of monks. It was haunting.

After a few more minutes, Gedz'iel kneeled by Dash's side and touched Eilir's cheek, sliding his cupped hand under her jaw. He sighed, a cheerless and tired sound, and held out his arms. Dash's eyes pleaded for what couldn't be, but he stood and passed Eilir's body to Gedz'iel. She looked like a child as he lay her onto a bed.

The Alchemae ceased their mourning song and afforded Eilir the same death rights as they had the Afflicted. They draped her with sweet-smelling herbs and sat a lavender wreath atop her head. Dash held her hand to his cheek and placed a soul stone into it.

Gedz'iel kneeled by Eilir's bed. "In the name of I'el and the Throne of A'vean, I call to you, Eilir of Crickhowell. Child of the Earth, I urge your soul to come forth," he placed a hand above her heart and behind her head. "Do not be afraid. Let yourself be free."

Dash sniffed back tears but couldn't halt their flow. A trail of silver glistened down his face as he lay her hand back across her chest.

My skin prickled.

A quiet moan arose from Eilir. It grew louder until it was a light, rhythmic song. Then it changed pitch to an unbroken scream, a terrifying and desperate cry.

I covered my ears.

"Don't be scared, Princess," Brennan said. "Her soul is trying to understand what's happening. She's accepting the separation from her body."

Enl'iel held Dash steady, whispering comforting words to him.

Gedz'iel worked his hands above Eilir's heart and head. Light arced from his fingertips and pulsed above her, imparting a marbled hue to her skin.

Eilir's mouth fell open, and her scream stopped. An opaque white mist emerged from within her throat. It eked out until it hovered above the bed in a cumulus formation. The moan returned, building again within the mist above her. Without warning, the gaseous entity shot around the room, spiralling faster and louder by the second. The scream which trailed the strange white mass evolved from desperation to laughter. It whizzed past me, blowing my hair into a mess. It zigzagged between the Alchemae and Dash. Eilir's soul halted in front of him. She glowed a little brighter and slipped around his neck like a smoky scarf. Small zaps of lightning lit up within her roiling cloud. Dash ran his hand over her, his fingers entwining with her soft form.

"Go, my love," Dash said. "Rest after all these years. We will see each other soon," he smiled. His tears had dried, and a rosiness had returned to his tanned cheeks.

Eilir slipped from his shoulders and spun around his head in a giddy display.

Gedz'iel reach his hand out to her soul, "Come, Eilir."

She halted, pulsed like a beacon, and stretched into an oblong. The shape bobbed a few times before materialising into a beautiful, ebony-haired young woman with eyes as rich as emeralds.

Eilir's spectral form spun in wonder, "Oh, look at me! Will you just look at me?" Her luxurious hair swirled down her back. She giggled with delight.

Dash gazed at her. "It's like the day I first saw you. You are so beautiful. You always have been," his voice caught, he pressed his hand over his heart.

Eilir smiled and ghosted a kiss onto his lips. "Don't get all blubbery now. I didn't feel a thing. It was time for me to move on; a blessing in disguise really. That body was no friend to me anymore, dearest Dash," she slipped her misty hand into his.

Dash hugged her into his chest. She nuzzled into him, a perfect fit.

"Despite the rules, despite the consequences, between this world and all the others, you are the only love I've had in all my days," he said.

Eilir brightened, more luminous than before. She pulled away and looked at us before turning back to him. She took Dash's face into her ethereal hands, and he leaned into them.

"Sweet Dash. Cry not for me or for us," she said. "Cry not for what could have been. You gave me more than anyone could ask for in a thousand lifetimes. Help dear Sophia and your kin. We will meet again when she wins this war and unites the realms."

They embraced once more; their foreheads touched before she relinquished him.

Eilir floated towards Gedz'iel and threw her arms up in the air, "I don't know at all where I'm to go. Can you help me?"

"Of course, sister," Gedz'iel said. "Take my hand."

Eilir looked back one last time, waved to me, and let her eyes linger on Dash.

"I will return soon," Gedz'iel said. He disappeared in a cracking flash.

A shocked quiet settled over us. Koi handed the Kaladai dial back to me. I placed it in my bag and sat by Dash, who squatted on the floor. His skin quivered slightly.

"I'm so sorry, Dash," I said.

He sniffed and wiped his nose with the back of his hand, "You don't need to be sorry for anything. She does," Dash pointed at the diamond remains of the Afflicted. He jumped up and ran to the skeleton. With a speed and force that defied all laws, Dash screamed and smashed the remains into dust.

Koi pulled Dash's arms, but he twisted away from Koi.

"Let me go Koi!" he grunted angrily.

"She wasn't in control of her ascension," Koi said, grabbing him again. "It was an accident."

Dash broke free and took a swing at Koi. His fist opened a fresh wound where it glanced off Koi's cheek. Jude tackled Dash to the floor. They rolled until they were smeared in dirt. Dash crawled into a squat; his eyes wide and wild. He swung at Jude again.

"Cut it out!" Jude grabbed Dash's fists and threw him onto his backside.

Dash scrambled up. "Get away from me! All of you!" he stumbled, glaring around the room.

"Dash?" Enl'iel called to him.

"Stay away!" his face glowed strangely. His mark flickered. One by one, each swirl and curve receded, its light fading as though it had never been there.

Jude raised his palms, "What are you doing, Dash? Stop, brother!"

Koi mirrored Jude. "Dash?" Koi asked, a nervous edge in his voice.

"Dash? Please, try to be reasonable," Brennan said.

Lorcan stood very still next to me. He swore to himself and clenched his fists. "Don't do it," he whispered.

"What's going on?" I asked.

A distinctly different energy had entered the room; heavy and hot, nothing uplifting about it at all. The Alchemae receded to the shadows.

"Dash, don't be a coward," Jude growled, less anger and more nervousness in his tough-as-nails voice.

Dash's wings emerged, soft and white. A strange serenity descended over him. A small power vortex emerged atop his hands which moved with speed, rolling over and over. The power pulled the Thanratos of the destroyed Afflicted's body into a plume. He dumped the glittery remains into a dish by the bedside.

"This may be of use, later," Dash said to no one in particular. He moved to Eilir's earthly remains.

Dash placed a handful of lavender and rosemary into her palms and closed her fingers. He threaded a strand of grey hair behind her ear. His hands clenched in time with the grinding of his jaw. He looked at us vacantly as he undid his weapons belt and threw it across the bed to Jude.

Jude stepped closer. "Stop this, mate."

"We need you, Dash," Koi said. "Now more than ever," his cheek had swollen into a shiny red lump. One of his hands lit, and he offered it to Dash. "Take my strength and stay."

Dash stared at Koi's hand and shook his head. "No," he closed his eyes.

I grabbed Lorcan's arm, utterly confused. "What's going on?"

"Eilir needs me more," Dash said. "She will be alone and scared. Forgive me."

Enl'iel began to cry.

"Dash, this was an accident," Koi said. "What you're about to do isn't."

"You're perfectly right," Dash said. "She wasn't in control of her ascension, but I am in control of mine."

My blood chilled.

Dash's wings enveloped him. The others rushed at him, but he was already untouchable.

Through the soft haze of his pulsating wings, Dash threw his head back and stretched his arms wide. The E'lan soared. Dash surrounded himself in a cyclonic electrical storm. He was like the nucleus of unimaginable energy. The iridescent cage forced us to retreat, just as with the Afflicted woman's demise.

A deep hum filled the room as Dash ascended by pure will alone. One moment, he was a tall, powerful soldier of the cosmos. The next, he was a frozen caricature of himself with translucent skin. His veins glowed as his life pulsed out of his rigid flesh.

I screamed through the chaotic noise, but there was no point. His attention and heart were elsewhere.

An intense opaque whiteness engulfed him and erupted in blue flames.

"Bury my remains with Eilir," his voice a deep echo. "I will see you all again when Sophia is victorious."

The flames exploded, leaving a pile of smouldering ash and a perfect diamond skeleton.

I couldn't take my eyes off the place where Dash had ascended. I hadn't noticed Gedz'iel return, but he kneeled before Dash's remains with his head in his hands.

"Do as he wishes," Gedz'iel sighed.

The Alchemae collected the skeleton and whisked it away. They shrouded Eilir and moved her on, too.

Gedz'iel shook his head, "This war is not worth the cost."

Koi's eyes glazed over, "Trackers are on the way."

Gedz'iel peered over his shoulder at Koi, "Where do they come from?"

"They'll arrive imminently with word of…"

Three bright lights appeared in the room and snapped into the form of female trackers, splattered with blood. An Alchemae began patting them down.

"Master Gedz'iel," the tallest one said. "It is the Unseen. Their realm has ripped wide open. We entered to find it practically deserted. They are all over Earth."

Gedz'iel balled his hands into fists. For the first time, his supernova eyes showed true fear.

"We traversed the Americas, Australia and Asia," another tracker said. "They are everywhere and openly attacking humans. The human populace is in panic. War will be irreversible if we cannot bring Yeqon to heel. Governments are concluding it as definite terrorism now, and the response is as you can imagine."

Gedz'iel pummelled his fists into each other and paced, "They've baited us into a corner."

"How do they attack?" Koi asked.

"In local places of gathering without care nor heed for being noticed. They released Rogues in a market on the outskirts of Osaka, to name just one. It was all we could do to contain them and repair the memories of those affected. And..."

"And what?" Koi asked impatiently.

"The vampires previously reported throughout Mexico have grown in number as well. They are running separately from the Rogues."

E'lan's anger licked the air with a barrage of electric snaps.

Koi's nostrils flared. "Vampires on their own?" he glanced at Gedz'iel and rubbed his knuckles. "She wouldn't, would she?"

Gedz'iel wrapped his hands over Koi's and nodded. Why did Koi seem so undone?

"She will if he has discarded her," Gedz'iel murmured. "Her existence depends on him and them."

"Are you talking about Lilith?" I plucked at my soul stone, wishing I'd never see her again. The familiar mix of fear and anger churned back to life in my gut.

"Yes," Gedz'iel said. "You may well have another enemy to worry about." The mark on his face blazed, "Koi, I'll meet you in the armoury. We will have to recruit the Hidden whether they like it or not. No one who is fit and able is to be left behind. Keep just enough sentries on guard here to protect the young. Lorcan, Brennan and Jude will stay with Sophia as she has requested. If he sets one foot wrong, you may descend Ben."

The boys shuffled and glanced at me.

"Enl'iel, call in all the medics you can to assist our healers," Gedz'iel said. "I fear we will have many casualties."

She nodded and headed to the prep table, where she pulled down dried herbs and collected bowls and pestles.

Gedz'iel turned to me.

"It's not what you want to hear, but the reality is that there is an incredible danger out there. You've seen it. I cannot leave humans to be Yeqon's cannon fodder. Somehow, he knows you are closer to the key, and he knows we can't ignore this diversion. We are relying on you to take your own lead," Gedz'iel said.

I bowed my head and didn't look up until they had disappeared. My heart hammered against my ribs. Hearing Lilith's name didn't at all suit me. Yet, I knew no Daimon, no vampire would stop me. There was a sting in my lip where I'd bit too hard.

All were gone but the Alchemae, Enl'iel, Brennan, Lorcan, and Jude. My back burned, my face ached, and my veins screamed. I let my wings release with sweet relief.

"I'm done with this crap," I said. "First things first, I'm finding Jaz." I pulled the rest of the hair out of my pocket, "And then this portal key will be mine, and I will ram it down Yeqon's throat."

Chapter
Twenty-Three

A gull squawked below a silky night sky. Buffeted by the growing gale, it rushed to a nest in a chalky cliff. Waves crashed below. Salty foam clung to the rocky coastline.

Anjou'elle slipped on the icy ground.

"Damn it! Look at my clothes, will you?" she shook a ragged Afflicted by his scruff. He cowered by her feet. "Find the Great Healer, sister says! She wishes me to chase a myth! Sister has sent me on a fool's errand. She just wants my pet to herself. You know, I do think she has a soft spot for humans, despite what she says. What do you think?"

She pulled the Afflicted along, his bare feet tripping and sliding across the frozen ground.

"Cat got your tongue?"

Anjou'elle throttled him. His eyes bulged; his crusty lips quivered.

"Do not ignore me. I asked your opinion, and I expect a timely answer."

Although taller and broader than her, the male shied from her every move.

Anjou'elle tutted. A wry smile tugged at her mouth. She leaned closer to his face, took in every curve.

"Hmm," she plucked up a piece of his hair and smoothed it behind his ear.

She licked her lips, "I see there was beauty here once."

He gulped. A grunt underpinned his rattling breaths.

"I wish… to be saved," he spluttered.

Anjou'elle laughed and pulled him faster across the muddy landscape. He tripped when lightning forked the horizon.

Anjou'elle stopped and turned towards him. He cowered under the thunderous sky and Anjou'elle's dark visage.

"I won't hurt you, you fool," she said. "Not unless you give me cause."

He stretched a little taller but didn't meet her eyes.

"You wish to be saved; you say? This is why you volunteered to assist me?"

He nodded and pulled his ragged clothing tighter against the cold.

"Pity you didn't think of this before you took the drug," she said. "So, tell me, is there any truth to this Great Healer tale?"

The ocean thundered behind them. Across the velvety black of the roiling waters, France and Nephr'eus awaited their return.

He coughed a few times to free his voice. "I… have only heard… rumours," there was a notable accent upon his words.

"Hmm, Russian. You're a long way from home."

He nodded.

"Not been in France for a long time, I would imagine?"

He nodded.

"Do you have a name?"

"Serg'ail."

"I like that," Anjou'elle said. "I'll call you Sergei for short. That's a lovely Russian name, don't you think?"

Sergei nodded again.

Anjou'elle pulled him into a faster walk. They traversed a grassy slope far away from the shoreline.

His condition worsened the further they went. Sweat poured from him in the freezing night air; white streaks settled in the creases of his face where the salt dried. Anjou'elle's eyes flickered over his sickly torso.

"You don't have long before you descend. What do you know about this healer?"

They crested a small hill and took in the sparse landscape ahead. Miles of rolling rock-strewn hills, moonlight their only beacon.

The male shuddered. He coughed and sniffed back a stream of snot.

"It is said… he moves underground, picking up those he deems…" he coughed harder, "…worthy."

She slapped her stomach and laughed, "Good luck to you then. I don't suppose he helps those who toil for the likes of us?"

Sergei stumbled over his bare feet and yelped. "No, I suppose… he would not," he coughed uncontrollably.

Anjou'elle crossed her arms and rolled her eyes as she waited for him to recover.

"There, there. It's okay, pet," she pulled at his arm to help him stand. She patted his hand. "I'll encourage him heal to you. I am very persuasive when I wish to be," she winked and fiddled with a wisp of static between her fingertips. "Where underground would one look? Have you ever known one of your own to be cured?"

The Afflicted shook his head and cowered.

"Oh, will you stop that," Anjou'elle tutted impatiently. "You bore me to my death. I'm not going to hurt you; you're doing that well enough by yourself!"

"Now, tell me what you know, and be quick about it."

He drew a deep, raspy breath. "A woman from my old clan was supposedly close to the Healer," his face contorted when he coughed again.

Anjou'elle pursed her lips. She lit her hand and held it to his back. He drew a deeper breath and sighed as his cough eased. His lips quivered a small smile of gratitude.

"Well?" Anjou'elle encouraged as they continued on their way.

"It is said she rescued him from a poor childhood as a prisoner to humans. She succumbed to the drug sometime after. That's what urged him to seek a cure."

"Hmm, interesting," she cooed. The power she could wield with such a cure… Anjou'elle's mark flickered to life but faded just as quickly.

The wind picked up. She brushed her hair from her eyes and cursed at the turning weather when a wet leaf smacked against her mouth.

"Perfect weather is the only part of A'vean I miss. None of this!" Anjou'elle pointed towards an abandoned church when freezing sleet began to fall, "Over there."

She pulled Sergei into a run until they came to an ancient waist-high stone fence, half-hidden behind stalky weeds. She pulled him past it, winding through gravestones that sunk and lurched under time's weight. They rushed through an arched doorway into the ruins.

The stone edifice missed its window panes where the wind whistled through. Leaves whipped up into a frenzied dance, sucked away on the storm's next breath.

Sergei slumped against the remnants of an altar, "I'm sick."

Anjou'elle paced in front of him, "Then tell me everything you know, and you might just get cured."

His sunken eyes widened at Anjou'elle, "I have never wanted anything more. This is torture."

"Well, don't expect sympathy now. No one forced Thanratos down your throat!" her hands slipped to her waist. "The moment this storm passes, I will leave. If you don't want to be left behind to descend alone, tell me more of who and where the Great Healer is."

Sergei pulled himself back up a little. His bony knees dug into the uneven stone floor. He leaned one shoulder against the altar to steady himself, licked his dry lips, and tried to rub warmth into his arms.

"I'll tell you what I've heard, but please, will you help me first if we find him?" his voiced wavered.

"You're not in a position to bargain," Anjou'elle's brows arched. "However, if your assistance pleases me, I may consider it a reward."

Moonlight reached through the rotten thatch roof. Lightning preceded thunder, and Sergei startled.

"Get on with it, pet," Anjou'elle flapped her hand at him to hurry.

"He's a hybrid, that's a common rumour. The son of a Daimon is another. It's said he is quite young too."

"Well, well. Interesting. Go on," she encouraged with a casual wave. Her pacing halted; her eyes more keenly fixed upon Sergei.

"He's never left Britain and stays underground near the place of his childhood. He draws strength and knowledge from the Watchers in secret. If that's true, he would need to be close to them," Sergei clasped his head and groaned. "The pain…. make it stop!" he slumped lower to the ground.

Anjou'elle tipped her head to one side, "And you know all this how?"

Sergei coughed and wretched. Mucous dribbled from his nose and mouth, and he shuddered with fever.

Anjou'elle sighed and used a lace kerchief to wipe his mouth. She burned away the defiled square and stayed by his side, kneeling close enough that he could smell her perfume.

"There, there. Tell Anjou'elle everything."

Her lips pouted; she bit them to draw a lustier blush. Heat flushed to her cheeks as her mark fired. Its light exaggerated the shadows on Sergei's face, which now had an altogether different kind of flush to it. The pulse in his neck quickened. Anjou'elle licked her lips, making sure he was watching as she ran her tongue across the lower one.

She nuzzled his ear, licked the edge of his jaw, "Tell me all your secrets."

Sergei sighed, his lips parted, "The one… who cared for him was…"

"Yes?"

"More, please?" Sergei begged for her touch.

She masked her disgust and ran a finger along his dry lips.

"Tell me, and I will take away your pains in a way that Thanratos cannot," she lowered her voice, nibbled his ear some more.

Sergei moved closer to her. His breaths came quicker.

"Alen'ael saved him. She was the leader of my old clan. Find her, and you'll find him," Sergei groaned.

His eyes rolled back in ecstasy as she nuzzled his neck.

"Keep talking, kitten. You're making Anjou'elle very happy."

Sergei's pulse surged under his paper-thin skin.

"Alena was the only one he detoxified with success."

"And where does she reside?"

"I'm not sure."

Anjou'elle pinched his ear. He yelped and talked faster.

"They lived below a river near a Watcher enclave, but I can't be certain. Brother Anton told me after we defected from Yeqon weeks ago, when he attacked the Watchers in Tewkesbury."

Sergei groaned some more as Anjou'elle moved her hand across his chest. She slipped it under the shirt. Her nails dug into his chest. He moaned.

"Go on," she cooed.

"He said he saw Alena with an unusual Watcher. No fighting gear, more like a monk. They were watching the Earth-born from the rooftops."

Anjou'elle tensed.

"Tewkesbury is near Katoika. The Avon runs beyond it. How delightful," she bit her lip in thought, ran slender fingers up to his throat and circled her nails along his neck. He groaned deeper.

Lightning struck nearby, and thunder roared. The wind howled. A thick patch of roof peeled away.

Anjou'elle leaned back on her haunches and looked up at the dark, pregnant clouds. A few white flashes, not of meteorological origin, dashed amongst the lightning. Raindrops splashed onto her face. Her mouth widened into a glorious smile.

"This world does not appreciate Anjou'elle," she laughed, a full and resounding cackle, and stood. Her wings emerged with a brilliance that lit the entire ruins. "Change of plan, dear Sergei. See what's coming?"

She pointed at the sky and at the ground. A thick sea of fog encroached the landscape; more white flashes merged with the lightning strikes.

"The Great Healer is small change. Anjou'elle has a better plan."

Sergei shrivelled away from her, "What do you mean?"

"This Earth and its pleasures so easily ruin the weak like you," she said. "The strong prevail, and I am the strength of the elements. I am your God. To me, your truth is your redemption and your demise."

Lightning pierced the ceiling and set the last of the ancient thatch ablaze. Rain poured in. She gathered Sergei into her arms, but the lust had drained from his skin.

"I shall fly with the lightning as the Watchers do, hidden in its beautiful song."

Anjou'elle sighed with satisfaction. She breathed in the stormy air as it lashed her face. She rose into the air, her wings snapped like liquid light. She sliced Sergei in two.

"Sorry, pet. I've my own redemption to attend to."

With the next lightning bolt, Anjou'elle had vanished.

Chapter
Twenty-Four

I stood in front of the Zythros stone, my body still burning from the anger-filled transfer. Brennan called for me in my mind, but I ignored him. I paced around the stone, the precious Kaladai dial pressed against my chest. One hand still clasped Jaz' hair. Her energy was strong, and that gave me hope.

People rushed about with more purpose than usual. I awaited the right moment to place the artefact back.

Nothing would move forward until I found Jaz, especially now Yeqon had shown his hand. It was distracting me too much. If that meant the search for the rest of the Kaladai was temporarily hampered, then I could live with that, but Jaz wouldn't if I didn't find her. She was integral to this journey, not just collateral damage. She was part of my past, and my past was part of me. My gut churned with worry. Where was she? Was it worse than Yeqon? Memories of how he treated me were raw. The way I'd found Rik brought bile to my throat.

As the hall became silent, I walked onto the platform where the beautiful salt stone sat in all its splendour. It was pulsing brighter than usual. I circled it, my hand rising and falling along its indentations. Halfway around, I rested my ear against it. A million voices surged through the geological world wide web. I couldn't make sense of any one conversation, but I did pick up a few alarming words; *attack*, *Rogue*, *vampire*, and *help*.

"Oh no," I whispered to myself. The world was panicking.

"What troubles you, sister?"

I gasped, startled. I'd thought I was alone.

"Rik?"

He leaned against a nearby column of rock which bordered the stairs. Unlike everyone else, he was still dressed in all black. His expression reflected his outfit. He flicked his fingernails against one another like a nervous tic.

He uncrossed his arms and tucked his hands into his pockets.

"You seem distracted. What are you doing here?" he asked.

"What are *you* doing here?" I was taken aback that he was actually talking to me. "Are you lost?"

"Lost? I am found, am I not? And by my dear sister, no less," he bowed with a sarcastic smile. That smile evaporated as he straightened.

Confused and hurt, I slung my backpack over my shoulders. I felt a strange sudden urgency to hide my prize from his prying eyes.

I kept my pack out of his sight, "You should go train, Rik. We might require you to go into battle… if you're ready, that is?"

"I'm ready," he sauntered over and leaned against the Zythros stone. He closed his eyes and seemed to breathe it in.

"You may not think enough of me to save me, but I'm ready to defend and serve, sister. I know my place," he pushed away from the stone and scowled as he walked down the stairs. He turned back as if to say something else, but instead ran his hands through his hair and sighed, "Finish whatever you're doing here. It's clearly not any of my business."

"Rik, please. I'm sorry."

"Me too, sister, me too," he disappeared into the shadows of the doorway.

I punched the stone. It pulsed where I'd hit it.

"Don't you give me crap as well!"

Before I began talking to other inanimate objects, I hid the bag where Brennan had and puffed out a relieved sigh. I readied myself to leave but a shadow swept past the door. It couldn't be that Asmodai, that thing was well and truly dead.

"Rik?"

No answer. I rubbed my temples. I was tired, frustrated, and just a tad overwhelmed. Maybe it was my imagination. I checked once more that no one had seen me and transferred away with a plan, and the feeling that someone was following me again.

I forced my mind back on task as I made my way through the bustling corridors. I wasn't sure my plan would work, but after the shock of Eilir's death and Dash's ascension, I wanted to leave quickly and quietly. I ducked vines heavy with flowers and rounded the last corner.

"Took your time," Brennan teased.

"Funny," I said. "Where are the others? I want to get going."

Brennan pointed to the door that led to the cells. We entered together.

"Why is it so dark?" I asked.

"Do I have to do everything by myself?" Jude grumbled. He tossed a small orb into the air and revealed what both he and Lorcan were up to. Jude had one of the guard's elbows wrenched behind his back whilst Lorcan clenched his fingers around the guards temples. The guard quickly slumped, asleep.

"Best that fewer people know we're travelling with a stinking Daimon," Jude grumbled.

I leaned forwards to check the guard's pulse, "You haven't hurt him, have you?"

Jude snorted, "Nothing you haven't already done, Sophia. He's just having a nap, don't worry."

I cringed inwardly. "I know this goes against everything you believe, but I need you, Jude," I replied, feeling guilty for what I was asking of him.

Lorcan lowered the guard's head to the floor. Jude helped position him comfortably, tucking his weapons in easy reach for when he awoke. He looked up at me and took my hand in his.

"I need this too," Jude whispered and nodded to the others. "Just don't tell them."

Unsure what he meant, I squeezed his hand, relieved.

"Right, let's do this," I said. "Did you ask Thomas for the extra weapons?"

"Told him where my best stash is," Jude answered.

"Awesome, thank you," I said. "I know I'm asking a lot of you all, but I promise the second we find Jaz, one of you can bring her back here and I'll move straight onto the next phase of my search for the rest of the Kaladai."

"I'll bring her home," Jude said rather quickly. He tried to cover his enthusiasm with a scowl, but the extra glow of his mark betrayed him.

I smiled, "Thanks, Jude."

He nodded, folded his arms, and stared hard at the two cells.

"We've all got something to track with?" I asked.

Everyone nodded.

I reached for the hair in my pocket. Every touch sent an electric shot up my arm. The visions were the hardest. One moment Jaz was panting, my own throat tight for her, the next, my stomach churned as bile dribbled from her mouth. The longer I held that small part of her, the more intense was the pull I felt.

"Let's find her before anyone else gets hurt," I said.

"I assume you want my help?" Ben asked from the shadows. "You know, since you've incapacitated my guard and all?" he appeared at the red bars, still battered and bruised.

"I do," I said. "You're a strong link to her, and you're more familiar with Nephr'eus and Anjou'elle. You can approach them and pretend you can lead them to me."

Ben edged closer. "Sounds like an adventure," the whites of his eyes blazed crimson from the red of the bars. They looked devilish in that light.

I hoped to hell I was right.

"Between the five of us, we should be able to find Jaz and hopefully deal with Nephr'eus and Anjou'elle," I said. "You have pretty much zero trust with this group, Ben, so this is a good opportunity to redeem yourself, at least on Earth."

He shook his head with a derisive smirk, "You assume so much."

"I assume you don't want to return to Yeqon, and I assume you'd like an opportunity to defend yourself against I'el."

His smirk evaporated, "So what's your plan?".

"We'll disguise ourselves whilst Ben diverts the sisters' attention," I suggested.

"Hmph. Could work," Ben muttered.

Brennan turned me around, "You want to conceal yourself?"

"It got me away from Yeqon," I said.

Lorcan and Jude shook their heads.

"You will all have to conceal yourselves," Ben said. "I know where they reside, but Nephr'eus is no fool. She will sense you from miles away if you turn up like that."

My heart raced, "You know where they live? As in, exactly?"

Ben smiled. It annoyed me intensely but also warmed a small part of my heart too.

"Chateau Pouancé Manor," he said.

"Damn, that's where we just were," Lorcan said. "She was probably right under our noses."

Brennan threw his hands in the air, "Bloody hell!"

A tremble ran through my body. I wasn't sure if it was excitement or fear of what we might find.

Jude bumped his fists together, "What are we waiting for? Let's go bust some arse!"

"You'll need to conceal yourselves in a manner that's attractive to them," Ben said.

Jude moved closer to him. "And what would that be, Daimon?"

I kept myself between them, not entirely convinced Jude wouldn't do something stupid.

"New fighters for their cause, of course," Ben said. "Afflicted who are drawn to their generous pay cheque, if you know what I mean?" he jerked his eyebrows twice.

Jude scoffed, "You want us to conceal as one of those?"

"I'll stick with this, thanks," Lorcan pointed at himself. He was looking more Viking-esque than ever. He'd stopped shaving. A thick, long braid ran from the crown of his head and down his back. He'd threaded it with prickles and twigs. Along with the weapons dangling by his sides, he looked scary as hell.

"You may as well just announce your arrival via a megaphone," Brennan said.

"What's a megaphone?"

I giggled at Lorcan's naivety of human inventions.

"Never mind your brother," I said. "Ben's right, we have to blend into their world. It's how I got away from Yeqon, remember?"

"Soldiers do as is required, Lorcan," Jude said. "Suck it up, mate."

"Means to an end, pretty boys," Ben added smugly.

"Call us that again and your head will decorate the end of my sword!" Jude threatened.

"It would be my pleasure!" Ben added.

"Get over your egos. Time is wasting whilst you all act like gorillas punching your chests," I snapped.

"When you find your friend, I will have the answers you need," Belial's deep, dry voice filled my veins with hot anger.

I stomped towards his cell, "What the hell does that mean?"

He didn't step into the light, but I saw him well enough. I wanted to descend him right there, but I also didn't want to pass up good intel.

"I've heard your mumblings. I know the drug ails her. If she is alive, I can help you. I have knowledge that may prove fruitful to her survival."

Just the sound of his voice infuriated me.

"Shut up. You know nothing!" I gripped my weapons belt to stop my hands from shaking.

"Then nothing you will receive."

I stepped back, affronted by his attitude.

"There's nothing of value you could offer me besides your death," I turned away from Belial, drew my sword, and slashed open Ben's bars. "Out. And keep your hands out front where I can see them."

Ben stepped out, and Lorcan glued himself to my side.

Ben complied. I formed a fresh set of shackles and bound his wrists. He winced. They were tight, but I hadn't perfected this little trick yet.

He smiled, "I like the pain."

"You're lucky it's her putting them on you," Lorcan grumbled. "I'd have made them much tighter… enough to shut your mouth!"

I glared at Lorcan," Cut it out!"

I pointed at Ben's wrists, "You'll lose those when required."

"*Sophia,*" Enl'iel whispered into my mind. "*Whatever you're up to, make it quick. The change of guard is on its way. Please, don't get yourself killed?*"

"*I'll tuck you into bed with tea tonight,*" I responded.

I pushed Ben away from the cell.

"Time to go," I said. "Group transfer. Ready?"

I urged them in close, Ben on one side of me and Lorcan on the other. Brennan and Jude tolerated each other's proximity, their eyes on me rather than each other. My wings unfurled, and they followed suit. We huddled closer, our wings touching to hold us together. Each one of us rigid with tension, especially Ben. I kept him close, ready to kill or save him. Both options stirred something in my gut.

His comforting smell of ashes and spice made my head spin before I shook the superfluous thoughts away. He wouldn't muddle my mind.

It was time to bring Jaz home.

Chapter
Twenty-Five

The five of us stumbled onto icy ground. An insulting winter chill slapped away Kaymakli's warmth.

I tightened my chest guard and checked on my weapons. All were accounted for. My fingers grazed the diamond dagger, the comfort of it the strangest of things.

A small country town panned away behind us. There was no rush of cars, no sound of industry, only the chirping of birds in an overcast sky. A crisp early morning fog hugged a green-and-white landscape of undulating snowy fields. Scant trees broke the horizon in front of us. Lorcan forged ahead towards them. We followed, Ben close to me; the other two only a breath behind.

"Time to power down," Lorcan called.

We turned off everything that screamed *otherworldly*. Facial markings faded; wings retracted. We kept our eyes low lest someone noticed the unnatural swirling blues.

"How far?" I asked.

Lorcan pointed ahead, "About two to three miles. If Ben is telling the truth, the manor is at the back of the estate. Have you still got the hair?" Lorcan called back.

I pulled it out and immediately felt drawn forwards.

We walked at a brisk pace, and I was glad of it. I needed to release the tension from all that had transpired over the past hour.

"You really think Jaz is here?" I asked Ben as we approached a small field.

He smiled, *"New tricks are improving, I see."*

I stepped over an old stone fence, *"Just answer, please?"*

Ben jumped over it. *"Yes, she probably is,"* he raised his hand to shield the snow glare and pointed past Lorcan, *"That's the ruins of Pouancé."*

I squinted at a dark smudge against the white horizon.

Jude pushed Ben in the back, *"Move it!"*

Ben stumbled, and I grabbed his arm. He tensed under my hand.

"What else?" I asked.

We jumped a fence on the far side of the field. The snow was deeper; its arctic touch nearly reached my knees.

"This is Nephr'eus's territory. She's done whatever she's pleased here for a thousand years. I wouldn't be surprised what we find here, actually."

The distant blot became clearer; a large expanse of roofline that peaked above a crumbling perimeter wall.

"How does she have the freedom to do what she wants?" I asked. *"Doesn't Yeqon rule you all?"*

"He invests energy only where there's a payoff. She has nothing he wants, not until now, apparently. If he knew she's interfering, she'd be fodder for the Pits."

I bit my cold lips and pulled him along to keep up with Lorcan, fiddling constantly with my pendant.

"Don't worry," Ben said. *"I'll find her. I knew Jaz long enough to sniff her out."* He eyed my fist full of her hair. *"I don't need a piece of her to do that."*

I felt a little jealous that he knew Jaz better than I in some ways. I tucked the hair back into my pocket.

"You think they're expecting us?" I asked.

"Absolutely, but they won't be expecting me," Ben poked his chest and smiled.

"What will you say to them?"

"That I offer my services. They know I was with the Unseen for a long time. They'll sweat over me sharing intel. Besides, Nephr'eus was sweet on me once."

That last comment shouldn't have annoyed me.

"You think you can fool them?"

Ben laughed out loud.

"Shut up!" Jude growled and poked Ben's back.

Ben sneered to himself but didn't respond to Jude.

"You wound my pride," Ben glanced at me; his eyebrow quirked along with a self-satisfied half-smile. *"Did I not fool you?"*

"Smug, aren't you?" I said.

"Just well-practiced," Ben's smile faded and something inside me seemed to sink. *"You'll have to stay hidden until I call that it's safe, Soph. You're like chum to sharks in the ocean, even with those arses as your back-up."*

"Those arses are only not eating you alive because of me, so mind your manners."

"I can take care of myself!" he snapped

Ben clasped his fists together. His wrists were flaming red. *"You will have to trust me,"* he said, as though he knew what I was thinking.

"That's a big ask."

"It is. I wouldn't trust me."

Lorcan pulled up.

"How far now?" I asked.

Lorcan pointed left, "Not far. Do you see those ruins?"

They were larger than life, and only a short walk away.

"That's where we found the lair, but Jaz isn't there. Look past it, behind those trees," Lorcan said.

Beyond the crumbling ruins of Castle Pouancé, the edifice of the grand-looking home loomed clearer with every step we took.

Lorcan wriggled his fingers, "Pass me some more hair."

I pulled it back out, and heat rushed to my face. I had the intense urge to run in that direction.

"She's over there!" my throat tightened; my mouth dried.

Jude squeezed between Ben and I, "So, what does stupid here know? I saw you two having a little chat."

The others stopped and stared at me. My cheeks blazed for a different reason. I sighed with annoyance, pushed through them and kept walking.

"He was just telling me about Nephr'eus and what he can do to help, that's all."

"I bet he was," Lorcan whispered into my mind. *"I'm sure he has a bucketload to say now he's out of prison".*

Brennan elbowed him, *"Shut up, Lorcs. We stick to the plan, Soph. Ben is only here because of you. He makes no decisions."*

"Ditto," Jude said.

I sighed. I was sick of the effort of mind chatter, so I stopped and faced them. A smattering of snowflakes fell and melted on my cheeks. Their crispness calmed my impatience.

"Just hang on! Yes, I get that he's a Daimon!" I stared hard at Ben, who kept his mouth shut for a change. "But he knows Nephr'eus. He said she's lived here a long time, so Jaz has to be here. I can feel her!" I began walking again, held up her hair and the breeze tugged it towards the ruins, "You can sense her too, can't you, Lorcan?" I waved the hair towards him.

His face tightened. Agreeing with a Daimon, especially this one, would be hard for him.

"Well?"

The three of them bounced their attention between a stony-faced Ben and one another. Their marks glimmered on and off as they had a quick mind collaboration.

I crossed my arms; I would have tapped my foot, too, if it hadn't been knee-deep in snow. Lorcan groaned when Brennan turned to Ben, his face grave.

"Alright, get it out," Brennan said. "What do we do?"

Ben smirked. He was his own worst enemy. The boys tensed, but he got on with it. He was smug, not stupid.

He readjusted his hands against the shackles.

"Nephr'eus isn't easily outwitted, neither is her sister. Me departing Yeqon's company would have been big news; word of him bashing me senseless would have been like paparazzi fodder to them," Ben eyed his battered, shirtless torso.

Our eyes met fleetingly. That beating was no laughing matter. The raised bruises and gashes were a testament to Yeqon's brutality. Jude seemed unaffected, but Lorcan looked the other way. Brennan winced.

"They'll know I've been your prisoner," Ben said. "If I turn up bloody and battered with a few lackies asking to join with them, then there's your open door. It'll be a whole lot easier than fighting our way in only to have Jaz murdered in the process."

"It makes sense," I said. "We should play to their desires."

Jude rolled his eyes and shook his head, "Shit, it's a bloody good idea."

"Let him take the lead? Are you kidding?" If Lorcan's mouth had been any tighter it would have sealed shut.

"Bro, pipe down," Brennan said. "This isn't about your ego. Jude's right, it's a good plan. It would blindside them. They'll gush over a catch like the great Nik'ael walking in and offering his services."

Lorcan cracked his knuckles against his thighs. Light snaked through his mark. He swallowed hard, and it settled.

"Lorcan, c'mon," I pulled in close to him. I didn't want to humiliate him in front of Ben. "Enough of this," I whispered. "Between the four of us, we've got him covered. As I've said, he puts one foot out of line, I'll kill him myself. He's either here to redeem or condemn himself, his choice," I squeezed his arm and turned back to the others. "Let's go!"

I led the way past the ruins without looking back. The pull I felt was getting stronger.

The township of Pouancé fell away behind us. Snow-capped provincial rooftops fenced the chateau on all sides.

Ben fell back in line next to me, "I can sense her, but she's weak."

I nodded; nerves were swirling in my gut.

"Hate to agree with the squib, but she's not well," Lorcan said.

I picked up the pace. The crunch of our feet in the snow seemed too loud, my breaths too anxious.

"I know where she'll be," Ben said, he picked up his pace.

"Why this place?" I muttered more to myself.

"This old house was owned by the Count of Anjou long ago. Anjou'elle cosied up to him before she murdered him and all subsequent owners out of nothing other than boredom. It's a no-go zone for humans. The locals think its cursed. Good proximity to

Pouancé castle for their Afflicted slaves. They'll be in the cellars, away from prying eyes and ears. Far enough from the township that no one can… hear the screams," his voice cracked on those last words.

I swallowed hard; my heart thudded heavier in my chest.

Lorcan's shoulder butted against mine. He nodded at me, a weak, reassuring smile. "She's definitely here," he fell back only to shove Ben. "You go ahead then, Daimon. You can be cannon fodder. We'll follow," Lorcan said with too much joy in his voice.

Ben grimaced but held his anger in check.

We moved away from the chateau ruins and towards the smaller manor at the rear. We took shelter under a copse of slumbering Blackthorn trees as a brief sleet storm blew through. Gnarled roots, sprinkled with shrivelled fruits, clawed up from the earth. Wind whipped through the naked branches, causing them to creak and moan. As the wind died away and the sleet melted on our skin, we listened for E'lan's warning whilst we observed the house from afar. It was subdued for now, a soft hum.

The run-down country home appeared deserted. The snow stopped completely and my feet hit gravel. The quiet was unnerving. No birds, no breeze. Extensive gardens had long turned to weed, the perimeter fence missing bricks here and there. The twisted branches of an ancient vine stitched the stone façade together. A mossy slate roof capped it off. A small gravel drive circled up to a gated front door. Rusty topiary birds guarded it all.

Amongst the desolation was a vibrant, yet melancholy energy, a silent vibration disturbing the E'lan. My pendant thrummed in time with it.

I knew it was Jaz.

Ben turned and put up his hand, "Wait here."

I followed him. He turned again, both hands up to stop me.

"I said wait. Listen to me, Soph. Jaz is their leverage and you're the prize. There's no other reason for them to have her. If they get wind you're here, we will never get her out in one piece, and I mean that quite literally. Do you really think you can just rock up and hope they'll politely hand her over? These two may look sweet and pretty, but they're as ugly as hell on the inside. Do you want to find Jaz in shreds?" Ben asked.

"You know I don't want that!" I snapped. My jaw clenched; I forced the picture of Jaz' dead body from my mind.

"Then let me help you. Didn't I already do that once before?" Ben askcd again.

I nodded slowly.

"But…"

"But what? For the love of the angels, you talk a lot," Ben mumbled.

"Pull it in there, Daimon! Remember your place!" Brennan said.

"We could stay here all day, or you can let me go on ahead to scout it out. If it's just me seen, it won't really ring alarm bells and Sophia will be safe and cosy here with you three," Ben smiled and bowed, testing their resolve.

Brennan shoved him in the back, "Get going then!"

Ben walked a few feet on, then turned back, his eyes hooked mine. "Don't move from here, no matter what you hear, see, or sense, got it?"

I nodded, "Hurry up then. And remember, I will descend you if one cell of your being thinks about betraying me."

"I believe you would too, and I'd expect nothing less," Ben's eyes sparked bright blue. My guts twisted as those eyes then dilated into that frightening Daimon darkness.

He sped off in a stealthy run.

"What do you think?" I asked the others as I settled back into a nook in the crumbling fencing.

"Well… it's a bit late now he's gone!" Brennan whistled lightly. "We'll see soon enough. I suppose he hasn't got much more to lose at this point," Brennan leaned next to me. Lorcan and Jude stood out front, eyes keenly trailing Ben's fading shape.

Ben disappeared behind the rear of the building, leaving me apprehensive that I'd made a huge mistake. I twirled my pendant. He was a master manipulator, had fooled me for years; however, that was then. I had a new set of senses now.

I reminded myself of what Gedz'iel had said about Koi. Daimon could change. I held onto that.

"Don't you dare betray me again," I whispered.

Chapter
Twenty-Six

The darkness in Ben begged for release. It teased and tugged at the bitterness that still coated his veins. He bit his lip and pressed on his still-broken knuckle with his thumb. The sting woke his senses, reminding him of all he had lost and all he still could lose. The closer the manor loomed, the stronger the memories and longing became.

Neren'iel's body felt heavy across his lap, her blood washing away in the surf that lashed closer with each heavy wave. He squeezed his eyes shut and shook his head, trying to eradicate the vision, replacing it with one of Sophia instead.

The betrayal, the pain, and the loss were etched so deeply into his soul, but somewhere beyond it, something else warmed that cold and filled the emptiness. It made his darkness run and hide in the shadows where it belonged.

Ben peered back over his shoulder. He saw her silhouette sequestered just behind Brennan's bulking frame. Her goodness, her warmth and strength, pulled at the white light of his soul. Her purity barked at the darkness to retreat, all with a single look. Even from here, her beautiful eyes reached him, but she stayed near her guard dogs. She was safe, and that gave him comfort.

He took a deep breath and headed around the back to the basement doors. Heaving them open with the shackles proved painful. They teased out new blisters with every flexion. Each bite a penance, each pain a step to redemption. Perhaps.

"Here goes nothing," Ben mumbled to himself as he descended into the dank corridor.

He was more than happy to be free of Kaymakli's cells, yet he wasn't free of his self-imposed prison of self-loathing. One stone at a time, he was mentally dismantling it. What would be left of him, for him, if he ever tasted true freedom? Ben closed his eyes and pictured Sophia again. He shook his head and continued.

Up ahead, he heard a mumbled scream. His face lit, and his muscles coiled. He tilted his head to listen more closely. Ben knew that heartbeat, knew that aura, but something was off. Jaz wasn't quite right, not altogether there.

Ben knew her so well. He had protected her from herself and saved her from her lunatic parents. He had insulated her from the confused rage boiling in her soul. For the past twenty years, Jaz had been one of only two things that had kept some humanity alive in him. She was as grounding to him as she was to Sophia.

His heart raced faster, and his mark curled to life, coiling around his eye like an ever-present friend. His wings threatened to unravel. Another deep breath and sweeping vision of Neren'iel drew forth his hate and put his head where it needed to be.

The door was only feet away. Neren'iel's screams had died away in his mind, far into the depths of his memories. It was now only Jaz' mournful cries that assaulted his senses. He reached for the wrought-iron handle, unsure what he'd find. Active torture? Was she alone? His fingers closed around the latch when a cold rush brushed them away.

Ben scanned the darkness… nothing but curtains of webs. He grimaced and swore. He wasn't alone.

"Show yourself!"

The cool energy circled him, its unsettled energy familiar.

"You play a dangerous game, Revenant. I really don't have time for this."

Ben reached for the handle again, and his hands were pushed away once more.

"Who trespasses on my home?" the revenant hissed.

"If this is your home, I'd choose a different place to haunt."

The entity swished past him and made him shiver.

"My home is my home and will remain so. I chose them to be here," a smooth, distant voice echoed along the corridor.

Ben still didn't see him. The spirit concealed itself, chose not to be seen.

"You keep dangerous house guests then," Ben replied.

"And you are any less so?" the revenant asked.

"I am worse. If your guests knew of the poor reception you're affording me, I couldn't say how they would repay your insolence."

The entity whooshed and squealed around Ben and materialised in a smoky haze. A well-dressed gentleman, willowy and crowned in a powdered wig. Worry crinkled his pock-marked features. Brass buttons marched down a heavy brocade coat.

"You know of my, erm, guests?"

"I do. That's why I question your co-habitation. They are my friends, but I very much doubt that they are friends of yours. You're fooling yourself if you believe so," Ben said.

The ghost stumbled for words. His fingers fidgeted with his lace sleeves.

Ben smirked, "They acquired your home, I suspect?"

"How did you know?" the revenant faded before brightening again. His eyes travelled up and down Ben.

Ben smirked at it, "I've been here before, long before you. How did you come by this old place?"

The ghost's cheeks puffed. "I won it fair and square in a rather marvellous game of roulette," he held his be-wigged head high.

"This place was gambled away?" Ben snorted. "What a waste."

The revenant tutted, "It was a December evening. Too cold to be out. We were snowed in for days after our meeting to discuss the unrest before the revolution. Terrible times." The spirit shook his head. "As luck would have it, the previous count had a loathing for boredom and a love for gambling. I was losing all evening, and then voila, I took the house down with a brilliant win on red twenty-one. He had nought to pay, so it was either a duel or this lavish home. He was a coward and had no stand-in, so the house was mine," the memory put a brief glow of happiness into the spectres sallow, dead cheeks.

"Hardly a win really," Ben scoffed.

The ghost shook his head.

"It is true. I was murdered the first night I lay my head upon my luscious new bed. The count did seem too eager to hand it off to me, when I think on it. I suppose he did not enjoy the mistresses either."

Ben was growing edgy. The sudden quiet of Jaz' screams worried him. He smelled her sweat, and it had the sourness of illness.

"I am sorry for your misfortune," Ben said, "But I'm here on business. Let me pass."

"I… cannot. They will do worse things to me. I am bound to them, you see?" the revenant pointed at Ben's wrists.

"Go to the middle realm, they can't follow you there," Ben said.

"You misunderstand Sir, I am quite literally bound to them. As you are bound to someone, so am I to them until they choose to free me," he pointed to Ben's wrists.

"Their witchcraft binds me to these walls to alert them of intruders. I am sorry, but I cannot let you pass."

"And if you do let me pass?"

Even in spectral form, the man paled, "It is unspeakable what they are capable of. I have descendants; their claims of murdering my lineage have proven true."

Ben now worried those fools outside would let Sophia barge in too early.

"I'm here to stop their devilry, but only if you let me pass."

The revenant clasped his chest. "I thought you were friends, Sir!" he leaned in and whispered. "None can match them," his ghostly hand quivered by his mouth.

Ben smiled, darkened his eyes further, and leaned closer. "Well, old man, you don't know me," he punched his fists clean through the revenant's chest.

The ghost screeched, grabbed his perfectly intact chest, and began to circle. "No, no, no, no, this is not good!" he muttered agitatedly.

"Calm down, you fool!" Ben threw his head back, sighing impatiently when he'd rather blast it into oblivion. "Be quiet!" Ben whispered through his teeth.

"No, no, no, no! They are too powerful. I'll alert them to your plan. I will not suffer because of you!" he spun more feverishly, blurring with his worries.

Ben's power surged to his face. His eyes darkened to the blackest black. His chest widened, baring his battle scars.

"You can help me, or *I'll* descend you to the pits of Hell right here and now," Ben growled.

The spirit shrunk away against the wall.

"I've no quarrel with you. Let me pass, and I shall free you," Ben said more calmly.

The spirit bit his knuckles.

"I haven't all day," Ben moved in to overshadow the spirit.

"Y-you can p-promise me this?" the revenant asked.

"Get out of my way and you shall have your freedom shortly."

"Very well," the revenant shrunk away, smaller and smaller, until he disappeared with a tiny *pop*.

Ben quieted his power down to nothing. The tunnel was dark and uneventful once more, but they'd know he was here now.

His fingers closed around the wrought handle, but the door flung open before he could twist it. Nephr'eus pulled him inside. Ben blinked to adjust to the bright contrast. Even the air was warmer and sweeter.

"Darling! To what do I owe such pleasure? I mean really, it has been much too long, *mon ange*!"

Nephr'eus shut the door with a soft thud, pinched her cheeks, and pouted her lips. She rushed to Ben, but stopped short when she noticed his appearance.

"And what is this?" her hands ran across the swellings and scars on his torso. She took his hand and gently rubbed the broken knuckle. Her tongue swept her lips with every touch.

Ben repressed a pained groan.

Nephr'eus rubbed her palms and ignited their light. "Let me help with this mess," she eradicated his shackles with a wave of her hand.

Ben rubbed the ulcerations. They stung like vinegar on an open wound. Neph'reus' hands glimmered and waved across his.

"No, I'll heal them later," Ben pulled his hands from hers. His eyes swept the room. He masked his shock by indulging her amorous advance. "But thank you, dear Nephr'eus, for your kind offer," he kissed the back of her hand. "You are as stunning as ever."

Ben pulled her in and kissed her deeply, nibbling at her eager lips. He cupped her head in his hands. She moaned and ran her fingers through his hair.

Nephr'eus' fingers fell to his shoulder, down to the delicate leaflets of his spine and back up again. Her touch ended with her nails grazing his chest. Ben closed his eyes and imagined vanilla and lavender, felt Sophia's soft hair run through his fingers, tasted her on his lips. He too moaned, and Nephr'eus took it as encouragement.

She plucked at his bottom lip with her teeth. He didn't resist. Her hands moved up his chest, behind his head, and drew him into another kiss. He stroked the nape of her neck as he slowly spun her. She moved her mouth to his neck, sucking and biting, and he groaned at what he saw behind her.

Jaz lay draped under a light sheet, still and quiet. Her pallor made even death look cheery.

Ben dug his fingers into Nephr'eus's back, and her lips found his again. Her fingers clawed through his hair. He pulled away, redirecting her mouth to his neck. Ben stared at Jaz; fear coiled through his stomach.

He had tolerated Nephr'eus for long enough. He untangled her arms, but she plunged her mouth back onto his. He pulled away but she bit his lip harder. A drop of blood pooled in the corner of his mouth. He wiped it away with a thumb.

He smiled at Nephr'eus while keeping an eye over her shoulder on the girl he'd raised as a sister.

"That was a welcome I don't usually receive," he said.

"I should hope not. I would be thoroughly jealous and would have to kill my competition."

Ben tucked one of her ebony curls behind her ear. Nephr'eus flicked through his shoulder-length hair.

"And what has happened here?" she asked. "You're greying out?" Neph'reus' eyes narrowed.

Ben darkened his eyes and shrugged, "The stress of torture. Even the best of us succumbs."

"They tortured you? I didn't think those lily-livered do-gooders had the stomach for it," she flipped her hand and sighed melodramatically. "I suppose when you steal the Earth-born, that will turn the most angelic to the dark side."

Ben felt nauseous as her greedy claws ran up his abdominal muscles.

Nephr'eus tutted at the green and purple hues. "Darling, let me fix those up for you," she set her lips on one of the bruises.

Ben lifted her face from his skin, careful to not offend her, "I like my souvenirs. Keeps the mind sharp."

"Your loss. My touch is legendary," Nephr'eus stepped back and crossed her arms. "So, the Earth-born. What happened? You had her in your grasp, as I hear it. How could you possibly lose her?"

"I was a fool and underestimated her. As you may have heard by now, she is maturing into a more powerful angel than even I expected. I chased her through Yeqon's realm and back to Earth, only to be outwitted by her."

"And then you were captured," Nephr'eus laughed. "How humiliated you must have been!"

Ben bit his tongue and bowed his head. He needed to keep her appeased.

Nephr'eus leaned back against the edge of a settee, she fluffed out her skirts so that they folded in neat pleats.

"She truly is as impressive as they say?" she frowned as she looked him up and down.

"All that and more."

Jude called to him, and his tone was beyond impatient; Ben needed to move this charade onwards.

He reached for her hand, "But there is no one like you, dear Nephr'eus."

She giggled like a schoolgirl, batting her lashes, but her sweet smile didn't reach her black eyes. A vindictive flash sparkled across them.

"Not even dear Neren'iel?" she nibbled the tip of her forefinger. "Hmm? Dear Nik'ael, do you burn for me more?"

Ben imagined eviscerating the evil witch right there. He imagined pulling the guts from her stomach and hanging her from the rafters with them. His skin burned with hatred. He took a deep breath and swallowed the murderous desire like the bitterest pill.

"You, my dear, are one of a kind," he nodded towards a sideboard. "A drink?" Ben took her hand, circling his thumb across her skin to divert her attention to the bottle collection, which was a few paces closer to Jaz.

"Oh, *mon dieu*, my manners! Of course!" Nephr'eus poured some claret into a metal goblet.

Ben gulped it down.

"How have the years treated your sister and yourself?" he asked.

"You know me, I like to live simply these days," she laughed. "The Middle Ages were so very tiring."

Ben forced a chuckle, "Indeed, they were. You two certainly got your hands dirty amongst human affairs."

"Ha! Yes, it was fun, wasn't it?" she trilled.

Nephr'eus poured herself another wine. Ben refused a second.

"Where is your sister?" he used the question as an excuse to scan the room again. It was neat and orderly apart from Jaz dying in the background.

"Oh, she's here, there, everywhere."

I bet.

A sigh bubbled from Jaz. Nephr'eus rolled her eyes and put down her wine. Her skirts swished as she wandered over and pressed the back of her hand against Jaz' forehead.

"This was meant to be less messy," she muttered to herself. "Sorry, dear Nik'ael, for this intrusion, though I do believe you are acquainted with this human?"

Ben forced his face to crinkle with disgust whilst his heart thudded painfully under his ribs. "It was a sufferance for years," he wanted to squeeze Nephr'eus' neck until her eyes fell from their sockets.

"Well, your pain is my gain, darling. She is the ticket to the next phase of my life."

Ben moved nearer to Jaz and forced another grimace. "A poorly human is going to improve your position? You must tell me your secret; I'm looking to turn over a new leaf too. Yeqon is bat-shit crazy." he poked Jaz' arm; her skin was so cold that he shivered inside.

Nephr'eus' hand fluttered to her chest; her eyes twinkled with delight. "No! I don't believe it! You have truly parted ways with him?"

She poured two more glasses of wine, and they chinked the goblets. Ben gulped it to dull the pain of seeing Jaz.

"To be fair," he threw his goblet across the room into the crackling fire. The flames whooshed high and orange. "I gave Yeqon plenty of time. He is lost in his own ego. I don't have the drive to war with A'vean anymore," Ben wiped his mouth with the back of his arm.

Nephr'eus sauntered closer, delicately sipping from her goblet, "So, you would stay here? On this forsaken planet?"

"Could be worse," Ben said. "There are fouler places than this to dwell, as you well know. If Yeqon wins, we suffer under him. If he loses, we pay the price with I'el. This place is a fairly neutral and less painful alternative. Besides, humans have rather grown on me… for amusement, that is," he pointed at Jaz. "Why do you feel this one is of any value? She was nothing but something to trip over," his heart climbed to his throat.

"You know very well why she's special. Don't play coy, Nik'ael!" Nephr'eus moved in closer again, ran a slender finger across his abdomen and peered up at him through her lashes. "I am less of a fool than you think. The whole world knows she plays the Earth-born's heartstrings," she spun away and drained her wine.

"She doesn't look so special now. Not sure how a corpse will leverage the Earth-born," he spoke low to hide the pain in his voice.

Nephr'eus clapped a hand to her cheek. "Oh yes, that is my fault. Poor judgement on my behalf," she adjusted her hair, picked up a water jug and cloth, and leaned over Jaz with a disgusted grimace. "She is a nasty piece of work with a foul mouth and constitution. I just couldn't stand the language and moaning," she pursed her lips as she tipped Jaz' flaccid face up. "I gave her a little Thanratos to shut her up… a little too much, it seems."

Ben went cold. He moved as casually as he could to the other side of the bed. His fingers flexed; his knuckles cracked in an attempt to reign in his rage. It simmered so close to the surface it made his head swim, but he kept it in check. Jaz' life, what was left of it, depended on his self-control.

"You gave her Thanratos? Are you as mad as Yeqon?"

Jaz would die. Humans and Thanratos were a chemical disaster.

Sweat gathered at his temples as he stared at Jaz.

Nephr'eus poked Jaz' shoulder three times. "Come on, show him you're not dead," she squeezed water from a cloth over Jaz' face.

Jaz groaned and mumbled incoherently. Her eyes shot left and right beneath the lids. Small tremors rumbled across her lips.

"What are you cooking up?" Ben asked. "I'll share Yeqon's intel if you share with me?"

Nephr'eus's eyes shot up at him. "You will tell me his plans?" she dropped Jaz' head, straightened and arched her brows.

Ben shrugged, "Why not? He's nothing to me."

Nephr'eus threw the cloth down and walked around to him, glancing a few times between him and Jaz.

"How can I trust you?" she gently prodded his chest and ran her finger towards his navel.

He pulled her roughly into his chest, plunging his mouth hard onto hers. He tasted her darkness, probed at the evil that permeated from inside to out.

He pulled quickly away, gently rubbing her lower lip with his thumb.

"What are you up to?" she gasped. A little breathy from the kiss.

"I bring you my services, and a gift."

She narrowed her eyes and stepped away; the tips of her fingers lingered over her mouth. "How do I know you're not Yeqon's spy, here to bring me down?" Nephr'eus' hands made their way to her hips. She cocked her head to the side.

"He has his dregs infiltrated everywhere," lust faded from her cheeks.

"You're a reader, aren't you?" he asked.

"The best, darling," she crossed her arms.

Ben offered her his hand, "Read me then. You can see our last encounter for yourself."

Nephr'eus held out her hands, and he placed his between hers.

She held his eyes a moment longer, "If you lie, as much as I'd be pained to hurt this glorious body, I will descend you."

Ben hooded his eyes as he looked down at Nephr'eus. She bit her lip until it plumped to a deep crimson. She pulled his hand in close, tightening her grasp on it.

She closed her eyes. Ben closed his without choice, she drew his memories like the Asmodai, but gained only information, not power, from the act.

Ben thought about the altercation in Yeqon's throne room. He showed her the beating he had received, the expulsion, and his wandering through the Pits, then threw in his capture by the Watchers for good measure. She *oohed* and gasped throughout.

Their eyes reconnected.

"My, my, you *have* fallen foul of him," she muttered. "What did you do?"

"Took my time with a mission. He became impatient, and frankly, I forgot to care anymore," Ben smiled and ran his fingers across her décolletage, skimming along the deep-green edges of her dress.

"Neren'iel is finally out of your heart then?" Nephr'eus guided his hands to her throat. "I thought you would pine eternally for her."

A tick twitched across his chin.

He bristled, "She is history."

They kissed until Nephr'eus squeezed his fractured hand and cracked another bone. She flung his hand away from hers.

"Shit!" Ben bent into the pain.

"I don't trust you," she said. "Yet…I have seen your memories. You are a conundrum. Are you here to join me or are you here merely for pleasures of the body?" she lifted his chin with a finger, saw the pain in his eyes. Her desires were too strong. She pulled him in and he complied, desperate to get the others inside, and Jaz out.

"Do you even trust your sister?" he whispered into her ear.

Nephr'eus laughed.

Jaz coughed and spluttered.

"Oh, be quiet, you filthy thing!"

"Where did you say Anjou'elle was again?" Ben asked.

Nephr'eus threw her arms in the air and huffed. "I sent her to find that Great Healer schmuck, if he even exists. I cringe to admit it, but I suppose you're both right," she looked down her nose at Jaz. "This human needs to live if I'm to get my hands on the Earth-born. Now, give me your gift, and let's start our new and rewarding relationship."

Relief washed over Ben's skin as he transferred out.

Chapter
Twenty-Seven

The clouds dumped on us again. The ground slushed with fresh snow and mud. The breeze strengthened, it weaved around my legs and tugged my hair.

"Hurry up, Ben," I muttered.

"He's got two minutes," Brennan said.

"*One* minute," Jude said.

"He shouldn't have any at all," Lorcan added.

"I'll give him thirty seconds," I said. "How does that suit?"

The rain fell harder, torrential and cold as ice.

Had Ben deserted me? I fiddled with my soul stone for strength.

The boys crossed their arms with three don't-mess-with-me faces growing more impatient by the second.

"Try to remember Enoch's prophecy," I said. "A devil will save me."

Jude retrieved his favourite dagger and tossed it up and down. "Words written so long ago. That could refer to anyone," he grumbled.

"Yet, all so far have come to be true," I responded.

"For the love of the angels, Sophia," Lorcan said. "Did you not once think that Ben might be playing you? He pretended to love you for twenty years. He's got a grip on your heart, that's all."

I sucked in my breath, bit the nasty words I wanted to spew back.

Brennan slapped him over the head, "That's enough!"

Lorcan shoved him away, "It's bloody true. And she's all over him too! We'll all be descended because of a frigging romance gone wrong."

I glowered at Lorcan. This was partly my fault without doubt, but he needed to chill the hell out.

"You can just back off," I said. "My heart is set on one thing, and one thing alone, and that's finding Jaz. If you've got something to say that's helpful, say it. Otherwise, shut the hell up!"

Jude pushed between us. "Shall we just let off a flare announcing our presence? I don't know what's going on here, but cut it out. Lorcan, show some respect. You should know better, she's young," he pointed the dagger at Lorcan. "Put your ego away, mate."

Lorcan's face reddened even further. He was embarrassed, so was I.

"I thought we sorted this out?" I spoke into this mind. *"There's enough stress without you adding fuel to the fire. I'm sorry; we are friends, but that's all. Good friends though. For all our sakes, work with me. I'm not trying to get you killed, I'm trying to save you."*

Lorcan screwed up his mouth, punched a nearby tree trunk and turned away. He slapped his shoulder and spun back around, "Get off, Brennan!"

"I didn't touch you," Brennan said. "I'm over here, you twit."

Lorcan looked at us, confused, still patting at his shoulder. He cleared his throat.

"Well?" I asked.

"Fine. Ben's got one minute," Lorcan acquiesced.

"I don't need a minute. I've found her."

My skin flushed. Warm relief flooded my freezing skin.

"Condition?" Jude asked.

"Not ideal," Ben's mouth was tight. He didn't look at me.

"I knew it," I said. "I felt her suffering," I clasped my mouth.

The darkness in Ben's eyes fought to rise.

"Nephr'eus has fed her Thanratos. Jaz is dying," Ben said, his eyes glassy.

I felt like I'd been punched in the gut. I fell against Lorcan. I was breathless, my head swam. I clawed at Lorcan.

"I've got you," Lorcan said softly. He stroked my hair, but nothing would make this better.

Jude wandered a few feet away and punched the same tree. Snow salted our heads. The cool a relief from the burning inside. Jude crouched and impaled the bark with his blade.

Watching him express his rage woke me from the mute terror that had paralysed me. My fingers shook, and my eyes flooded. Pain crushed my chest.

"No! No! She'll…" I couldn't say it.

"Let's get her out of there," Brennan said. "She should be comfortable and with people who love her."

Jude stabbed the tree over and over, his eyes murderous, "I'll rip the bitch to shreds! She will see no mercy!"

My pendant thudded hard and slow, like it was mourning. The chain tugged at my neck, and I listened to its elemental chime. It drew me to the manor. It urged me to rise above my pain so that I could relieve hers.

I felt for my weapons. Kea's sword comforted me when my thumb grazed it. My nostrils burned from the cold as I sniffed away my tears.

Jude leaned his head into his fists, then yanked his dagger free. He slowly lifted his eyes to mine. They were red-rimmed, his mark bright. Pain and a regret I'd never seen in him before seem to shade his face.

Lorcan clenched his fists, his attention on Ben.

Brennan's face was red with cold. A tear steamed over his searing mark, "I'm sorry, Princess."

I cleared my throat. "Let's go." I said hoarsely and made to run, but Ben grabbed my elbow and yanked me back.

"Let go of me!" I snapped.

"Quiet, will you?" Ben shushed me. "She'll see a worse death if we just barge in," he said. "We need to conceal, remember?" he glanced at the others, who had rushed forwards to my defence.

I pulled away and sidled next to Jude. He squeezed my hand. Ben was right. My grief had muddled my thoughts. I was about to say as much when I noticed Ben's hands were free.

"Where are your restraints?" I asked.

Brennan created a new pair.

"Wait," I said. "How did you get them off?"

"Nephr'eus removed them," he replied. "It was fortuitous to be trussed up. Made me a believable escapee."

I waved at Brennan to relax, and he lowered his hands.

"So, how do we get Jaz out?" I asked.

"You all need to stay calm," Ben said. "Nephr'eus doesn't completely trust me, but if you control your emotions, you'll have your turn with her, as will I." His nostrils flared; his lashes barely restrained what looked like tears. Was he actually worried about Jaz?

The rain fell harder, and the sky rumbled in the distance.

I swallowed the energy that raced to my face, that pushed at my wings and the fire inside me, "Why would they hurt her?"

The blue of Ben's eyes filled out. They glistened with what looked like pride, "She fought them, she was true to herself."

"Of course she did," a new tear slipped down my cheek.

That was my feisty best friend. She'd killed a Rogue without even smudging her mascara, after all.

"They're in a panic now though. Anjou'elle has gone to search for the Great Healer to keep Jaz alive long enough to bargain for you. This is a good thing, because Nephr'eus is alone."

"She's not that stupid," Jude said. "There'll be someone watching out. And that healer thing is bull-dust, he doesn't exist. Just a fairy story to tease the Afflicted," Jude looked more like himself again. His dagger flipped up and down in his palm.

"Not necessarily. I've heard enough in my time to think more of it than a mere rumour," Ben said.

"I've heard of Santa Claus too," Lorcan said. Ben grimaced at him.

"Cut it out Lorcan!" Jude grumbled. He stepped closer to Ben, looked him up and down, "Neph'reus is alone? You're sure?"

"Yes, appears so." Ben peered back towards the manor. His wind-swept hair seemed lighter every minute.

Jude sheathed his dagger. "So, we storm the place, light it up, and get the hell out with Jaz."

"I said she seemed alone, but Nephr'eus will most certainly have warriors close by. There will be a den of Afflicted nearby at her beck and call, you can be sure of that," Ben added.

I couldn't believe they were talking productively.

"We descended them all," Lorcan said.

"They replenish pretty quickly," Ben replied.

A devilish smile crept from Jude's mouth to his eyes, "So, we light it up quietly then."

Ben pointed at one of my weapons, "I'll need one of those."

Jude bustled close enough to Ben that their noses could have touched, "Good try, fool. We'll shackle you again if you don't watch yourself. Remember you're here at Sophia's pleasure, not ours."

I pushed Jude aside. "Stop it. Let's hear him out," I turned to Ben. "You do have a plan, don't you? And you're *so* not having a weapon."

"Nephr'eus will know she needs more than she has to be any competition to Yeqon. I'm a prize for her with a strong link to Sophia that she never expected to have. If I drag in extra soldiers for her, extra cannon fodder, all the sweeter," Ben answered. "I know you all don't like it, but Nephr'eus will lap it up."

Jude's eyes swirled; he tapped his fingers impatiently against his thighs.

Brennan kept one hand hooked over his weapons. Lorcan didn't take his eyes off Ben, whose eyes flickered between me and the others. Despite the cold, Ben sheened a nervous sweat. This had to be a rocky road for him.

Clouds blew in faster, releasing a new freezing rain from a green-hued sky.

"You guys need to conceal yourselves as Afflicted, Daimon or Rogues, doesn't matter which, and I'll take you in," Ben said. "I'll convince her that I've converted your loyalties. Nephr'eus will love it, particularly as she's just lost her whole den as Lorcan has just told me. Like Yeqon, she's always looking for new soldiers to do her dirty work."

My heart thrashed with impatience, "Let's do it."

Ben gathered us closer, and we spoke in a huddle as the wind whipped up a notch.

"Follow me in," Ben said. "I've already set the scene. I told her I rescued one of the Afflicted that she sent to Kymakli."

"She's ascended you idiot," Lorcan replied.

Ben grimaced with annoyance.

"Neph'reus doesn't know that! Sophia can conceal herself as that one and say she's returned with intel. You three can just make yourselves less ugly somehow so she doesn't recognise you," he smirked at Brennan. "Grow some horns or something."

"Seriously? Do you have to needle them like that?" I rolled my eyes.

"It's the small things that make life worth it!" Ben responded with a little too much joy.

The boys' faces couldn't have been more murderous.

"Soph, you sure you're okay to do this?" Brennan asked.

I pulled the lock of hair out of my pocket. "Jaz would do it for me if she could," I passed it around. They all touched it before handing it back.

I shut out the storm, ignored the freezing rain that fell heavier by the minute. I closed my eyes and pictured the Afflicted that had killed Eilir. It hurt, but I brought every detail to the forefront of my mind. A shiver, cooler than the wintery gusts, ran through my body. I opened my eyes… Brennan's jaw dropped, "Freaking hell, Soph!"

For a few moments, they gawked at me, half in awe, half repulsed.

"Get on with it," my voice was scratchy, my arms too long and scrawny. I felt too much like Spider, and I hated it. I pulled at shreds of fabric that were apparently clothes. They barely covered my middle.

The E'lan prickled and buzzed louder as the others prepared themselves. Three more shudders in the Earth's energy field saw a motley crew squatting under the trees.

Jude and Lorcan, almost hairless and as pale as the snow, grumbled next to me. Brennan on the other hand, admired a short pair of horns he'd sprouted amongst a crop of black hair, and his eyes swirled a darker blue as he indulged his ego.

"Super model amongst Daimon," Brennan smoothed his hands over his horns. "Hmm, nice."

Ben glared at Brennan with disgust, "You look too much like Yeqon. Get rid of them."

The horns retracted into nothingness.

"Damn, I quite liked them," Brennan said.

I pushed at Ben to get going, "We'll follow your lead."

The rain eased into drizzle, but the wind still blew as bitter as the bile at the back of my throat. Jaz was effectively dead. Who else was going to die?

The storm had actually been a blessing. Despite its discomfort, it meant the locals stayed in; we made it through the outer gates without fuss, without a witness. A *No Trespass* sign gusted against the metal bars.

"Just follow my lead," Ben strode around the back, his feet crunching on the frozen gravel. The manor was a shambles. Grey brickwork sagged and crumbled. A melancholy structure dotted with glassless windows. Shutters flapped against second-floor windows, only a few of their louvres remaining. One chimney stood proud upon a mildewed slate roof. We stepped over the remnants of another. Nature had claimed as much of it as it was able. Brown grasses hugged the manor's foundation. Hundreds of years of weather had stained the lower brickwork a murky brown.

Lorcan ducked the branch of a tree which grew from the manor's roof. "If anyone saw us…"

"It's an improvement, trust me." Brennan flicked the same branch back into Jude's face.

"Arsehole!" Jude said.

"Shh!" Ben whisper-shouted, "Are you trying to blow your cover?"

Ben squatted and indicated for us to do the same. He directed us to a set of weathered doors at the rear of the house. We sneaked in a huddle.

Ben patted the grey wood, leaving a handprint in the snow dusting. "These lead to the cellars. Whatever I say in there, it's just an act. For Jaz' sake and Sophia's, don't blow it."

I nodded, urging him onwards.

The door whined when Ben opened it. He stepped down the first few steps and reached up for my hand.

"I'm fine," I stepped down behind him.

Ben shrugged and let his arm fall.

The others followed.

"The game starts here," Ben said and pushed me ahead into the dark. It smelled old and wet with a hint of decomposition.

"You three, in front of me, now!" Ben barked at the others. He was in character and it was alarming.

The boys' eyes impaled Ben as they pushed ahead of me.

Ben kept up the rear as we wandered through the dank corridor. Webs strung overhead like morbid curtains, parting over ancient doors which pocked the stone walls every ten feet or so. Outside, there was snow. In here, there were slimy puddles.

A moan echoed through the darkness and chilled my Afflicted skin.

Jaz.

"She's here," Jude whispered.

"No talking," Ben ordered. "You're lucky I've not descended you filthy vermin already. Pray for the mercy of your new queen."

"You'd better be right about him Princess," Brennan whispered into my mind. *"He's falling into this convincing act too easily".*

"Means to an end," I answered with more conviction than I'd anticipated.

Up ahead, a number of wall sconces burned with fire, not orbs. To hide herself? To limit how much of her energy was detected?

The floor felt uneven, like stones were missing.

A scream echoed up the corridor. I quelled the urge to run towards it.

"Hurry," I whispered to Ben.

He forged ahead and stopped us in front of a door that seemed less time-weary than the others. Its wood retained a gloss the others had long lost. He knocked.

"Enter," a trill came from within.

Ben faced us, "Bite your tongues and play along until I give the signal."

He opened the door. A bright room, ornate to the last sparkling crystal trinket, welcomed us. Lined with cabinets crammed full of colourful vials, the room brimmed with comfort.

Nephr'eus stretched out on a chaise longue. Her arm dangled over its side; perfect fingernails tapped rhythmically against the dark wooden leg.

"Well, well. So, it is true," she eased herself onto one elbow and eyed us through lush lashes. "You have indeed brought me presents, Nik'ael. How exquisite," she clapped.

Ben pushed us inside and made us sit in a circle by an open fire.

"I rarely arrive anywhere empty-handed," he said.

Nephr'eus rose to greet him. A lingering peck on Ben's lips sent a horrifying jolt of jealousy through me. She seemed to sense it and pointed at me.

"Come here!" her finer curled at me.

I walked over; head bent; eyes downcast.

"Come, pet. Oh, aren't you an insipid, ragged thing?" she gently turned me this way and that, plucked at the strands hanging from my head, and pinched my arms. "Skin and bone, tut- tut! You will need a solid feed before you are any good to me," she leaned down to pick up a shawl. "Your skin is ice. Here, put this on."

I saw Jaz at the back of the room beyond Nephr'eus. It was almost impossible to restrain the desire to run to her. Jaz was still as stone and pale as death. Her fatigued gasps for life chorused the crackling of the hearth. My eyes swung to Ben.

Nephr'eus finished wrapping the woollen knit about my shoulders. "There now. You dress far too indecently," she leaned in and whispered. "Oh, he is a catch, isn't he? Yearn all you want, but a true warrior like him will never be so desperate as to lower himself to a drug-addled freak like you," she blew me a kiss. "There you go pet, back to your little herd." Nephr'eus prodded me in the back, "I will source what you need to buffer you up. And you, Daimon…" she sidled up to Brennan. "What's your name?"

I sensed his hesitation and willed him to play along.

"A name? Have you lost your tongue?" her eyes travelled all over the breadth of his body.

"Uh, forgive me, madam," Brennan said. "I am speechless in the presence of your beauty."

Nephr'eus trilled a fake laugh. "Oh, stop!" she waved him away melodramatically. "Now, a drink, and then we shall discuss what exactly it is we have here, Nik'ael."

She poured wine for us at a silver service trolley.

I kept glancing at Jaz.

Jude sat close and whispered into my mind, *"I will kill her for what she's done. She will pay for this horror."*

"I'll hold her down for you," I answered.

Nephr'eus placed a goblet of red wine into my bony hands and pulled a vial out of her deep skirt pocket.

"A little sprinkle to ease into the day?" her eyes blinked in an innocent, almost benevolent fashion.

My eyes widened. I nearly put my hand over my cup to stop her.

"I wouldn't advise that," Ben said. "I fed them yesterday. I like to keep them on the lean side, keeps them more agreeable."

Nephr'eus nodded. "Very wise. I do the same," she slipped the drug away into her pocket.

Jaz groaned. Nephr'eus looked over her shoulder and back at us.

"Forgive the intrusion over there," she said. "It won't be here long."

She smiled and I felt like I died inside.

Brennan pointed at Jaz, "Who's this?"

Nephr'eus waved Jaz away. "Oh, it's nothing. Give it no mind," her attention fell heavily on Brennan again. "And your name was?"

"Dash'iel."

Raw hurt forced a cry from me. I smothered it with a hacking cough.

Nephr'eus eyed Brennan as hungrily as she did Ben. "You may join Nik'acl and I on the settee," she patted his arm in invitation. Her expression towards us was immensely cooler, "You three can stay by the mantel. The fire shall warm you."

Ben and Brennan settled on either side of her, and we did as she'd said.

My concealment was waning; I put all my energy into maintaining the illusion.

Ben flicked his hand in our direction. "I have more where these came from. Yeqon is too hard a master. Leave him to his Rogues. There are plenty more Daimon wishing to defect, I assure you," he snaked his arm around her shoulders. "What can you offer me in return for my loyalty and fighting power? Equal billing when we squash him?"

She cast her eyes sideways at him, her smile broadened when she looked at me.

Lorcan chewed the side of his sallow face, his torn nails raked the old carpet. Jude goggled at Nephr'eus like a Rogue never would. The energy peeling off them both panicked me as I struggled to remain hidden.

Nephr'eus battered her eyes at Ben and fiddled flirtatiously about her décolletage. "That, my dear, is most interesting. Your undivided loyalty? A king to rule alongside me? A very tempting offer, Nik'ael."

Her suspicious eyes landed on me way too often. I faked another coughing fit. Jude pulled at the rags that were his clothes. Lorcan scratched his arms. All of which were the hallmarks of Afflicted hungry for Thanratos. Seemingly satisfied, Nephr'eus focussed on Ben.

"Unlike darling Yeqon, my dears, I don't wish to return to A'vean. I would prefer to never lay eyes on the Throne again. I have seen the universes, and I have been to so many worlds. Being trapped here has worked in my favour. There is much to amuse me. I am quite contented here," she stretched her arms. "I find these forms quite satisfying," she readjusted her corset and pushed her cleavage a little higher.

"You wish to rule the humans?" Ben asked.

I was relieved that her flirting didn't affect him, but it irked me that I noticed. Why the hell should I care? I closed myself to the answer before it undid my concentration.

"Why not?" Nephr'eus asked. "They are obedient and easily manipulated, even pretty to the eye. After all, they are in our image. Those who resemble our best traits are quite the temptation," she eyed the length of Ben's body and lingered on his groin.

I bit my lip; it made me feel sick.

Ben pushed her face back up to his, "And?"

"Their governing bodies are like putty in my hands, crammed full of sleepers, as you well know, darling," Nephr'eus kissed his fingers but noticed Brennan's eyes widen. "Oh yes, darling. It's not only the Watchers and Yeqon who have their people walking the halls of this world's monarchies, parliaments, and congresses. Anjou'elle and I have entertained ourselves endlessly by meddling in their affairs from afar. But you know this, surely?" She tipped Brennan's chin with a fingertip. "Why open the portal and assure damnation upon ourselves? I've no stomach for vengeance, only indulgence," she ran the back of her hand along Brennan's jaw. "Aren't you more inclined to indulge desires of the flesh than the sword of war?"

Brennan leaned into her touch, "Desire fires my soul."

"Hmm, I bet it does, dear one," she cooed.

The ornate swirls around her right eye glowed with lust. She sipped more wine without taking her eyes off Brennan.

"You are pretty, aren't you?" she prodded his pecs. "Alas, as with Nik'ael, unfortunately I sense great passion in you for someone else." She sighed through another delicate sip.

"I…"

Nephr'eus placed her finger on Brennan's lips. "Hush. It means little to me. I fulfil my needs when I require; although, you both would be such fun," she batted her lashes at Brennan, who played the role too well.

I tried to keep up my concealment, but pins and needles rippled from my head to my feet.

Ben reached for Nephr'eus' neck, readjusting an earring, making sure he grazed her skin as he did so. He leaned into her ear and whispered softly.

"Whilst your pleasures are most definitely also mine, I am here for business at present," he said. "We will have plenty of time to fulfil our other needs once we have achieved our goals. Do you have a plan for foiling the portal opening?" Ben asked, breaking the fiery tension she was cultivating with Brennan.

Nephr'eus's lips were inches from Brennan's. She sighed and passed a fresh goblet to them. Ben drank from his cup and threw it to the floor once it was empty. It rolled in front of me. He wiped the claret from his lips.

"How can I help with your plans?" Ben asked.

"Oh, darling, you already have," a broad smile reached her rapidly blackening eyes.

Tension ripped through my muscles. Jude and Lorcan straightened and shuffled closer to me. Brennan glanced at us; his hands curled tight.

"How so?" Ben asked.

"Revenant?" Nephr'eus called. "Where are you?" Neph'reus trilled lightly as though she may be calling a dog.

A soft white light oozed through the solid wood of the door. It buzzed past us and stopped in front of Nephr'eus, where it materialised into a gentleman of another era. A powdered wig sat atop a thin face with a bulbous nose. His lanky frame was dressed like an aristocrat, and he held himself as such. He dabbed a delicate kerchief at his ghostly face.

Nephr'eus smiled, "Good morning, dearest Sir William."

He bowed and wrung his kerchief through his fingers.

"May I ask, dear sir, if this is who you met earlier today in my corridor?" Nephr'eus gestured towards Ben.

A muscle twitched under Ben's eye. He glanced at Brennan whose eyes rolled around the room.

"Yes, M'lady," his thin voice quivered.

"And?" Nephr'eus' eyebrows arched impatiently, she leaned away from Ben and Brennan.

Sir William fiddled with is cuffs.

He regarded Ben, peering down his nose at him as though he was something that smelled past its used by date.

"We spoke in the corridors for a time. He inquired about you."

"And what of his companions?"

Sir William's beady eyes swept over us. "They were not present," he pointed a thin finger at us. "Strangers skirted your lands, however."

My heart leapt into my throat, eclipsed by cold fear. I smeared the spring of sweat on my palms down my sides. The fire crackled brighter, fuelled by E'lan's rising pitch. It flickered across Nephr'eus's black eyes. She stood and walked to the end of Jaz' bed.

"She knows!" Ben caught my attention, his eyes swept between Lorcan and I. I reached for Lorcan. His fingers slid into mine and squeezed them.

"Prepare yourselves," Jude whispered into our minds.

"Tell me more, Sir William," Nephr'eus said. "Tell me about your fascinating investigation," her eyes were bright, her smile knowing.

I swallowed so hard it hurt.

Sir William glided overhead and dove into our huddle. He weaved between us, stopping in front of each of us before he drew back and screeched. His beady eyes widened, he threw his kerchief away and flailed his arms.

He spiralled above us, "M'lady, beware! They are Watchers, hidden in shells!"

"No time like now!" Ben yelled.

We snapped back into our true forms. Heat flooded back into my body.

Ben and Brennan leapt from the settee and placed themselves between Nephr'eus and I. Jude swirled his sword in a wide arc, ready to defend us. Its power urged my pendant to hum. E'lan sparked across the ceiling in a glittering cosmic wave.

Nephr'eus clapped. "And here we are!" she had positioned herself in front of Jaz. "You did bring me what I needed. You brought me the Earth-born. Good boy, Nik'ael!" her wings lit and spread; their heat dangerously close to Jaz. "Call for backup, Revenant!"

The ghost whorled out of the room, straight through the whitewashed walls.

Fear burnt the back of my throat. I felt like I might choke. I was so close to Jaz it hurt.

Nephr'eus laughed. "He will be back shortly, and then this will be a true celebration of might!" Orbs erupted upon her hands. She rolled them around her palms. Her wings spread wider until only Jaz' silhouette was visible through their hazy glow.

I edged closer to Jude and Lorcan, but Brennan elbowed me back. I pushed ahead anyway, drawing power into my hands so fast it stung.

Ben glowered at Nephr'eus as his hands burst to life. A growing orb pulsed and orbited his palm, "You're outnumbered, Nephr'eus!"

Nephr'eus threw her head back and laughed. "Oh, you really do amuse me, Nik'ael. I knew you were up to something."

I coaxed a warm rush of power to my hands.

Nephr'eus' head snapped back, her eyes black marbles. Her two orbs exploded at our feet in a controlled warning. "Not... a... muscle!" she aimed a new orb at Jaz.

I froze. She laughed softly. Her smile faded; her eyes thinned.

"You never liked me, Nik'ael. I know that. You deliberately got in my way with Elizabeth and Edward. *She* wouldn't have been born if it hadn't been for your lot."

"What's she saying, Ben?"

He was too focussed on Nephr'eus, but she focussed on me.

She pointed at me. "We could have erased her lineage if you'd left well enough alone, Nik'ael!" her wings pulsed, and the whites of her eyes fluoresced like crescent moons. She hovered just off the ground, hands fully armed.

No one moved.

Nephr'eus had implicated Ben in my very existence; my past, my present, and how much would he be in my future?

Emotions hurtled through me. A haze of confusion was quickly replaced by a moan from Jaz. I tuned into her energy. It was faint, hard to feel with all the simmering elemental energy about to erupt, but I sensed her heart. Its every contraction was an effort. It would fail soon. If we made the wrong move, I might never recover her at all.

I lowered my arms and stepped away from my companions.

"You want me?" I asked. "Fine. Just hand over Jaz. She's no use to you now," I demanded.

Nephr'eus's mark curled farther across her cheek. Ben raised his hand for me to stop, but I ignored him and stepped closer to her.

She smiled, like a crocodile smiles at a zebra, it held nothing but death in its shadows.

"So, it's true, you will sacrifice yourself for those you love. I am impressed," she said, nodding as though she truly was impressed.

I slipped my hands into my pockets and cocked my head. "Unlike you, I look after my family," I scowled. "Sacrifice is a big word, but I do what it takes."

"Sophia," Jude grumbled behind me.

Ben's eyes caught mine.

"Back off!" I whispered into his mind. *"Trust me, please?"*

I laughed hysterically. "Isn't that what I was born to be? A means to an end for everyone but myself," my right hand slipped out of my pocket and sat on my hip. The first sting of a fresh orb radiated in my palm. "Let's be realistic, Nephr'eus, I was never going to outwit you all. This nightmare may as well stop here," my hand edged away from my hip. "You going to stop your show and calm down? Let them leave, let Jaz go, and you and I can do whatever you want," I coaxed her ego.

Nephr'eus opened her mouth to speak but paused and lowered her feet back to the floor.

Everything quieted. The pressure in the room eased.

I shaped the orb into a razor-sharp shard behind my back.

"Why would you do this?" Nephr'eus asked suspiciously, her wings fanned behind her. Her eyes and mark calmed, but her brows knotted in thought. Her orbs continued around her forearms like a magician's trick meant to mesmerise.

"I was raised human," I said. "Being selfless is a very human thing to be."

Nephr'eus cocooned both orbs between her palms and formed a single orb, "Indeed. Or one could say, they're stupid."

I flicked my head at Jude, and he edged towards the bed. Nephr'eus's eyes followed us, her orb glowing red.

"Let him take her, and I'll come to you of my own free will. Let's not mess up this nice old place."

I reached the foot of Jaz' bed. My heart sank. She appeared as wrong as she possibly could. The closer I came to her, the farther away she felt. My heart sank. She was dying right before my eyes.

The door slammed against the wall. Glass jingled in the cabinets. A dozen Afflicted entered, chittering and crouching like pale cockroaches.

My heart hammered. Sweat ran down my neck.

"Hold them off, Nephr'eus!" I sharpened my orb-spear. "I've made my bargain with you."

Nephr'eus held up a hand.

The boys were in a tight formation, back-to-back. Ben and Brennan edged behind me.

"*I got your back,*" Brennan said.

"Step away from the Earth-born!" Nephr'eus retracted her wings and pointed at me. "You stay right where you are," she waved at the boys. "Take that thing away."

My body felt set to explode. My fingers ached as they gripped the shard tighter.

"Hurry on now, take her away," she urged with a casual and disdainful wave of her hand. Jude lifted Jaz into his arms and held her close to his chest. Her head lolled against his shoulder like a doll.

He studied Jaz' face.

"What have you done to her, you evil bitch?" he back-tracked towards the others. Ben rushed in and rested his hand on Jaz' forehead. Jude flicked it away, hugging her closer. Ben's face contorted with anger. My hand shook with fury. The shard bit into the back of my leg, and I relished the burn.

"She's barely there," Ben said through his teeth, his eyes full of hate as he fumed at Neph'reus.

"Oh, Mini Princess," Brennan whispered.

Nephr'eus placed herself between the boys and me.

"Oh, stop your whining! There's plenty more where she came from. You all fret too much." she gestured for her bedraggled guardians to desist. They dulled their energy, but their beady eyes watched the others move towards the door. Lorcan had his hand on the frame. I nodded for him to keep going.

Nephr'eus reached for my hand, as though I would just take it and skip happily away.

"Come, child, let's be on our way. No need for a fuss, as you so adeptly put it."

I walked to her, and she took the lead.

"You give in too easily, Nik'ael," she looked down her nose at him. You disappoint me."

I slowly pulled my arm in front of me.

"You believe whatever you wish," Ben said, "But I never give in."

I nodded, and we all moved.

Ben spun on his heels. His wings were so quick that the closest Afflicted had no time to dodge before his head slipped from his torso. Lorcan and Brennan followed suit whilst I flipped backwards. When Nephr'eus spun for me, her slashing wings fell short.

I jumped over the bed and flipped it on its side. It thumped heavily between us. Nephr'eus stretched her wings and walked around the bed towards me. I mirrored her until we circled each other.

She screeched, "Liar!"

Her wings lashed across the bed and set the linen ablaze. I ducked below the flames, the black smoke hiding my movements.

"Where are you?" she screamed.

Flames licked close to my face as I peered around the bed. Someone coughed on the thickening smoke.

"Sophia?" Brennan yelled

"I'm fine! Get rid of those things!"

"Argh!" Nephr'eus yelped when her hem caught fire. She stamped it out, and I dashed behind her. My spear pierced one of her wings, and she howled.

She spotted my reflection in a mirrored cabinet. As quick as a whip, she spun around. I rose into the air until I grazed the ceiling. My feet burned in the flames.

Nephr'eus lunged. I closed my eyes and transferred to the other side of the room. She screeched like a banshee but clenched her teeth and zoomed back towards me.

"Get Jaz out of here!" I screamed.

Brennan yanked Jude through the door, but they hesitated when Nephr'eus throttled me into the wall. I dropped my spear.

"Leave, *now*!" I yelled.

"All… I… want… is… for you… to stop…what you're doing!" Nephr'eus screamed in my face.

Our hands clamped together as we struggled to push each other away.

"Never… gonna happen!"

I headbutted her. Her eyes rolled back, and she wobbled.

Two Afflicted crawled up behind Brennan.

"Look out!" I called.

Lorcan cut one down with his wings. I threw an orb at the other's head. They erupted in bright flashes, leaving diamond remains behind.

Ben flung the last Afflicted from his body and flew at Nephr'eus. She tried to dash at me, but he pulled her back by her hair. He punched her back until her wings disappeared.

"Argh!" she screamed. "Traitor!" she gnashed her teeth at him as Ben scooped her arms up behind her, holding her in the air, flailing.

"You could have had it all, Nik'ael!"

Blood trickled from a gash across her forehead.

His eyes flashed to me, "I do have it all."

His implication made me feel stronger, empowered. I grabbed Nephr'eus' neck. Ben and I spun with her between us. She struggled and hissed, but I dug my nails deeper into her flesh.

"So big of you to pick on innocent little humans," I growled.

I nodded at Ben, and he let go. I flung Nephr'eus down through the blackened air, swooped after her, and picked up the spear I'd dropped. I landed atop her, the shard over her heart.

She thrashed. Spittle sprayed from her mouth, "Brat! Get off me!"

I grabbed her neck again to hold her down. My hand shook; the spear wavered across her chest.

Ben landed next to us, his wings warm and bright behind me. "Descend her, Soph!"

I wanted to. I ground my teeth, "No."

"He's right," Lorcan called, "Kill her!"

My fingers loosened around her neck. Nephr'eus coughed.

I shook my head, held my spear firmer. Blood sprouted where it bit into her chest.

"Prepare some shackles."

She moaned and laughed, a thin cackle.

"You won't be laughing in our cells," I said.

"Don't bother yourself with such troubles," Nephr'eus coughed again. "That horse has already bolted."

The tension left her body, and she went flaccid. The E'lan tingled.

I yanked her hands up, "The shackles!"

Ben conjured a pair and flung them towards her...

He was a moment too late. They ghosted through her wrists. Nephr'eus had transferred.

I screamed and pummelled the floor. I speared the shard into the settee, setting it alight.

"You should have killed her!" Lorcan yelled, "You're a fool, Sophia!"

I dug my fingers into my temples, "God, I had her!"

I was so weak. She'd hurt Jaz, and I let her go. Jude had left with Jaz, but she would die.

A cry escaped me. "What have I done?" I fell forwards and hid my face in my hands.

Ben put a hand on my shoulder and leaned in, his voice soft and sympathetic, "You're not a killer, Soph. One of us should have done it. We have Jaz, and you're okay. Let's get out of here."

I sniffed and sat back up.

Lorcan ran his hand over his sooty face. "He's right, you're not a killer. That's what makes you, you," he quickly circled the room dousing the fire, easing off the choking smoke.

I swallowed my disgust at myself.

"We've got Jaz. That's something," I sniffed again, tasting blood in my throat.

"Let's go," my lips trembled. "I need to be with her before she's gone forever."

Chapter
Twenty-Eight

No one had any clue as to how to treat Jaz. She was breathing and her pulse continued its chaotic rhythm, yet her energy was dull, like it was trying to leave. I tightened my fingers around her limp hand and licked tears from my lips. My healing vibrations bounced back like she was repelling them.

Guilt pressed down on me like the ocean's depths. Darkness crept into the light that buoyed my soul, its enticing tendrils like thorny vines clutching my conscience. My fingers plucked at my lips trying to quell their tremor. I never should have allowed Jaz to enter this world.

Enl'iel and the Alchemae tended Jaz with equally gaunt expressions. They burned all manner of herbs to ease her suffering. Cael rested a hand over her heart; his heavy eyes barely left her.

"Will anything help her?" I asked.

Her sallow skin screamed the answer at me.

"No one survives Thanratos," one of the Alchemae said.

I sniffed and coughed back another cry. The tears were gone and replaced by a stony heaviness in the pit of my stomach.

"What about this Great Healer?" Lorcan asked. "Is he really just a myth?" he leaned in to touch her skin. "She's so cold," he pulled his hand away and stepped back.

"Of course, it's a myth, you fool!" Jude said. "It's garbage," Jude paced at the base of the bed. He reached out as though he wanted to

334

touch Jaz, but jerked his hand back and ran it through his hair. His pained eyes narrowed in anger, "I'll be in the training room with Rik if you need me," he slammed the door shut, followed by the Alchemae's hushed scolding.

Enl'iel dabbed a bunched cloth across Jaz' forehead, "He feels responsible, but the fault lies with Nephr'eus and Anjou'elle and no other."

I squeezed Jaz' hand harder, trying to draw out the stagnant darkness inside her. It ate away at her and tapped into me, nauseating me.

Enl'iel soaked a cloth in fresh water, "Follow Jude, Brennan. Keep an eye on him, please?"

"Of course, Li Li. When you're ready to go, Soph, call me," he blipped out in a flash.

I had to leave Jaz. I'd found my friend, and now I had to fulfil the other end of the deal, perhaps to never see her alive again. My lips tightened in an attempt to hold the angst at bay.

"It was too easy," I murmured.

"What was?" Lorcan asked.

"Overcoming Nephr'eus. I mean, I've never met her before, but I thought she would do anything to get me. Instead, she fled with barely a punch," my nostrils flared as I drew in an angry breath.

"Agreed," Ben said. "And those Afflicted were too easy to dispatch."

I'd forgotten he was standing in a corner a respectful distance away. No one had tried to get rid of him.

I shook my head as I dipped a cloth in a pungent herbal liquid, "I was right under her nose, practically in her grasp at one point. She barely raised a hand to any us."

I took over dabbing the constant sheen from Jaz' skin. My eyes stung, my heart a slow, uncomfortable drum. I felt like I was sweating on the inside.

"Well, her sister wasn't there," Ben said. "They've always been a team. Perhaps she thought it better to run than to fight alone?"

I drew in another deep breath to quell a delicious anger that was tempting me to give in to it.

"What was it Nephr'eus said? The horse had already bolted?"

I squeezed my watery eyes shut, blinked a few times. They were burning.

Ben stepped closer to us, chewing on a thumb nail. "I think we've underestimated her. She knew you guys were there," he stared at Jaz, his eyes as heavy as everyone else's. "Shit. She played us. But how?" Ben slumped against the wall and banged a fist into it.

"I thought you were the one playing her?" Lorcan asked, "Or are you playing along with her?"

"Lorcan, enough!" I flung the wet cloth at him, "Just shut up!"

Lorcan picked up the cloth and dropped it into the bowl. He glanced at Ben, "He shouldn't be here."

Enl'iel walked to the prep table, "Lorcan is correct, dear."

He crossed his arms, snorting with satisfaction.

"Maybe none of you should be here!" I peered at Ben through the haze of my aching eyes.

Enl'iel gasped, but I ignored her. My guts writhed in nauseous conflict. From the heavy shadows, Ben's disconsolate eyes rested on me. They were always on me. I knew I did the same to him. I needed him. I didn't fully trust him, but he had helped me achieve two goals.

"Go back to the cells," I said. "It will cause less tension. You don't have to be locked up, just a guard outside will do."

His eyes narrowed at my flat voice.

"Are you okay?" he whispered into my mind.

"No. Go!" I pinched the bridge of my nose, trying to squeeze the pain away.

Ben pushed off the wall, "Please let me know how she is?"

I nodded, "Maybe you can drag something useful out of Belial while you're there?"

My burning eyes pounded behind my lids.

Enl'iel dropped her herbs, "What in I'el's name do you want to ask him?" Her pestle tinkled inside the mortar as she stirred the contents.

I peeked through a fresh flood of tears, not emotive ones, but those that wash dust from your eyes.

"He made some strange statement about helping Jaz if we found her."

A moan ricocheted through Jaz' chest, and I squeezed her hand. At the same time, an electric pain stabbed my forehead. I slapped my hand between my eyes and groaned.

Enl'iel stopped bashing the pestle into the mortar.

"Are you unwell, Sophia?"

"No," I said. "It's just a headache."

"You probably need fluids."

She had an Alchemae bring me a cup of water. I slapped the cup to the floor.

"I'm fine!"

"Clearly not, or you wouldn't consider dealing with Belial," Enl'iel sent over a new cup. She worked the pestle again, its thumping like a jackhammer in my head.

"Listen to her, Soph," Lorcan said. "He's a murderous beast."

The skin on my face was too tight. Cold sweat trickled down the back of my neck. There was a tremble in my body that wanted to explode, to rage, to burn everything away… to burn *everyone* away.

"Sophia?" Cael's voice was close and far away. He rested his hand on mine. *"You're struggling."* his voice was so soft in my mind.

The desperation not to let go of Jaz was overwhelming, yet I placed her hands into Cael's for a moment. I forced my eyes open; the light was too bright. I looked at Ben, barely able to keep my voice steady. I wanted to scream.

"I've got no more time for bullshit. Do you think Belial will help?"

"He might," Ben narrowed his eyes like he was trying to read my thoughts. "I wouldn't bet Jaz' life on it though. Move on with whatever it is you need to do, and quickly," he said, one last distraught glance at Jaz. I looked away when he headed for the door. "Come on, pretty boy," he said to Lorcan. "Take me back to prison."

Fury blushed Lorcan's neck, "Don't tempt me, Daimon."

Lorcan clicked his fingers. A guard grabbed for Ben, who jerked away.

"I'm going," Ben said. "Keep your hands off."

"I'll take him," I kissed Jaz' cheek. "Fight this, damn you," I whispered into her ear and stood.

"Let me in," an unearthly rasp whispered into my thoughts.

Heat burned my cheeks. Panic squeezed my head. There was a high-pitched ringing in my ears. I clutched my head, breathless, whilst the voice sniggered in my mind.

"Sophia?" Enl'iel's voice was distant.

An odd weight fell over me.

I rushed towards Ben and dug my fingers into his arm like I was hanging on for dear life. I relished the transfer's release from so many querying eyes.

Cold gloom seeped into my skin. I wrapped my arms around myself to ward it off, but felt an uncomfortable urge to embrace it.

Ben returned to his small cot with the door open and a guard outside.

He kicked off his shoes, "You're exhausted. Your psynostris is due, Soph."

Was that why I felt so weird? I rubbed my eyes. They felt gritty.

"Let me in." The strange voice probed again.

'Shut up!" I snapped.

"What's going on?" Ben asked.

I sunk to my knees. The voice reverberated through my head, a repetitive tease that drove my heart into chaos.

"Sophia?"

Ashes and spice. Ben put his arms around me as visions of Jaz flooded my mind.

She's dancing under flashing lights in her favourite club. I call her, and she turns around. The happiness on her face fades rapidly. The lights dim, the pumping music dies, and she's alone under a spotlight.

"Soph? Where are you?" her voice is weak, scared.

I call to her, but I'm mute. Jaz hugs herself and shivers. I try to get to her, but my body doesn't move.

We aren't alone.

The air is hot, then freezing. Invisible things jostle Jaz and knock her to the ground. I don't see her face, only her jerking boots. She screams.

Jaz was never frightened.

"Why did you bring me here?" she asks.

A bone-chilling cold sucks the air out around me. The unseen things conglomerate into formless shadows. They descend on her like a wicked blanket. She screams my name one last time, then she rises and spins, her eyes bulging and her mouth agape as her chest heaves for breath.

A spotlight on a stage erupts behind her. It lengthens, and the shadows fall away. Footsteps click on the ground.

"There, there, petal."

My heart stops.

Nephr'eus steps into the light — the light of her own orb, which hovers above her hand. She pulls Jaz closer until her head is just below the orb. Her eyes flick up, Daimon-dark and glittering with delight. A devilish smile thins her black eyes.

Nephr'eus throws her head back and laughs, "You shall never rise above me."

She rams the orb into Jaz' mouth. The explosion throws me back. The floor is cold, my body rigid, and my heart stone.

"Get your hands off me!"

I roll onto my knees. When had I fallen to the ground? I felt strange, dissociated.

"Soph?" Ben asked.

I ignored him.

He kneeled in front of me. "Look at me!" Ben tipped my chin up. "No…" His blue eyes bored into mine, flicking left and right in disbelief.

I pushed him away and released my wings. Relief rushed from my aching chest.

Ben grabbed my shoulders, "Don't do this!"

I turned away from him.

"Please…don't be like me!"

His voice fizzled away into the transfer as I escaped Kaymakli and its rules.

The fresh snow was soft beneath my feet, the air so cold it stung my lungs. It sunk its tendrils into my guts and stirred them into a comfortable indifference. Pouancé's manor was an antique blot on the horizon, a blot I needed to stamp into nothingness.

I flew over the landscape, my feet scraping through the Blackthorn trees. I didn't care about the bloody gashes, because I felt only one thing… hatred.

I landed outside the front door and splintered the ancient oak into kindling with a flurry of orbs. Laughter rumbled over my lips at the sheer ease of it.

I entered the corridors, "Nephr'eus!" I screamed.

My voice was deep and distant. At every turn, at every missing reply, I ignited a room. Radiant heat filled the house as curtains melted and cobwebs vaporised. Floorboards cracked and snapped behind me.

I screamed from my soul. My skin felt like it might peel away.

I found a door in the kitchen and blasted it open. Basement stairs appeared most conveniently. I smiled and descended, leaving fire and billowing smoke in my wake.

"Nephr'eus!" the scream burned in my throat.

I entered the room where we'd found Jaz. Nephr'eus wasn't there. I waded inside and re-ignited the settee. Another orb licked the last of the cloth from the upturned bed. A vortex of heat circled the room and squeezed my heart into darkness.

I shot through the ceiling and crashed through walls. Plaster snowed over me. Lights exploded, leaving only the fire to light my path. The comforting smell of burning wood mixed with whatever eye-watering toxic chemicals painted the walls.

I saw her. Nephr'eus's eyes beheld as much hatred as was drowning me. I rushed forwards, arms raised and ready to strike her down. I skidded to a stop, orb aloft—

And froze.

I hadn't seen Nephr'eus. I stood in front of a mirror. I stared at myself, mouth open, hair billowing as the fire behind me burned like the lava rivers of the Empyrean realm. Smoke made the image hazy, and a crack splintered the middle of the glass. My breaths quickened, but not with fear.

I let the voice in. It was my voice, and the feeling that followed it was seductive. I smiled at my reflection —

And looked deep into my gleaming black eyes.

The End

To continue reading
The A'vean Chronicles
Scan below for the final instalment.

Redemption
Book 4

ACKNOWLEDGEMENTS

When I wrote Awaken, I was shocked I actually finished it. It was just an idea that kept growing. When I finished Surrender, I knew I had a series to write. Surrender flowed easily and Sophia's story was strong in my mind. Then life happened.

Allegiance and Redemption were originally one book to finish a trilogy, but this book grew and grew. Sophia's story was bigger than I had anticipated. So, with the guidance of my amazing editor, Sarina Langer, and my wonderful friend, and fellow author, Beverley Lee, I decided to split the last book into two. The moment I did it, it all made perfect sense and I knew it was meant to be. The journey of Allegiance has been a long one in the making, but I'm so grateful I gave it the time it needed to have.

I would like to thank Sarina Langer, Beverley Lee, Becky Wright and James Fahy for beta reading Allegiance for me. To fellow author and friend, Julia Blake who read an early ARC and wiped out some nasty Grammar Gremlins that had slipped through, many thanks. Immensely grateful Julia. Without the generosity of their time and constructive feedback, it would be difficult to publish a well-rounded piece of writing.

To Sarina Langer, what I've learned through your developmental editing is utterly immeasurable. Thank you for helping me to sculpt my ideas into a smooth story that I'm really proud of.

To Katrina Young of katartillustrations, your imagination in bringing Sophia and my characters to life through your art has been incredible. I am very lucky to have had your creativity in developing my well-loved original book covers and artwork.

To Platform house Publishing, for designing the stunning new covers and for taking my plain manuscript and sculpting it into a thing of beauty.

To my readers, thank you for your enduring support.

ABOUT THE AUTHOR

G.R. Thomas is an Australian indie author. An avid reader since childhood, it has only been well into adulthood that pen was put to paper to capture the stories that have always been her mind.

In between working as a theatre recovery nurse, being mum to three beautiful children, wife to an ever-supporting husband and running a hobby farm, writing is the passion that glues a very busy life together.

Follow me
Please keep up to date with what I'm up to on social media:
Instagram: @grthomas2014.
TikTok: @grthomasindieauthor
Website: www.grthomasbooks.com
Facebook: G.R. Thomas Author

If you enjoyed this or any of my other books, please leave a small review on Amazon, Goodreads, or wherever you prefer to review the books you enjoy. Reviews are the gold dust that make books sparkle and are forever appreciated by authors.

Thank you for reading Allegiance.